I felt a coldness in my soul . . .

The teenage girl simply stepped in the void and virtually winked out of existence. Above, one of the evil low-lying clouds pulsated briefly. It had done that when the dog disappeared too. Something in me shuddered in sympathy.

Some members of the procession saw this. They broke away from the others. Into the patch they leaped, lemmings on two legs. Into the void they vanished.

A booming voice lifted. "Humans! Escape into the void! Escape and you will not be consumed. Escape into death! There is freedom in death. And from the new masters of Earth!" It was a centaur.

A surge of humanity responded to that hellish promise. They stampeded for the blackness. Some were trampled. Others stumbled over them to seek dark oblivion. Soon, the greater portion of them were gone. Utterly gone. I felt a coldness in my soul. . . .

Above, the clouds pulsated wildly, as if laughing uproariously in delight.

—from "What Brings the Void" by Will Murray

CTHULHU'S REIGN

EDITED BY
DARRELL SCHWEITZER

DAW BOOKS, INC.
DONALD A. WOLLHEIM, FOUNDER
375 Hudson Street, New York, NY 10014

ELIZABETH R. WOLLHEIM
SHEILA E. GILBERT
PUBLISHERS
http://www.dawbooks.com

First Printing, April 2010

1 2 3 4 5 6 7 8 9

DAW TRADEMARK REGISTERED
U.S. PAT. AND TM. OFF. AND FOREIGN COUNTRIES
—MARCA REGISTRADA
HECHO EN U.S.A.

PRINTED IN THE U.S.A.

ACKNOWLEDGMENTS

Introduction copyright © 2010 by Darrell Schweitzer
"The Walker in the Cemetery," copyright © 2010 by Ian Watson
"Sanctuary," copyright © 2010 by Don Webb
"Her Acres of Pastoral Playground," copyright © 2010 by Mike Allen
"Spherical Trigonometry," copyright © 2010 by Ken Asamatsu.
    English translation © 2010 Edward Lipsett.
"What Brings the Void," copyright © 2010 by Will Murray
"The New Pauline Corpus," copyright © 2010 by Matt Cardin
"Ghost Dancing," copyright © 2010 by Darrell Schweitzer
"This is How the World Ends," copyright © 2010 by John R. Fultz
"The Shallows," copyright © 2010 by John Langan
"Such Bright and Risen Madness in Our Names," copyright © 2010 by
    Joseph E. Lake, Jr.
"The Seals of New R'lyeh," copyright © 2010 by Gregory Frost
"The Holocaust of Ecstasy," copyright © 2010 by Brian Stableford
"Vastation," copyright © 2010 by Laird Barron
"Nothing Personal," copyright © 2010 by Richard A. Lupoff
"Remnants," copyright © 2010 by Fred Chappell

CONTENTS

WHEN ALL THE STARS ARE RIGHT ON THE EARTH'S LAST NIGHT

An introduction
by Darrell Schweitzer

"**A**ll my tales," H.P. Lovecraft famously wrote, "are based on the fundamental premise that human laws and interests and emotions have no validity or significance in the vast cosmos-at-large. To me there is nothing but puerility in a tale in which the human form—and the local human passions and conditions and standards—are depicted as native to other worlds or other universes. To achieve the essence of real externality, whether of time or space or dimension, one must forget that such things as organic life, good and evil, love and hate, and all such local attributes of a negligible and temporary race called mankind, have any existence at all."[1]

That, we must admit, is a pretty stringent "ideal," which even Lovecraft could not stick to all the time, it being inherent in the nature of fiction that a certain amount of human interest is necessary to keep human

---

[1] Lovecraft to Farnsworth Wright 5, July, 1927. In *Selected Letters II*, p. 150

readers interested. Nevertheless he clearly stated the underlying philosophy behind his literary corpus, and had done so at a significant moment, because that letter accompanied the submission of the classic "The Call of Cthulhu" to *Weird Tales* in 1927.

It is probably unnecessary in this age of Google and Wikipedia to go into great detail about who H.P. Lovecraft was. Suffice it to say that Lovecraft (1890-1937) was the greatest writer of weird and horrific fiction in English in the 20th century. He published most of his work in pulp magazines, particularly in *Weird Tales*, and saw only one very limited, shabby book publication (of the novella *The Shadow Over Innsmouth*) in his lifetime. Were he not a strict mechanistic materialist who did not believe in such things as "spirit" or an afterlife, he might be looking down in utter astonishment to see his work not only published all over the world but reprinted under such prestigious imprints as Penguin Classics or Library of America, this latter explicitly placing him on the same level as his own literary idols, Edgar Allan Poe and Nathaniel Hawthorne.

One can only guess what he would have made of those plush Cthulhu dolls you can get from The Toy Vault, which are actually manufactured in China, and if anyone had told him, back in the '30s, that he would become a world-wide cultural phenomenon adapted into everything from films to comic books (just being invented in his time) and manga (unknown) to role-playing games (likewise), he would have thought his informant stark, raving mad.

A good deal of the reason for Lovecraft's enduring fame is his invention of the body of lore we call the Cthulhu Mythos—although he did not use that term. The core of it is to be found in three key stories, "The Call of Cthulhu," "The Dunwich Horror," and "The Shadow over Innsmouth," all written in the space of five years, between 1926 and 1931. Certainly other Lovecraft tales contain elements and allusions—for example, Abdul Alhazred is mentioned for the first time in "The Nameless City" (1921) and the dread *Necronomicon* is introduced in "The Hound" (1922)—but if you read just these three stories you will get the basics.

Not only is humanity negligible in the cosmos at large, says Lovecraft, but humans are only one of the many masters of the Earth, neither the first nor the last. In "The Shadow out of Time" (1935), a contemporary man's brain is exchanged through time with that of a member of the Great Race, cone-shaped beings from a civilization (ultimately of extraterrestrial origin) that flourished in Australia about 150 million years ago. From other kidnapped minds, the hero gains a hint of the earth's post-human future, when, thousands of years hence, there will arise a civilization of intelligent beetles.

"The Call of Cthulhu" deals with the still lingering "god," Cthulhu, who sleeps in the sunken island of R'lyeh below the South Pacific, and who once possessed the Earth and may one day awaken to reclaim it. But even Cthulhu may only dimly spy even vaster powers, the Old Ones of "The Dunwich Horror," about whom we learn something in what is perhaps the most famous of all *Necronomicon* quotes:

"Nor is it to be thought that man is either the oldest or the last of earth's masters, or that the common bulk of life and substance walks alone. The Old Ones were, the Old Ones are, and the Old Ones shall be. Not in the spaces we know, but *between* them. They walk serene and primal, undimensioned and to us unseen. *Yog-Sothoth* knows the gate. *Yog-Sothoth* is the key and the guardian of the gate. . . . He knows where the Old Ones broke through of old, and where They shall break through again. . . . Man rules where They ruled once; They shall rule soon rule where man rules now. After summer is winter, and after winter summer. They wait patient and potent, for here shall They reign again."[2]

In "The Call of Cthulhu," the sunken island of R'lyeh actually *is* heaved to the surface of the Pacific by an

---

[2] *The Dunwich Horror and Others.* Arkham House, revised text, 1984, p. 170

earthquake and the awful, squid-headed god walks (or shambles) beneath the clear sky for the first time in "vigintillions of years," but conditions are not *quite* right and the island sinks again, and mankind has had a narrow escape more through sheer luck than anything anyone actually *did* about the matter. In "The Dunwich Horror," a degenerate back-country sorcerer manages to impregnate his daughter with the seed of Yog-Sothoth, resulting in twins, one of which, Wilbur Whateley, superficially resembles a human being, whereas his brother (the "horror" of the title) decidedly does not. In "The Shadow over Innsmouth," the tourist narrator discovers an entire town taken over by cultists of the Old Ones and especially of the sea-god Dagon. The Innsmouthites have a peculiar "look" which becomes more pronounced as they age, because they have been interbreeding with the Deep Ones, minions of Dagon, and eventually transform into an aquatic, post-human form in the course of their very long (possibly immortal) lives.

What we are intended to take away from these stories is the notion that humanity's existence is a transient and precarious affair, and that most of us are better off with the delusion (encouraged by most of the world's conventional religions) that we are the center of the universe, watched over by benevolent angels and deities. The truth, says Lovecraft, is likely to drive you mad. While Lovecraft did not personally believe in any supernatural beings or forces and had invented the *Necronomicon* as a tongue-in-cheek hoax, he did, through the Cthulhu Mythos, express in an indirect yet dramatic way his most firmly held beliefs about the nature of our existence: that the virtually limitless universe revealed by science is a vast, impersonal, mindless chaos, in which we exist purely by biological-chemical accident and only on a very small scale. His utterly inhuman monsters are symbols of forces in that cosmos-at-large that he described to Farnsworth Wright, for which human endeavors have no significance or validity.

Lovecraft's fictional mythology developed during his lifetime. That it is not entirely self-consistent and changed from story to story is only to be expected from a body of ancient lore which is only imperfectly understood from possibly unreliable texts and fragmentary hints. He encouraged his friends and colleagues, notably Clark Ashton Smith, Robert E. Howard, Frank Belknap Long, and August Derleth, to use Mythos elements in their stories, and he incorporated *their* invented gods and forbidden books into his. In "The Whisperer in Darkness" (1930), there is even an in-joke allusion to "the Commoriom myth-cycle preserved by the Atlantean priest, Klarkash-ton," a reference to Smith's Hyperborean series.

After Lovecraft's death, August Derleth, who had founded the publishing firm of Arkham House to preserve Lovecraft's writings and who edited numerous anthologies of Lovecraftian and Cthulhu-slanted fiction, in addition to continuing Mythos pastiches of his own, attempted to catalogue and systematize Lovecraft's mythos, as if it were the Greek or Norse or Hindu pantheon, with each "god" assigned a place and role. This was probably a mistake. You can't categorize chaos, and Lovecraft's fiction, if it is about anything, is about cosmic chaos. More seriously, Derleth misunderstood Lovecraft's philosophy (or chose to reject elements in it) and turned Lovecraft's nihilistic, impersonal universe into a dualistic one, in which there are forces of "good" opposed to the forces of "evil," and which sometimes come to mankind's aid. For Lovecraft, there is no such moral order and no such hope.

There have since been thousands of Cthulhu Mythos stories by other writers since Lovecraft's time. Fortunately most of them have (at least in recent years) discarded the dualistic, Derlethian "heresy" and have gone back to Lovecraft's own ideas. There have been numerous Cthulhu Mythos anthologies, of which the book you hold in your hands will certainly not be the last.

But this book does attempt to go all previous ones one better. Where previous Mythos collections and stories have uncovered more forbidden lore, explored the crazed cults which might seek to bring the Old Ones back, or otherwise deal with the ever-present threat of Their return, *Cthulhu's Reign* asks the Big Question which very few others ever have: what happens when the Old Ones *do* return? What happens when Cthulhu "wins"?

There are only the vaguest hints of this in the Love-craftian canon itself. If the puny efforts of mankind can do little to stave off this doom, what is to stop the catastrophe from happening at any time? Cosmic forces have to line up, we are told. The stars have to be "right." But what can most of us do about it? Answer: nothing.

We turn again to the key story, "The Dunwich Horror," in which the half-human Wilbur Whately writes in his diary and describes (on p. 184 of the Arkham House edition) how he intends to go to "the inner city at the 2 magnetic poles" when "the earth is cleared off." He speculates further, "I wonder how I shall look when the earth is cleared and there are no earth beings on it. He that came with the Ako Sabaoth said I may be transfigured . . ."

This leads us directly to the question of survivors. If everyone just dies hideously and quickly, there aren't many story possibilities. The writers in this book have to do better than that. The results are, of course, not entirely consistent with one another, any more than Lovecraft's mythos is entirely consistent. These are speculations, possibilities, forebodings, based on dreadful, ghastly, mind-numbing hints from the beginning of time and the furthest depths of space. The entirety of the Answer is not something the human mind can grasp.

Undoubtedly, an Earth ruled by Cthulhu or his minions (or even his enemies, other beings who may in turn displace Cthulhu, as seems to be happening in Fred Chappell's "Remnants") will be transformed beyond recognition. At least during the transitional period, some human beings may continue, overlooked by the Old Ones even as humans overlook cockroaches when they aren't too obvious. Is there some inferior ecological niche humans may still occupy? Some folks may figure, "if you can't beat 'em, join 'em," and try to join one of those rumored cults which supposedly sides with the Old Ones against the majority of mankind.

Such cults, we are told, have existed since remotest antiquity, very likely inspired in humans by dreams sent by sleeping Cthulhu himself. Cultic worship figures largely in a great number of Lovecraft's Mythos stories, not just in the Big Three mentioned above, but in such works as "The Festival" and "The Thing on the Doorstep." Then there is the town of Innsmouth, where the entire society has gone over to an alliance with the Deep Ones. I once (jokingly, I'd like you to believe . . . heh, heh . . .) produced a chapbook of *The Innsmouth Tabernacle Choir Hymnal*, which we imagine laid out on the pews during services at Dagon Hall, where the faithful may sing (or croak) along to familiar tunes and such lyrics as:

> *It's a gift to be squamous,*
> *it's a gift to have fins,*
> *it's a gift to have gills*
> *when Cthulhu wins.*
> *When all the stars are right,*
> *on world's last night,*
> *we will swim in the glory of R'lyeh's light.*

But will they? Do vast cosmic intelligences like Cthulhu and Yog-Sothoth make deals, much less keep their promises, with beings they must perceive as vermin or bacteria, if they are even aware of mankind's existence at all? Are the Cthulhu cultists as deluded and doomed as anyone else? A couple stories here address that very point.

I suppose I should warn you that this isn't a very cheerful book, what with all that cosmic nihilism inherent in the Lovecraftian worldview. What these stories do is go bravely where few others have, following the Cthulhu Mythos to its ultimate, logical conclusion.

THE WALKER IN THE CEMETERY

Ian Watson

When our tourist bus arrived at the side gateway to the necropolis of Staglieno on our tour around Genoa, a couple of cheery garbage men were loading floral tributes into a crusher truck. The afternoon was bright and breezy. Twenty meters' length of the high perimeter wall and the pavement were stacked with huge arrangements of roses, irises, lilies, and tropical blooms interspersed with palm fronds and other foliage, undoubtedly several thousand euros' worth of beauty. Into the crusher those were all going, either crammed into a big wheeled green bin first or, if too large, bourne on their wooden frames in the arms of the garbage collectors. Bird of paradise flowers passed by me, as did giant blooms in the shape of large lacquered red hearts from which protruded what looked like long thin white penises with green foreskins.

And all of the flowers and foliage were fresh and perfect, at least until the crusher compacted them.

Questions flew. Our guide, Gabriella, said that the tributes were from just this one day. Owing to cremations, there was no space to let that glory of blooms remain on display.

"But cannot they go to brighten a hospital or an old people's home?" asked a German woman indignantly. English was the language of this tour.

Her husband said, "Suppose you're in hospital, or

very old, do you wish to see flowers of the dead?" His grey hair cropped very short, he had a noble bearing; I thought of a Prussian general of olden days.

He turned to me sharply, as if to say, *Am I not correct, madam?*

Startled, I said nothing.

And so we entered a gallery of that amazing cemetery which was to become for us a huge prison and abattoir of mystifying horrors.

Like any good guide, Gabriella began discoursing as we gazed along the first of the lengthy gloomy arched galleries, statues on plinths inside niches, ornate plaques crowded between the niches, the regular slabs underfoot covering the dead sealed away beneath.

"... perhaps our cemetery here in Genoa is the most astonishing in Europe ... The revolutionary Enlightenment no longer wished to use churches and churchyards to bury the dead ... The posh old families, some rich ever since Genoa contended with Venice for mastery of the Mediterranean ... New nineteenth-century bourgeois wealth demanded sculptural realism like three-dimensional photographs in stone ... At first a classical romanticism, then symbolism, and ultimately art deco ... Angels of consolation becoming disturbingly erotic and sensual ... Death becoming an uneasy ambiguous mystery—"

"Excuse me," said a tall skinny Dutchman, "why the different colors of the candles?"

We were beside a memorial to a nun, whose photograph taken long ago was surrounded by dozens of little imitation candles jostling on ledges, with lavish fresh bouquets to either side; she was still adored. The pseudo-candles, squat tubes with a protected bulb shining dimly atop each in the shaded daylight, were like feeding bottles with plastic teats for babies or maybe squeezy bottles of skin cream. Some were blue, others red, though all bore an oval image of the Pope gesturing a blessing.

"Some," said Gabriella, "shine for a week, others for a month."

Ah, different sorts of battery.

We would need those pathetic little lights later ...

A profusion of galleries was here, and a huge population of marble statues seeming particularly lifelike because of darker dust upon them. As Gabriella escorted us, talking now and then, I came upon a bald-headed, long-bearded monk, his hood resting on the back of his neck, who had turned away—permanently—to consult a little book. He was yet another statue, as if petrified while alive. Trickles of white stains seemed caused by windblown rain that had reached him; but what took my attention most regarding the masses of more sheltered statues was how the dark grey dust of a century and a half had added a velvety shading to all the pleats and folds of drapery, intensifying the naturalism. Too vast a task, presumably, to keep so many hundreds, or thousands, of statues clean. I licked my finger and rubbed a sculpted leg. The moisture made a little dark mark, yet my fingertip came away clean, not coated in grime.

"The dust becomes united with the stone," said Gabriella, noticing. "That adds chiaroscuro."

Indeed. Some of the realism was astonishing. The sheer details of stockings or of a baby's bonnet, for instance! Families or individuals in perfectly rendered clothing of the nineteenth-century middle class stood or knelt by memorials, grieving or consoling or gazing. Stone doors stood ajar, as though the soul of the departed had only just disappeared through them.

And then the sensuality of female curves, and drapery, and petrified flesh! A beautiful young woman nude to the waist swooned in the arms of a robed Death, his veiled skull apparent; yet at the same time this couple might well have been dancing a tango.

Emerging into sunlight, we took in a fieldful of more orthodox modern gravestones and flowers, lined with many tall slim cypresses and junipers, beyond which a great stairway ascended to a domed Pantheon flanked by monumental colonnades. Behind and to the sides, a wooded hill arose, from which hundreds of white mau-

soleums reached up like temples or the spires and towers of cathedrals.

Yet by now we'd used up the time alloted for our
glimpse of the necropolis of Staglieno. Shepherded by
Gabriella, the twenty-odd of us trooped back along a
gallery towards the gateway.

Just then the tombstone-slabs, which composed the
floor of the gallery, trembled. The gallery itself shuddered, and daylight dimmed. Dust didn't exactly stir into
the air, yet visibility lessened considerably as though the
air itself had become grey.

Gabriella called out, "I think that's an earthquake
tremor, but don't worry." She was a busy, practical
woman, mid-forties. "Genoa is actually on a fault line.
However, a big quake offshore in 1887 didn't do much
harm to this cemetery even though many buildings in
the city were badly damaged." Was our guide being to-
tally honest? "So you're in a safe place. Probably there'll
be no more tremors. I've lived here all my life."

So we proceeded onward.

Could clouds have suddenly darkened the sun at the
very same moment as the tremor? No doubt that was a
coincidence, yet I almost felt as if—so to speak—reality
had shaken somewhat. Strangely, we seemed to walk for
ages, as though we were treading the same slabs over
and over again, although we weren't, for I looked down
in puzzlement at the progress of my feet.

From the office inside the gateway, a couple of middle-
aged men in shirtsleeves emerged. The cemetery's superintendent and a subordinate, a caretaker maybe?
Jabbering at one another, they stared up at what we
could see, now we were in the open, was a dull pearly
sheen masking the sky, as if a peculiar bank of mist had
descended over the cemetery—and I was surprised to
see the very same just outside the gateway, as if that was
an exit to nowhere and nothing rather than to parked
cars and a tour bus.

"Signora Vigo!" Of course the superintendent would
know all the tour guides by name. Urgently he ges-

tured Gabriella to come—along with the rest of us, who crowded as best we could, in the wake of the two men and Gabriella, into an office where a largish TV set was showing silently in flickery black-and-white what I took to be an old Japanese monster movie.

An enormous tentacle-headed thing with a scaly body and what looked like stumpy, spiky wings was standing up in the sea near an ocean liner. The creature was a grotesque blend of octopus, humanoid, and dragon, and dwarfed the boat, which seemed the size of a toy. Waves from the monster's motion through the water caused the vessel to tilt alarmingly, though it righted itself. What giant bathtub had this epic been filmed in?

I couldn't understand any of the rapid-fire Italian, perhaps Genovese dialect, being exchanged between the two men and Gabriella, who looked ashen. Abruptly the movie changed its scene to a view of New York, where another of those monsters stomped in the Hudson River as if that was merely a shallow gutter. The malign creature *towered* above the skyscrapers of Manhattan, which it began to wreck, flailing elephant-trunks of arms before turning and heading seawards, as if toward its proper home, capsizing merchant ships and ferries like scraps of flottsam.

To my astonishment the channel was CNN, an English-language banner running along the bottom of the screen. *An old monster movie showing on CNN? And in flickery black and white? With no sound?* I realized that the TV hadn't been showing CNN when we crowded into the office; spontaneously the TV had jumped channels. And now I caught up with the words as they scrolled sideways.

. . . GIANT SEA MONSTERS ATTACK SHIPS WORLDWIDE . . .

The channel hopped again. Paris, obviously; Arc de Triomphe in the distance. Creatures exactly the same in appearance as the enormous "sea monsters"—yet now more like two storeys high rather than two thousand—were proceeding with a rolling gait along the Champs Élysées destroying cars either by collision or by treading upon them. All silently. I glimpsed two of the tentacled dripping behemoths themselves colliding and *fusing of a sudden into one*—while further along the avenue I could swear that a single creature became two identical creatures. Suddenly the TV went blank.

The people in our group were babbling, and the three Italians were voicing off wildly, until the German man drew himself up and bellowed, "*Silence!*" Our uproar diminished to a few whispers. The German glanced at me and nodded approvingly since I hadn't been contributing to the noise. Then he tapped his watch significantly.

"Here in Genova it is 2:30 in the afternoon. In New York it should be 7:30 in the morning, maybe 8:30, I am not sure exactly. But I am *sure* I saw an oval shape of light *to the west*, way beyond the New Jersey heights. Presumably that was the sun, although looking distorted. Unless it was the fireball from a nuclear weapon . . . But assume it was the sun. Right now it should not be evening in New York. Did any of you feel something strange about time after the shock while we walked here?"

I raised my hand, and he beckoned me to him, while Gabriella was apparently translating for the benefit of her two fellow citizens.

I said, "I felt as if I was walking over the same space many times. I even watched my feet to make sure they were moving forward."

"And you are?" he asked.

"My name's Sally Hughes. I work at CERN in Geneva. The big particle accelerator."

"So you are a physicist!"

"No, I'm an administrative assistant in the Director-General Unit, Relations with the Host States Service. That means I deal with the various French and Swiss authorities, update regulations about the site we're on, that sort of thing."

Less than three per cent of the people at CERN were actual physicists. The site employed masses of engineers, electricians, low temperature specialists, just for instance. How else could CERN have functioned?

"But you are English?"

"My mother is Belgian. I went to school in Liège for a few years."

"So you're a bureaucrat, not a physicist."

"I'm fairly familiar with what we're doing scientifically at CERN. As are most of the staff."

"Is anyone here a scientist?" demanded the German, but everyone shook their heads.

"Miss Hughes, was any important experiment at CERN scheduled for today?"

"All the experiments are important, and they happen constantly. But it can take a bit of time to interpret results."

"Your physicists are trying to recreate the earliest primitive state of the universe, is that not so?"

"That's an important part of it."

The superintendent pulled out his mobile and jabbed, but then he frowned at its screen; whereupon he resorted to a fixed line phone on the desk, before gesturing helplessly, non-plussed. Quickly I discovered that my own mobile had no signal. Nor did those of others in our party. We were cut off.

"Did you observe," our German asked me, "that the enormous *krakens* in the sea and the smaller but still sizable creatures in Paris had *exactly* the same appearance? As if the latter were identical to the former, merely on a smaller scale?"

I nodded. "I think I saw two of them join into one, and another suddenly divide into two."

Ruefully: "I missed that. This suggests to me that both sizes are iterations of the same thing. Assuming that we were indeed watching reality, not a hoax."

"Iterations?"

"The repetitions of a process, for instance in a computer program, or in fractal geometry such as the Mandelbrot set where the same figure is generated at ever diminishing scales. Or the pattern of a *Blumenkohl*, a cauliflower. Chaos theory gave rise to this."

"You ain't kidding about chaos!" cried a buxom American woman. "That was chaos from hell itself we saw in New York. Hell has broken through into the world! This is the end time *right now*. That's the very Antichrist, as prophesied."

"Verily it *is*," called out her presumed husband.

"Be calm, madam, sir," said our German. "We must analyse. That is why we have brains."

"*You* seem to be a scientist," I said to him quickly, in case the Americans might take offense.

"I am Thomas Henkel, a historical novelist of some reputation, but I have wide-ranging interests, particularly in the history of science present and past, including Chinese, which I taught myself. This is my spouse Angela." *Ann-gay-la*.

"I'll see if our bus is waiting for us," announced Gabriella, perhaps clinging to a lifeline of routine.

"Excellent idea," said Henkel, and we all filed out quickly in her wake.

The gateway, and that shimmery mist pressing upon the entrance . . . Gabriella strode towards and into the mist, promptly disappearing; just a moment later she was returning, and gaping at us all.

"I did not turn round!" she cried out. "Mother of God, *I did not turn round*. I walked straight. I swear that."

"Come back here," Henkel said in a consoling, though authoritative tone. "We must all stay together now." He alone was standing still, tall on a step, while the rest of us milled about. "Listen to me, while you, Gabriella, translate for your countrymen. If this is no hoax, such as we saw on the television before it failed, and if we are not somehow miraculously protected by nothing external being able to enter here, analogous to Signora Vigo being unable to leave—an assumption that we dare not make!—and if those *krakens* multiply and iterate themselves at progressively smaller scales, being all essentially reflections of the same entity, then we might encounter one or more within these very walls, of a scale more in accordance with our own size. For which reason, we must all arm ourselves with whatever suitable maintenance tools the Superintendent can make available *immediately*."

This certainly made sense, as did the wisdom of acting

in an organised manner as regards morale, which might have been Henkel's major motive. Major or general, I thought. Well, someone needed to take charge.

"Miss Hughes," he called out to me, "I need an aide, or rather an adjutant." So Henkel was indeed thinking of himself as a sort of high-ranking officer. "I believe your job qualifies you. We shall see to introductions and assess our skills just as soon as we are all armed."

From a storeroom near the entrance we were soon equipped, like some band of medieval peasants cajoled to war, with spades, various forks, a scythe, a couple of sickles, shears that could stab, hammers. I myself took a fork and Henkel a spade that could deliver a flat blow as well as jabbing or slicing; and now our impromptu general could get on with formal introductions, to the extent that we hadn't already spent a whole morning together informally. Dutifully I listed the names and occupations in a notebook taken from the office.

Thomas Henkel, historical novelist, German
Angela Henkel, ex-archivist, researcher, German
Hans-Ulrich Kempen, literary translator, German
Sally Hughes, CERN administrator, British
Gabriella Vigo, guide, Italian
Rudolfo Grasso, cemetery superintendent, Italian
Gianni Celle, cemetery assistant, Italian
Jimmy Garrett, evangelic Protestant pastor, American
Mary-Sue Garrett, business secretary, 1970s Kansas
    beauty queen, American
Paul Goldman, Harvard University Press, American
Betsy Goldman, romantic novelist, American
Alice Goldman, their teenage daughter, American
Wim Ruyslinck, architect, Dutch
Anne Gijsen, art student, Dutch, Wim's girlfriend
Dionijs Ruyslinck, Wim's elder brother, computer as-
    sisted designer, Dutch
Nellie van Oven, art historian, Dutch
Anders Strandberg, bank manager, Swedish
Selma Strandberg, financial consultant, Swedish

Bruce Ballantyne, wine merchant, Australian

Jack Ballantyne, teenage son, Australian

Iain Mackinnon, gap year student of geography, Scottish

Katie Drummond, ditto but archeology, Scottish, Iain's girlfriend

Laszlo Michaleczky, computer programmer, on honeymoon, Hungarian

Zsuzsa Michaleczky, lawyer, on honeymoon, Hungarian

Our ages ranged from a guesstimated 65 for our general down to 15 or 16 for the American girl Alice who kept chewing at her lip, looking scared, scythe in hand. Fortunately there were no small children among us.

"Here is our defensible base," announced Thomas Henkel, gesturing at the office and other structures beside the gate. "Next we must consider water and food and toilet facilities."

An enquiry by Gabriella quickly elicited from Rudolfo that only some bread and sausage and cheese was in the office, although of course the building contained a toilet. Gianni went back inside, and emerged to declare that a tap was producing water at about half the usual pressure.

"At least there's water," said Gabriella.

"Not to be wasted in a toilet," said Henkel. "We shall resort to latrines in the grounds, behind trees or bushes. We have ample digging tools."

The two Scottish students had wandered, whispering, to the near end of the innermost gallery of slabs and statues.

"*Something's coming!*" the Scots lad called out. "*Jesus Christ!*"

Most of us rushed to witness. What had come into sight at the far end of the sepulchral gallery had nothing to do with anything divine according to human understanding and everything to do with what we'd glimpsed on TV. Two and a half meters high, tentacle-faced, it was a human-scale iteration of one of those monstrous crea-

tures from out of a nightmare, or from the warped mind
of some special-effects genius on drugs, or from somewhere utterly *other*.

As the thing proceeded towards us, we gripped our
various gardening implements, in my case with trembling hands. A hissing invaded my awareness, similar to
static on a radio or a breeze through holes in ancient
stones on some windswept mountain: *thoooo-loooo,
thoooo-loooo*, a mesmeric sound that seemed to be rustling within my mind rather than coming from outside
to my ears.

The creature's great warty body was gherkin-
green. Under the swollen, thick-veined dome of that
pulpy head brooded baleful red eyes. Suckery tentacles or feelers dangled, writhing, from those inhuman,
inhumane-seeming features. Webbed frills jutted where
ears might be—or was I seeing some sort of fin, even a
vestigial *wing*? The body seemed covered with rubbery
warty scales. Two principal muscular tentacles appeared
to serve as arms, branching at their tips, and branching
again into clusters of anemone-like fingers. Huge triangular feet, that left a glistening snaily trail behind them,
bore savagely hooked claws. . . .

    thoooo-loooo, thoooo-loooo

A vile odor assaulted us, like the glutinous stench of
some coral newly torn out of the sea, although more intense, a penetrating smell of primitive biological slime
that oughtn't to be released into the air but should stay
masked underwater, a concentration of the reek of
seaweed-coated rocks at low tide.

    thoooo-loooo, thoooo-loooo

Abruptly the romantic novelist screamed, setting
off likewise the Dutch art student. This broke a kind of
paralyzing horrid enchantment, as felt in dreams where
you can't flee, or can but feebly and very slowly, from
what menaces you. We retreated so as not to see what
was coming—except for the Australian wine merchant,
Bruce, and the burly Hungarian who must have felt
that he was defending his bride. Those two stood their
ground, armed with a fork and a spade.

What happened next was abominable.

As if the creature had speeded up, or even shifted instantaneously, all of a sudden it was upon the two jabbing men, its arm-tentacles wrenching their weapons from their grip with evidently great strength, to be hurled aside. A clawed foot casually tore open the Australian's clothing and abdomen. A tentacle snaked into the bloody wound to jerk free the tubing of his intestines, hauling his bowels out and out, two meters, three. Bruce Ballantyne may have died of shock before his body hit the flooring, since it didn't flop about like a beached fish. At the same time, the other tentacle gripped the Hungarian's neck—and impossibly hoisted his head aloft atop his spinal column coming right up from out of his shoulders. No natural force could have done that to a man! Could the creature manipulate matter by thought, by malign imagination, as well as physically? Head and spine were discarded even as Jack the son howled, "Dad!" and the newlywed Zsuzsa shrieked.

My list, drawn up only a few minutes earlier, began to seem futile except as a probable In Memoriam. Yet the creature didn't proceed to hurl itself upon the rest of us as we variously cowered back or made a show of defending ourselves. It regarded us, almost as though the two hideous deaths constituted a demonstration of power.

thoooo-loooo, thoooo-loooo

The American evangelist and his wife sank to their knees, praying loudly, "*O merciful God* . . ." And the creature's feelers began to move as though conducting an orchestra, almost as if it understood it was sardonically accepting obeisance and encouraging more.

"Kneel and pray for salvation!" Pastor Jimmy Garrett urged us before resuming his chant. Although Rudolpho and Gianni probably didn't understand what the American said, the two Italians collapsed to their knees, crossing themselves repeatedly.

"Pray to *that?*" bellowed our general. "For that's what it looks as though you are doing, sir! Come, we must retreat in an orderly manner! You," pointing at the Swedish bank manager who had an avuncular look, "see to the Australian boy. And you," indicating his wife, "guide the shocked widow. Signora Vigo, you take us all to some safer and higher place. From the look of it, the *kraken* may have difficulty climbing. Quickly now, but do not run in case instinct impels it to give chase."

Instinct? Or was that creature intelligent, maybe far more intelligent than ourselves, and cruelly so, so that we were to it as a rabbit or a rat is to a human being . . . ?

Presently we'd cut across the huge open area of more modern and simpler graves, most with fresh flowers in vases, hoping that the closely-set white marble grave-stones might obstruct the bulky *thoooo-loooo* creature (I still heard its whisper). And we were ascending that broad flight of steps we'd seen earlier—Selma Strand-berg hugging and pulling bereaved Zsuzsa—towards that scallop-tiled pantheon from which colonnades stretched away, behind which, and beyond, groves of cypress and juniper and other trees rose steeply and extended afar, innumerable tall mausoleums poking up amidst the foliage like miniature churches topped with small domes, stone lanterns, finials, crosses, so many or-nate habitations of the dead. Could we take refuge in one of those; achieve sanctuary?

Shady pathways wound upward through the groves. As a child, how enchanted I would have been to ex-plore this place, thinking of it as a secret garden. But now . . . !

At the top of the flight we paused to regain our breath.

Thomas Henkel, unwinded by our journey, surveyed where we had come from. He was a field marshal, if the grave-crowded expanse beneath us were a field. He should have worn a monocle and pointed with a swagger-cane.

"Straight over there!"

Where a broad, tree-lined pathway led from the triple rank of galleries abutting the threefold principal arched gateway stood the thing that Henkel chose to call a *kraken*, gazing at us from afar and directly opposite. A shiver ran down my spine, for in that moment, despite the distance, the creature seemed to fix on me, like the pin that fastens a butterfly in a display case.

Just then—could it possibly be by the agency of that beast?—a giant oval lens opened in the pearly mist that cloaked the cemetery. From this elevation we could see right over the high perimeter wall. Far beyond the roofed gateway where the creature lingered, beyond where I knew the city's wide shallow river curved, part stony, part vegetated, I saw part of the raised riverside roadway and many of the apartment blocks, their concrete faded yellow or faded rose.

"Traffic!" Yes, others saw the same. Shimmering, cars and trucks and buses were driving along the highway, undisturbed by any trampling behemoth. No police vehicles nor ambulances were racing, emergency lights flashing. Nor trucks of armed soldiers. Normality, so it seemed. A vision of this part of the city as we'd seen it just an hour or two before.

Or as it was *right now*, yet in some other reality . . . ? The lens closed up, having taunted us.

"We're no longer part of that reality!" I said to Henkel.

"We shall talk of this later," he told me.

Zsuzsa was still sobbing inconsolably. The Australian adolescent was trying to behave like a man, although I saw him quiver. We needed protection.

I pointed at what appeared to be the topmost ten meters or so of a Gothic cathedral amidst trees, the railed area around it apparently choked with bushes.

"Could we take shelter in that spire, for instance?"

"Most of the mausoleums are locked," observed Gabriella.

"A spade can break a lock."

"Forget all those pseudo-buildings," said Henkel. "Anywhere with only one entrance is a trap. We'd be fish in a barrel."

Of course he was right. The yearning to be inside protective walls had made me stupid. My orderly world, my past, was melting away like wax. What twisted shape would result?

Henkel conferred with Gabriella *sotto voce*, and we set off, presently to arrive at a tall gap where a wall several meters high, inset with caskets, confronted an equally high blank wall, coarsely plastered with concrete except where the covering had cracked off, exposing bare mortared stones. This narrowest of alleys extended for maybe forty meters, and only one body's width, terribly claustrophobic—what if something appear at the far end when you were halfway along? To relieve slightly the intense gloom, quite a few lanterns, each containing a battery-powered Pope candle, hung from caskets at various heights. Our field marshal ordained that we should each take one of the feeble lanterns with us, along with our gardening weapons—maybe, if lucky, we might later take the monster by surprise.

And so we came, passing by grieving statues, to a most unusual part of this singular cemetery. Although we were still quite high above ground level, we entered a labyrinth of several balustraded levels linked by stairways, walled with more caskets. On a dismal midway level Henkel decided that we should settle ourselves upon the paving stones.

"We shall take turns to be lookouts at the up-stairway and at the down-stairway. I think the *kraken* may find those stairways a hindrance. If it does come from one direction, we shall escape the other way."

To sleep eventually on the hard stone floor in our fairly lightweight clothing? After no food or drink? Meanwhile, doing nothing but wait?

"Signora Vigo," asked Henkel, "are there water taps nearby in the area outside, to fill flower vases?"

Seeming uncertain—does a tour guide pay much attention to taps?—Gabriella asked Rudolfo, whose response was obviously positive.

"Ask him to go, Signora Vigo, to show where . . . Jack Ballantine, would you go with two or three others to bring water back?" Yes, give the shocked lad something to do; already he was nodding yes.

"But what do we carry the water in ... ?"

"Why, in vases which you empty and rinse out. Mijnheer Ruyslinck, will you go too? And Mr. Goldman, to keep watch?"

"No," said his wife Betsy.

"I'll be all right, honey."

"But the other Italian guy *knows* the cemetery."

"Precisely for that reason," said our field marshal, "he must remain with us as a source of information in the temporary absence of his superior."

Just in case Rudolfo met his death vilely outside ...

As soon as this little expedition departed, to loud prayers from Jimmy Garrett, Henkel came and sat by me.

"So," he asked softly, "you think there may now be two separate realities? In one reality our world has been invaded by these multiple iterations of *krakens*, on various scales? And in the other reality, another world carries on as normal?"

"It was you who mentioned recreating the primitive earliest state of the universe ... before physical laws became fixed. A sort of no-time when a different sort of universe could have burst forth and inflated instead."

"And maybe that universe *did* come into a parallel existence, remaining faintly linked to our own universe by early ... I think the correct word is entanglement."

"By and large I know what that means, but I'm only a bureaucrat, as you pointed out."

"Never mind, at least you know something! Maybe as much as I know. If our physicists have recreated that earliest stage of the cosmos in miniature, does this permit a kind of *bridge* between two possible cosmoses? Or rather a *hole*, which can be forced open by a powerful and evil intelligence?"

"How do I know!"

"Miss Hughes, surely it's better to think rationally along such lines than to imagine that *hell* has invaded us, especially as that creature corresponds to no religion that I know of."

"At least we won't die deluded."

"We mightn't die. If those *krakens* are all linked, and

are aspects, *avatars*, of the same entity, we might come across a tinier iteration of the beast *and stamp on it*!"

Was our field marshal himself deluded, or was this for the sake of morale?

"If they're all aspects of the same, what did you say, evil intelligence, that must be one very highly developed intelligence."

"Compared with which we are stupid? Maybe so, maybe not. But maybe we are very stupid to bombard the consituents of matter into a state which hasn't existed since the dawn of creation, alien to the universe we know today. Stupid to meddle with the fundamental basis of reality. Maybe that's how the rift happened, when something broke through—something which may even have been able to touch our world in the past by entanglement, though not as sustainedly as now. Supposing that at the beginning the cosmos divided, one of the twins pursuing our own everyday course, the other cursed twin torn away from its mirror image into a ghastly dimension or between-dimension where vile intelligences arose hungry for the substance of our world. How the invaders are reveling now."

I thought that Henkel too was reveling somewhat in rhetoric, but I had to ask, "What about the normality we saw through that lens? Which cosmos is that in?"

"I think that was an illusion, a lure to attract us back to the gate, as if we are sheep. The *kraken* is experimenting with us."

"If the creature can create illusions . . . and you saw how *impossibly* it pulled the spine out of . . . " I couldn't continue.

Thomas Henkel patted me on the shoulder. "There now, be brave. As you have been until now. If the *kraken* possesses such powers, which seem to us paranormal, well, it isn't exerting them all the time."

He stood up, and addressed our huddled company, declaring his theory that we might come across a much smaller *kraken* and be able to destroy it, thus striking a maybe mortal blow at the larger one which menaced us in the cemetery.

Personally I thought that, if what we'd witnessed on TV was authentic, then nuclear weapons would have destroyed at least several of the greater monsters. Unless of course the monsters could neutralise missiles.

At least our group seemed somewhat comforted by Henkel's idea.

I'd often wondered in what way I would die one day. That's the big question which most people avoid asking themselves, not least because there's no answer until it happens, and even then you mightn't know the answer, supposing your mind has degenerated prior to death, as my mother's did. Whereas the truck that skidded and mowed down my dad from behind might have obliterated him before he could even realize. So somehow— due to family history—I thought that I wouldn't know about death when I died. I would simply cease, the way I once ceased due to anesthetic when I needed a kidney stone broken up by laser. Did I hope simply to cease or alternatively to know the very threshold of death? Had the creature come to teach me?

"There's still no mobile phone signal," said Wim Ruyslinck's girlfriend.

"Did you just try to call Mijnheer Ruyslinck?" demanded Henkel.

"Yes, but his phone's set to vibrate, not ring. I wouldn't draw attention to him like that."

"Wise. However, we should conserve batteries, in case there's any future use for them. Everyone should switch off their phones. I'll keep mine switched on in case there is any change. When my charge runs out, I'll appoint someone else."

"Runs out?" queried Betsy Goldman, who was plump. "When's that? In a week or a fortnight? What do we *eat* till then?"

"The human body doesn't normally die of hunger for forty or fifty days provided it can drink. Fasting is normal for many people in the world, often involuntarily."

"You mean I'm starting from a good baseline?" Betsy laughed, perhaps a shade hysterically, but others chuckled or grinned, the first hint of good spirits.

"Very good!" Henkel said approvingly.

Fortunately, her husband and Rudolfo, Jack Ballantyne, and the Dutchman all returned safely soon enough, bearing vases brimming with water.

That, comparatively, was the good time, the time when there was still some hope, even if meager . . .

We're allowed our sanctuary, here in this dusty shadowy minor labyrinth of stairways and galleries where the warped oval sun only reaches through a grimy round skylight or so at the top. A place resembling a library, except that instead of books on shelves there are almost identical caskets containing the dead, blessed to have died when they did.

Maybe the creature cannot easily mount or descend the stairs, though I doubt it. So far at least, Cthulhu hasn't done so. There comes a click in our minds, and the drawn-out whisper inside us, of *thoooo-loooo, thoooo-loooo*: that might be its name, or maybe a call of power akin to an abracadabra.

Yet the stairs don't stop Cthulhu from taking us one by one to play with. And then to discard, vilely and agonisingly used. Maybe beyond any agonies caused by human torturers, since I believe its tendrils can reach into our brains to push the buttons of pain. For we must eat. And Cthulhu feeds its pets.

After half a week of hunger for us, our water-bearers of the day sighted a small heap of dead fish and fruits on a path they used. *Was that bait?* Iain McKinnon darted ahead bravely to scoop the food into his empty vase, and survived. He returned for the rest of the rations, and survived.

On the following day, a pile of raw meat and vegetables was further away. Subsequently, some cheeses and salamis were outside the house-size version of the Pantheon of Rome. Presently we needed to hunt through statued galleries of the cemetery to find wherever our food might be. On all expeditions, near or far, we carried forks—the gardening, not the dining, kind—to defend ourselves and each other, however feebly.

A week passed before, half way along a gallery, Iain Mackinnon trod on a patch of the strongest of glues of the same colour as the flagstones. He couldn't wrench his sneakers free. As he stopped to untie the trainers, so that Katie Drummond and Paul Goldman and Jack Ballantyne could then try to jump him out of that stickiness, *k-thoooo-loooo, thoooo-loooo*, towering Cthulhu came. The tines and blades of the gardening tools jerked down to clang against the flagstones as if a powerful magnetic field dragged them. It was, said Paul afterwards, like some bizarre salute to a potentate, the lowering—then the necessary letting go—of swords. Katie could only scream and wave her arms at the advancing entity. Neither she nor Paul nor Jack were going to throw themselves bodily at that monster. One of its feet seemed to suck the glue back into itself as its arm-tentacles immobilized and lifted the Scots student who bellowed, then tried vainly to bite at face-tentacles . . . as he was rushed away. The forks and spade were no longer fastened to the flagstones. Snatching them up, for what use those might be, the trio did give chase led by Katie, but when they rounded a corner the next gallery was empty except for mournful statues. Thus they related when they returned to our labyrinth—carrying the day's food, yes; Katie having to be commanded and cajoled by Paul Goldman, for *what else could they do, what else*?

That night we all heard the thin, piercing screams, for what seemed hours, dying away, starting again. Henkel had to restrain Katie. Of course no one slept. The next day the hideous mess that had been Iain Mackinnon lay on the space outside the Pantheon. He almost seemed to have been turned inside-out by an insane vivisection.

It was . . . slippery to bury him in a copse as close nearby as we could. Pastor Jimmy Garrett managed to say words and quote parts of the Bible that weren't excessively evangelistic; and I noticed that his hair, now lank and stringy where it had been lovingly tended and conditioned before, was falling out after these weeks. So hair doesn't always just go dramatically white overnight with shock.

Katie begged our field marshal to strangle her; she promised not to struggle. Then she begged the taciturn German translator, Hans-Ulrich. Of course nobody would strangle her. In due course, might suicide by assistance become easier to contemplate?

No one went to fetch food for four days. Eventually hunger pangs prevailed. The instinct for survival is so strong. Katie didn't try to smash her head against the hard stone that was all around us, even though we had no sedatives, only some painkillers and stomach settlers in a couple of the women's shoulder bags, and a few tampons, soon used. Most bags including mine had been left aboard the bus for our brief stroll into Staglieno.

As time wore on, Zsuzsa was taken similarly, and Selma Strandberg and Nellie van Oven and Wim Ruyslinck and Hans-Ulrich. The monster only rarely resorted to glue, preferring the direct approach. Nevertheless, not each far sortie resulted in a victim. Cthulhu preferred to fool us that by luck or at random we might return safely. Hence the rabbits would scurry to snatch their suppers.

No one spotted another lens in the prevailing mist, supposing that the original lens was designed for us to see. Of course we didn't venture outdoors more than was essential—oh, the crushing endless fearful misery, even though for distraction we took turns telling our life stories. I think there was only one lens, and that it showed a memory of our world just before the Cthulhu creatures arrived, not an image of normality continuing in some parallel reality that might even be reachable. Nor did anyone stumble upon a mini-monster to stab and slash and crush.

Monster? More like a baneful sadistic *god*, if it could multiply itself on different scales all across the world! If it weren't simply this cemetery of Staglieno that had been abstracted from ordinary reality by a potent entity from another universe that could conjure up illusions ...

Nor did every abducted victim scream through the night. Maybe a tongue was removed first of all.

"Each person lost," said Garrett one day, "is a sacrifice to *it*. A human sacrifice. As in pagan antiquity. But worse. I think it's . . . rationing out its sacrifices. Or maybe it's like a serial killer who gets satisfied for a while until the head of steam builds up again."

Garrett frequently goes outside to keep watch, from the top of the steps to the Pantheon. Thomas Henkel doesn't object to what might seem to be a desire for martyrdom on the evangelist's part—at least, until martyrdom actually commences. Any additional information is valuable in our field marshal's blue eyes, sometimes cool, sometimes almost twinkly. I think we're all losing our sanity somewhat, or else we no longer remember what sanity is or was.

And I accompany Garrett, despite a dark look of mistrust from ex-beauty queen Mary-Sue.

"I quite often see him walking in the garden," Garrett tells me. "That's to say, *it* walking in this cemetery. I'm still a witness of the Lord's, whatever has happened."

I feel more sympathetic to the evangelist now than at any previous time. He's trying to cope without ranting nonsense.

"Look, Sally."

And there is the Cthulhu thing in the distance, pacing slowly, rollingly, as I imagine a sailor newly on land after a very long voyage. On *our* land, of which Cthulhu has taken possession. The Cthulhu thing turns, aware of our scrutiny, and once more I experience the sensation, *thoooo-looo thoooo-loooo*, that it's staring directly into my eyes, into my mind which may seem very simple to it, like a seashell with a soft little body inside.

Rudolfo gone. Paul gone. Dionijs Ruyslinck gone. Anders Strandberg gone, to join his wife, as it were. And Angela Henkel gone—our field marshal needed to send her out voluntarily more than once to bring food back, otherwise he might have seemed to be protecting her, thus impairing his authority. The available pool of food-bringers is diminishing all the time. What an unbalanced game of chess, wherein pawn after pawn is removed from one side only when we make a wrong move, as is inevitable. Despite Thomas Henkel's laudable pretensions, our side only consists of sacrificial pawns, no king or knight or queen.

All the cut flowers in vases died long ago, but rain falls frequently and suddenly to lubricate the cemetery, whereupon Cthulhu walks in those heavy showers to lubricate itself, wafting its face tentacles. What does the creature muse about? Maybe it had a million years previously to muse, and now it *a*muses itself. Creator and creature are quite similar words.

I total the days scratched by me, as Henkel's adjutant, on the wall in five-bar gates. Does a week of five days, rather than seven, make the time pass more quickly, even though that system produces more weeks? Look: we survivors have lived for twenty-three weeks by now. August should be the current month, although the temperature stays much the same as that mild April day of our imprisonment; the brightish oval wavery yellow shape which we sometimes see above the mist, and which moves across the sky, should be much hotter by now if it's the same sun we knew.

The piles of food put out, or materialized, in unpredictable places for us pets to find grow smaller in proportion to our diminishing numbers; Cthulhu is keeping tally. It plays like the wicked boy inflating a frog with a straw through its anus until the poor creature explodes. Or pulling the legs off a spider one by one to test its balance. Only much more so.

Discarded playthings are sometimes still alive when we reach them, maybe without teeth, or with a tiny worm swimming in a single gaping double-yolked eye, gibbering softly, leaking, no longer seeming human; we dispatch those with a spade blow, those of us who remain.

Our leader has gone; Thomas Henkel is taken. So am I in command now, promoted from adjutant on the disastrous field of battle, or rather of massacre? The others seem to expect this, and I can't reasonably demur. Jimmy Garrett blesses me.

Garrett is taken, to meet his new master, intimately.

*   *   *

By now, those of us who remain are myself and Katie Drummond and Anne Gijsen and Alice Goldman and Jack Ballantyne. Four young women, one young man. Is a vile parody of Adam and Eve to be enacted? To my best knowledge no one has fucked anyone else since this all began, for mutual comfort. Stone floors, for a start; and who would sneak off into the softer sheltering groves? I think Anne and Dionijs came close, some time after brother Wim's death, but they were too upset.

Even though there's supposed to be an instinct to propagate the race, in extremis . . . Can it be that we're the only surviving human beings? Or are other iterations of Cthulhu playing variations on this vicious game all over the world? The latter seems more likely than that we should be the . . . *privileged* ones.

thoooo-looo thoooo-loooo

When we awake from dire dreams this morning, Katie is dead, apparently strangled, to judge by bruise marks. Of course we gave up posting guards weeks ago now.

"If one of you doesn't confess," I say, "then we must assume that *it* can come here while we're sleeping."

"Naw," says Australian Jack, "that would be too merciful."

I wait for him to fess up.

"It was me," says Anne. "I go, I went, to judo classes in Holland. It's a judo strangle." She crossed her hands, back to back, grips an imaginary shirt or blouse collar, and rotates her wrists. "Pressure of the wrist bones on the carotid arteries. Unconscious in fifteen or twenty seconds, death in maybe a couple of minutes. Katie begged me. She was so scared." Anne looks from face to face, almost expressionlessly. "Well. Does anyone else want this? If only," she adds, "I could strangle myself."

"*Yessss*," comes from Alice Goldman. "Yes, please . . ."

Jack and I have kept quiet.

Anne nods. "I shall not strangle more of you, though. No more of us. Only Alice. I don't wish to leave myself alone."

"Do you want," Jack asks Alice, "that we leave, then come back after a few minutes?"

"No! Watch! Witness me!"

In what sense, witness? Witness her being *brave*, of all things? Cowardly brave?

Alice lies on her back across two slabs. "Like this?"

Anne nods.

"What if my blouse snaps?" Our clothes are by no means in tatters, merely very soiled.

Anne advances on hands and knees, then she lowers herself beside Alice, one leg across her body as if to restrain her; and her reversed hands slide round the American girl's neck as if lovingly.

After several seconds Alice does slap her entire free arm upon the slab as if in submission at a judo contest, but only once. Her exposed feet drum a little, then are still.

Anne remains pressed upon Alice for what seems a long time, before the young Dutchwoman rolls aside.

"See," she says, sitting up, "I can be a murderer too, just as well as *the thing*."

"I'd hardly say—" begins Jack.

"Say nothing."

None of us wish to be left alone, so we all go out together to hunt for our food, or be hunted. Like an offering, we find two vacuum-packs of sliced mortadella sausage and half a dozen oranges on the step under a grandiose melancholy memorial attended by a kneeling, praying woman and a bearded man who stands respectfully with gaze downcast. That woman's crocheted shawl is so intricate. Her ruffled cuffs, the teardrop the size of a lemon pip spilling upon the side of her nose . . . He, with a coat over his arm, clasping his hands before him, a couple of fingers loosely—though inseparably—holding a grey bowler hat. Midway between the petrified pair, our meal.

"*Two* packets," says Anne, a quaver in her voice.

And Cthulhu comes . . .

. . . for her.

*   *   *

At least there's no distant screaming tonight. Maybe
a tough tentacle is down her throat, no doubt allowing
her to breathe, though, as she writhes.

Jack and I don't catch sight of Anne's corpse anywhere on today's search for more food. This takes us
hours, but there are no birds to steal. Finally, we find
what we seek upon the simple marble tomb of Mazzini's
mother, within a railed little garden in front of the squat
Doric columns supporting the massive architrave carved
with the name of the great Italian patriot, wrapped over
by creeper-clad rocks—for the atrium and then the crypt
beyond, very dark within, burrow into the hillside in this
part of the wild woodland. Paradoxically, quite close to
our sanctuary, almost the last place we think to look.

On his mother's tomb by a towering tree: a single
plate of white pasta scattered with clams. Brought from
where, and how?

"Ladies first?" enquires Jack with an effort at humour.

Together we advance into the little railed garden.

A soft stirring sound from within the mausoleum.

k-thoooo-looo

comes.

I do hear the shrieks tonight, and try to stopper my
ears. Maybe I should jam into my ears the long-expired
Pope candles. The scene repeats in my mind: stooping
to pass under the architrave, the tentacled monster had
surveyed us. No point in fleeing; we knew it could catch
us.

Heads or tails, male or female, Jack or me?

Then Cthulhu had swooped upon Jack and swept
him away howling back inside that mausoleum. Is it so
shameful that I seized the plate of pasta and clams and
ran off with it?

So I'm all alone in the labyrinth now; and I'm hungry.
Does something *really* special await the solitary, and female, survivor?

Maybe a boiled lobster, and no evil consequences on this particular occasion ...

I'm in the gallery where a boy and his sister, hair and clothing perfectly rendered, are witnessing the departure of their mother's soul to heaven—the bronze door of the sepulcher above is already half-closed as the boy gestures upward, his other arm tenderly embracing his sister. Beside the children's feet lie a big bar of nut chocolate and an overripe banana. Chocolate! Immediately I'm tearing off the paper and silver foil, and biting into the sweetness.

But for the sudden assault of stench, I almost fail to notice Cthulhu coming until it is upon me, entangling me, its suckers tearing off slacks and shirt and underwear. The suffocating smell is of sewers and rotting fish.

Face tentacles sliding into my ears, *thoooo-loooo thoooo-loooo*, arm tentacles probing my anus, my cunt.

A storm of ecstasy like a blinding enveloping light! A momentary shaft of terrible agony as if I'm burned alive!

The ectasy again! I would crawl begging to the beast for this, like those rats that burn off their paws by pressing a red-hot plate that stimulates the pleasure centers in their brains.

Cthulhu is ... calibrating me as, yes, it copulates with some organ or tentacle or other.

And I'm alive, lying naked and used—*for how long?*—upon flagstones bearing names of the dead. Alive. So violated but alive. Cthulhu has gone, though leaving his odor upon me.

At the tomb of Mazzini it must have been choosing whether its *bride* should be an Australian youth or me ...

And what is a bride but a receptacle for seed?

A movement. *What?*

The statue of the boy has lowered its arm and removed his hand from his sister's shoulder. She turns and steps down, and he copies her. The chiaroscuro of dust still remains on these nineteenth-century children as they step towards me, as I roll with difficulty on to my hands and knees so as to press myself up from the floor, and haul my aching abused self upright. The children remain marble, yet that marble has become a flexible, mobile parody of what it represented so faithfully for a century and more. Those clothes of theirs wouldn't come off them, I know that—the bodies are as one flesh with the garments. The boy and girl pause, looking up at me now.

Confused words come from their softened mouths.

Not Italian words, no.

Words with a Swedish lilt, I'm almost sure . . .

The voices of Anders and Selma Strandberg, the bank manager and his wife . . .

"... help us ..."

"... how small we ..."

"... where we been ..."

"... what we ..."

"... hurt ..."

"... hurt ..."

Within half an hour a score of statues have found me, arriving slowly, step by step.

The pious little old proletarian peasant woman, long-skirted, aproned and shawled, whom Gabriella had said sold peanuts all her life to save up for a statue of herself in Staglieno—she still carries strings of inedible peanuts as if those are rosaries.

The tall young swoony woman, nude to the waist, now detached from the grasp of the veiled skeleton.

A suited businessman, crumpled bowler hat in hand.

More children, dressed like miniature adults . . .

Some of the minds in the statues seem insane from the experiments they suffered. Others are very confused. Two can only speak in what must be Hungarian.

Eating or drinking is plainly impossible for them. Do they envy or resent my chocolate? Impossible to tell. Will their minds emerge more, and maybe heal, as time passes?

For what capricious purpose have we been reunited? So that a score of animated statues can provide company while *something* grows inside me—until at last I give birth surrounded by mobile dusty marble people, in a reverse of their previous roles as mourners at death-bed scenes. How often will Cthulhu play with me stinkingly again ... ?

Jack is the brightest of the children. He knows how his father died, and how he himself died. And how, but for me, he would now be bearing spawn in his belly.

SANCTUARY

Don Webb

It was the third year after the Aeon of Cthulhu had
begun. The second year after Nat's wife had walked
off into the sky, and the three weeks since he driven into
Austin to raid a drugstore for antidepressants and vita-
mins. It was noon; three years ago he would have been
at Precision Tune scanning cars whose "Check Engine"
light had come on. Now, since it was noon, he would be
walking across the street to Tacos Arrandas #3 with Wil-
lie, Juan, and Mike. The chicken flautas with sour cream
would be pretty good right now with a *cerveza*. Someone was crying in the Church, but someone was always
crying. They would quiet down. Everyone sat upright
at Santa Cruz during the day, unless they were praying. If they weren't out growing vegetables, they stayed
here. There were non-Catholics here—Mr. Jones, over
there, with his black shiny face, he had been some sort
of Baptist minister. The once-fat blonde lady who taught
science had been an atheist—what was that word they
used in Mr. G's class? *Her **hypothesis** must have proven
wrong. There were gods; mainly they ate us.*

Nat hated the Church except for Jesus. Jesus never
looked too good to Nat growing up, stuck on that damn
cross, couldn't help anybody, could he? He used to make
stupid jokes with the *cholos* he hung out with: "Why
can't Jesus eat M&Ms? 'Cause they fall through the holes
in his hands." They would tell him that he was going to

37

hell. *Guess they were right about that.* He still carried his baby-blue rosary from back in the day. It seemed like those from Below didn't give a shit about colors.

He liked Jesus now. He didn't understand why Jesus was white when the *Virgin* was Mexican. Don't you know that had been a shocker to Joseph? The brown eyes were large and shocked with pain—*we should'a known; he was telling it was coming for years. We all look like that now.* Jesus had caught up with the times or the times caught up with Jesus. The crying had stopped and praying had started. Prayers were pretty free-form, mainly to Jesus or the Blessed Virgin, but occasionally someone worked in a call to Yog Sothoth; as Keeper of the Gate, he was pretty popular. Maybe he would gate them all back. It was one of the few Names everybody knew. CNN had lasted for twenty-three days after the Rising. So everybody knew something. Even in Double-sign, Texas.

He thought of his youngest brother Xavier. Nat hadn't been there to witness what had happened to Xavier, but he'd heard about it from people who had, and he could envision it so vividly in his mind that he might as well have been. Not that it would have made any difference.

Xavier had decided the thing to do was get with the program. He rented some horror DVDs from Blockbuster—he figured that he would get in good with the New Bosses. He studied the ritual sequences, the sacrifices. So he drove into Austin, found an occult shop, bought some black candles, some chalk, a fancy knife, and a big chalice to pour blood into. Mama told him to have faith. It was a stupid argument. Had faith kept Cody from getting HIV? Had faith kept Esmeralda's pickup from being hit by the eighteen-wheeler?

Xavier drove to the parking lot of Sam Houston high school that night. The Moon was full and high and it had not yet opened its Eye. He spray-painted two big circles one inside the other. A crowd of people watched. It was better than listening to what was going on in Japan. *You'd think after all them Godzilla movies they could have handled it.* No one had told Father Murphy.

The witnesses later said they'd wanted to see if Xavier was right. He lit five black candles in the shape of a star. Then he opened a used black paperback book that he had paid top-dollar for in Austin. He read some gibberish by flashlight.

Then he went to his old Chevy half-ton and took his red-nosed pits out. He had them tied up with bungee cords and they were squealing and barking. He dumped them in the center of his circle, put on his black graduation robe and got the Chalice and Knife from the front of his truck. He carried an MP3 player with him and lay it next to the dogs. He cranked up *The Symphony of the Nine Angles* and started yelling stuff about the "Blood is the Life" and "Passing through Angles Unknown." *I guess I should have paid more attention in Mrs. Gamble's geometry class,* Nat thought, well after the fact, hearing about this.

Xavier picked one of his dogs up and cut its throat. It was not easy to manage this and hold the Chalice and the paperback. The dog made a terrible sound, and maybe someone was going to rush in and stop all this, but no one did. Everyone was scared. Everyone had seen the Terrible City on CNN and the Thing at the North Pole.

He dropped the squirming and whimpering dog. "¡Venga adelante y aparezca O Utonap'stim! ¡Venga! ¡Venga! ¡Yog Sothoth! ¡Beba la sangre se ha ofrecido que! I call you by the Seal that is at once Four and Five and Nine! ¡Venga! ¡Venga!"

The dying dog tried to crawl away. The other screamed like no one had never heard a dog scream. Xavier's flashlight went out, but it wasn't very dark because of the Moon. Then the Moon went dark. It was as though every piece of light was sucked away suddenly. People who told Nat about this later claimed they could feel sound being sucked away, too. In Robert E. Lee Park, next to the school, there were the usual late spring lightning bugs flashing on and off. Suddenly they all flew toward the parking lot. They clustered all over Xavier. Everyone could see him struggle, but couldn't hear a word. He fell over and the dark went away; even his flashlight flickered back on. Finally, someone ran up to him. The bugs had eaten his skin and eyes. Juan found a gun and put the dog out of its misery. The others had trouble getting the cords off the other dog without getting bitten. When they did, she ran away. Somebody burned the book. CNN reported a few days later that if you called them by night they came.

Nat didn't like thinking about that. But you couldn't think otherwise. He looked at poor white Jesus. Poor bastard. Even being white didn't save you now.

Nat was rich right now; he had made a run into Austin with Jesús' truck. He had found an HEB that hadn't been looted. Dried pinto beans, jalapenos, canned ham, tangerine jello, soup, flour (without too many weevils), and a large can of fruit cocktail. Mama invited over the MacLeods from next door. Dr. MacLeod had taught classes in chemistry at the University of Texas. His wife had taught painting classes for adults at the community college here in Doublesign. They had been great neighbors since before the Rising. They were Mormons so they had over a year's supply of food saved up. They loved Mama, even when Nat and Jesús and Juan were sowing wild oats, they took her applesauce bread, and had had her over for "Mormon Beans" back when ground meat was available. Dr. MacLeod had been so helpful when the Rising happened. He knew all about the Masons and the Illuminati. He spoke at one of the last town meetings and everyone agreed to crucify the old men in the Masonic Lodge. It was easy to catch them; not one was under eighty—besides they died quickly, which everyone says is a Good Thing these days. Dr. MacLeod explained how the One World Government was really about Cthulhu. After the Moon opened its Eye, it was clear what the "All Seeing Eye" on the dollar bill had been about.

Mama didn't have electricity, of course. But Nat had driven to Barton Creek Mall the day after one of the Shining Waves had passed through Austin. It had paused at the Mall, breaking it into three big pieces. Nat and

Juan had loaded up their trucks two times each with the
stock of a Wicks and Sticks. At first (before Victoria had
walked into the sky) Nat had kept all the candles at his
place. But when his wife was Called by the Thing Behind
the Winds, he had moved everything (including Stephanie) to Mama's. They lit candles everywhere, and only
once had the house caught fire by one burning too low.

Dr. MacLeod was explaining the world, as usual.
"What we didn't understand is that it is all personal. I
never understood that the many nights I researched stuff
on the Web. All the scholars said it was impersonal."

Mama just smiled. It was not that she lacked intelligence, but like so many, something had shut down in her.
She never left the house except to get water at *el rito*. By
day she read old *fotonovelas* and copies of the *Reader's
Digest*. At night she prayed in her *sala*. She would not go
with Nat to Church. Safety was here, in her home. She
was happy when she could serve food to other people
and when people brought her things.

"What do you mean, Dr. MacLeod?" asked Nat.

"It isn't about what happened in the Pacific or the
Arctic," he said, "It's your brother. It's my son. Some
Thing out there interfaced with us."

Mrs. MacLeod said, "Is it because we were bad? Because the world was bad?"

"No, honey. We weren't bad. We were just good
food."

"We weren't the ones that were eaten or," she said
looking at Nat, "called."

"Our suffering feeds them. When they take poor
Stephanie there," he began.

The child looked up, frightened.

Nat yelled, "They are not taking Stephanie!"

Mama began to cry. Stephanie looked down at her
knees, afraid to move.

"Come on, Nat, face facts; everything we've heard
tells us it runs in bloodlines," said Dr. MacLeod.

"Shut up, honey. This isn't the place," said Mrs.
MacLeod.

"They just need to face facts. The Others have a fix

on their family, just like they got our Billy for meditation. Something was wrong with Theresa. She belonged
to Them, and They Called her."

Stephanie had put her hands over her ears. She
sobbed.

"You go away, you bastard. We know what you are.
Maybe they got your Billy because you had us nail up
those old men. You go away and don't come back."

"Nat, you're being emotional. You know they won't
let her in the Church building now. We just have to face
facts."

Mrs. MacLeod got up and was pulling her husband by
the short ecru sleeve of his shirt. "Shut up, Bob. Nobody
needs to face anything. We've all faced enough. Don't
ruin another night."

He pulled his arm away from him. He drew back his
arm as thought he might hit her, and then just started
sobbing.

"Come home, hon." She said very gently, "I am so
sorry. So so sorry."

Nat put Stephanie to bed. She was ten and would be
in fourth grade if there was any school left. For a while
Miss Farmer and Mrs. Martinez tried to do classes, but
as it sank into people's minds that man's time as Earth's
master was over, classes ended. Nat and the people on
the block raided Bowie Elementary School for books
and globes and scissors and glue and colored paper. He
had raided Terra Toys in Austin. There were still people
or things like people in Austin. Then that was before the
Shining Waves passed through. The empty houses across
the way were filled with stuffed animals. He thought it
would make the world less scary for Stephanie if she
saw windows full of white bears and blue horses.

He usually slept in the hall between Stephanie's and
Mama's rooms. There had only been one incident. One
night a little crack opened in the air about six inches
below the ceiling and a black slime had *dripped* down
into another crack about six inches above the age-
dulled hardwood floor. He had set up for hours watch-

ing it, hoping it would go away, praying that neither of the females would wake up and see it. It faded away before dawn. Some people thought the whole process was driven by dreams. Others thought dreams were driven by the process.

He couldn't sleep tonight. Dr. MacLeod's words had slipped under his skin. He thought about his little girl all the time. He played with her every day, not for the joy of play but to keep her focused on human things. Other parents wouldn't let their kids play with her, not after her mother . . .

She liked the swing sets in Robert E. Lee Park. That was only two blocks away. He carried her on his shoulders, like she was a much younger girl. They would swing, and he would spin her around on the roundelay. Then one morning he found that something had taken a *bite* out of it in the night. After that he kept her at Mama's. Nat wanted beyond all things to be able to take her to the Church, which he figured for the only sanctuary. Father Murphy had said no. He didn't think the girl was Marked, but you know how everyone is these days.

Dawn came and he made breakfast for himself and Stephanie. Grits with a little molasses. She looked cute rubbing the sleep out of her black eyes. She wore her pale blue shorts and her little yellow top. She was growing out of the top, beginning to have the buds of breasts. Nat doubted that she would grow up to become a woman. There was no future for humans any more. He wondered for an instant if she would "marry" one of the gray-skinned ghouls in Austin, and the thought turned his stomach. Fortunately he did not lose his breakfast— food was rare.

"Hey, I need to go to work now."

"You don't need to work. *Abuela* dreamed we won the lottery."

"There is no more lottery, my little bluebonnet."

"Sometimes grandma says strange things."

"She is just playing, my little orchid."

"What's an orchid?"

"It's a pretty flower like you."

"I'm not a flower. I'm a girl."

"Then I will call you 'flower-girl' because you smell so sweet."

"The next time you go to ATX, can you bring back some perfume so I really can smell sweet?"

"I will, Flower-Girl. Chanel Number Five."

Today he was going to work in his cousin Tony's field. Tony was bringing in a crop of corn, some tomatoes, and *yerba de manso* for sore throats. Even before the Rising weather was hot in Texas by April, and smart people didn't work at midday. He woke up *Mamacita*. "I am going to Tony's today. I will bring you some tomatoes and a little oregano, OK?"

"You are a good boy, Juan."

"I'm Nat, not Juan."

"Be careful, Juan, bring us some chicken from that place on Goliad Street."

He kissed Mama's brown forehead. The light went out a little each day. He remembered the line from that poem from Mrs. Phillips's class, "Rage, rage against the dying of the light." Poetry made sense these days; history, not so much.

At the edge of the village stood walls made of galvanized iron and plywood. Two men were watching the road. Doublesign had been a tiny town, hence its name. "The sign that says Entering and the sign that says Leaving are on the same pole." It was a couple of miles to the fields. He drove. As long as they could get gas out of the tanks, they wouldn't walk. It made for too easy a target. The guards were Father Murphy, with a gray crewcut and a stained priest's collar, and Nick Flores, a light brown man with a big gold tooth. Nick had a 512 tat and a People's Nation star. They drank out of thermoses, rifles by their sides.

They got off their lawn chairs and began to swing the gate open. Father Murphy waved him over. Nat rolled down his window.

"Natividad Moreno—just the *hombre* I needed to see." The father's Irish accent had not died away after twenty years in Texas. Nor had his potbelly shrunk in the last three years. He was the only fat man left in Doublesign.

"What can I do for you, Father?" asked Nat.

"You can do something for our little town." The father's gray eyes were about to shoot out the guilt trip ray that only priests, nuns, and mothers can use. It could turn Nat into a teenager, into someone half his age.

"I do a lot for our little town. No one else makes the run into Austin since the flying things came."

"You are a brave man, Nat. That's why I thought of you. I need you to bring me something powerful. In Comesee there is a used bookstore. Eligio Mondragon told me that it has a *curandero's* Bible. It has some of his charms and recipes written in it. As our supply of medicine runs out, we need to know about oshá and Alamo tea. Some of the charms may be helpful against things."

"Why don't you go get it?" asked Nat. He knew the answer: the priest was important and he was some peon, but he wondered how the priest would say it.

"Because I am afraid," said Father Murphy.

"You think I am not?" asked Nat. "Fear and bravery are not enemies. But isn't the book of a *curandero* taking from you used to call the 'other side'?"

"I am not making rash judgments these days. If I thought I could get the leprechauns to help us, I would be calling for them."

"Why is Eligio remembering this now? Wouldn't this have been a good thing last year or the year before?"

"Psychology is not my forté."

"I am not going to risk my life for a book."

"If you bring me the book, I will make your life much sweeter."

"How?"

"Nat, I will allow Stephanie back into the church. I will let her stay there during the days, be in the storm shelter when needed. Your mother will not have to watch her during the day."

This had been the first good news in so long that it almost puzzled Nat, as though he had lost his hearing and was suddenly greeted by the cry of a mourning dove.

He tried hard not to let his voice break, "You would do this for us?"

"The book is important."

Jesús' old Chevy Custom 10 dated from the Reagan Administration. It had belonged to Dr. Chainey, who ran the cancer clinic. Nat could've got a new pickup after the Dying in Austin, but he didn't like to steal from the dead. Comesee lay twenty miles to the south. No one drove there because it lacked large grocery stores to loot—besides, as a small town, it might still have people.

The sun looked like the sun today, which Nat always felt was a good sign. He left on FM 1193. The first three miles held no surprises. About four miles on he saw one of the webbing cities. Roaches, the kind called palmetto bugs in Texas, had increased in size after the Rising. They were about as big as his fist and their shiny black carapaces were marked with bright green angular signs. They built cities. On the last day CNN had been on the air, there had been some remarks about them as the "Great Race." Nat couldn't see anything great about oversized bugs. People knew that they weren't a thing of nature because their web cities were illuminated at night. The city took up the better part of what used to be a cotton field, so Nat knew it was at least forty acres in size.

He couldn't see any of the bugs, which made him feel better. One time a couple of them flew into town and seemed to be checking everything out. Mr. Franks had run inside his house and grabbed a bottle of Raid and ran after them spraying the air. They stopped and sort of hovered. The poison seemed to do no harm, but after thirty seconds Mr. Franks just sank to the ground. His skin showed angry red blotches in the shape of the angular designs on the bugs' wings. He never came to and passed a few hours later. Now when a bug flew by, people ran indoors.

As he continued south, the sky changed from blue to the color of lead. Comesee had been a little anglo town. In the old days (which seemed so far gone), it survived by its junktique stores that sold to the Austin tourists on weekends. Nat hadn't thought about the town since the Rising, even though it was just a few miles away. Since then you just assumed anything that could be bad was. The billboards still welcomed folks in the name of the Lions. Historic Denton's BBQ still promised the best Elgin sausages and brisket. Even the Dairy Queen was up ahead nine blocks on the left. A few burned-out cars were on the highway, but the passage into town looked clear. Nat glanced at the pair of loaded Glock 37s on his passenger seat. Bullets worked against most things. If it didn't hurt your eyes to look at it, generally bullets would hit it. He slowed down as he came into town, waiting for either for signs of humans or of the Change.

It was the latter.

The Chevy dealership was covered with gray mucus. Nat could see angular things of metal that jerked inside. He gave it wide berth and drove on into the center of town the corner of 2nd and Main. *Calabazas*—what do they call them—jack-o-lanterns stood in front of every business on Main. It was spring, no time for fresh pumpkins. At least it was spring back in Doublesign. Father Murphy said he had to look for Two Guys from Texas Books. Time was pretty leaky these days.

There it was. Middle of the block between to the karate place and Hickerson's Video and Game Rental, it had big plate glass windows. It wasn't covered in slime; it looked normal. Maybe there was a healing book inside. He hated getting out of the truck. Nothing swooped or buzzed or squelched. The air smelled clean and hot. He left the motor running. He walked to the door. It was dark inside; faded reds and pinks dominated the window display. The Rising had happened in February, and many places still commemorated a faded Valentine's, when earth's old lovers had come back. The door was locked. He got a cinderblock out of the back of the pickup and smashed the glass. All of the jack-o-lanterns had rolled closer to him while his attention had been elsewhere. Reality was melting; he would have to be quick. Dr. MacLeod had explained to them that the "Otherness" had to seep in through "liminal" things. Nat thought that "liminal" meant scary. He kicked two of them away from the door, grabbed a flashlight and went in, careful not to slip on the broken glass. The store didn't smell right—it didn't have that acid tang of *Tia* Rebecca's yellowing romances. It stank of fire and copper, but the books looked OK.

There it was. The Bible. It sat on a shelf beneath diet books, with other Bibles and Books of Mormon and old Methodist hymnals. But it was big and black with gold lettering *Biblia Santa*. It had a nice heft in his hands, but as he picked it up something laughed in his head. Voices in the head weren't unusual, but they made him miserable. Outside the shop, the jack-o-lanterns weren't round or orange any more. They were becoming one of those clear snot-looking things that seemed to have rusty machinery and mercury inside. They were dumb but fast. He grabbed some paperback novels and flung them on to the street. The snot-thing formed several eyes that focused on the books and squelched off in their direction. Swallowing hard, he ran toward it, since he needed to get to his truck. It didn't turn until he was inside. He threw the truck in reverse and pulled into the crossroad. It had sensed him and shot out two long runners of snot to pull itself toward the backing Chevy. It grew mouths. Some yelled "Tekeli-li!" Others made the sound of fire engines and turkey buzzards. One mimicked a reporter from Channel 42, "Tex DOT has no explanation of the mysterious slime on I-35."

He turned his truck toward Doublesign. The creature was gaining speed. It had made some of the strands into tentacles that were holding on to his tailgate. He put the pedal to the metal. 40, 50, 60. At 75 the main mass couldn't keep up, but about a gallon of the goo had managed to plop itself in the bed of his truck. It was making little green eyes that looked like zits and little centipede legs to scuttle across the bed. It slimed its way up his back window and its little eyes just spun around. Two mouths formed, their voices thin and high like a kid that has breathed in a helium ballon. One yelled, "Tekeli-li!"

and the other said, "¡Si usted ve un soggotho escaparse!"
Nat laughed. That was—what's his name on KHHL out
of Leander. Man, he was funny.

Before.

Yeah, before.

Nat tried to concentrate on his driving. He rolled his
window up as far it would go. A tiny thick tendril was
pushing itself against the window, a tiny eye forming
at the tip. He didn't want to take it into the village. He
had some bug-spray, a Crip-blue bottle of Raid Flying
Insect Killer. He braked hard and leapt out the passenger side window and let the loathsome mass have
it. *Jesús, Maria y José.* It pulled itself into a dirty white
ball and flung itself on the asphalt. It was rolling away.
Some days you got the bear; for Steph's sake he hoped
the bear would never get him. Dr. MacLeod said that
all life on Earth came from the shoggoths. He said they
had never gone away, just "hidden up the spiral stair-
case of DNA." All of the things that showed up three
years before had always been here, but most humans
couldn't smell them or hear them or see them. When
that city had Risen in the Pacific, we could touch them
and they could touch us.

The sky looked blue, hazy, but not dangerously so. The
sun was white and some turkey buzzards were flying off
to the west. The ground had grass and a few late-season
bluebonnets on it. Figuring it was not against the law
to pick them now, Nat gathered a few and one Indian
paintbrush for contrast. He put them in his truck on the
passenger's side next to the Bible. He decided to open it,
to look for cures. Father Murphy had disgusted him by
suggesting that some *curandero* bullshit would be good
against the Otherness. Real crosses and real rosaries
hadn't worked. At his worst moments, Nat thought that
the *campo santo* of the Church didn't really work either.
Some day They would come, some ally of the Thing in
the Pacific. Doublesign was a small village. It couldn't
feed them the fear and misery they drank like wine.

He opened the Bible to find that it too was a trick.

The book had been hollowed out. There was no

curandero's herbs, no list of spells against the coming of the night. It was little spiral-bound book from Lulu Press. The chapters made no sense to Nat.

1. "Archaic Techniques of Ecstasy in the *Ryleh Text,*" Mircea Eliade
2. "Divinatory Deep Structure in *Seven Cryptical Books of Hsan* and the *Yi Ching*"
3. " Prophetic Patterns in Innsmouth Jewelry," Ellison Marsh
4. A selection from "Crave the Cave: The Color of Obsession." Esther Harlan James. Diss. Trinity College 1996, pgs 665-670
5. A selection from "A Refutation to Shrewsbury's 'Elemental Schemao.'" Mary Roth Denning. Diss. University of Chicago 2007, pgs. 118-126
6. A selection from "Fieldwork with the *Brujos Ocultados* of Barret, Texas." Carlos Cesar Arana. Diss. UCLA 1973, pgs. 93-118
7. "Cthulhu in the Necronomicon," Laban Shrewsbury
8. "The *Black: Sutra* of U Pao in relation to Left Hand Path Cults of South east Asia," Patrica Ann Hardy. Diss. MIT 2001, pgs. 23-40
9. "The Prehistoric Pacific in Light of the 'Ponape Scripture' (Selections)," Harold Hadley Copeland

"Alles Nahe werde fern"
Everything near becomes distant—Goethe
AD MEIORVM COVLHI GLORIAM

As usual, Nat did not know who was tricking whom. The small black book with its simulated leather binding had probably been one of those books college kids buy for a class. Juan had bought one for his Southwest life and literature class and another for his HVAC class at the community college. Juan had been working in Dallas when the Rising had occurred. Mama loved Juan better; he was the gang-free smart son. Nat smiled at his brother's favorite joke, "What do you call two Mexicans playing basketball?" "Juan on Juan." Nat started to throw

the book away, but who was he to judge? Certainty went
out of the world three years ago. Daymares and night-
reams were the scaffolding of reality now; loved ones
walked into the sky.

He opened the hollowed-out Bible; on the flyleaf
someone had written two verses in heavy pencil. **Genesis 28:16-17: And Jacob awoke out of his sleep, and he
said, Surely Jehovah is in this place; and I knew it not.
And he feared, and said, How terrible is this place! this
is none other than the house of God, and this is the gate
of heaven.** And **Job 3:8: May those who curse days curse
that day, those who are ready to rouse Leviathan.**

He drove on to Doublesign. Felix Washington stood
on guard duty. He was the Rev. Jackie Jones' uncle. Felix
was a very popular man, and at 78 certainly the oldest
left. He had been a jazz pianist back in the day; he'd
played gigs in Austin as little as five years ago. He had
also saved a coffee can full of marijuana seeds. Marijuana
provided a good buzz and it was good for trading with
the some of the other little towns that still remained,
like Thalia. Felix still tickled the ivories at the Kuntry
Kitchen, and Nat had seen his name on yellowing post-
ers for The Soft Machine and The Mahavishnu Orchestra. He liked to piss people off by saying, "Cthulhu ain't
no worse than white people." Felix opened the gate and
waved him on.

Nat drove to Santa Cruz. Father Murphy sat at the
wooden picnic table near the entrance. He had his pock-
etknife out, looking for all the world to be carving something in the rotten wood. He indicated that Nat should
sit beside him.

Nat realized how angry he was. His heart pounded.
The fat bastard had had him risk his life for a book. A
book wasn't going to solve their problems, certainly not
the Bible. Hadn't we seen hundreds of people using the
Bible to lay It back in the sea? Who was this fat Irish-
man, telling his family and friends what to do for the
last two decades? He had preached against his cousin
Cody's queerness, so Cody had run off to Houston to
live in the gay community there, sealing his death when

the waves that came with the Rising wiped Houston off the globe. He denied the Mass of the Dead for the scores of suicides, saying the Rising was God's test of our faith. As though the death of millions was a little algebra quiz. Nat wanted to start smashing him with the Bible—hit that red uneven face that always reminded him of a potato. Nat couldn't sit down.

"I brought your damned book."

"Thank you, Nat," said Father Murphy.

"It's hollow."

"Many people find the Bible hollow these days."

"No, I mean it is really hollow. You sent me there for nothing." Nat took out the little book from inside and tossed in front of Father Murphy. Murphy showed no surprise. Murphy continued his carving, some complicated sign.

"When did you really know the human world was over?"

"Three years ago, like everyone else." Nat wanted the guy to finish. He looked at the church door.

"Oh, she's in there with the others. I am as good as my word. I understood the world was over when the Bishop sent me here. I was sent to this little hellhole as a punishment. The Mother Church doesn't like its priests to stick their dicks in altar boys' cherubic little mouths. Did you know that? So they sent me here and I knew the world was over when I saw Christ's face in there. All that look of suffering. He had been mutely telling the human infestation for years and years."

Nat didn't like that he had had the same thought as this kid-fucker.

"You're a fucking pedophile?" Nat felt his stomach heave.

"I never liked fucking them; anyway age has taken care of that. Besides, I don't really like brown boys as much as blonde ones. Do you know why the Rising happened?"

"¡Chingada!"

"Remember all of those talking heads on TV? *When the stars are right,* they said, they know nothing. The great

Priest Cthulhu took a little nap, and a great deal of what is hidden by matter slept. We are the alarm clock. The shock. We figure out things, and as our tiny brains correlate the contents of our minds, their shock, their agony at glimpsing the true cosmos sends out a nice jolt. There are so many things waiting to Waken still; roses in your garden wanting to sing weird songs, pebbles wanting to shoot forth stony blossoms. Human time is done."

Nat wanted to hurt him. He would check on Stephanie, and he would tell some of the others first.

"Why did you want the book?" asked Nat. "I know it is about bad things, but why now?"

"The collector of these little texts was special to Cthulhu. His moment of endarkenment actually impressed It. This little *Liber Damnatus* is dear."

"You work for It."

"I have always worked for It. Most humans do, and those that don't serve as well. Hasn't your good doctor explained the Octopus to you? Humans' shock, their horror, and, for a rare few, their ecstasy works for It. At this point all we can do that is meaningful in the world is to increase the aesthetic value of this blue marble of a planet for a Will older and better than our own. Humanity is its last decade will finally have a purpose."

Nat took the hollowed shell of the Bible and smashed it as hard as he could against Father Murphy's cheek. He knocked the priest off the bench onto the grass. Murphy just laughed. Nat stomped on his chest.

"Beautiful." Father Murphy gasped, "Just beautiful. Oh Loathly Lord freed from the Angles of the Water Abyss I am but a shard of black rainbow to adorn the world to which you awaken. *Gurdjiatn Cthulhu gurdjiatn ekd szed mem-zem zmegnka!*"

"Fuck you, asshole!" Nat left him. He needed to see Stephanie now.

"Look, my son, I am turning the other cheek." Father Murphy rolled over. "I have made my garden beautiful for You. By the green star of Xoth I adore Thee, Domine."

* * *

About twenty people knelt in the church. Stephanie was a couple of rows from the front. Candles flickered around the Virgin, and the noontime sunlight came through the stained glass, but the church seemed dark.

"*Calabaza,* are you OK? Stephanie, we need to go."

She didn't move from her prayer. No one moved. He ran to her, neglecting to genuflect as he passed the altar, even though the light burned signifying His presence. As he came up to her, her face confused him. She had the naughtiest smile ever, and her eyes were crossed. Then he realized that something slick and shiny was coating her face. He touched her. He flinched. She was cold and sticky. A little sob died in his throat. All of them. They had faces of idiocy or leering lust. Some fixative had been sprayed over their faces. Someone had fixed their hands into obscene gestures. Miss Abelard was chewing on a crucifix; Joel Sanchez was whacking off.

He fell on his knees next to Stephanie. His weight knocked her little rigid body sideways. She would be a praying fool forever. He looked up at Christ. *How could you let this happen?*

Murphy had sawn Christ's ivory colored head off. He had replaced with an ivory-colored flying octopus. The image that the whole world had watched on television and feared. The image that had been in the dark spiral tower of their DNA. The part of Nat that was holding his world together, had its last moment. Nat felt the world stop. He heard a snap inside his head and his psyche dissolved into shock. He actually felt no amazement when the little flying octopus relaxed its grip on Christ's body and began flying so slowly, ever so slowly on its stubby wings toward Nat. Nat's last coherent thought was that it couldn't move that slowly and stay in the air. He was trying to scream.

He heard Father Murphy entering the church continuing the strange chant he had begun outside. He saw the green banner Father Murphy carried with the strange yellow design, and felt the tentacles as they surrounded his head. He almost laughed because they felt like something familiar—IcyHot muscle rub. He felt them slip over his open eyes and push their way into his nose. He felt one wriggle through his mouth and crush his larynx.

After that, there was no more linear thinking. What had been Natividad Moreno was now another art object. A tiny part of the Remaking of the world.

(For Robert Price)

HER ACRES OF PASTORAL PLAYGROUND

Mike Allen

Lynda chews her peas. Her husband watches, his wary gaze fixed on the beauty mark beneath her left eye, no bigger than a felt-tip stipple, a fetching accent to the delicate sweep of her cheekbone.

When Delmar first placed her plate in front of her, that mark wasn't there.

"Your pork chop okay?" he asks. "Not too dry?"

She nods, mutters "It's fine" through a mouthful. The muscles at her temples flex as she chews, drawing his attention to the lovely streaks of gray that flare above her ears, so exotic, so witchy—the angle of her head projects in his mind just so and a sleepy flutter of lust stirs deep within him. And a flutter of alarm, too, though why that is, he doesn't understand.

Then the black spot on her face moves. It's larger now, no longer a beauty mark, a lumpy mole with a thick black hair sprouting from its center. The hair twitches again, like a bug's antenna.

A whippoorwill starts its saw-motion song outside as a warm breeze stirs the kitchen curtains. Through the window Delmar notes two of the Appaloosa grazing in the pasture closest to the barn. Despite the brooding, overcast sky, sunlight washes the farm in soft watercolor hues.

Lynda picks up her ear of corn, peers out the window just as a faint spatter of rain belies the filtered sunlight.

"The Devil's beating his wife," she says. "Meaghan would love this. I hope she's better soon."

"She will be," Delmar replies. He says it automatically, like it's a programmed response, a catechism. The growth on the side of his wife's face thickens into an articulated tentacle, long as a tablespoon, and like one of those, it flares and bulges at its end. The growth waves up and down as if it's sniffing the air. Lynda brings the cob to her mouth, paying no attention to her new deformity.

Delmar goes to the stove, where he has set a wooden-handled butcher knife so that the top half of its blade rests on a red hot coil. He picks up the knife. "Honey, I'm sorry, but I need you to hold still a second."

What he does next he does with the impassive face of the parent who must every day hold his daughter with cystic fibrosis upside down and beat her to make sure she can breathe another day. Lynda holds still, closes her eyes, seems to *shut down*, almost. When he finishes, there's a raw circle on her cheek, like a cross-section of severed sausage, bloodless; and in seconds it's stretched over with new skin, pink and healthy. She starts again as if nothing has happened, picks up her ear of corn and starts to gnaw.

The black thing squirming in Delmar's hands screams when he drops it in the pot, but he has the lid over it before it can crawl out. Before it can speak. He knows he can't let it speak. *Why* he knows this, he can't really say, it's as if someone is whispering in his ear, whispering frantically, *don't let it, don't let it, don't let it*, but there's no one else in the room, just him and Lynda.

Outside, the rain-sound stops, and the landscape brightens, though the clouds stay gray as ever.

"Sweetie," calls Lynda, "could you bring me the butter?"

"You bet," he says, keeping the pot lid pressed down hard. "In a minute. Just a minute." He eyes her sidelong. "Just don't forget who loves you."

She smiles widely over the decimated contents of her plate. "I haven't. Ever."

After lunch, he trudges out to the vegetable garden, not a trouble on his mind. Though there's no break in the clouds, the light that so kindly warms his land makes its gentle presence known on his face. Most of his farm is given over to pastureland—he likes to joke to Lynda that he's renting from the horses—but he keeps a half-acre tilled and the animals, with preternatural discretion, leave it alone. He's never even had to put a fence around it.

He's imagining a sweaty but productive day spent plucking hungry bugs off the potato leaves, pulling weeds from between the beanstalks, harvesting the ripest ears of corn. How easily the work comes to him, a lifestyle he once knew only from the half-listened-to tales—more like shaggy-dog complaints, really, long growly rants with no real point—from his grouchy father, God rest his soul. Delmar agrees now with his father; that he really was born to this work. He can hardly remember his life before he brought Lynda and Meaghan here.

The cornrows tower at the edge of the tilled square furthest from the house. He gets to that task last of all, and once he's there something in him grows uneasy, and a sensation crawls through his shoulders—like the prick, prick, prick when a wasp alights and starts to scurry across exposed flesh—but he feels this on the inside of his skin, not the outside.

And at once his mind fills with the sight of the black limb twitching on his wife's face. The texture of her flesh when he cut into it, spongy and yielding not a speck of blood. He doubles over, his insides pricking, but that voice is back, soothing in his ear, *Don't think about it, just don't think about it, don't let yourself think about it.*

And though his heart is racing he can stand up straight. The pricking sensation is gone. He breathes deeply; his eyes take in the beauty that surrounds him, the grass-green slopes, the fecund garden, thriving as a result of his proud handiwork. Yet he's still not at ease.

Beyond the corn lounges a long stretch of pasture that the animals hardly ever visit. Beyond that rises a gray haze of fog. He thinks nothing of it—this wall of fog is always there, misting up in a thick curtain to join with the low-hanging clouds overhead.

Instead, a spark of light in the pasture catches his eye, orange and pulsing like fireplace embers. A brush fire? Couldn't be. Something pricks in his belly, once, sharp, and stops.

His boots whisk softly through the grass.

For as long as he can remember, there's been an oddity present in this particular pasture, a blackened spot, perfectly circular, about the size of a manhole, where nothing grows. *It's a lightning strike*, that internal voice always tells him, whenever he gets close. *Nothing special. Not important.*

But now the burnt circle in the ground has rekindled. He comes upon it to find it alive with curling lines of pulsating orange and yellow light. Stranger still, the lines etched by the glow form patterns, some of which he recognizes, though it's as if a brick barrier stands in his mind between recognition and understanding. The patterns throb.

A sound from the fogbank. A sob.

The pricking beneath his skin returns. Delmar takes a step toward the foggy veil, despite the voice whispering, *Stay away. Stay far away.*

"Who's out there?" he means to shout, but the sound barely leaves his throat.

The sobbing within the fog continues. It's unquestionably the sound of a man, weeping.

Delmar goes pale. It's been months at least since he's ever heard another human voice out here. There's been no one save him and his wife and his daughter, safe from the rest of the world, the way he's wanted it to be. Confusion and anger and that hideous pricking fear all slither inside him.

Worse, he thinks he recognizes the voice, but he can't place it. The man's sobs grow louder, the sound of someone unhinged with grief, a father finding a child's murdered body in the trunk of a car.

Delmar takes another step toward the gray wall.

"Get out of here," he says, louder, but still not with the strength he'd like. "You're trespassing. Go back where you came."

The man in the fog starts to scream. It's a sound ripped from the belly, and the screams keep coming, like the man is being shredded inside by something small and burrowing. And Delmar has heard this agony before, this man screaming in torture, and he covers his ears, because he can almost make out words. He reels and steps back—

No, no, no! hisses the voice in his ear.

He looks down. He nearly stepped into the black circle, which is no longer burning, no longer glowing. And he shudders. He doesn't know why, but he knows he should never step in the circle. Never cross its edge.

The screams in the fog have gone silent. He feels no desire to know who it was, whose voice shrieked from the fog, no more than he feels desire to know why that fog never moves, why the sky never clears.

Go to your family. Love them. Let them love you.

And he goes back to the garden, not a trouble on his mind. Before the light starts to fade, he's filled a big wooden basket full of fresh-picked ears of corn. He'll shuck them so Lynda can slice off the kernels and can them. They like to do this together, let their smiles do all the speaking. They'll do it tomorrow. He so looks forward to it.

But things in the house take a turn for the worse. His heart won't settle. His mind won't stay quiet.

Dinner goes wonderfully enough, built around two thick steaks he set out to thaw early that morning. He even speaks to Meaghan for a little while once the rich meal lulls her mom into an evening doze. While Lynda slumps comatose at her end of the sofa, he settles comfortably at the other end and listens to his daughter's high, sweet voice sing the alphabet, or mouth nonsense syllables to the same calliope tune, and he feels consciousness drifting off.

An electric hum accompanies a constant, steady rattling. It takes him a moment to place what he's hearing: the rapid-fire click-click-click of a home movie projector. Delmar hasn't heard that noise since his twelfth birthday, when his father dug out that seemingly ancient machine to show the gathering of school chums embarrassing footage of the family dog wrapping her leash around a younger Delmar's stumpy legs.

It's now Delmar's father who sits with him, hunched at the other end of the couch. His father's head turns on a neck mutated by swelling cancer lumps. *You asked me to dig out this one*, his father says, the sound coming through the surgery hole in his throat. *Don't whine to me. This is all your cross to bear.*

The beam from the heard-but-not-seen projector shines on a wall of fog that conceals the other side of the room. Distorted on the fog, Meaghan's face flickers in close-up, framed by straight dark hair just like her mother's. The footage is black and white, rendering her bright green eyes a moist gray. He recognizes her unicorn pajamas.

A large hairy arm, a man's arm, reaches into frame, takes her wrist. Her eyes bug, her face contorts. Delmar feels the prickling inside as the huge hand turns her wrist palm up, as another hand, the right to match the left, stabs a butcher blade into her forearm, slices a long black line.

All this has unfolded free of all sound save the rattling projector, but when Meaghan's mouth stretches open to scream it's loud and piercing and absolutely real.

Delmar starts awake. Lynda is beside him on the couch, still comatose. Meaghan screams again, somewhere in the house. Lynda doesn't stir.

Delmar can't bring himself to move, paralyzed by a gut-dragging-and-twisting spin of disorientation. He can't remember a time when he's heard Meaghan's voice without Lynda close by, and he knows something is wrong with that, really wrong, and the voice that protects him is saying that too, that something's wrong, he can't really be hearing that. Yet upstairs—she has to be upstairs—she cries again, "Dadd-eeeeeeee!"

The noise as raw and loaded with pain as if she'd fallen on a bed of nails.

He runs for the stairs pell-mell. His daughter screams again, the sound like pins stabbed into his eardrums. When he reaches her bedroom door, her shrieks hardly sound human.

But he throws the door open, and she isn't there. There's nothing there. The room is empty, even of furniture.

Meaghan shrieks again. Now, the noise comes from downstairs.

The voice in his ear is whispering, *It's gotten out of control. You need the book. You need to get it* now.

Delmar doesn't understand what the voice wants. Or something in him doesn't want to understand.

At Meaghan's next howl, he plunges back down the stairs. But stops halfway.

On the couch, in Lynda's place, a monster writhes, a black sunburst of ropy worms. The shrieks he hears are coming from somewhere in its center. It lurches to the floor, dozens of snaky limbs flopping blind, turning over lamps and end tables, capsizing the TV.

The book, hisses the voice in his ear. This time, he understands, and knows he has to obey.

He dashes through the den, toward the hall and the utility room at its end, but one of the black ropes twines around his ankles, and then the thing is pulling itself on top of him, wailing in Meaghan's voice. Keening syllables that are almost words.

His bare hands tear at the cables of black flesh sliding against his skin, but it's as if two tendrils replace each one he breaks, lashing around his forearms and thighs and belly, struggling to hold him still. The thing is still screaming, now with Lynda's voice. A snake-smooth band of contracting muscle coils around his neck, starts to tighten.

But he is stronger. He shoves to his knees, rips out the boneless limbs by their roots, hurls the thrashing tangle across the room.

Lynda screams, screams, screams.

He returns from the utility room with a huge book,

its leather binding on the verge of crumbling, its pages flopping as he holds it open. The symbols in dark brown ink mean nothing to him, though they radiate a head-spinning wrongness. If these scribblings form words, he doesn't know what they say—and yet he does. It's as if another person inside him uses his eyes to see, his mouth to speak, knows the precise rhythms and pauses. And as this happens the squealing black thing in the den begins to foam, to buck, to lengthen and thicken and lighten in hue. Delmar's vision blurs, with tears that he understands no more than he does the incantation.

His voice rises in crescendo, and all the space around him seems to ripple, in a way that can't be seen physically—yet his mind still senses it. The ripple starts where he's standing and spreads through the room, the house, even the land beyond, and he knows that the power in that subtle wave is setting things to right. The voice tells him so.

The black thing is gone. There's only Lynda, resting peaceful on the couch, her only motion the soft rise and fall of her breath. There is no sign of Meaghan, but the voice is telling him not to worry about that. He might not see her, yet whenever he asks, she'll speak, and he'll know she still loves him.

Lynda's limp as a bag of straw, but he's strong enough to lift her. He carries her to bed.

Using the book always makes him uneasy—vaguely, he recalls he's had to before—but now all is restored. Outside, there are no stars, but neither is there darkness. Just as with the sunlight, an unseen moon bathes his farmland in its shine. He can make out the shapes of the horses, straight-legged and still possibly sleeping.

He snuggles in beside his lovely, witchy wife, no troubles on his mind, and settles his head in the pillows.

He's back on the sofa, and behind him the projector rattles. Meaghan sits next to him, kicking her legs, which don't quite touch the hardwood floor. *I asked Grandpa to get this out again*, she says. *We haven't watched it since forever.*

The film unspools in grainy black and white, just like before. But now it resembles hidden camera footage, the view angled down from a corner of the ceiling. From this vantage point the disembodied observer peers into a large room with cinderblock walls, its carpet and other objects, mostly large plastic toys—a playhouse, a hobby horse, a Sit-and-Spin—shoved hastily against the far wall to bare the cement floor. Three figures huddle at the center of the bare floor, a man, a woman, a girl maybe seven years old. And the man has a book, a huge ominous tome. There is a small window in the far wall, placed high, indicating a basement room. The window is just out of the camera's range of clear focus. Beyond it, through dingy glass, shadows move with chaotic fury. Sometimes blinding light flares there. Sometimes the window goes completely dark.

The man is drawing frantically on the ground. The film speeds, somehow recorded in time lapse, an effect that drastically accelerates the chaos seen in silhouette through the high window. The man completes a huge circle inscribed along its entire circumference with headache-inducing sigils. The circle encloses him and the woman and child.

"You were always so good at drawing when you worked at that school," Meaghan says beside him.

"University," he corrects out of reflex.

She giggles. "I remember how you came home all the time with those weird drawings in your coloring book."

"Sketchpad, darling. It was a sketchpad."

"How you said you got 'em from some book you were studying and you never let me look at 'em. Never."

He turns to tell her to stop sounding mad, it was all for her own good, but she's gone. Yet he's not alone: he's looking at a copy of himself, but with bruises on his face, a cut down one cheek, dressed in an oxford shirt with a deeply stained collar, a torn sweater vest, fancy slacks ruined by more flowing stains. He looks like an academic who just escaped from the mouth of hell. He's dressed just like the man in the movie. He *is* the man in the movie.

I try to stop you from remembering, this new self says, *but you fight me. Some part of you is always warring with me, trying to remember everything. And when you do, you'll understand why you have to forget again. Understanding means madness.* The man's voice, the voice of this other self, is the voice he always hears whispering in times of terrible stress.

His guardian self keeps talking, but Delmar stops listening, because a new voice distracts him, murmuring right in his ear. It's Meaghan again; he can practically feel her lips against his skin. "Don't listen, Daddy. He can't stop you from knowing."

Delmar watches himself in the film, scrambling to draw a second, smaller circle, about the size of a manhole, at the center of the larger one. It's an agonizing, slow process, taking time even in time lapse, with the activity seen in shadow at the far window getting more and more frenzied, impossible to comprehend. Often times the mother, who his mind admits is Lynda, must be Lynda, seems like she's having an exasperating time keeping the little girl inside the circle.

As Delmar watches, his immediate surroundings fade. Soon there's nothing left but the picture show flickering on the fog and Meaghan's voice in his ear.

"Sweet Daddy. Don't you worry 'cause I still love you. I understand it all. You tried to use evil to do a good, good thing, but you had to be evil to use evil. But you did it 'cause you love us and love can be evil and good together."

The time lapse reverts to normal speed. In black and white, Delmar and Lynda are arguing. She turns hysterical, terrified as his gestures grow more frantic. In the background, unnoticed by either of them, the little window rattles. Darkens. Bizarrely, it looks like hair is growing around the frame.

The voice changes oh-so-subtly, still with the timbre of a child, but more adult, more knowing. "What you did was so powerful it could never work, never, without the blood of an innocent. I know, Daddy, I know."

In the film he screams, the contortion of his face grotesque in total silence, and his wife pushes his daughter toward him. He takes her wrist, produces the knife. Still unnoticed, the window pushes open, just a crack, and the hair-tendrils that have worked their way into the room begin to thicken and lengthen into streams, into ropes. Something huge is oozing through the gap around the glass, pouring down the wall as if made from soft clay.

"I should have been smarter, Daddy. I shouldn't have been so scared."

The image goes out of focus, becomes a crazy split screen, left and right visions going out of sync. In one lobe, Delmar, weeping as he chants, holds his daughter's bleeding arm over the inner circle, its black designs coming to life, shining, burning as the blood strikes it. In the other lobe, the windowpane bows and shatters as a slimy mass of dense hairy jelly shoves its way through, unfurls in an explosion of sucking lamprey mouths and clusters of lidless human eyes.

Staring down from the corner again as the insanely hideous thing lands on the debris and springs—and it is as if the creature strikes a wall where the outer circle is drawn, as if it crashes straight into curved aquarium glass. The creature is not repelled by the barrier, but hangs there in the air, sticking to the invisible wall like a tarantula hugged against a fishbowl, its dozens of limbs splayed out radially from its squirming core like a spider escaped from a schizophrenic's most deranged hallucination.

Delmar has released his daughter's arm. He's kneeling by the circle, the book beside him, cords standing out against his neck as he chants. And the little girl sees the horrid thing hanging in the air. And she screams. And she runs. Away from the center of the circle. She runs out of view of the disembodied ceiling observer, and the thing crawls so fast around and across the surface of the invisible barrier, scuttling spider-fast, as Lynda lurches too late to catch her daughter.

All through this, Meaghan's whisper has never stopped.

"Don't you want to know really why we love you so? Because you're just like us, just one of us, all part of us and us part of you. We ate you all up, we did. You made the spell work, you made the monster back into mommy and me with that magic from my blood, but we're still it and it's still in you, it's always been in you, changing you inside, one slow cell at a time, because your spell can't protect you that small."

The dream camera coldly documents what follows. The burst of dark fluid that sprays into the circle. A woman's severed arm lands on the floor, a foot lands another place, snakelike black limbs greedily snatch them up, gulp them down. The man's face a mask of horror, but he doesn't stop his chant, even as the multi-limbed thing joins him within the invisible aquarium, squeezing in through the opening made when the outer circle was fatally crossed. The dream-Delmar doesn't stop his chant, even when the creature sends long hooked limbs around the burning inner circle to hook into his vulnerable belly, punch in and drag out the gray ropes coiled inside. The man's face contorts in unspeakable agony and mystic ecstasy as he howls his final syllables. And it's at that moment that the inner circle surges in a pillar of blinding fire, and the film changes to color, *Wizard of Oz* technicolor.

"But, Daddy, the part of us inside you is going to wake up. And then we'll be together like we should be and you'll never be alone again. You'll never, ever, ever be left alone. When you hear my voice, I'm saying other words too, words that you can't hear, but the sleeping part of me that's inside you can. It hears me and it wants to wake up. And when it does, that voice you always hear won't really be yours. It'll be ours. And we'll trick you, and you'll ruin the spell. We'll trick you, Daddy, when we wake up."

The burning circle, now a blackened spot in a beautiful pasture. And the man, his body whole, his clothes changed to suit his surroundings, picks himself up as he watches a black mass shrink and thicken and transform into a new, familiar shape. But only one shape. Never two.

And behind them, at the edge of the pasture, the fog. And above them, the grey clouds that will never, ever lift.

A tickling at his ear, a whisper.

"Wake up. Wake up. Wake up."

He springs awake and gropes for the lamp. The bulb casts its light across the comfortable contours of his bedroom.

His wife lies on her side, sleeping peacefully, her back to him, the cartoon cat on her favorite nightshirt flashing its inane grin.

From under her collar a dark tendril stretches, no thicker than a strand of yarn. Its end rests on his pillow, bulging out into a plush-lipped mouth that nestles beside the indentation where his head had rested. It continues to mouth words as if it doesn't know he's not there any more.

Delmar trembles, staring at the tiny mutant mouth that mutters in his daughter's voice. His eyes bulge. Tears smear his cheeks. All the barriers he's built inside his own mind to survive day to day in this world he created for his family, for what remains of them, have crumbled. He comprehends everything.

He only ever hears Meaghan's voice when it speaks from Lynda's body. Confronting this truth isn't what was causing him such disgust and dismay. What rips deep inside him, aggravating once again that pricking beneath his skin: never before has that voice turned against him, said things that Meaghan herself would never have said.

He leaves the bedroom, comes back with the book. Sets it down. Sits on the edge of the bed beside Lynda, sets to work with a blowtorch and knife. His tears never stop.

He returns to the book, starts to read aloud.

It's dark beneath the ever-present clouds, but he knows the way. He walks across the verdant pastures that always stay green and thick with grass no matter how long the animals graze. He walks past the burnt circle, its ember glow patterns pulsating brighter than he's ever seen, a silent blare of strident warning. He leaves the circle behind, strides into the fog, consumed by the message he needs to deliver.

The rustling of his feet through the damp grass grows muffled in the dense mist, then fades altogether. It's as if his steps alight on the fog itself.

He takes ten strides, twenty, thirty, and then, as abruptly as a bird striking glass, the fog ends. His land ends. The entire world ends.

Beyond the edge: an ocean of inhuman flesh, seen from undersea.

Just as the protective circle he drew in his horribly failed attempt to save his wife and daughter gave rise to a clear fishbowl barrier against the things it was intended to keep out, so does this island of sanity built from his daughter's blood and his father's rambling stories terminate at a barrier, one that shuts out the madness that swallowed the earth whole. He and what's left of his family—that disgusting black thing, forced to take the form of his wife when the spell touched her piecemeal remains, but not enough of his daughter left to take form too, only a voice—he and his family dwell now in this single pocket of peace, a bubble in the belly of the all-consuming beast.

On the other side of that barrier, pressed hard against it, pink translucent ropes thick as tanker trucks pulse and swell as rivers of ichor flow through their veiny channels. These titanic kraken tentacles move slowly, like slugs on glass, and plasma churns and boils in the spaces between them. Sometimes the bubbles look like faces. Sometimes smaller things squeeze in between the vast squirming limbs, enormous urchins with eyes lining and crowning the spines, or amoebic creatures that spontaneously form mouths or multi-jointed arms as they flow bonelessly through the cramped liquid spaces. Sometimes gray skinless beings, sculpted crudely humanoid, emerge and scrabble desperately against the invisible barricade before the currents sweep them back into the sickening organic soup.

Delmar understands all now. If the clouds ever parted above and around his farm, these sights would form his heaven and his horizon.

He stares into the nausea-inducing chaos, unblinking, and speaks. "I'll keep them alive, as long as I can." He spreads his arms. "I'll keep this alive, as long as I can. I'll never, ever give you what you want."

Behind the sliding pink tentacles, a vast eye peels open. Even through the layers of wormy flesh, he can see it.

And when it opens, pores gape all along the massed coils of pink, translucent flesh. They gape and flex like octopus siphons sucking water. Perhaps it's these that make the noise Delmar hears as countless whispers speaking in one voice. *Inside your shell, time still flows forward, but that time will end. Outside, time is still. Outside, your future is now. Outside, you are with us and have been forever and will be forever. Your future is our now.*

While the orifices whisper, an immense mouth yaws apart above the eye. Things crawl inside its lips. And somewhere inside the crawling darkness, a man screams. He howls in such a magnitude of pain that Delmar can't begin to imagine what's being done to him. The man screams and screams, over and over—then perhaps there comes a fraction of respite, for the howls crumble into high-pitched and pathetic sobs. Maybe there are words, repeated pleas, but Delmar can't make them out before the screams start again, and the mouth closes, sealing them away.

The voice of the screaming, sobbing man—it is his own voice. The voice of his future self, once his safe haven has perished.

Delmar's eyes are wet and bright and knowing. But his voice doesn't waver. "I'll keep them alive. As long as I can."

As he retreats into the fog, the million-strong voice whispers back. *We wait.*

*　　*　　*

Light streams through the open kitchen window as Delmar slices onions for the omelets. The soothing breeze accepts his invitation to drift inside.

Delmar has the vaguest memory of an upsetting night, but a voice whispers in his ear, his own voice, telling him he has to forget for now, compartmentalize, or the weight of knowledge will keep him from what happiness he has left, with what's left of his family, in the time he has left.

Whatever it was, it hardly seems to matter now. He breathes in the warm, sweet air that mingles with the smell of his own cooking and knows he can handle whatever life has to throw at him.

The sizzle of the bacon in the skillet doesn't completely drown out water rushing onto tile as Lynda showers. He can do this almost without thinking: the bacon first, then eggs to soak up the flavor. Lynda always *tsk*ed him for that vice, frying eggs in bacon grease, but she can't stop herself from wolfing down the results. *Just an evil way to show my love*, he likes to tell her.

He raises the knife above a helpless onion, then stops short. There's singing, coming from the shower. He freezes, listening, because it's Meaghan's voice that sings, and that doesn't seem right, and part of him knows the many, many reasons it's not right, but that part of him refuses to share its concerns aloud. And so he shrugs it off. It's not important.

Back to his task. He realigns the onion and steadies it for the killing stroke. Then something catches his eye. He lifts his hand to his face. His heart starts to pound.

A black growth shivers on the back of his ring finger, just below his wedding band. It extends as he watches, reaches out with twin protrusions akin to a snail's eyes. They twitch toward him. He feels a painful, pricking sensation, but *under* his skin, and for a brief flicker another vision imposes over his own, a vision of his own face, monumental in size and monstrous. The inner voice he always hears, the one that comforts and warns him, speaks again, but only says, *We wait.*

His wife's singing has stopped. The bathroom door opens.

"Sweetie," Lynda calls from the shower, "can you bring me a towel?"

"Sure," he answers, as he positions his hand on the cutting board. "In a minute."

SPHERICAL TRIGONOMETRY

Ken Asamatsu
Translation by Edward Lipsett

1

What I saw just before I awoke—the mountain road, winding away beyond the front windshield of the car. Darkness crowding close to the left, the right. Bulging, pallid beasts appearing and vanishing again in the headlights, beams always stabbing on. Their faces, human, on the heads of wild-eyed, shambling *things*. The monitor built into the console and the scenes of the city it showed. The city was crumbling, turning to rubble from the sky down. The images, washed away under a flood of noise . . . noise wavering like jellyfish tentacles. The woman wearing glasses in the passenger seat, smoking. I could sense her irritation clearly. I glance into the rearview mirror, see the couple in the back seat. He's mid-fifties, she's maybe around thirty. His arm around her shoulder, he whispers something in her ear, then unexpectedly looking forward, speaks.

"We're here, Kanako. See, the Womb!"

At last a giant white sphere, half-buried in the ground, looms ahead, then suddenly changes into a giant eyeball, staring at us. *Their* eye.

I scream, half jumping out of bed. Nightmare. No, what I just saw wasn't a nightmare, was it . . . it was a fragmentary memory. A memory of the night of April 30, well after midnight, when I arrived here at the Womb.

The *Womb*, Manabe had named it, keeping the pronunciation even in Japanese. He said the name suited the birthplace of the next generation of humanity. Manabe never refers to it as a "refuge" or a "shelter." Whatever. So I'll call it the Womb. But the Mother who holds that womb within her is terrified, facing death.

My name is Tatsuya Izumo. I'm a painter. Hardly the sort of person fit to be the "father of the next generation of humanity," as Manabe says. He really wanted my wife, not me—I was just sort of baggage she happened to bring along.

My wife Sayoko was a scientist and the architect of the Womb. When rich occultist Manabe asked her to design it, she accepted and took complete command of the project. Then, Sayoko had never thought that the Change he always spoke of would really come.

After all, there were a fair number of rich men and women who believed Nostradamus' prediction that the world would end in 1999, or the Mayan calendar's prophecy of catastrophe in 2012. Rich people always tended to lean a bit toward the occult ... In Japan, there was no shortage of company presidents who would consult fortunetellers to learn the most propitious date to sign a contract, or turn to *feng shui* when decorating their company headquarters. So when Manabe asked her to build a shelter without angles, in preparation for the coming "Change," Sayoko figured it was just another wacky job and accepted. The money was excellent, and as a scientist and an architect she was intrigued by the challenge of building a shelter "without angles" where people could live in safety for fifty years.

Manabe bought up a huge tract of land deep in the mountains of Nagano prefecture, the site for the Womb. The occultists, fortunetellers, and psychics hired by Manabe all agreed that it was the most sacred spot in Japan. In fact, a certain "new religion" had designated it as holy, building their headquarters and temple there. During WWII, their surging strength lead the feared *kempeitai* police to accuse the religion of *lese majesty*, destroying the temple and arresting all officials and believers at once. He said nobody had set foot on the land in the eighty-odd years since. And now Manabe was building his Womb on that sacred spot, no matter the cost.

At the beginning, Sayoko thought Manabe was simply using a metaphor when he demanded a shelter without angles. She thought he just wanted a safe refuge. She realized he was speaking quite literally when he saw the first design drawings and refused them outright.

With the haughty expression the rich reserve for their lessers, he berated her: "What do you call this? This is nothing more than a simple bomb shelter! And full of angles! The entrance, the walls, the ceilings . . . angles, angles everywhere! How could you possibly imagine this could be a shelter! Do it again, and better!"

"Yes sir, President Manabe," she asked. "Can you provide some specifics for the design?"

"I need a facility without angles of any kind," he answered, changing instantly from the president of a megacorporation to an occultist. "You seem to be bright, but obviously haven't a shred of esoteric knowledge. Fine. I'll teach you.

"Since it was created, our universe has been the battleground for a never-ending conflict between curves and angles. What we call 'good' is expressed in the abstract by curves, and what we call 'evil' by the angles. The black magicians of the West treasured the pentacle because it held five angles. The mandalas of the East were round, curves without angles. Atzous says that the purest evil in all creation is symbolized by the triangle: it is the evilest shape, because it is formed of the smallest number of angles. The ancient Chinese knew the esoteric meaning of triangles, and so named the triangle formed by the triangle of Sirius the 'Evil Stars' for just that reason. Even Homer knew Sirius was evil . . ."

And he ordered Sayoko to build him a shelter without angles as quickly as possible, because there was so little time left.

Sayoko thought it was just a figure of speech, his saying there was no time left. She didn't worry too much about it, shrugging it off as just another obsession of an occultist client.

A little less than a month after Manabe urged her to push ahead, though, *it* happened. Four prefectures facing the Pacific Ocean—Ibaraki, Chiba, Kanagawa and Shizuoka—suffered a catastrophic earthquake and *vanished*. They didn't burn down, or sink, they literally *vanished*. Naturally the government, the earthquake experts, the mass media, even my wife and I, believed it was the work of some giant earthquake and the resulting tidal wave.

Manabe called us very early the next morning. I distinctly remember being rudely awakened at four in the morning by the phone. I picked up the receiver, and the first thing I heard was "Put Sayoko Izumo on." Manabe was extremely excited, sounded almost furious.

"It's started," he told Sayoko. "Exactly where Teizo Akechi predicted in his *Traditions of Esotericism*, and exactly as catastrophic. They are returning, and the Gods and Buddhas cannot save us any longer. It is the End Times. We must flee to the Womb in Nagano at once!"

"Sir? Excuse me, sir?" Sayoko broke in. "The Womb is still incomplete. Your plan calls for fifty years, but I doubt it would support people for even twenty the way it is now."

"It's too late now. Even twenty would be excellent. You mustn't waste a minute—my wife and I are fleeing to the Womb at once. You and your husband should join us."

"My husband and I?" she countered, unable to stop herself. "But why?"

"The more people we have, the better, for saving the human species. The ideal would have been to build a huge Womb, a colony holding ten thousand people, but no longer. You are healthy and intelligent, and from what you have told me your husband is as well. You will bequeath excellent genes to the next generation of humanity. . . . Make ready at once, and come with your husband to pick us up. Within three hours. And keep the Womb secret . . . not a word to your families!"

Then he cut the phone, leaving us no chance to refuse.

"He's out of his gourd," said my wife, putting the phone down with a frown. "I've been playing along with him until now, because he's an important client and a sponsor for my research . . . but this! This is just insane! I'm not going to work for someone who's plain nuts!"

"Of course you can't! Even painters wouldn't work for anyone that far 'round the bend! And especially . . ."

The world shook around me, and nausea and dizziness cut off my words. I thought for a second I must be having a stroke, but then the books began falling off the shelves and the paintings on the walls began banging. *It's an earthquake!* And even as I framed the thought, the shaking intensified. It was like no earthquake I'd ever felt before, more like standing on top of a record player and spinning around and around and around . . . and counterclockwise, at that! The feeling of rotation jumped yet again, and suddenly I felt as if I were standing on the deck of a wave-tossed ship at the mercy of the storm.

And my brain was shattered by a piercing impact. Pain seared through my head, as if a thick nail had been driven into my brain through my retina, bringing a host of visions. The waves of the nighttime sea, rolling back as the seabed surged to the surface. Soft mud, seaweed, flopping deep-sea fish unable to escape in time. Like flash shots in a movie, the pictures appeared and vanished again, a bursting flood of imagery. Giant *structures* rising out of the ocean depths, covered in millennia-old mud. They looked as if they were of ancient stones, but the structures themselves writhed and quivered constantly like something alive. And from the shadows of the columns something crawled out, something shining . . . something that could only be called the natural enemy of humanity itself.

Sayoko shrieked before I had a chance to. When I saw her white face and hollow eyes, I knew she had seen what I had, in that brain-shattering instant.

No, not only Sayoko.

In that instant all of humanity saw the same visions, the same horror—the instant when the Damned Gods returned.

2

Sayoko always wore glasses, suffering from both near- and far-sightedness. Even so, her face was attractive, the type you'd describe as an intellectual beauty.

Maybe Manabe brought Sayoko and me with him to the Womb was because he had some plans for her.

Whatever disgusting plans he might have had, though, they were shattered before she ever entered the Womb.

What am I saying? Every time I think of it I lose it again . . . cool, gotta stay cool . . . calm, rational . . .

Reeling from illusionary visions, attacking my senses like some cerebral stroke, I turned on the cable TV and clicked to the all-news channel. The newscaster who popped up on the screen looked almost like he was smiling.

"The Tokyo city government office building is collapsing."

Simultaneously the screen switched to a video feed, showing City Hall shining metallic blue under dozens of searchlights in the early morning dimness. Covered in metal frames and huge sheets of glass, City Hall's surface was covered in angular shapes, a huge crystal reflecting the searchlights. When it was built people had laughed, saying the mayor had built a modern pyramid to cover his own underground mausoleum, or Godzilla had come out of the ocean and turned into a robot. That had been back in the '90s . . . a gigantic building fusing postmodernism with New Gothic architecture in the height of the economic boom years.

And now from protruding angles covering its surface, hundreds and hundreds of yellowish ropey things stretched out, quivering up into the pre-dawn sky. Semi-transparent tentacles like some huge jellyfish writhed and slimed from angular alcoves and setbacks inside the building. A newspaper copter drifted in a bit closer, trying to capture the metamorphosis of City Hall more clearly, and suddenly a piss-yellow rope snapped up, whipping around the copter and yanking it from the sky. The blades snapped off, still whirling as they flew toward City Hall, smashing into the side of the building in a glittering waterfall of glass shards. The waterfall poured down on the heads of the emergency personnel clustered below—police, JSDF, fire and ambulance— slicing through heads and hands and legs with bloody abandon. The tentacle obliterated their screams in an explosion of greasy flame as it smashed the crumpled helicopter down on top of them, smoke and fire shooting up the walls.

"...a monster movie..."

I turned the TV off.

"It's just special effects, computer graphics. Things like that just don't happen!"

Behind me, I heard Sayoko hang up the phone.

"That was President Manabe. He said to come to his house at once. He said he was watching City Hall on the TV. He said they attack from other dimensions, through the *angles*..."

"*They*?"

Her face began to crumble, tears and fright shining through.

"He said something... something about *Tindalos*... and, I think, *Atzous*... Who cares? It's *THEM!* Those *things!* Those tentacles, reaching in through the angles and killing and killing and killing! He said we have to escape to the Womb, with him and his wife, before the invasion really begins. He said right now!"

The shock of a distant explosion rocked the building, and I instinctively looked toward the sound. South. I could see brilliant orange light there, through the curtains. I ripped them open, and heard Sayoko gasp at my side. Huge pillars of flame rose from the bustling city center of Ikebukuro.

3

As I drove toward Manabe's mansion, my wife switched the Garmin over to TV and sat eyes glued to the screen. As a scientist, I guess she couldn't wrap her mind around what was happening. She was whispering to herself, and when I glanced at her, her profile was beaded with sweat, feverish. I noticed she had starting smoking. She said she'd quit, but I guess she still had some hidden away somewhere. I didn't say a word. If I smoked I'd damn well have wanted one myself right then.

It was stop-and-go all the way to Manabe's mansion west of Tokyo. I wondered what was happening. No more details showed up on the TV, the radio, even the Internet sites, after that first flash. I did see a column of JSDF tanks racing along the expressway, and here and there police were out setting up roadblocks and inspection chokepoints. I didn't stop to look, just kept on driving, silent.

When we got to Manabe's home we switched to his shiny van. He said it could carry a lot more stuff that little Prius we drove. I guess his housekeepers and employees had all fled, because he was loading the van himself.

The boxes he was loading so lovingly, though, weren't crammed full of cash or securities or food or clothing or medical supplies, but moldy old books . . . a pile of occult rubbish, magic, sacred texts from bizarre cults, collections of forgotten myths and the like.

. That was when I met Manabe and his wife for the first time. He was in his mid-fifties, a striking, tall man with graying hair and a pale face. Had I met him under normal circumstances, his piercing gaze probably would have made me think of a successful entrepreneur, a fine judge of people. These weren't normal times, and what I knew of him showed me nothing more than an eccentric millionaire.

"We can exchange greetings later," he snapped. "We have to get out of Tokyo at once!"

And, taking his wife Kanako by the hand, he slid into the back seat.

As I slipped into the driver's seat, I asked "Wouldn't it make more sense to use a company helicopter than have me drive all that way?"

I wasn't trying to be smart, I was serious. I thought Manabe could flee Tokyo faster that way.

"Even if we did go by chopper we wouldn't be able to land near the Womb, up in the mountains like that. We'd have to land at a local airport and drive . . . and there's just not enough time before *They* come in force. The government has begun quietly flying officials out of the country in Self Defense Force choppers and military transports, too, and if we happened to be in the wrong place at the wrong time they'd shoot us out of the sky."

A laugh bubbled up from the seat next to Manabe. Hysterical, forced laughter . . . I glanced back, and Kanako Manabe giggled, "Funny, isn't it?"

"What is?"

"It's all just so unreal! Like a shot from a movie, or a play. I mean, it's like we're on *Candid Camera*, right? Or I'm having a really bad dream . . . That must be it. This can't be real! It's just too impossible!"

"Sorry, it's real. Unfortunately."

Manabe's voice was as flat as his expression. Then he told me to drive on.

4

And I kept driving, no sleep and no rest.

We couldn't stay focused on news broadcasts on the TV, radio, and the Internet sites on our cellphones throughout the whole long drive to Nagano. We began to talk, slowly. Manabe and my wife didn't want to say much at first, but Manabe's wife turned out to be a real chatterbox and I finally learned a little bit about her. And him.

She said she'd be thirty-three soon. A little short, maybe about five feet, but she was the embodiment of female beauty: jutting breasts, slender waist, firm ass. My dad would have smacked his lips and called her a hot dame. She was beautiful, and the coquettish smile never left her round face. She always seemed to be smiling in invitation, I thought. And it turned out I was right, I guess, because until last year she had been a hostess at a Ginza club, until regular patron Manabe snapped her up.

Manabe described her quite a bit differently, though, in his disinterested tone: "I needed a healthy woman, with a healthy womb." It sounded to me like he was just being bluntly honest, no more, no less. He hadn't said a single kind or loving word to her since we left.

And when Kanako glanced at him, from time to time, I thought I could see cold disdain shining through.

Manabe had taken over the company founded by his grandfather about twenty years before, when his own father has suddenly died. He had been studying ethnology at the university then, he said. He had spent vast sums from his inheritance on occult books, and seemed likely to spend the rest of his life locked away in research by himself. Maybe because he hadn't come down out of his ivory tower into the real world until his thirties, or maybe just because of his rich boy background, his insufferable attitude made it impossible to get along with him for more than an hour or so. His total lack of human warmth, his coldness, really got under my skin. He suddenly ordered the rest of us to "Stay away from angles!"

After a half a day in the car together, I was through with him. I spoke only with my wife, and Kanako.

Our flight continued, and as we crossed into Nagano prefecture I noticed that there weren't any other cars on the roads. Driving up the winding mountain roads, there were no people at all. In fact, there were no deer, or bears, or squirrels, or even a single bird. But as dusk that day approached, we began to catch glimpses of grotesque creatures in the woods around us.

We saw a group of four-legged beasts, with hides the color of human skin, huge bodies lumpy with roiling fat, distended bellies swaying. And though many of them had brown hair on their heads, their faces were bare.

"They aren't people . . ." whispered Kanako, voice trembling. "But their eyes and noses and mouths were . . ."

I ignored her and kept driving. My wife sat in the passenger seat, cigarette lit. Uneasy silence filled the cabin, pressing down on us all.

Manabe shattered the silence with his monotone. "The locals are regressing, just as Atzous wrote."

I stepped on the gas a bit harder.

As the sun set, the darkness along the narrow road grew even blacker. There were no more houses visible, no fields, just the depths of the mountains. Sometimes we saw a pale shadow passing in the dark, a four-footed nightmare with the face of a human being . . .

When we finally reached the Womb, the world was wrapped in iron blue, the darkness just before dawn.

The Womb looked like a giant tennis ball half buried in the earth, I thought, seeing it for the first time. It didn't seem to have any windows or doors.

"The surface of the sphere irises open and shut, like a camera shutter," explained my wife. "I'll tell you where the door is. Go ahead and get out."

"Um," I mumbled, opening the door to an uncanny, bestial roar from the forest. It sounded like a wild beast, but at the same like a cry of anguish a child might make.

"I hope there aren't any juvenile delinquents up here!" half-giggled Kanako as she got out, clasping her shoulders and shrinking.

Manabe's lips twisted. I think it was the first time I saw him smile, if smile it was. Perhaps he meant it as a wry grin, but all I saw was a sneer, disdain for his wife.

"If they were here we'd be eaten by now," he said, smiling more broadly than before.

"Stop it!" she cried, terrified.

Sayoko had been walking toward the Womb, and now stopped to take a remote controller from her handbag, pointing it at the dome. No doubt built to Manabe's specifications, it was a rounded, triangular shape covered with round buttons. She pressed one, and a black hole appeared in the face of the Womb, irising open rapidly to create a circular doorway big enough to walk through.

"We can get the baggage later. First we have to get Kanako to safety," said Manabe, prodding her toward the circular doorway.

"Not alone!" she wailed, shaking her head violently.

"Izumo, go with her and carry her bags, then," he ordered.

"There's a switch on the right just inside for the lights," added my wife, and I nodded thanks as I picked up one of the huge clothing cases Kanako had brought and began walking toward the Womb. Kanako, relief clear on her face, came with me, and as my wife had said, there was a light switch just inside. The lights snapped on, blinding, white . . . and illuminating the side of the Womb, tiny glyphs and symbols cut into every inch of the walls.

"What is all this weird stuff?" shrieked Kanako, eyes flying.

"I had them specially carved into the walls to make sure *They* can't come in from another dimension," said Manabe. "Walls, ceilings, even the floor are covered with runes, Naacal and Pnath script. And the sigils and seals they fear have been carven here and there as needed, too. Our magical defenses are perfect!"

"Isn't that right, Izumo . . ." he began, turning back to Sayoko, and suddenly stopped, speechless, transfixed by the *thing* that had snuck up behind her.

I saw it, too. So did Kanako. Only Sayoko didn't see it.

She saw the horror in our eyes, and even as her own face began to twist, the white *thing* leapt on her, hammering her to the ground, atop her. Her handbag and the remote fell from her outstretched hand, and as she reached for them instinctively the white *thing* leaned over, teeth still showing their human origins chewing into the back of her neck, stripping off skin and flesh. Her screams snapped me out of it, and I dropped the bag to run to her rescue.

... Except that Kanako grabbed hold of my arm, hard, shouting at me: "Stop! No! It'll eat you too!"

"Let me go! It'll kill her!"

But she didn't. She wrapped her arms around me, holding me, leaving me no way out but to strike her down. I drew back my fist to punch her away when suddenly Manabe moved.

I thought he was running to save her. But he ... Manabe was a man without a single shred of humanity in him. My wife was still alive, even with that white monster sitting on her back, shredding her neck. Her hand was still reaching toward the remote, twitching. And Manabe, instead of turning to her, snatched up the remote controller, leaping back to the safety of the Womb. He punched a button on the remote as soon as he was inside, and the shutter began to iris shut; like watching my wife through a camera.

"Sayoko!"

And the shutter irised tighter in front of my eyes. My wife, being eaten alive by that damned white *thing* squatting astride her: the image pierced my eyes, my heart, my sanity. I could see other white shapes rising from the darkness, my wife lifting her bloody face, looking up at me. Trying to say something, and vanishing under a vast rush of grunting, squealing, hungry flesh.

And the shutter closed, searing my wife's end into my soul.

5

The three of us—me, Manabe, and his wife—descended into the Womb. My wife's design was perfect, with not a single angle anywhere. Chairs and tables stood perpendicular to the floor, but surfaces flowed seamlessly together, as if they had grown from it. Floors and table legs of such were of course rounded, no corners anywhere. Lights and furniture were circular, but so were cutting boards and knives and forks and even the screens of the TV and the computer ... Everything was circular or curved, *everything*. It was monomaniacal.

"*They* come in through the angles," repeated Manabe again and again. "*They* can invade anything through the angles, but not here! They can't get inside the Womb!"

Kanako and I already knew it far too well . . . the radio, the TV, the Internet all told us how bomb shelters, even secret military bases, has been effortlessly invaded, their human occupants torn to bloody shreds. Usually it was tentacles, like a squid or a jellyfish, seeping in through an angle, but sometimes there were reports of the white beasts, or speaking mold, or huge mobile plants with human eyes.

"It's all over," laughed Kanako, laughter breaking into jagged shards.

We lived on in the shelter, no angles and no knowledge of when it all might end. We continued to receive reports from the outside world for three days, then suddenly the TV stations went off the air. The Internet continued until the fourth day, but that night the remaining few blogs and boards began displaying meaningless strings of consonants, or rows upon rows of unreadable characters, until dying completely on the fifth day.

On the sixth day Kanako began acting strangely. During meals or while drinking coffee she would wait until Manabe was looking elsewhere, and flash desperate glances in my direction. Her expressions were not wholly sane, but were packed with pheromones by the abnormality of our situation. I ignored her, shutting myself in my room, and painted. Driven by hopelessness, I felt that only by painting could I retain even a shred of my sanity.

On the seventh day, Kanako slipped into my room as I painted.

"Help me, Tatsuya. Hold me. I can't bear it any more!"

She wrapped her arm around me from behind, naked, and when I turned to face her began kissing me with wild abandon. The sight of Sayoko being devoured by those white creatures flashed through my heart, and I shook my head, trying to push her away. Kanako thrust her tongue into my mouth, soft, sweet, a faint scent of perfume . . . the latch of my sanity slipped, and as I eagerly sought her tongue with my own, my arms tightened around her. We fell to the floor, and found solace in each other until the night. It was not love, nothing so beautiful, it was hungry sex, two people seeking refuge in the flesh, trying to escape inescapable terror. We spasmed in climax, brought each other back again and again with our mouths and our hands, losing ourselves in each other in timeless repetition, a mindless drive to forget the terror that seized us.

And as the sun rose again we returned to our senses, whispering together. What did we need? How could we escape the hopelessness, the terror? We reached a conclusion, sealed it with another brief bout, and broke apart. She returned to her room, and I to the shower.

At dinner, Kanako came wearing one of her favorite outfits, and a neutral expression.

The dining room was of course circular, as was the table. The chairs, the plates, even the steaks and the vegetables in the salad were round, free of angles.

She had a white scarf round her neck, matching her white suit, and she had made herself up as she hadn't for days, chic and beautiful. Manabe, as always, was in his ratty jacket and slacks, glittering eyes peering from his pale face, looking like a successful businessman on his day off.

I wore my old black turtleneck sweater, a cheap jacket and jeans. Not nearly the sort of dress appropriate for a dinner invitation.

After pouring us all glasses of red wine, Kanako asked what we should toast.

"To life without angles," said Manabe, without even stopping to think about it.

I lifted my glass in response, but Kanako shook her head.

"No. I hate that!"

"Well, then, to the beautiful suit you're wearing, Mrs. Manabe," I proposed. She giggled.

"This scarf looks good on me, doesn't it?" she asked, grasping it by the end.

"Yes, it doesn't have an angle on it," said Manabe,

and Kanako burst into laughter. Her wineglass toppled, red wine seeping into the tablecloth in a blotch that was also rounded.

"What is the matter with you?" demanded Manabe, brow furrowed.

"All you ever talk about is whether or not there are any angles. That's all you ever think about!"

"It's a crucial issue. The Womb is safe because it has no angles. I can sit here drinking wine because of it."

"Of course. It's safe because it has no angles, and I . . . I . . ."

She pulled on the end of the scarf, unwinding it to reveal her slender, white neck, and the red mark, like a scar, that flamed there.

"What is that?" asked Manabe, quizzically.

"All you worry about is future generations, and you've forgotten what men do here."

"What in the world . . . ?"

"It's a kiss mark!"

She laughed triumphantly, white teeth flashing. I joined her in laughter, captured by her spirit.

"So you slept with Izumo . . . so what?"

"Are you jealous?"

"No," denied Manabe, shaking his head. "If you have sex with both of us, the chances of being impregnated will increase. Your infidelity fits perfectly with my original plan to save humanity."

Her laughter faded as Manabe continued.

"Was it good? Maybe we should try it together, then, tonight, all three of us. I don't mind either way. As long as we preserve the species."

"Hold on one minute, Manabe!" I broke in, unable to hold back any longer.

"What?"

"Are you serious? You spend a fortune building this spherical coffin, you leave my wife to be eaten alive, and then when a painter steals your wife you just suggest maybe we should try a threesome! What the hell do you think is going on outside? The world is ending! And you! All you can do is . . . !"

"It's not ending," he broke in. "There are no angles here, so *They* can't get in. The world will not . . ."

He suddenly broke off, slapping his hand to his mouth, eyes blinking wildly, searching left and right. From behind his hand, the sound of a clogged drain oozed from his mouth, a pause, then the sounds of his stomach violently surging back up his throat. His hand slipped from his mouth, letting thin, translucent tentacles snaked out, like wet slugs or tired noodles. They writhed, squirmed, heads twisting and seeking.

"It's *Them!* Oh God, it's *THEM!*"

Kanako leaped from her chair, shrieking.

A jellyfish gently began testing the air from inside his nostril . . .

"But how . . . ?" he asked, voice muffled, and his right eyeball popped out, little ripping noises, as tentacles lifted it up from the inside.

"No angles . . . there are no angles!"

I drew back from the table and the shaking mass that was Manabe, and answered him: "There are angles, you fool! The oldest angle of all, the human triangle!"

"Ridiculous!" he tried to cry. His right eyeball fell, trailing the debris of nerves and blood vessels, and dozens of jelly-like tentacles writhed in the gaping wound.

"You're an occultist! You of all people should know that metaphors and analogies can be truth! We painters have known that for centuries!"

"Just playing with words . . ."

A smile bloomed on Manabe's face. A smile of understanding? A sneer of self-mockery? Before I had a chance to find out which, his face was hidden behind a twirl of ropey tentacles, wrapping him up.

Tentacles were already bursting from his ears, from the bottom of his pants legs, squirming, writhing.

"Kanako! Where's the remote?" I cried.

"Here! But . . . what?"

I answered as I took the remote control from her outstretched hand. "We're leaving. Getting out of this spherical hell!"

We ran toward the exit, urged on by a bestial roar from the dining room behind us. Kanako flinched.

"It's all right. That's Manabe's death rattle."

A horrible *tearing* sound came from the dining room, and the smack of raw meat slapping into the floor. A pause, and then innumerable milky tentacles, jellyfish or squid or whatever, came creeping from the dining room. I tore my eyes away, and pressed the button.

The doorway irised open, a camera shutter revealing a pitch-black world awaiting us.

"Beasts, global catastrophe ... Bring it on! Even with angles, it's better than staying here!"

Wrapping my arm around her shoulders, we plunged through the circular doorway.

WHAT BRINGS THE VOID

Will Murray

I

"Things Are in the Saddle ..."

It was the dark season of the portmanteau word. Ragna-geddon. Yog-Narok. Demondammerung. None of them caught on.

It was not the twilight of the gods long prophesied. It was sunset for the human race. Or sun blot. For the sun's fate was the first cosmic sign of the uber-apocalypse.

In the Western hemisphere, it was past midnight when the moon simply winked out. Few noticed. It was still there, of course. In the Eastern hemisphere, the sun just shut down. No sun, no moonlight. In the darkness of the void, the stars brightened. Yes, there were fewer of them than before. That hardly seemed to matter.

A bluish filament of light traced across the utter night like a crazed comet. The Sothis Radiant had touched the sun with a groping tendril, extinguishing it with appalling finality. But few cared. Things shifted so fast that the past and its causes were lost in the torrent of violent ever-present change.

I was walking the streets of Washington, D.C. that first night of First Dark. I sensed the moon's death. Darkly luminous, a weird cobalt-blue cloud rolled in, smothering the night sky. It seemed to hang lower than any terrestrial cloud had any right to hang.

91

Down from it had fallen two cloudy appendages, like fat tails of some boneless monster. I turned a street corner and there they were. Where they fell, they right-angled like torpid boas. At the blunt tips of each, the misty heads seemed to have taken on the form of squat dogs—a sheepdog and a bulldog. Or was one a chow? They were dull impressionistic apparitions. Both stared at me with their hollow cloudy unreadable eyes.

I reached out to touch one, thinking it some trick of the night fog. It shrank from my touch.

This cloud is alive, I marveled. The doggy form collapsed in on itself as the tentacle silently withdrew.

I found a rope and threw it toward the other—the bulldog. I thought to dispel it with its manila weight. Instead, the rope caught in its shadowy mouth—or was caught.

I felt a distinct tug. Dropping the rope, I fled.

Mankind was in a new reality.

The sun never rose again and what the moon did no one knew. An extinguished lamp, it was never seen again. Nor were most of the Milky Way stars. Without them, time simply stopped. It became 2012 forever.

No one knew what killed the global power grid. It simply stopped functioning. A greater night clamped down. Machines stopped cold. But just as importantly, world currencies—reduced to electrons moving unseen through fiber optic cables—collapsed. With no gold or silver to back paper bills or coin, the global economy popped like a soap bubble.

Civilization as we knew it was over within a month.

Two unknown satellites rose in the sky eventually, twin orbs of emptiness, one a sickly bone white, the other the hue of coal. Those who knew their *Necronomicon* gave them names—Nug and Yeb. Need I say more?

The Old Ones were back, and Great Cthulhu drinking up the vast Pacific in his vaster gullet was the least of the legion. The Poles ignited, burning with a dark electronic fire. New place-names sprang up. Lake Ohio. Chesuncook Pit. Transyl-Pennsylvania. Kalifornia. Nyarlathotep again strode the whelmed Earth, reverse-engineering centuries of human civilization. It was terrible.

Mankind stood prepared to battle this hellish host—only to learn that the invaders regarded man as parasites on their newly reclaimed world.

Some said they merely wished to exterminate us. But there was more to it. Far more.

I was in a unique position to observe it all. Never mind my name. Call me ORV 004—Operational Remote Viewer #4. I was attached to the External Threats Directorate of the Cryptic Events Evaluation Section of the National Reconnaissance Office.

"External threats" was our euphemism for extrasolar or other-dimensional concerns.

The Old Ones kept us hopping. But that was Back in the Day. Now there was no day—only endless night.

We had our first post-change briefing session by guttering candlelight, like a coven of damned witches.

The Director kept it simple. "I don't want to hear any crap about end times. This isn't the Rapture or Ascension. It's a goddamned invasion, and we're running a counterinsurgency out of this office." Pounding his desktop, he growled, "I want intelligence—local and non-local." He looked at me, the only surviving ORV.

"On it," I said.

"Get cracking."

"I'll need a tasker and a monitor," I pointed out.

Remote Viewing is an intelligence methodology devised in the 1970s for special military applications. One definition calls it "The ability to perceive, by purely mental means, persons, places and things usually inaccessible to normal senses, regardless of time, distance or shielding." I was trained under Department of Defense RV protocols, at a sleepy place nestled in the Virginia foothills called the Monroe Institute.

The secret of Remote Viewing is to blind the viewer to the target. If you have no idea what you're supposed to look at, your imagination can't run away with you.

No deduction, induction, or adduction possible. Just pure psychic signal.

I lay in the dark and listened to the monitor's voice. He had no clue as to the target any more than I did. The tasker simply handed him the coordinates, and the monitor read them to me. That way I couldn't inadvertently access his mind and glean clues by common telepathy.

"Your coordinates are 8646 7944. Target is to be viewed in present time. Good luck."

I went in. It was like walking through a dreamscape. Fleeting multisensory impressions swept across my mind's eye. I scanned for resolution.

"I see a black blot," I reported. "Huge. The size of a city."

"Can confirm blot."

I probed the image. "Blot was once a major city. City is no longer there. Not even ruins. I don't even perceive a soil base . . ."

"Keep going," the monitor encouraged.

"Nothing exists there. It's like a drop out in reality. There's no matter there—as we understand matter. It's vibrating on another level—slower, colder, darker."

I shuddered in contact with the anomaly. That told me I had successfully bilocated to the target area. My senses felt like they were swimming through static.

The monitor commanded, "Move to a point northwest of the center of the black area, please."

I found myself perceptually at a far different place. Something familiar about it. I reported my aesthetic perceptions.

"Concept of factory. Sense of purpose. Darkness and secrecy around the latter. I see beings. Bipeds. A mixture of human and not. Decoding as centaurs, but not centaurs. No horse attributes. Some type of bioengineered half-human hybrids. They function as slaves and slavedrivers."

"Enter factory."

I tried. I really did. But I was blocked. I felt an impenetrable membrane.

It reminded me of the time I viewed the current location of the Ark of the Covenant. I got in, but something forcibly ejected me. Something powerful.

"Denied area," I reported.

"Recon vicinity for impressions, Number 4."

The ground gave up nothing but a cold staticky energy. But when I shifted my focus skyward, I detected something.

"Sense of clouds above. But these are not meteorological clouds. They pulsate, then brighten. No recognizable atmospheric phenomena correlate to these changes. But I sense a connection between the activity in the factory and the clouds above."

"Describe this connection."

After a period of struggling with inchoate impressions, I reported, "Cannot."

"Are you blocked, Number 4?"

"Negative. Feels more like I lack a frame of reference to comprehend the exact nature of the activity within as relates to the overhanging clouds."

"Okay. Come back."

When I attempted to sit up, I felt like a truck had hit me. My brain expanded against the cavern of my brain pan like a fat balloon. I closed my chakras down as best I could.

By candlelight, I wrote my report. Secondary impressions of a rendering plant danced in my head, but I left them out as imaginal artifacts.

The director had me in his office within the hour. My report was on his desk.

"Number 4, I want you to recon this so-called factory."

"In person, sir?"

"Only someone with your clairvoyant abilities can get close without detection. Determine what's going on in there."

"But—"

"This is not a request. You are not a volunteer. Is that clear?"

"Yes, sir." It was a death sentence, but how could one care? The entire race was under a death watch.

The locality was outside the former Richmond, Virginia. A short ride. I took a train. Some were still running.

As the engine pulled me through the unrelieved night, I looked up at the star-starved sky. A narrow face stared down from the clouds. It was a confusion of luminous contra blue and purple, suggesting a sharp-featured demon with a round open mouth. Too round. Like a black orifice.

Once you train up to Master Remote Viewer, you are always in viewing mode. The only question is whether or not your inner perceptions reach the conscious mind's level.

This time they were. I had the distinct feeling that the demon of the clouds was looking exclusively at me, and would swallow me if he could. Was it a presentiment—or a warning?

The demon passed from view. But I still felt its hollow eyes upon me. They reminded me of those nightmarish canine apparitions.

The train let me off short of the dormant crater that had been Richmond. I walked from there. It was like a trek through a minefield of the unknown. Even the leaf-less locust trees had a stark look, as if shocked by their new habitation.

Three miles along, I encountered trouble breathing. I backed up and worked around it. No-oxygen zones. They were growing. The Old Ones didn't need oxygen, people said. I wondered if the factory was dedicated to atmosphere conversion.

Even as the thought glimmered my mind, I intuited that the truth was more dire. Far more dire. But I could not conceive how much . . . .

People filed along the road, coming from somewhere, but going nowhere.

Everyone understood that, so talk was shunned. I was reminded of Springsteen's mournful end-of-the-world song, "The Ghost of Tom Joad." Welcome to the new world order. . . .

You don't fully understand time and timelessness until the sun and moon and the familiar planets are no longer there to help mark the celestial procession. Against a fading blue web spun by the star-quenching Sothis Radiant, Nug and Yeb careened crazily through the vacant sky, confusing matters.

I walked for hours, but it felt more like an elastic eternity. Nothing to look forward to. No hope of natural light. My flashlight helped to guide me. Then I encountered a darkness it could neither penetrate nor dispel.

A black ovoid lay in the road. It looked unnatural, so I approached it gingerly.

Vibrationally, it reminded me of the black blot I had mentally come into contact with—the old Richmond. This was smaller. Superficially, it resembled a hole in the earth. But my light failed to illuminate the sides of the "hole." And it lacked any sense of dimensionality.

I dropped a stone into it. It abruptly vanished, as if relocating to another reality.

Only then did I sense a disturbing connection between this hole and the gaping mouth of the demonic cloud face that had regarded me so singularly.

I rushed on.

When I came upon an orderly file of people, I joined them, as if to lose myself in their numbers. They walked along in a single file of the condemned.

I turned to one and asked, "Where are you going?"

He pointed to the others ahead of him. "Wherever they are," he said dully.

"Don't you know?"

He nodded. "This is the food line."

"There's food up ahead?"

"No, we are the food." He said it without hope, fear, or caring.

I stepped out of line.

I saw my first centaur then. That is, with my physical eyes. My non-physical vision had detected one during the RV session.

This one stood taller than a man. From approximately the thorax up, he looked human. He was a big burly black man, muscular in the extreme. His skull was shaven and his torso rippled with undraped muscles.

Where his pelvis devolved into legs, no legs as we know them supported the rest. The pelvis instead flared out into a wide skirt of some unappetizing flesh, like a columnar snail. It stood on this pad, moved on it via some snail-like form of locomotion.

But the lower appendage was not flesh, or even organic matter. I sensed this, and my perception was confirmed when the centaur glided over a great patch of unrelieved black that lay off the roadside like a pool of tar.

The black patch supported it. It would never support a physical man.

Confirmation of this came almost immediately.

A maddened dog tore running out of somewhere and lunged for it. The dog charged across grass and brush and seemed oblivious to the blackness until its paws came into contact with its unreflective surface.

Then its snarling was swallowed whole—as was the damned and doomed dog.

Seeing this, a teenage girl detached from the line and approached the spot where the dog had vanished. I moved in to intercept her. She got there first.

"What do you think is down there?' she murmured as she stared into the unrelieved abyss, Gothic eyes blank.

"Nothing," I said firmly, reaching out with care.

"Nothing," she said dreamily. "Sounds like a better deal."

I snatched at her too late. She simply stepped in and virtually winked out of existence. Above, one of the evil low-lying clouds pulsated briefly. It had done that when the dog disappeared too. Something in me shuddered in sympathy.

Some members of the procession saw this. They broke away from the others. Into the patch they leaped, lemmings on two legs. Into the void they vanished.

A booming voice lifted. "Humans! Escape into the void! Escape and you will not be consumed. Escape into death! There is freedom in death. And from the new masters of Earth!" It was a centaur.

A surge of humanity responded to that hellish promise. They stampeded for the blackness. Some were trampled. Others stumbled over them to seek dark oblivion. Soon, the greater portion of them were gone. Utterly gone. I felt a coldness in my soul . . . .

Above, the clouds pulsated wildly, as if laughing uproariously in delight.

Recoiling, I put distance between me and the patch of voidy non-matter. As I ran, the glowing eyes of the centaur tracked me. They burned a weird pumpkin orange, like a seared jack o'lantern.

"Beware the voids!" he called after me, as if to taunt my flight. "Voids become vortices. Vortices become vornados. And vornados—" He began laughing raucously. His laughter boomed and cannonaded like thunder.

The rest was lost to hearing.

I reached a hill and found shelter among the dying trees. They drooped, blackened leaves wilting, as if in despair.

As I watched the ragged line of humankind close up and reform itself to trudge on toward an unknowable destination, like some segmented worm, the great black void that lay upon the field began to swell. It spun. Black as it was, I could sense this inner churning. No sound came forth. But the void rose up and began to wheel and lift ponderously, growing in size as it reared to life.

It became a vortex. And as the vortex found coherence, it elongated, became towering, mighty, *hungry*.

Vornado! I thought wildly.

The vornado twisted and spun on its ever-changing ropy funnel, got itself organized, and moved for the line of humans with deliberate intent.

"Alive! It's alive in some way!" I cried.

The vorando sought the last stragglers and ingested them, lunging after the rest. The screaming that followed was wild, but brief. The line broke, scattered, but the vornado moved about, with unerring instinct and consumed them all.

None were flung about or ejected by its centrifugal force, nor wasted.

When the last of the fleeing ones was gone, the vornado spun and searched in forlorn disappointment. Finally it sensed the laughing centaur.

It bore down on him too. His laugher chopped off. He turned to flee, urging himself along on his semi-fleshy pedestal. But it was designed for non-matter. The pad dragged on earthly grass, retarding him.

The centaur screamed until the last possible moment of life. After he was gulped up and digested, his scream seemed to linger, and the vornado gobbled up the echoes in a final voracious effort.

Then, howling with hunger, it moved along the road in search of new prey.

Above, the clouds danced with an unholy bluish-gray light.

II
"... And Ride Mankind."

Somewhere in the deep of the night, I came upon a man in black. He was fiftyish, with a deeply-lined face and gray stubble hair, charred eyes set in bony craters like spent meteorites.

I did not recognize him for what he really was.

"Can you show me the way to the plant?" I asked.

"Have people lost their faith so much that they seek hell itself?" he countered.

Then I noticed his soiled collar and crucifix.

"Sorry, Father. I'm with the government."

The priest spat. "And you're here to help, I suppose?"

"That's classified."

I noticed his crucifix. The broken hands and feet of Christ were present, still nailed to the cross, but the body had been forcibly wrenched off.

"Where's Jesus?" I asked.

He lifted a gnarled hickory cane in my face. "Where's Jesus, you say? That's the question of the hour. Of the century! Isn't it?" His voice rose in righteous indignation.

"All my life I preached the lesson of the cross. Now the world is tumbling into the abyss, and where is our Lord?

The greatest battle between good and evil in human history and Jesus Christ is nowhere to be found!"

I could see he had a point. But I said nothing. He charged on.

"If this is the Day of Judgment, where is our Savior. Late? Overdue? Perhaps he's busy on some other planet saving the sinful souls of lizard men. Do you think it likely? How else to explain his absence? For if the Second Coming is tomorrow, he's a bit bloody late, isn't he? Can he put back the entire world? Can he restore sanity? Has the Rapture been postponed? Or rescheduled like a damned pink tea?"

"I don't have answers for you, Father," I said gently.

"The world of our fathers is no more. It was all for nothing. Nothing, I tell you. Nothing! A sham. Not just the Holy Church. But the Jews and the Muslims and the Hindus. They too followed a lie. A damned lie!"

"Father," I said carefully, "we still have our souls."

"Yes! Our immortal souls. Death is our only hope now. One solitary means of escape from this earthly torment. Jesus has turned slacker. We must take salvation into our own hands. Look!" He took two long needles from his tunic. "Do you see these?"

"I do."

"All my life I have railed against the mortal sin of abortion. But now I perform them. And do you know why?"

"It's better not to bring children into the world as it now is," I replied.

"Far, far better!" he thundered. And he broke like a rainstorm, weeping uncontrollably, his dark threadbare shoulders wracking with unleashed sobs.

"Direct me to the plant, Father."

He croaked the words out. I had no words of comfort for him. He was a broken priest, but yet also a driven man. Something was about to snap in him and only death would cure it.

"Go with God, Father," I said.

After I had moved on, he seized control of himself and cried out, "Heed me! Trust not the Lord! Look to

Satan himself for succor! Lucifer was at least once an
angel! But these hellish things, they—"

I walked away from his retching anguish. I was a
lapsed Catholic. I had long ago put all belief systems
behind me. I had been out in the matrix of all creation.
I knew what the real score was. God was more of a ho-
logram than a unitary being. But human consciousness
was inextinguishable. There was no death, only transition to other realities. This hard-won knowledge kept
me sane through all the horrific earth changes. Detach-
ment became my baseline emotion. What was the worst
that could happen to me? Death was inevitable, Old
Ones or no Old Ones. If in the end the universe were
devoured by the eternally-beating nuclear chaos called
Azathoth, there were other universes, adjacent dimensions in which my immortal soul might dwell.

It was a strange unanchored courage, but I had
learned it in the matrix. Thus fortified, I prepared to
brave the locus of local activity that should explain the
One Ones' fell objectives.

The factory sat in a dell or hollow not far from the
corpse-choked James River.

It looked like a coal plant, but smelled like a crematorium. The flaring smokestacks reminded me of that
time I RVed Dachau. The spiritual emptiness was op-
pressive and overwhelming. I never wanted to go back,
physically or otherwise.

And now, here I was—facing a far worse environment. I could sense it.

Lines of yoked and chained people were being driven
into the main gate by a dozen centaurs, some of which
had birdlike heads and tentacles for lower limbs, like
the ancient representations of the suppressed Egyptian
godlet, Abraxas.

I made a nest of branches, brush and other debris and
hunkered down to observe closely.

When I had absorbed all my physical eyes could perceive, I closed them and eased into an alpha brainwave
state, then cycled down to theta. I do my best work in
theta. When I don't click out . . .

I focused on the line of victims filing into the factory. What did they represent to the Old Ones? What was their value?

My first impressions were representational and confusing. I saw soda cans, milk cartons, liquor bottles. Clearly I was operating on my right hemisphere. I tried to switch to the left to invoke the clairaudient function.

I heard a single clairaudient word. A mere whisper bubbling up from my unconscious mind: *containers.*

My eyes snapped open. "For what?" I said under my breath. Can't be blood. Or H2O. The Old Ones are non-physical. They were busying terra-deforming the Earth—clearing it as the *Necronomicon* once prophesied—so that it will be vibrationally supportive of their kind. Could they be energy vampires?

I shut my eyes and tried again. This time I set a different intention: *containers for what?*

A vivid image sprang up. Clouds. The cobalt clouds that had been forming above the Earth, growing by the immeasurable hour. What did that mean? I focused on those eerie apparitions.

In my mind's eye, they brightened and pulsated. I saw turbulent faces, boiling like thunderclouds shown in time-lapse photography. Demonic faces roiled and shifted and regathered madly. The clouds spread. I recalled reading about the phenomenon of noctiluminescent clouds—mysterious atmospheric vapor formations that had been reported for over a century now—were they somehow more than mere clouds?

Orifices opened in those clouds. Many of them. Thousands. They irised wide, then snapped shut. I was reminded of gulping piranha. What were they doing? Making faces at hapless mankind?

I gave it up. Rolling over in my makeshift shelter, I stared up at the night sky. Metallic-blue cumulus clouds began gathering over the factory like scavengers to a corpse. That meant something. But what?

I upshifted my breathing and climbed back to a beta state. I needed a clear head. The deeper I went into non-ordinary states of consciousness, the fuzzier my thinking would be until normal baseline beta consciousness reasserted itself. The dreaded downside of being operationally psychic.

An hour passed. Two. A dismal line of people continued filing into the factory. Chopped-off screams broke the stillness. But I could glean nothing further on any level of perception at my command.

It had been years since I had astral-projected. I was never very good at it. Just looking and down at my body lying there was enough to give me a jolt and send me snapping back into my physical self.

Yet I had to try. It was the only way in—the only safe way. Or so I assumed.

I lay on my back and drifted into a deep meditation. Fighting a rising fear, I pushed my jagged beta brainwaves flatter and flatter, till they were sine waves, then shallow waves. As they moved toward flatline, I unexpectedly went delta.

The delta state is trance sleep. I don't know my way around it. But somehow I achieved separation.

Below, I saw my body entangled in brush and hoped I'd get to return to it.

Carefully, I moved away. I was now in the thought-responsive aspect of reality. I had but to think of a place, and I would translate there. I approached the factory with the care of a visible man—which I was not.

At a far corner, away from all centaur activity, I eased in through a broken window. Inside, furnaces massed. The place was full of great smelters and electrical furnaces and the like. Whatever this had been, it was the fiery pit of hell now.

Centaurs with their scourges stormed about. Some wielded clubs. They drove people into the fire. Some humans quailed before the flames. Centaurs quickly dashed out their brains and flung them bodily into the glowing furnace maws.

This was a crematorium!

I was almost disappointed. That's all?

No. Not all.

It was not a voice. I would not have heard a voice. For I had left my ears behind.

It seemed to be coming from above. I moved to the shadowy vault of a ceiling, through it, and floated above the roof.

Above hung the low-lying clouds. Dull blue, they stared down at me with hollow interest.

Suddenly I felt an irresistible force, pulling me up, higher and fast.

I willed myself back into my resting body. But the force tugging on the eternal me was strong.

Frantically, I looked around and saw the silver cord that anchored me to my mortal form. Still intact!

With a dawning horror, I spied the smoky tendril drifting down from a nodular cloud. It quested coilingly for the silvery filament that guaranteed my survival.

Just as its leading edge bloomed into a scorpion with snapping claws, adrenalin kicked in—and I was yanked back!

I sat up, gasping, clothed in flesh once more. A coldness settled into the pit of my lower chakras and I knew a hyperventilating terror beyond anything I had ever experienced.

"What are those damned clouds?" I called out to the Almighty.

As if in answer, the clouds above pulsated menacingly. God, if he still ruled the created universe, said nothing.

Cold fear turned to hot anger and I resolved to complete my mission.

When my brain cleared, the obvious became obvious.

Back in my days as a lowly NRO Signalman, I was taught that every thing in creation had a unique energy signature, and from it flowed non-local signal information about its identity and fundamental nature. You just had to learn to tap into it.

For a Signalman—and here I mean a Remote Viewer in training—it was as hard and as simple as sending a telepathic interrogative to the target. They explained it that it was like bouncing a signal off an orbiting satellite. Or transmitting an IFF—identify friend or foe—transponder signal to an approaching aircraft.

You simply directed a thought at the target. But the thought couldn't be couched in words. Sometimes the target was not human or did not speak your native language.

Other times the target was inanimate. They had us practice on vehicles to train us how to interact with non-conscious targets.

The trick was to formulate the question conceptually, or visually, without brain-based language. It was tough, but we learned to do it.

Lying there under the mocking cloud, I mustered up that old training.

I had little to lose and less to fear. After all, it had already attempted to seize my incorporeal form, and failed miserably.

What are you? I beamed up.

Back came an inchoate chaos of thought impressions—largely consisting of roiling cumulonimbus clouds enmixed with gaseous nebulae, and a sense of ultra-deep spacial regions.

Are you cosmic?

The cloud pulsated. I sensed an affirmative and a secondary sense of greatness. Extra-cosmic, I intuited that to mean.

I sent up another interrogative, and waited for the bounceback signal.

I didn't quite catch it. Was it calling me the N word? That made no sense. I'm white. I tried again. This time instead of asking what it was, I inquired of its name.

It was sentient. Therefore it must possess a name—if only for self-reference.

The bounceback decoded on the wrong side of my brain. I saw an image. It was a lowly shrub. I had no idea what it meant, and sent that puzzlement upward.

I sensed laughter. It was cruel. It mocked and threatened the way a storm cloud threatens rain. I felt as if any minute now I would be rained on by the most hellish precipitation imaginable.

Visions of viscous black rain came to my mind. I could not tell if this was precognition or in the nature of an imminent threat.

But no rain came, black or otherwise. I relaxed, remembering that it had not rained since the night of sun blot.

I got up and reached into my backpack where I carried my E-reader. It was standard issue, loaded with only one text—the *Necronomicon*.

I started a word search. First I tried "shrub."

Not Found, it read.

I next tried "cloud." I got several hits. But the first was "cloudy." I almost skipped on to the next one when my eyes fell upon a phrase: "The Black Goat of the Woods with a Thousand Young."

Not "shrub." *Shub-Niggurath!*

I looked up. There was nothing goatlike about what was floating above my unprotected head. Nor was it truly black. Dark yes, but in the way a thundercloud is blue-gray.

Could the ancients have got it wrong . . . ?

I raced through the other hits and they made my blood run cold. Finally, I was back at the first hit. This time I read more carefully.

The *Necronomicon* described in spare terms the malign intelligence called Shub-Niggurath as "a vast cloudy entity of unknown source or purpose," almost always spoken in the same breath as the Black Goat of the Woods, which has long been identified as Shub-Niggurath.

What if Abdul Alhazred was in error? What if they were two separate beings, linked ritualistically, but not otherwise?

What if staring down from the unreflective sky where the alien satellites Nug and Yeb raced drunkenly was the hellish incomprehensibility, Shub-Niggurath?

They say if you possess the name of a thing, you gain control over it. So I made my next move.

Are you Shub-Niggurath?

Back came a splintery confirmation. I did not understand the splintered aspect of the nonverbal reply, but since more clouds had gathered under the perpetually night sky, perhaps Shub-Niggurath was in the nature of a colony of beings, or something that could separate and reform like amoebae.

What is your purpose?

Back came a stark clarification. It was virtually in English.

To help clear.

Clear what? I beamed back.

The Earth.

Of what?

Of all.

What is your specific function? I was thinking in English now, and was answered in kind.

Back came a sense of a box being opened. It turned into a tableau—a sea of humans seen from the waist up, eyes dead, the tops of their heads opening like a soft-boiled eggs being shelled, and a golden light streaming upward toward waiting clouds.

Hungry clouds, with rapidly irising orifices.

"Knowledge? You drink knowledge!"

Shub-Niggurath only communicated a thirsty impression.

I ran then. Foolish flight or fight conditioning, I knew. But I had to get this intelligence back to headquarters. Damn, for a cell phone that worked!

The cobalt cloud followed me, hurling a chilling thought at me: *No escape. No escape for any human.*

Three towering centaurs abruptly converged on me, responding to commands from my pursuer, I sensed. Loops of some rubbery matter dropped over my head, constricting my neck. Helpless, I was dragged back to that hellish factory.

We came to a fenced-in yard where debris and detritus lay in forlorn heaps, lit by fitful flames. A charnel odor hung over all.

There was an altar. And before it a great black statue in the shape of a man.

But the man had no face. It was gargantuan, uncaring,

pharaonic. It struck me as hauntingly familiar. But my oxygen-starved brain couldn't process anything.

I sent out an interrogative. Back came an accursed name: *Nyarlathotep.*

But it was not the literal Crawling Chaos, only an idol created in his image, formed of fused bonemeal—human bonemeal. For the carbonized cremains of those who were processed through the human rendering factory were not wasted. All this I sensed in a pounding heartbeat.

They laid me on the altar, which had the coolness and shape of a gigantic anvil—an anvil on which mankind was now being hammered into extinction.

My wrists and ankles were held down. I struggled, but the centaurs were irresistible in their obdurate strength. I was finished and I knew it. A curious calm came over me then. I relaxed. Suspecting a trick, the centaurs tightened their grips.

I took several slow breaths and prepared to die.

When death is this close, the mind shifts into a pre-death mode. Inevitability helps the process. I would be killed, after which my soul could escape from my body. This time for eternity.

But I possessed spiritual tools most ordinary people don't have. I made a prayer to the Infinite Spirit God whom I acknowledge, and prepared to commend myself to the Vastness.

Various theories and belief systems kaleidoscoped through my unnaturally calm mind. Would I be absorbed into the Allness like a drop of spiritual water into the ocean of God, surrendering all individuality? Would I transition to a place of astral regeneration, there to await a future existence? Would I plunge into eternal life, according my earned rewards?

I let all these concerns wash over me, then let them go. I would die soon.

And I would know the ultimate truth almost as soon. I had no fear.

For I was about to go beyond the reach of the Old Ones and their terrible universal hegemony. The Earth was now theirs. I only hoped that the realm which awaited me was greater than the spent one I was about to vacate.

I harbored no Earthly regrets. But I did have a spiritual ace up my sleeve. I waited for the beginning of the death stroke. It soon came.

One of the centaurs lifted a crude tool I could barely make out in the smokestack glow. Was it a cudgel? A blade? I could not tell. And I felt myself disassociating from all concern.

When the downstroke began, I departed from my body. Pop! Clean separation.

This way I would feel no pain of slaughter.

I floated face down. Fascinated yet detached, I watched my very brains being spattered about. The silver cord severed. I could feel it, see it—and I accepted it.

Slowly, with my mortal form jittering in death, I began ascending heavenward. A peace washed over me. I was going home. I knew that now. Home. I didn't know its name or its form, but I could feel it tugging me toward its uncharted territory.

Smooth as a swimmer, I rolled my orientation skyward to focus on my immediate if unknown future. I half expected to see archangels in flight.

Instead, I beheld the awful nodular countenance of Shub-Niggurath. It gazed down with sharpening visage.

Out of my way, I directed. *You can't hurt me now.*

Not knowledge, it said clearly.

What?

Humans have no knowledge we seek.

Then what—?

I sensed a lascivious energy. *Your container is broken.*

My soul froze.

Then its maw opened—empty and black as interstellar space . . . and I understood what Shub-Niggurath meant and more dire, what it sought on earth.

Humans were containers—*for souls!*

As I was sucked into that blackest of black holes, cheated of all hope of an afterlife, realization crystallized. All over the Earth the globe-girdling clouds hung poised to capture freshly liberated souls every time men died. And we are all predestined to die . . .

Around me, others like me continued collecting. Soon we began pulsating in resonance to our swelling host. All one. Yet also individual. Parasites, yet prisoners. Powerful, but helpless. Nothing but something. Something yet nothing. Neither matter nor energy. Not particles and not waveforms. Only blind self-aware voids in an unknowable plenum.

I send these thought-forms out to my surviving colleagues. Take drugs. Seek madness. Pray for the gift of amnesia. For there is no other escape.

Absorption finally came, and I became another cold, yet still conscious corpuscle of the insatiable, eternal void that is and always will be Shub-Niggurath.

THE NEW PAULINE CORPUS

Matt Cardin

Seated at a small wooden desk, a humble piece of cypress wood furniture elevated to veritably mythic status by a heaping of fabulously ornate decorative flourishes, he spreads out the papers on the smooth surface before him. A rushing murmur, like the sound of ten thousand voices melding into an oceanic hush, flows through the doorway that stands open and waiting on the far side of the equally ornate room.

The papers are crammed to capacity with a chaotic jumble of handwritten markings. Rows of text run from left to right and then, often, meet the edge of the page and instead of breaking to the next line simply continue on, rebounding from the barrier in curling coils and tracing the paper's edge in circles that effectively form a written frame around the rest. Some lines appear in ink, others in pencil. Some words are minuscule to the point of near-indecipherability. Others shout hugely in hysterical looping letters.

None make sense. Not on their own, at least. Fragments. That is what he has in his possession. Pieces of a puzzle. Scraps of a portrait. Shards of a mirror, each reflecting and refracting the image of all the others to create a dazzling maze of meanings whose infinity encompasses enormous blank spaces.

*   *   *

The more I dwell on it, Francis, the more I am convinced that the single most fruitful result of the frightful transition which has overtaken us is the resurrection of our collective passion for *story*, for the specifically *narrative* understanding of our lives on this planet. I now view the trajectory of my former theological writings toward an almost exclusive emphasis on ontological matters as an egregious error. More than any other religious tradition in human history, our own Christian faith, along with its Jewish forebear, has always been centrally rooted in a cosmic-narrative understanding of human life and the cosmos itself. A reverence for story—as we have now been forcibly reminded—is not symptomatic of a regressive intellectual and theological naiveté but of an unblinking realism. It may simply be the case that the story in which we find ourselves existentially involved as living characters lacks any obvious correspondences with the charming drama we were told from childhood about the Eden-to-Fall-to-New Eden arc of our race. Or perhaps these elements are indeed discernable in our new tale, but in a jumbled order or—more likely—as inversions of themselves. I hope to say more about this in a future letter.

In any event, happily for me, since it means that I do not have to jettison the entirety of my former theological corpus, is the fact that theology-as-story does not *preclude* ontology but *incorporates* it. In fact, what has now been revealed to us in our dreadful recent disruptions is the express unity of these two categories of thought. That is, we are *living the story of a war between levels of reality*. Our metanarrative is the tale of how space-time, the cosmos, the created order, was usurped by a reality that is more fundamental, primary, and ancient.

This story, our story, is a tale of the deeply *inner* and *primordial* turning with hostility upon the objectively *outer* and *evolved*, and reshaping it according to a set of principles that are incomprehensible and, as we can see all around us in the fact of our wrecked cities with their new and growing populations of squamous, octopodan,

and quasi-batrachian inhabitants, thoroughly revolting
to the latter.

*Under red-glowing smoke-filled skies I thread my
way through a boulder field of shattered buildings. Fires
blaze and smolder in places where no fuel ought to burn.
Twisted chunks of steel and concrete burn like dry-rotten
wood. Sparkling shards of shattered windows and doors
and street lamps catch the flickering orange glow and
ignite from the pressure of the images on their glassy
surfaces. A sea of flaming rubble, fifty miles wide. This is
what remains of my city and of all the others like it dot-
ting the surface of the round earth like piles of autumn
leaves raked together for burning.*

Here is the heart of the matter, Francis, in a rush of
analogies intended to distill the essence of the insights
I lost when I shredded my manuscript on that terrible
day.

ITS OMNIPRESENCE: my theological namesake
quoted approvingly to his Greek audience a common
bit of philosophical wisdom from their own cultural
milieu when he spoke of God the Father as "the one
in whom we live and move and have our being." Does
not such a formulation recall Yog-Sothoth, who walks
with the other Old Ones between the dimensions, and
in whom past, present, and future are one? Does it not
recall Azathoth, the primal chaos that resides not only
at the center of infinity but at the center of each atom,
each particle, perhaps serving as the unaccountable
subatomic bond that has categorically escaped scientific explanation? But here I overstep the limits of my
formal authority, so effectively does this demonic pantheon inspire a plethora of transgressive and exhilarat-
ing speculations.

ITS ANNIHILATING HOLINESS: in the Hebrew
Scriptures, in the desert, under the merciless sun, the Is-
raelites witness repeated outbreaks of Yahweh, Who "is
a consuming fire," an untamable force, a burning pesti-
lence, a plague of serpents. And so is He revealed not

just as the Holy Other but as Wholly Other, possessed
of a cosmically singular *sui generis* nature that cannot
and will not abide contradiction. In the words of Luther
himself, if you sin "then He will *devour thee up*, for God
is a fire that consumeth, devoureth, rageth; verily He is
your undoing, as fire consumeth a house and maketh it
dust and ashes." As Otto wrote with such frightening
clarity of apprehension, there is something baffling in
the way His wrath is kindled and manifested, for it is
"like a hidden force of nature, like stored-up electricity,
discharging itself upon anyone who comes too near. It is
incalculable and arbitrary." To see His luminance shining from the face of Moses is a horror. To see His face
is to die.

This incomprehensible, inconceivable, incalculable,
arbitrary horror serves as the font, finish, and focal
point of our entire tradition. I trust my attempts at com-
mentary would only weaken the blow of the brute fact
itself.

"My son." The voice speaks behind him, and he looks
sideways in acknowledgment of its presence without actually turning to face it. "Have you read them again?"
The voice is thin as a reed, like a sick child, and also
thick and murky, like a chorus chanting together in im-
perfect unison. But even now, with the world having
passed beyond its own farthest extremity, the voice exudes a supernal calmness and control that still, astonish-
ingly, serve to comfort and soothe.

"Some of them, yes," he replies. "But something is
eluding me. They seem to contain two different strands
or stories. One of them is like a dream narrative that follows an alternative plot and—perhaps—posits a world
in which the efforts of the other narrative have failed or
were never made. But I'm not at all certain of any of this.
I need to read the pages once more."

"Then read," the voice says. "But remember that
we are waited upon." As if in confirmation, the ocean
roar of voices swells momentarily to a peak, washing up
from below the balcony outside and telling of a tensely

waiting throng before settling back into an undulating trough.

He nods and returns to the pages.

ITS TRANSCENDENCE. In the Book of Isaiah we encounter a Yahweh who protects the cosmic order from destructive incursions by the ancient chaos serpents but also launches His own cosmos-shaking assaults against that order, all leading up to a concluding note of horror in the book's worm-infested final verse that has resounded down through the ages and brought no end of trouble for biblical exegetes, since its literary and theological effect is to stamp the book with the impossible message that *Yahweh is the ultimate chaos monster* who only saves His creation from the others so that He can destroy it Himself. (Surely you remember this subversive reading of the Isaian text from my last book, which sold relatively well but drew such scathing condemnation from my fellow theologians.)

Is it possible, can we conclude, that these and a thousand other aspects of our tradition were always both more and less than they seemed—that they were, in a word, *other* than they seemed; that instead of pointing directly toward spiritual and metaphysical truths, the great concepts, words, and icons of our tradition were in fact mere signals, hints, clues, that gestured awkwardly toward a reality whose true character was and is far different from and perhaps even *opposite to* the surface meanings?

Consider: humanity's dual nature—conscious and unconscious, deliberate and autonomic, free and determined, physical and spiritual, cerebral and reptilian—has always singled us out as the earth's only true amphibians. We have always acted from two centers and stood with feet planted in two separate worlds. Now we have seen this duality ripped apart or brought to fruition— how to regard it is unclear—as those elements of reality represented by our reptilian brainbase, and by the darkest archetypes of our collective unconscious, and by the corresponding monstrous elements in our mythological traditions, have fulfilled a nexus of ancient race-level fears.

Does this perhaps indicate something of our role in what is transpiring? Do we perhaps serve a necessary function as bridges between the realms, *simply by the fact of our fundamental duality*?

I turn my eyes skyward and see the gargoylish figures still commanding the open air between the coiling columns of smoke. Rubbery black demonoid shapes with smooth blank faces and leathery wings swoop and careen like flakes of ash on a hot wind.

A moment later I stumble on a fragment of granite, and the involuntary ducking of my head proves perfectly timed for avoiding a surely fatal encounter with a squid-like shape twenty feet long that bloats and shimmers through the air in a rhythmic pulsating pattern like a sea creature propelling itself through deep water. I stare at its underside, sick with terror, as it slides past and over me, but then note with relief that the fat torpedo-shaped body is turned so that its great blank eye looks laterally instead of downward. Had the thing been looking down, it would have done what these sentinels always do when they detect their prey: it would have paused directly over me and regarded me through that alien eye with an equally alien intelligence. Then it would have bunched itself into a knotted mass of claw-tipped tentacles ringed around a dilating sphincter-mouth set with concentric rows of needled teeth, and dropped upon me with inconceivable speed and ferocity. I have already seen those serpentine tentacles enmesh many a man in their deadly loops. I have heard the human flesh sizzle and scorch on contact with that corrosive extra-dimensional matter. I have watched shrieking people disappear into that churning meat grinder of a mouth.

As incongruous as it may sound, I now express *thanks*, not just passive resignation but a positive gratitude, for the waking nightmare that has overtaken us. For those things that otherwise seem so horrific in their surface appearances can actually serve to awaken us from our dogmatic slumbers and lead us to a more vital and viable faith, a faith that is unshakeable, unassailable, impervious to doubt: a true theological exemplar of Luther's *Ein Feste Burg*, although this mighty fortress, if rendered in literal brick and stone, would embody a warped architectural schema of a pointedly nonhuman and nonrational nature.

It would be so easy to rearrange some of these fragments, to clarify their individual and collective meanings by connecting some of their philosophical edges where they obviously cohere. But despite his pleading for permission to do so, the rule is firm: the pages and their contents must remain in their received order, and must be met and dealt with in that order and no other. Any interpretation must emerge from and pointedly account for that canonically unalterable jumble in its precise given form. *A new Revelation*, so many members of the hierarchy have said to him and to each other on so many different occasions since the papers first came into their possession at a time when the global nightmare was just beginning to invade from the shadows. *A new scripture. A third testament.* They have said such things in tones of awe, and exultation, and confusion, and horror, and, increasingly, with a dogmatic air of fanatical certitude.

We were both weaned, Francis, you in your Roman tradition and I in my Protestant one, on the winsome belief that "All things work together for good for those who love the LORD, those who are called according to his purpose." I am writing to you now simply to say this: our global eruption of nightmares, which would otherwise seem to disprove this canonical statement from my theological namesake, actually serves to confirm it—not directly but by demolishing the presumptuous prison of axioms in which it lay incarcerated for two millennia. "All things work together for good for those who love the LORD"—ah, but *what* good? And *which* LORD?

"Those who are called according to his purpose"—ah, but w*hat* call, and *which* purpose?

The quotations and their implied questions point to our pressing need. What confronts us as an awful necessity, if we and our faith intend to survive, is a reconciliation of what we have always believed with what now presents itself as a contrary but incontrovertible truth. The classic theological antitheses—Jerusalem and Athens, the City of God and the City of Man, Christ and Belial—no longer apply. The only one that still retains any potency is that which refers to the enmity between the "seed of the woman" and the "seed of the serpent." But it requires a substantive modification.

Our antithesis, our dilemma in the form of a sacred riddle, is simply this: *what has Christ to do with Cthulhu?*

It comes with a corollary: *what has Jerusalem to do with R'lyeh?*

In these letters I intend to present you with the rudiments of a viable theological recalibration that will explore the avenues opened up by these shocking juxtapositions, and that, in doing so, will safeguard the possibility of our salvation, albeit in a much modified and, as I fear we shall be unable to keep from feeling it, far less agreeable form.

As I navigate the burning wasteland, another environment flickers intermittently into view around me: a crazy-tilted maze of stone columns and temples vying with the reality of the blasted city and attempting to supplant it all at once in a cinematic superimposition. The ocean, hundreds of miles from here, laps momentarily at my feet, while a monolithic mass of ancient stone towers glimmers darkly offshore. I blink, shake my head and refuse to accept the vision. After a furtive hesitation, the inland wasteland regains its foothold.

ITS AWFULNESS. Especially in Mark's gospel, but also throughout the New Testament and also the Hebrew scriptures, manifestations of divine reality are portrayed consistently as occasions for sheer terror. Jesus calms the storm; his disciples are filled not with sweet sentiments of divine love and comfort but with terror and awe. The women find his tomb empty; they do not exit the garden singing hosannas but stumble away in soul-blasted fright, unable to speak. When angels appear in bursts of light and song, shepherds and Roman soldiers alike faint, tremble, avert their eyes, raise their hands to ward off the sight of those awful messengers of a reality from beyond this world—a reality that is *inherently* awful *because* it is from beyond this world.

He pulls his attention out of the pages like a swimmer hauling himself naked and shivering out of icy black waters. He makes to inhale deeply, to suck in cleansing air, but finds that his breath remains frozen at mid-breast, just as it has been for months now, ever since reality first went mad with the collapsing of the distinction between divine and demonic, leaving him internally paralyzed, gripped as if by a fist in his diaphragm while grotesque supernatural impossibilities erupt all around.

The voice behind him remains silent, but its presence is palpable and its command unmistakable. With fixed stare and only slightly trembling hand, he resigns himself again to the task and begins reading from the first page, scanning not only for the meanings contained in the words themselves but for evidence of the interstitial semiotic glue that binds the whole insane edifice together. As always, his attention is soon swallowed whole by the dark and deranged philosophical cathedral it has entered.

Perhaps a recounting of how our new Great Awakening (a term whose traditional, historical use seems gallingly blinkered now) first made itself known to me will serve to purify and clarify our mutual apprehension of these matters.

As you know, I was hard at work on my third book of theology, a substantial and career-defining exercise in theological trailblazing to be titled *The Fear of God*, in which I took on the same theme treated by John Bunyan in his classic treatise with the same title, and agreed with him that "by this word *fear* we are to understand even God himself, who is the object of our fear." I took for my orienting point Luther's subversive declaration—which exerted a veritably talismanic power over me—that God "is more terrible and frightful than the Devil ... For therefrom no man can refrain: if he thinketh on God aright, his heart and his body is struck with terror ... Yea, as soon as he heareth God named, he is filled with trepidation and fear."

One day—I distinctly remember the sun was shining sweetly through my living room window while a few birds twittered in the yard, so it must have been during the spring or summer, although my sense of time has lately become as confused and chaotic as the natural elements, which, as you know, have now taken on a schizophrenic kind of existence—one day I sat poring over a stack of pages that I had recently written, and was struck without warning by a thoroughly hideous vision. As I looked at my pages, I saw peering through the typewritten words, as if from *behind* the lines of text, a face more awful than any I had ever conceived. I need not describe it to you: the bloated octopoid visage with its obscenity of a fanged and tentacled maw, and with saurian and humanoid characteristics all mixed together in a surreal jumble. It conjured involuntary thoughts of the great Dragon of John's Apocalypse, and of the watery waste of Genesis, and of the waters beyond the sky and below the earth, and of the chaos serpent Leviathan. But there was far more than that. Staring into the red-black effulgence of its awful eyes, I saw the skin of those biblical images peeled back to reveal great Mother Tiamat, the ancient archetype of all dragons and serpents and extra-cosmic chaos, wearing the more familiar imagery like a cheap rubber mask.

It was more than just a visual image, it was a veritable convulsion in my total being, and its ripples spread through the very air of the room. You well remember your own experience as you knelt praying before a statue of St. Jude and raised your eyes to his benevolent face, only to be greeted by the same sight I am describing. So you know, too, the violent illness that overtook me. I was gripped by a kind of mania even as my stomach and bowels twisted into searing knots, and I began turning frantically from page to page in an effort to escape the vision, but still the words of my *magnum opus* appeared as the bars of a cage holding back that impossible face, that locus of all nightmares, that source of all ancient, evil imaginings. I dimly remember ripping the book to shreds and even—I cannot remember why—eating portions of it, and then vomiting them back up; the half-digested paper had been transformed into tiny scrolls which I then ate again, and they tasted like honey, but then they turned so bitter in my mouth that I vomited yet again.

These events are all peculiar to me, but the rest I think you know. For my personal story is a microcosm of that greater story in which we are all now trapped. Each of us has his own story of how he personally experienced that terrible moment when our world was overturned by the eruption from beyond, and all of them bear a generic character that marks them as belonging to this new proclamation, this New Testament, which we are not reading but living.

"And did you truly experience such a vision with a statue of Saint Jude?" the voice asks, still located behind him. Its tone is overlaid with a scummy film, like the surface of a thick and slow-boiling stew, and he maintains his reverentially averted gaze. After pausing to regain his bearings in the relatively solid surroundings of the chamber, he softly shakes his head.

"I don't think so. Or rather, I don't remember. Reading the documents is like reading the transcript of a dream that I never knew I had experienced. Every line feels like a half-memory of something I had forgotten without ever knowing it at all."

He considers the description of the demon-dragon, and imagines it transplanted onto the patron saint of desperate cases and lost causes. The apostle's beard is a nest of writhing gray-green tentacles. Their tips caress the image of Christ hanging at the figure's breast.

He asks, "And how did these papers come into the Church's possession?" Maybe this time the answer will contain something new.

"By strange channels and unknown messengers," the voice replies, as if chanting a litany, "the writings of the new apostle came to the Church to illuminate the shadows of these dark days."

"But the timing is all wrong," he says, unable to restrain himself. "The author must have written these things *before* the cataclysm began. Weren't they delivered on the very day when the great face appeared in the sky and the cities erupted into madness?" The voice remains silent, of course, for these details have already been analyzed and discussed *ad nauseam* within the Roman episcopate. He considers for the hundredth time the ramifications of the fact that some unknown individual who shared the name of the last apostle had written of these things in the past tense, before they actually happened, and had addressed his dark visionary rantings directly to the Holy See in Rome. The Church's frantically launched investigation had been hindered at every turn not only by the fantastic events unfolding around the globe but by false and disappearing leads that appeared positively supernatural in their abrupt and strategic occurrences. No publisher knew of a book offering a blasphemous reading of Isaiah. Only the vaguest of hints spoke of a renegade theologian writing a self-described *magnum opus*. The papers had been sent via a route that looked impossibly circuitous when staked on a map. The trail dead-ended simultaneously at indistinct locations in North America, Central America, Eastern Asia—and Rome itself.

The more he ponders it, the more it sounds and feels like a narrative being altered and overlaid by multiple redactions, each intended to accomplish a greater opening to an emotion compounded of equal parts bafflement and spiritual revulsion. In the latest revision, the letters are addressed directly to him, and their author is rendered fictional, to await complete obliteration in a version yet to come.

"Why me?" he asks, even though he is growing increasingly terrified at the thought that the specific identity of the New Paul may be supremely unimportant in one sense and all-important in another.

The voice responds to his unspoken fear: "In the beginning was the Logos, which speaks not only in the lines of Holy Scripture but in the lines of the real itself. Our new apostle's writings and their accompanying signs and wonders declare a great rewording in which the notions of 'me' and 'thee' may be forgotten."

A pen, formerly unnoticed, rests beside the pages on the desk. His hand begins to itch. The voice intones, "The Word is a living thing. Like a farmer sowing seeds, one sows the Word but knows not how it grows. If all were written down, the world itself could not contain the books."

The multitude gathered outside in the piazza emits a sigh of anticipation and agreement.

He watches with shock and fascination as his hand picks up the pen and begins to add to the words of the final page, defiling its inviolable sanctity, writing in clean, crisp, orderly lines that cut across the jumbled chaos like the bars of a cage.

ITS IMMANENCE: Jerusalem and R'lyeh—might they always have been interlaced with each other? The physical Jerusalem and also the mythic vision of its bejeweled celestial fulfillment—both revealed as mere shades, devolutions, abstractions of the primary reality of those crazy-slanted, green-dripping towers and slabs emerging like the archetype of a chthonic city from the subterranean waters of the collective psyche, like bony black fingers rising up from Mother Ocean.

Christ and Cthulhu—might they both be hierophanies of the same awful transcendent reality? Christ as high priest in the order of Melchizidek, Cthulhu as high priest in the order of the Old Ones, both of them bridging the gap and healing the division between our free-fallen souls with their burden of autonomous, inward-turned selfhood and the greater, all-encompassing reality of God-by-whatever-name; both implanting their own deep selves *within us*, thus undercutting and overcoming our categorically contradictory attempts to heal the primordial rift through conscious effort. These psychic disturbances that have so terrified us of late, all of the collapsing distinctions between thought, imagination, and physical reality, so that a stray wish or undisciplined notion may cause finned, clawed, and tentacled atrocities to appear, or may even alter one's own physical body in awful ways that some of us have been unable to undo afterward, as in a nightmare from which one cannot wake because one has awakened inside the nightmare itself—may these not be the fulfillment of Jesus' promise to send the paraclete to "guide us into all truth" and "convict the world of sin and righteousness and judgment," and of his promise that his followers would perform even greater miracles than he himself had performed, and of the apostle Paul's teaching that the divine spirit living within us will show us directly those primal mysteries which "no eye has seen, no ear has heard, no mind has conceived"? Surely these last words, quoted by Paul from the prophet Isaiah, aptly characterize the marvels and monstrosities we have recently witnessed.

Still writing, still horror-struck, he sees in his peripheral vision the Voice moving away from him in a swirl of smoky shapes. The new scriptural corpus is complete. The Church can now achieve alignment with that which truly is. What might be a wholesome human form dressed in liturgical vestments and wearing the papal mitre might also be a mutated manshape sprouting dragon's wings and surmounted by a head like a cuttlefish, and this dual superimposition of high priest might be walking on the floorstones or gliding above them.

The crowd assembled in the piazza might be a wild-eyed multitude of ragged and terrified survivors or a stalk-eyed horde of flopping fish and toads.

The vast visage painted across the dome of the twilit sky might be a white-bearded transposition from the nearby chapel ceiling or the imprint of an extra-cosmic monstrosity now burned eternally onto the face of heaven.

The granite obelisk planted in the piazza's center might be a skeletal black finger rising from Mother Ocean. The curved walls enclosing the crowd might be alien stone hewn into an architectural impossibility.

The incarnate voice emerges onto the balcony. The crowd roars, raising hands or fins or webbed claws and screaming in desperation or delight, singing a hymn of horror to the face in the sky.

The voice begins to speak, delivering its opening blessing: "*Iä! Cthulhu fhtagn!*"

Inside the ornate room he continues to write, binding the pages with a meaning that can only be known, not spoken.

The answer, Francis, must surely be found in the implicit order that lies buried in all of this chaos. Embracing it is our salvation. God's ways are not man's. To Him a thousand days are as one, and one as a thousand. He is terrible to behold. Our religion, all the world's religions, may once have kept Him out, all unknowing of their true role, but now they, we, have become His conduit, again ignorant of our purpose until it is upon us to fulfill.

Gaunt faceless gargoyles hover on black leathern wings above the assembled multitude, showering whitefeather plumage as they beam benevolence from gold-glowing countenances.

The Lord God sits on His throne above the throng, towering above the basilica in a redblack inferno. His crown burns black. His beard coils green.

In these letters I intend to present you with the rudiments of a viable theological recalibration that will

explore the avenues opened up by these shocking juxtapositions, and that, in doing so, will safeguard the possibility of our salvation, albeit in a much modified and,
as I fear we shall be unable to keep from feeling it, far
less agreeable form.

GHOST DANCING

Darrell Schweitzer

By the time he's on the beltway around Boston, heading north, he's got the road to himself. But the radio still works and, although it mostly picks up static, every once in a while there's a clear voice, often just babbling or screams or frenzied prayers, but once or twice something approximating a coherent news summary, describing incredible scenes all along the coastlines of the world: mountains of flesh, miles high, roaring up out of the depths, tidal waves and tsunamis wiping out major cities in minutes. New York, Philadelphia, Baltimore, and Washington are gone. The air overhead looks overcast, but he can smell the oil and smoke, and he knows that's Boston burning.

North. He has nowhere to go, really, but he's driving north, all because of a last-minute email:

> Eric—Why don't you come up and see me? Now's as good a time as any. Cthulhu fhtagn, old pal.
> —Robert Tillinghast

He hasn't seen Robert Tillinghast since college, almost thirty years ago, but Tillinghast is right, it is as good a time as any, because as far as Eric Shaw is concerned, time has ended, and his life ended too the day his wife and two daughters went to New York to see a show and just happened to be there when something the size of

128

several dozen blue whales misshapenly lumped together with several giant squids tossed in for good measure heaved up out of the Hudson and came slithering up Broadway with tentacles flying like whiplashes, toppling buildings until the whole of lower and midtown Manhattan looked like "one vast pyroclastic flow," in the words of a newspaper reporter filming it all from a helicopter before something suddenly shot up and snatched him out of the air like a frog's tongue zapping a fly.

Once, when he stopped at a deserted rest stop along I-95 in Connecticut, he sat down in the McDonald's concession after helping himself to a cold hamburger, and he opened his laptop, got on the Internet, and saw that footage again.

The net was still up then, miraculously. But that was *hours* ago. It's gone now. In a fast-moving world, hours ago is *forever.* Now, he doesn't need the net and its wild speculations to tell him the nature and cause of the worldwide catastrophe, of the *ending* of the reign of mankind on earth. He knows that. Robert Tillinghast knows too. It's their secret.

Their guilty little secret, because just maybe they might have had something to do with how things have turned out.

So he can only drive, and by the time he reaches that little stretch where 95 crosses a narrow strip of New Hampshire it is getting dark, and a thick fog has set in. He is still too, too terribly close to the coast, when he hears a bellow like a thousand foghorns, deafening, and *something* best described as a centipede the size of the *Queen Mary* with legs as thick as telephone poles comes lumbering out of the woods to his right, grinding up the highway into rubble as its legs slam/slam/slam down in front of him, behind him, as the black shadow of the thing passes overhead and by some dark miracle he is not crushed. This is no dream, no hallucination brought on by fatigue or grief, but something definitely there. A minute later he is alone again, desperately trying to pick his way by the light of his headlights through the less mangled bits of the road surface until he can reach a more or less undamaged portion. By then there are more bellowing sounds, more of those things coming out of the woods from the direction of the ocean, but he is, at last able to reach solid, flat asphalt and speed away.

Maine, when he was a child, into his adolescence, was a summer wonderland, where the family went for month-long vacations every summer, his home away from home, where he had a whole different set of friends, where he met and dated his first girlfriend.

He starts to see familiar signs now: Kittery, York, Portland, Yarmouth, Bath. There he has to get off I-95 onto the more winding, semirural Route 1 and *follow the coast*. Too damned near to the water all the way. Why the hell couldn't Robert Tillinghast live in, say, *Kansas*, for God's sake?

He knows perfectly well why. It is their little secret and has a great deal to do with the present circumstances, if very little to do with God.

So it is when he finally, *finally* reaches the vacation-land of his youth, and winds his way through a half-destroyed, still smoldering Rockland, and has a bizarre encounter with a dozen men and women who come streaking out of the darkness clad in white, trailing tatters like something out of a mummy movie, screaming and babbling, clawing at the windows of his car. After that little snapshot of mass insanity, and a slow crawl through a deserted but picture-perfect Camden—yes, there's the library, the Village Restaurant, that over-priced bookshop, the schooners in the harbor; he knows every brick of this place; nothing has changed in twenty years, except of course that the world has ended in the meantime—after all that, with no time, alas, for wallowing in nostalgia, Eric Shaw, grieving father, widower for less than forty-eight hours, finally arrives at the address he has been given, one of those huge half-gingerbread, half gothic Victorian piles he'd driven by so many times during vacations in the past, the sort of place that tends to get broken up into apartments or turned into resort hotels these days; except for this one, because the Tillinghast family has always been unbelievably, fantastically wealthy.

After suitably spooky preliminaries, including standing on the cavernous porch for a moment and looking down over sloping lawn into the blackness where something like a series of enormous, glowing paper lanterns seems to be rising out of the waters of Penobscot Bay, after he enters the darkened house through the conveniently unlocked door, makes his way upstairs, cringing at strange sounds, some of them like grunts or muted barks—at the top, in a fully-lighted room he finds his old "friend" Tillinghast seated in front of an immense flatscreen TV, control device in hand, clicking through picture after picture, *laughing hysterically.*

Eric can only stand in the doorway of the room, too stunned to react, thinking, *Yeah, sure, why not? Millions of people are dead and I just risked my life to drive hundreds of miles to sit and watch TV with a crazy guy I don't even like.*

But he does sit down on the sofa indicated, with Tillinghast beside him, because they have their little secret.

Eric can only stare at this gaunt, hawk-nosed, half-balding, but wild-haired man who bears hardly the slightest resemblance to the fascinating, overpowering, and slightly terrifying Robert Tillinghast he had met when he was eighteen and Tillinghast was twenty, but then Tillinghast reaches over and grabs him by the scruff of the neck the way you would a cat, and twists his head toward the screen and says, "Now be a good boy, and *watch.*"

Tillinghast had always done that in the old days, because he was taller, had a longer reach, and was stronger. He'd treated Eric like a child, called him his "good boy," but was not the sort of person, back then, any more than he seems to be one now, inclined to take no for an answer.

"Now look at this," Tillinghast says, as he picks up the control and switches the scenes. It's not a live broadcast, obviously, because nothing is being broadcast anymore. It's something he must have saved off cable in the past few days.

There are scenes of religious ceremonies all over the world, a candle-lit procession up the side of a mountain in the Andes, great crowds of saffron-robed monks bowing down in front of a pagoda in Thailand, another candle-lit affair, but with people waving American flags and crosses and preachers screaming hellfire over a PA system, somewhere in a middle of a field in the Midwest, and then Tillinghast interrupts and says, "This one's really good."

St. Peter's Square, Rome. Night. Lots of floodlights. Cut to: inside the great basilica, the Pope himself conducting mass, surrounded by dozens of cardinals. Cut to: outside, in the square, the packed crowd (thousands of candles like flickering fireflies). His Holiness and the cardinals loom above the huddled masses, projected on two enormous screens for the benefit of those who couldn't fit inside the basilica. The Pope raises his hands and calls out to God to rescue the faithful in this time of greatest need, and he calls on the multitudes to renew their faith in Christ and look to the scriptures for some hope in the days to come—only by then the multitudes aren't paying much attention because St. Peter's Square has broken out in a bedlam of panic and carnage as something black and oily and huge starts pouring out of the sky, splattering across the floodlit dome like an immense, palpitating stain, pouring onto the crowd below.

"Shoggoths," says Robert Tillinghast, chuckling softly. "It's raining shoggoths in Rome. I don't think there's anything about that in *Revelations.*"

He *spits* in disgust and contempt.

Eric can't think of what to say in response. He's exhausted, drained, disoriented. It's almost as if he hears someone else muttering, with his voice, "What happened in Mecca?"

"Pretty much the same," is the answer. "Nobody knows, really. Mecca's not there any more."

The scene cuts to actual US Navy footage of the rising of the lost island of R'lyeh in the South Pacific. Something like green smoke pours out of crevices between the impossible angles of buildings the eye cannot quite bring into focus, and there is a hint of a massive shape rising up, writhing and wriggling, a cloudy outline of hunched shoulders; then wings spread wide, the screen goes blank, and Robert Tillinghast, in his best Porky Pig voice, cackles, "Th-th-that's all folks!"

Eric places his elbows on his knees, holds his head in his hands, and begins to sob, not even consciously thinking of the deaths of his wife and his daughters, or of the end of the world, but merely because the tears just flow of their own accord. Only after a while, with great effort he is finally able to gasp, "Would you kindly tell me *what the fuck your point is?*"

Now Tillinghast puts his hand on Eric's shoulder gently, as if to comfort him.

"My point is that it's all ghost dancing."

"Ghost dancing?"

"Yeah. You know how, at the end of the nineteenth century, when the American Indians—or do I mean Native Americans?—no need to be politically correct any more—*knew* they had lost everything to the white man, they started a new religion that held that if everybody put on their ghost shirts and did the magical ghost dance, then bullets would bounce off them, the white men would go away, the buffalo would return, and everything would be just peachy. That's what people do, at the end, when they have no realistic hope left. They lapse into fantasy. That's what's going on right now. The ghost shirts and ghost dances didn't do a whole lot of good against the Gatling guns at Wounded Knee. You saw what happened to the Pope. The spheres are conjoined. The gateways are open. The Old Ones return. That's it. *Ding!* Game over."

Eric just stares at him, and Tillinghast continues.

"Now I imagine you are exhausted, and have been under a great deal of stress, and you could use a good hot meal and a comfortable bath and a good night's sleep before we calmly discuss our future plans, or even why I brought you here—"

"Yeah," Eric says. "I really could."

But suddenly Tillinghast leaps to his feet, grabs him by the scruff of the neck and hauls him off the sofa. "Well, that's entirely *too bad*, because the evening's festivities *won't wait*, and have been delayed as long as possible so that you could arrive. So, I'm sorry, but we have to go *right now*."

Eric is too befuddled to resist as he finds himself hustled over to a closet and handed a robe of some kind, which, as he unfolds it, he recognizes. Black, hooded, embroidered, covered with sigils and signs copied from the pages of the *Necronomicon*. He struggles to put it on, over his clothes, remembering that in the old days it was customary to be naked underneath one of these things; but, as he hesitates, Tillinghast assures him that tonight such details are not going to matter.

Robed, the two of them take in hand ancient, golden lanterns of bizarre design, which allegedly came from beneath the sea, and, lighting the little candles within with an ordinary cigarette lighter, they proceed out of the house, across the porch, down a flight of wooden stairs, and then along a path along the edge of the lawn, downhill, toward the bay.

From somewhere up ahead he can hear chanting, and it occurs to Eric Shaw that on such a night as this—as dark as this anyway, overcast, starless—way back when, when the two of them were young, before their parting of the ways when he supposedly turned from the sinister life's course he had found himself upon, moved to New Jersey and become a respectable illustrator of children's books, most of which seemed to have something to do with happy bunny-rabbits—on such a night as this, one Cindy Higgins had, as it was whispered at the time, come to an exceedingly nasty end. The police never solved the case. Afterwards, Eric and Robert had parted, Eric to supposed respectability, Robert to his celebrated, scandal-ridden career as a poet and artist and alleged cult-leader of truly remarkable extravagance and rumored depravity.

All this comes rushing back to Eric now, the traumatically repressed details, the veils of hidden memories torn back, as he realizes that he is now on the *very same beach*, in the *very same spot*, where the aforesaid Cindy Higgins, who *hadn't* been his first girlfriend from Maine vacations when he was a kid, but his first girlfriend's younger sister's best friend, whom *he* had lured into the orbit of Robert Tillinghast and his cronies with the promise of a really good time, had met her hideous fate, very much in the manner that the girl who is there now seems about to meet hers.

Eric, physically and emotionally exhausted to the point of delirium can only exclaim, rather ridiculously, "Jesus Christ, what *a fucking cliché!*" when he realizes that he and his host have now joined the company of about a dozen similarly robed cultists who are standing by torchlight around a stone altar, on which is stretched, bound with the requisite leather thongs, a genuine *naked virgin*, a pale, blonde, teenaged girl, probably about Cindy's age, or his own younger daughter's age, who screams and whimpers and sobs begs to be let go, promising she won't tell, as if that somehow matters now.

It is, Eric realizes, just like old times. There are certain things in life that you can't just walk away from, and being a member of a human sacrifice cult is probably high on the list. No good saying you didn't mean it or you're sorry. It's way too late for that.

The only difference between this time and what happened to Cindy is that now there are *things* the size of small elephants, but spiny and rough and vaguely humanoid, crouched in the *water,* almost out of view beyond the range of the torchlight. They would be hard to see if their eyes weren't glowing. You might think they were rocks if they didn't make a chittering and hissing sound.

The last time he and Robert had done this, after they *were* done and Cindy was gone, taken by something that reached for her out of the darkness, Robert had shouted something out across the water, and from the distance had come a *reply,* followed by a thunderclap, and a flash of light on the horizon, then a cold, rushing wind that whipped up waves like a sudden squall.

"We've opened the gate just a crack," Robert had said then. "It is a beginning."

Now, as the cultists begin their chanting and the girl whimpers, Robert whispers to Eric, "We have to open the gate all the way, to make ourselves useful to our new masters, so there will be a place for us in the new world." After a pause he adds, regarding the girl, "Oh, by the way, she's not a virgin. Not anymore. It turns out that doesn't matter. So I took care of it myself. It's one of the *perks* you get in this line of work." Then he nods toward the hunched monsters in the surf and says, "You know what I've always said. If you can't beat 'em, join 'em. That is why we are gathered here today, dearly beloved in the sight of Dagon."

Inevitably, as the frenzied ceremony reaches is climax—as Eric plays along and waves his arms and chants along with the rest, because he's been here before *and he knows his lines*—Robert Tillinghast produces from within his robe the vast, curved, polished ritual knife that the well equipped cult-leader always brings to a occasion like this, and it is only as Tillinghast stands over the altar with the knife upraised like something on a glowing, black-light poster you'd get in an occult shop back when they were kids, that Eric is able to formulate even a vague semblance of a plan.

He reaches up. He grabs Tillinghast by the wrists and prevents him from bringing the knife down.

"No. Let me do it!"

Tillinghast draws back, startled. The other cultists stop chanting.

"You?"

"Let me do it," Eric says. "You know. To show commitment. I have to be a part of this. I'm not just here for decoration."

"That's right," says Robert Tillinghast. "You're not. Try to get the heart out in one piece. That's what they like best."

And looking down at the now silent girl and remembering Cindy Higgins and his own daughters, Eric suddenly rams the knife into *Tillinghast's* gut as hard as he can, and pulls upward with a savage yank until he can feel ribs starting to give way, and he twists the handle, knowing he's probably ruined the heart.

Nevertheless Tillinghast manages to cling to life for several more seconds, long enough to gasp, "What are you doing . . . ? The ceremony must be completed . . ."

He may even still be alive when Eric whispers in his ear, "No! It doesn't matter. Can't you see that? You're just ghost-dancing like all the rest. You're the biggest goddamn self-deluded ghost-dancer of them all. Not the Pope, *you!*"

But he is almost certainly dead when Eric holds him up, still impaled on the knife, turns him around as if he's about to address his astonished, faithful flock, then heaves him face-down into the surf.

"Look!" Eric shouts. "Look! It's all bullshit! This isn't going to *save* you!" He points at the *things* now lumbering toward the beach. "*They* don't give a damn about what side you think you're on, and it's not a case of fucking *if you can't beat 'em, join 'em*, because *they* aren't going to let you join 'em except the parts of you as they forget to pick from between their teeth!"

Now the monsters roar and come splashing out of the water and the cultists are screaming as teeth and claws tear them to shreds. Eric starts sawing away at the girl's bonds with the knife.

From over the water come several thundering, honking sounds that might be foghorns or ships, but he knows they are not.

Gunshots ring out. Something slams into him in the side, hard, and he feels a burning pain that begins to spread as he works. But he has the girl free now, and he hauls her up off the beach, onto the sloping lawn, driving her toward the house, his car, and a possible getaway. He's having trouble breathing now. He's coughing up blood. He's not going to make it. But she might. He tries to take off his robe and give it to her, but just loses his grip on her and falls down painfully onto his injured side, then rolls onto his back. He fumbles for his car keys, under the robe.

Above him, the fog has cleared, and the stars shine in all their distant, cold, pitiless brilliance.

He doesn't know if he's accomplished anything. This is probably just more ghost-dancing, but it sure felt good to try.

He catches hold of the girl by her ankle. She kneels down beside him. He gives her the car keys.

Above, the mad auroras roll.

THIS IS HOW THE WORLD ENDS

John R. Fultz

They always said the world would end in fire.

Mushroom clouds, atomic holocaust, the pits of hell opening up and vomiting flame across a world of sin, corruption, and greed. The world would be a cinder, and Christ would come down from the clouds to lift the faithful skyward.

I used to believe those things. My daddy taught me the Bible, and Revelations was his favorite chapter. He believed in the wrath of God, and he feared the fires of Hell.

But the world wasn't burned away by righteous fires. There was no great conflagration.

The world didn't burn.

It drowned.

One thing the Bible did get right: the sea did turn to blood.

The coastal cities were the first to go. Two years ago the first of the Big Waves hit. The newscasters called them "mega-tsunamis." Los Angeles, San Diego, Seattle, San Francisco . . . so many sandcastles flattened and drowned. Watery graves for millions. New York, Miami, even Chicago when the Great Lakes leapt out of their holes like mad giants. A single day and all the major cities . . . gone.

After the tsunamis came the *real* terror. The waves washed terrible things onto the land . . . things that had never seen the light of day. Fanged, biting, *hungry* things. They fed on the bodies of the drowned, laid their eggs in the gnawed bodies. Billions of them ... the seas ran red along the new coastlines. Survivors from Frisco fled inland, carrying tales of something even *worse* than the vicious Biters. Something colossal ... some called it the Devil himself. It took the fallen skyscrapers as its nesting ground, ruling a kingdom of red waters.

I heard similar tales from western and eastern refugees. They fled inland, away from the stench of brine and blood, and the drifting islands of bloated bodies.

The military tried fighting back, but there were too many of those things claiming the coast. That's when the plague started. It floated across the land in great, black clouds, like dust storms during the Depression. Those who breathed the stuff didn't die ... they *changed*. They grew gills, and fangs, and writhed like snakes, spitting venom. Feeding on each other. Soon there weren't any more soldiers.

I heard they tried nuking Manhattan, where something big as the moon crawled out of the ocean. The missiles didn't fire. Something shorted out all the technology, every computer on the continent ... probably the planet ... every piece of electronic equipment ... all dead. Air Force jets fell out of the sky like dead birds. Somebody called it an electromagnetic pulse. As if the rules of the universe had shifted. In a flash, the modern world was done.

There was nothing to do but run. Hide.

Hordes of the Biters took to roaming the plains, the hills, the valleys and mountains. Those poor souls who didn't get taken by the rolling clouds eventually got rooted out by the Biters or the worm-things that followed them around. Big, saw-toothed bastards, like leeches the size of semi-truck trailers. I saw one of the Biter hordes hit Bakersfield, saw a school bus full of refugees swallowed whole by one of those worms. Still see that in my nightmares sometimes ... the faces of those kids ... sound of their screams.

Whiskey helps, when I can get it.

About fifty of us from farms in the San Joaquin Valley had banded together, loaded up with guns, ammo, and canned food from Lloyd Talbert's bomb shelter, and headed east in a convoy of old pickups and decommissioned Army jeeps. We figured out that the black clouds usually preceded the Biters, so we stayed one step ahead of them. We tried to pick up some relatives in Bakersfield or we would have avoided it altogether. Barely made it out of there, and we lost twelve good men in the process. Nobody got rescued.

It had rained for two months straight in California, nonstop ever since the Big Waves. Farther inland we went, the less rain we got. We figured out that the Biters liked the wet . . . they hated the dry lands, so we went on into Nevada. Thought we'd find kindred souls in Vegas.

That was a mistake.

Sin City had been smashed flat by something terrible that came out of Yucca Mountain, where they buried all that nuclear waste. We couldn't tell what it was, but we saw it slithering through hills of rubble, rooting up corpses like a hog sniffing for truffles. We watched it for a while from a high ridge, until it raised itself up and howled at the moon. Its head was larger than a stadium, and it split open like a purple orchid lined with bloody fangs. What grew along the bulk of its shapeless body I can only call . . . tentacles. Looked like something from a B-movie filmed in hell. It was the Beast That Ate Vegas.

Then it belched out one of those black clouds, and slammed itself back into a sea of debris that used to be a sparkling dream of a city. This cloud wasn't like the others. There were things inside it . . . flying things . . . maybe they were miniature versions of the Vegas-eater. We thought our vehicles could outrun the cloud, so we headed back west, until the Flyers came down on us.

I was riding in a jeep driven by Adam Ortega, a man I'd known since Iraq. We were two lone wolves who had gone through a lot of shit together and somehow came out alive. One of those Flyers swooped out of the dark and landed on his face. It smelled like fish guts. He screamed, and the beast pointed its orchid-face at me.

A cluster of pinkish tongues quivered between the rows of fangs, and I raised my shotgun just in time to blow that thing to hell. My shot took Ortega's head off. God knows I didn't mean to do that. I was scared.

The jeep veered off the road, hit an embankment, and sent me flying. I blacked out, and when I woke up the entire convoy was in flames, every man lost beneath a mess of black-winged monsters. But they had forgotten me, at least for a few minutes.

They were good men, all of them, but there was no helping them now. Some had brought families with them. I heard women screaming. And children. Me, I'd always been alone, ever since my divorce. Farm life was lonely life, but it was good. My daddy passed away three years previously. Now that I think about it, I'm glad he went before all this happened. And that I never had kids of my own to see all this evil shit coming down. But some of my friends had loved ones they weren't about to leave behind, so there they were . . . deep in the middle of the shitstorm with the rest of us. I hid in a ditch and watched a few stragglers try to escape, but the Flyers tore away from carcasses like flocks of ravens and flapped after them.

I still had my .45 Desert Eagle and knew I was probably dead anyway. I could run, maybe live a while longer. But one of the women trying to outrun those things was pregnant. So I started picking off the Flyers chasing her, one by one. A man ran behind her, and the things took him down. He screamed her name and I knew who she was.

"Evelyn!"

That was Johnny Colton and his wife. They hadn't been married more than a year.

Johnny's blood spouted as the damned things tore his heart out, then set to work on his face.

I ran toward Evelyn, shooting two more Flyers out of the air. I'm a pretty good shot. Got a lot of practice in the Mideast. Kept up my skills at the shooting range over the years.

One of them landed on her back and she fell not twenty feet from me. I was afraid of shooting her, so I came at it with the hunting knife from my boot. Sliced it clean in half, but its blood was some kind of acid, splashed across my left cheek ... burned like the Devil's piss. Still have one helluva scar from that.

I helped Evelyn to her feet, and we ran together. She cried out for Johnny, but I wouldn't let her look back. The black cloud was bearing down on us, blotting out the stars and moon. I smelled the stink of the ocean rolling over the desert ... the smell of dead and rotted marine life.

I grabbed a satchel of gear from the overturned jeep, and we took off into the desert. The Flyers must have forgot us after a while. They had a big enough feast back on the highway.

As the sun came up, red and bloated in the purple sky ... it had never looked right since the Big Waves ... we came into Pahrump. The tiny town was deserted, and corpses littered the streets. We saw they had been gnawed up pretty good, probably by the Flyers ... or something just as bad. There wasn't a single living soul there. But we did find a good supply of canned food, bottled water, a gun shop full of ammo and a few rifles, and some other odds-and-ends.

It was Evelyn who told me about the old silver mine on the edge of town. She was a Nevada girl before she married Johnny.

"Maybe we can hide there ... in the mine tunnels," she said. "Maybe they won't go underground. Those mines are pretty deep. We'll be safe down there, Joe."

I didn't believe we would, but I looked into her big, blue eyes, crystalline with tears shed for her dead husband, for her dead relatives in San Joaquin ... for the whole damn world gone to hell.

"Yeah," I lied to her. "We'll be safe down there. Good idea."

We loaded wheelbarrows with provisions, water, guns, blankets, and I picked up an old ham radio from the gun store. I didn't expect it to work, but it was something. Something to pin our hopes on. When the world is ending, you'll take anything you can get.

Evelyn was five months along when we moved into the mine. We weren't exactly *comfortable* down there in the belly of the cool earth, but it was as close as we were going to get. Even a blanket laid over hard stones feels good when you're half-dead from exhaustion and worry. She tended the wound on my face, and I told her hopeful lies to settle her nerves. I said this would all blow over and things would be back to normal in a few months. I didn't believe a word of it. Maybe she did, or at least she wanted to.

I started playing with the radio, hooking it up to a portable battery and listening to the static. I scanned every frequency, every day for weeks, but there was nothing out there. Nothing at all. I imagined all those ham radio geeks out there, lying dead in their basements, or their bones in the bellies of nameless beasts, their radios crushed to splinters or lying in forgotten barns covered with dust.

Slowly, the months crept by. It turned out Evelyn was right. We were safe underground. Her belly grew bigger, and she stopped moving around so much. I started mentally preparing myself to deliver the baby, something I had never done before. But I'd seen so much blood and suffering, first in the war, now at the end of the world, that I knew it wouldn't matter. How hard could it be to pull this little bugger out of his momma's belly? *She* would do most of the work.

"I'm gonna name him Johnny," she said. "Like his father."

I smiled as if it mattered. The kid had no future in a world like this. I cleaned my .45 and contemplated putting us both out of our misery. Why go on living? What was the point? We'd both be better off dead. I loaded a clip into the chamber and tucked the gun behind my belt buckle. I went over to sit by her on the makeshift bed we'd been sharing. I had never touched her sexually, but we'd hold hands in the dead of night. It brought some measure of comfort . . . more for her than for me, I told myself.

The baby was kicking today, and she was excited.

I lowered the flame in our lantern and told her to get some sleep. I might sneak out later and hunt a hare for dinner, I told her. I always said that, but I'd never found any living game outside in the three months we'd been there. Still, sometimes I'd sneak out between the rolling black clouds and scavenge, or look for signs of life. I knew I was kidding myself, and I was tired of it.

She would nod off soon and I would end her life painlessly, one clean shot through her skull and another to finish off the unborn child.

Then one last round through the roof of my mouth and right into my brain pan.

All this suffering would be over for us. The baby would never know a world of crawling Biters and hungry Flyers. It was the right thing to do, I told myself, my mind made up.

But Evelyn . . . she stopped me without ever knowing my plan.

She looked up at me with those big, blue eyes, her dark lids heavy, and she raised her head a bit.

She kissed me, damn her.

She kissed me like she loved me, and I took her into my arms. We lay there for a while, then fell to sleep. After that I knew I could never kill her. Not even to spare her the pain of living in this dying world.

Two weeks later, she went into labor. I had the towels and the boiling water, and even some pain-killers I'd looted from a burned-out drug store in Pahrump. She started screaming, and I could see the baby pressing outward from inside her belly.

She screamed, and I coached her to breathe, breathe, breathe. She pushed, and she screamed. A gout of blood and placenta flowed out of her, and I knew something was wrong. Her screams reached a higher pitch, and she called out for Jesus, for her mommy and daddy, for poor old Johnny.

I fell back when her stomach burst like a ripe melon, a gnarled claw protruding like a dead tree branch. She writhed like a snake, and her wailing was a white noise in my ears as the thing inside her *ripped* its way out. It slithered across her splayed abdomen, and she fainted. I couldn't move . . . I stared at Johnny Colton's baby, my mouth hanging open, my heart a hunk of lead in my chest. The stench of the deep ocean filled the cavern, overpowering the human odors of blood and afterbirth.

Its head was a bulbous thing . . . emerald and coated with bloody slime. Two lidless eyes bulged like black stones, but it had no other face to speak of. A mass of quivering tendrils writhed below the eyes, headless snake-things dripping with gore and mucous. It crawled out of Evelyn's body, and I knew she was dead. Nobody could lose that much blood and still be alive. She was a hollow shell. Her vacant eyes stared at the tunnel's rough ceiling. I remember thinking it was a good thing she didn't live to see this thing that had grown inside her.

It hopped from her corpse in a splash of dark fluids, walking on its clawed arms and feet. Two more appendages grew from its hunched little back, and as they spread I heard a crackling sound like stretching leather. They looked like the wings of a big bat, though far too small to carry this thing with its melon-like head and bloated stomach. It had to weigh at least twenty-five, thirty pounds, I was sure.

It looked at me for a timeless moment, then turned to explore its dead mother's body with those twitching facial tentacles. I heard a horrible sucking sound as it lapped up Evelyn's blood like mother's milk, and then the cracking of bones as its tendrils encircled and *squeezed* her body into pulp. Already it looked somehow larger.

The sound of her bones snapping broke my trance, and I leapt for a sawed-off shotgun I kept near the blankets. It turned to face me again, as if it knew I was about to put an end to it. The big, black eyes narrowed in their sockets, and the remnants of its own afterbirth sluiced from its hidden squid-mouth. It stared down the twin barrels of my gun, and I swear it *spoke*.

Even though it was only minutes old, it hissed at me, a single word I had never heard before, but somehow sounded familiar. Maybe I'd heard it in a nightmare.

Cthulhu, it whispered before I blew its head off.

I've heard that word for months now. Every time I close my eyes.

Sometimes I dream of New York, or Los Angeles, or even London. I see the great landmarks of the world that was . . . the towers that once conquered the sky . . . I see them tilted and crumbling and fallen into the sea, and a mass of cold-blooded amphibian things swirling about them like maggots on a decaying corpse.

I see Evelyn Colton's baby, too, or something like it. It stands above those ruined cities, wings spread like thunderheads, singing a wild song of triumph and murder. It squats like a colossal ape on the skeleton of the Empire State Building, as if it were no more than a fallen log in some world-sized swamp.

I see its *children*, spreading across the globe, filling the low places with brackish seawater, turning the high places into wastelands. A billion-billion monsters spew from the angry seas, screaming its name beneath the bloody moon.

Cthulhu.

Flocks of Colton-babies fly down from the cold stars, soaring around their god like masses of buzzing flies.

That's what it is, I come to understand . . . it's their god.

It's the god of this new world.

It's been a year now since I buried Evelyn. Her grave sits in one of the mine's westernmost tunnels, marked with a cross I took from the husk of an old church.

I listen to the endless static on the ham radio every day. Found a little generator in the ruined town, and I've been siphoning gasoline from an abandoned filling station to power it. The static fills my ears, and sometimes it even drowns out the echoes of Evelyn's wailing as that thing tore itself out of her. Sometimes I broadcast, not giving away my location, but hoping someone—anyone—will answer. I feel like those SETI scientists who used to beam radio messages out into space, into the darkness of infinity, on the off chance that someone out there is listening.

But there's only static.

It rains all the time now, up there. I can't even go top-side anymore because strange things move through the rain clouds, and the puddles breed miniature terrors.

The world is still drowning.

The stink of oceanic brine rolls down into the tunnels of the mine.

I tune the dials of the ham radio, call out a few more S.O.S. messages.

The .45 sits on the blanket before me. I stare at it, gleaming with silver promise.

Evelyn isn't here to stop me this time. One quick, clean shot, and I won't smell the ocean stench any more, won't have the dreams anymore, won't hear the static. The unbroken, white static.

My bottled water is running out. I can't drink the rain, but I know sooner or later, I'll have to. I don't want to think what it will do to me. But thirst is a demon no man can outrun for long. I sit staring at the gun, listening to the radio static, making my decision.

I pick up the .45 and slide the barrel into my mouth. It tastes cold and bitter. Static fills my ears. I fix my thumb so that it's resting on the trigger. I say a silent prayer, and think of my daddy's face.

Something breaks the static.

A momentary glitch in the wall of white noise. I blink, my lips wrapped around the gun. I pull it from my mouth and fiddle with the knobs. There it is again! A one-second break in the static . . . a voice!

I turn the volume up, wait a few moments, then pick up the mike, dropping the pistol.

"Hello!" I say, my voice hoarse like sand on stone. "Hello! Is anybody there?"

White noise static . . . then a pause, followed by a single word, ringing clear as day from the dusty speaker, thick as mud.

Cthulhu.

I drop the mike. Something twists in my gut, and I step back from the radio like it's another monstrosity burst from Evelyn Colton's belly.

Again it speaks to me, a voice oozing out of the cold ocean depths.

Cthulhu.

The word sinks into me like a knife, a smooth incision . . . a length of cold metal between the eyes would be no less effective. The pain is a spike of understanding. I bend over, my hand hovering between the silver-plated pistol and the radio mike. I grab the mike, not the gun, and raise it to my lips.

I stare into the darkness at the back of the cavern and sigh out my reply.

"Cthulhu . . ."

I drop it to the floor and kick over the little table on which the radio sits. It crashes against the stone, spilling the lantern. Flaming oil ignites the blankets, and the cavern fills with noxious smoke. I turn my back on it and walk toward the smell of briny rain, my throat dry as bone.

As I come up out of the silver mine for the last time, the storm rages, winged things soar between the clouds, and I hear a chorus of howling and screeching punctuated by moaning thunder. Thirst consumes me.

I open my mouth to the black skies and drink the oily rain. It flows down my throat like nectar, quenching my terrible thirst in the most satisfying way. It sits cool and comforting in my belly, and I drink down more of it.

I'll never again be thirsty, I realize.

This isn't the end of the world.

It's the beginning.

My body trembles with hidden promise. I know I've got a place in this new world.

Towering things with shadow-bright wings descend to squat about me, staring with clusters of glazed eyes as I crumple . . . shiver . . . evolve.

I raise my blossoming face to the storm and screech my joy across the face of the world.

His world.

Cthuuuuulhuuuuu . . .

Spreading black wings, I take to the sky.

THE SHALLOWS

John Langan

"Il faut cultiver notre jardin." —Voltaire, *Candide*

"I could call you Gus," Ransom said.

The crab's legs, blue and cream, clattered against one another. It did not hoist itself from its place in the sink, though, which meant it was listening to him. Maybe. Staring out the dining room window, his daily mug of instant coffee steaming on the table in front of him, he said, "That was supposed to be my son's name. Augustus. It was his great-grandfather's name, his mother's father's father. The old man was dying while Heather was pregnant. We . . . I, really, was struck by the symmetry: one life ending, another beginning. It seemed a duty, our duty, to make sure the name wasn't lost, to carry it forward into a new generation. I didn't know old Gus, not really; as far as I can remember, I met him exactly once, at a party at Heather's parents' a couple of years before we were married."

The great curtain of pale light that rippled thirty yards from his house stilled. Although he had long since given up trying to work out the pattern of its changes, Ransom glanced at his watch. 2:02 . . . PM, he was reasonably sure. The vast rectangle that occupied the space where his neighbor's green-sided house had stood, as well as everything to either side of it, dimmed, then filled with the rich blue of the tropical ocean, the paler blue of the

150

tropical sky. Waves chased one another towards Ransom, their long swells broken by the backs of fish, sharks, whales, all rushing in the same direction as the waves, away from a spot where the surface of the ocean heaved in a way that reminded Ransom of a pot of water approaching the boil.

(Tilting his head back, Matt had said, *How far up do you think it goes? I don't know*, Ransom had answered. Twenty feet in front of them, the sheet of light that had descended an hour before, draping their view of the Pattersons' house and everything beyond it belled, as if swept by a breeze. *This is connected to what's been happening at the poles, isn't it?* Matt had squinted to see through the dull glare. *I don't know*, Ransom had said, *maybe. Do you think the Pattersons are okay?* Matt had asked. *I hope so*, Ransom had said. He'd doubted it.)

He looked at the clumps of creamer speckling the surface of the coffee, miniature icebergs. "Gus couldn't have been that old. He'd married young, and Heather's father, Rudy, had married young, and Heather was twenty-four or -five . . . call him sixty-five, sixty-six, tops. To look at him, though, you would have placed him a good ten, fifteen years closer to the grave. Old . . . granted, I was younger then, and from a distance of four decades, mid-sixty seemed a lot older than it does twenty years on. But even factoring in the callowness of youth, Gus was not in good shape. I doubt he'd ever been what you'd consider tall, but he was stooped, as if his head were being drawn down into his chest. Thin, frail: although the day was hot, he wore a long-sleeved checked shirt buttoned to the throat and a pair of navy chinos. His head . . . his hair was thinning, but what there was of it was long, and it floated around his head like the crest of some ancient bird. His nose supported a pair of horn-rimmed glasses whose lenses were white with scratches; I couldn't understand how he could see through them, or maybe that was the point. Whether he was eating from the paper plate Heather's uncle brought him or just sitting there, old Gus's lips kept moving, his tongue edging out and retreating."

The coffee was cool enough to drink. Over the rim of the mug, he watched the entire ocean churning with such force that whatever of its inhabitants had not reached safety were flung against one another. Mixed among their flailing forms were parts of creatures Ransom could not identify, a forest of black needles, a mass of rubbery pink tubes, the crested dome of what might have been a head the size of a bus.

He lowered the mug. "By the time I parked my car, Gus was seated near the garage. Heather took me by the hand and led me over to him. Those white lenses raised in my direction as she crouched beside his chair and introduced me as her boyfriend. Gus extended his right hand, which I took in mine. Hard . . . his palm, the undersides of his fingers, were rough with calluses, the yield of a lifetime as a mechanic. I tried to hold his hand gently . . . politely, I guess, but although his arm trembled, there was plenty of strength left in his fingers, which closed on mine like a trap springing shut. He said something, *Pleased to meet you, you've got a special girl here*, words to that effect. I wasn't paying attention; I was busy with the vise tightening around my fingers, with my bones grinding against one another. Once he'd delivered his pleasantries, Gus held onto my hand a moment longer, then the lenses dropped, the fingers relaxed, and my hand was my own again. Heather kissed him on the cheek, and we went to have a look at the food. My fingers ached on and off for the rest of the day."

At the center of the heaving ocean, something forced its way up through the waves. The peak of an undersea mountain, rising to the sun: that was still Ransom's first impression. Niagaras poured off black rock. His mind struggled to catch up with what stood revealed, to find suitable comparisons for it, even as more of it pushed the water aside. Some kind of structure—structures: domes, columns, walls—a city, an Atlantis finding the sun again. No—the shapes were off: the domes bulged, the columns bent, the walls curved, in ways that conformed to no architectural style—that made no sense. A natural formation, then, a quirk of geology. No—already, the hypothesis was untenable: there was too much evidence of intentionality in the shapes draped with seaweed, heaped with fish brought suffocating into the air. As the rest of the island left the ocean, filling the view before Ransom to the point it threatened to burst out of the curtain, the appearance of an enormous monolith in the foreground, its surface incised with pictographs, settled the matter. This huge jumble of forms, some of which appeared to contradict one another, to intersect in ways the eye could not untangle, to occupy almost the same space at the same time, was deliberate.

Ransom slid his chair back from the table and stood. The crab's legs dinged on the stainless steel sink. Picking up his mug, he turned away from the window. "That was the extent of my interactions with Gus. To be honest, what I knew of him, what Heather had told me, I didn't much care for. He was what I guess you'd call a func-tioning alcoholic, although the way he functioned . . . he was a whiskey-drinker, Jack Daniels, Jim Bean, Maker's Mark, that end of the shelf. I can't claim a lot of experi-ence, but from what I've seen, sour mash shortcuts to your mean, your nasty side. That was the case with Gus, at least. It wasn't so much that he used his hands—he did, and I gather the hearing in Rudy's left ear was the worse for it—no, the whiskey unlocked the cage that held all of Gus's resentment, his bitterness, his jealousy. Apparently, when he was younger, Rudy's little brother Jan had liked helping their mother in the kitchen. He'd been something of a baker, Jan; Rudy claimed he made the best chocolate cake you ever tasted, frosted it with buttercream. His mother used to let him out of working with his father in the garage or around the yard so he could assist her with the meals. None of the other kids—there were six of them—was too thrilled at there being one fewer of them to dilute their father's attention, es-pecially when they saw Gus's lips tighten as he realized Jan had stayed inside again.

"Anyway, this one night, Gus wandered into the house after spending the better part of the evening in the garage. He passed most of the hours after he returned from work fixing his friends' and acquaintances' cars, Hank Williams on the transistor radio, Jack Daniels in one of the kids' juice glasses. In he comes, wiping the grease off his hands with a dishtowel, and what should greet his eyes when he peers into the refrigerator in search of a little supper but the golden top of the cherry pie Jan made for the church bake sale the next day? Gus loves cherry pie. Without a second thought, he lifts the pie from the top shelf of the fridge and deposits it on the kitchen table. He digs his clasp-knife out of his pants-pocket, opens it, and cuts himself a generous slice. He doesn't bother with a fork; instead, he shoves his fingers under the crust and lifts the piece straight to his mouth. It's so tasty, he helps himself to a second, larger serving before he's finished the first. In his eagerness, he slices through the pie tin to the table. He doesn't care; he leaves the knife stuck where it is and uses his other hand to free the piece.

"That's how Jan finds him when he walks into the kitchen for a glass of milk, a wedge of cherry pie in one hand, red syrup and yellow crumbs smeared on his other hand, his mouth and chin. By this age—Jan's around twelve, thirteen—the boy has long-since learned that the safest way, the only way, to meet the outrages that accompany his father's drinking is calmly, impassively. Give him the excuse to garnish his injury with insult, and he'll take it.

"And yet, this is exactly what Jan does. He can't help himself, maybe. He lets his response to the sight of Gus standing with his mouth stuffed with half-chewed pie flash across his face. It's all the provocation his father requires. *What?* he says, crumbs spraying from his mouth.

"*Nothing*, Jan says, but he's too late. Gus drops the slice he's holding to the floor, scoops the rest of the pie from the tin with his free hand, and slaps that to the floor, as well. He raises one foot and stamps on the mess he's made, spreading it across the linoleum. Jan knows enough to remain where he is. Gus brings his shoe down on the ruin of Jan's efforts twice more, then wipes his hands on his pants, frees his knife from the table, and folds it closed. As he returns it to his pocket, he tells Jan that if he wants to be a little faggot and wear an apron in the kitchen, that's his concern, but he'd best keep his little faggot mouth shut when there's a man around, particularly when that man's his father. Does Jan understand him?

"*Yes, Pa*, Jan says.

"*Then take your little faggot ass off to bed*, Gus says.

"What happened next," Ransom said, "wasn't a surprise; in fact, it was depressingly predictable." He walked into the kitchen, deposited his mug on the counter. "That was the end of Jan's time in the kitchen. He wasn't the first one outside to help his father, but he wasn't the last, either, and he worked hard. The morning of his eighteenth birthday, he enlisted in the Marines; within a couple of months, he was on patrol in Vietnam. He was cited for bravery on several occasions; I think he may have been awarded a medal. One afternoon, when his squad stopped for a rest, he was shot through the head by a sniper. He'd removed his helmet ... to tell the truth, I'm not sure why he had his helmet off. He survived, but it goes without saying, he was never the same. His problems ... he had trouble moving, coordinating his arms and legs. His speech was slurred; he couldn't remember the names of familiar objects, activities; he forgot something the second after you said it to him. There was no way he could live on his own. His mother wanted Jan to move back home, but Gus refused, said there was no way he was going to be saddled with an idiot who hadn't known enough to keep his damn helmet on. Which didn't stop him from accepting the drinks he was bought when Jan visited and Gus paraded him at the V.F.W."

Behind him, a pair of doors would be opening on the front of a squat stone box near the island's peak. The structure, whose rough exterior suggested a child's drawing of a Greek temple, must be the size of a cathedral, yet it was dwarfed by what squeezed out of its open doors. While Ransom continued to have trouble with the sheer size of the thing, which seemed as if it must break a textbook's worth of physical laws, he was more bothered by its speed. There should have been no way, he was certain, for something of that mass to move that quickly. Given the thing's appearance, the tumult of coils wreathing its head, the scales shimmering on its arms, its legs, the wings that unfolded into great translucent fans whose edges were not quite in focus, its speed was hardly the most obvious detail on which to focus, but for Ransom, the dearth of time between the first hint of the thing's shadow on the doors and its heaving off the ground on a hurricane-blast of its wings confirmed the extent to which the world had changed.

(*What was that?* Matt had screamed, his eyes wide. *Was that real? Is that happening?* Ransom had been unable to speak, his tongue dead in his mouth.)

Like so many cranes raising and lowering, the cluster of smaller limbs that rose from the center of the crab's back was opening and closing. Ransom said, "I know: if the guy was such a shit, why pass his name on to my son?" He shrugged. "When I was younger—at that point in my life, the idea of the past ... of a family's past, of continuity between the present and that past, was very important to me. By the time Heather was pregnant, the worst of Gus's offenses was years gone by. If you wanted, I suppose you could say that he was paying for his previous excesses. He hadn't taken notice of his diabetes for decades. If the toes on his right foot hadn't turned black, then started to smell, I doubt he ever would have returned to the doctor. Although ... what that visit brought him was the emergency amputation of his toes, followed by the removal of his foot a couple of weeks later. The surgeon wanted to take his leg, said the only way to beat the gangrene that was eating Gus was to leap ahead of it. Gus refused, declared he could see where he was headed, and he wasn't going to be jointed like a chicken on the way. There was no arguing with him. His regular doctor prescribed some heavy-duty antibiotics for him, but I'm not sure he had the script filled.

"When he returned home, everyone said it was to die—which it was, of course, but I think we all expected him to be gone in a matter of days. He hung on, though, for one week, and the next, and the one after that. Heather and her mother visited him. I was at work. She said the house smelled like spoiled meat; it was so bad, she couldn't stay in for more than a couple of minutes, barely long enough to stand beside Gus's bed and kiss his cheek. His lips moved, but she couldn't understand him. She spent the rest of the visit outside, in her mother's truck, listening to the radio."

Ransom glanced out the window. The huge sheet of light rippled like an aurora, the image of the island and its cargo gone. He said, "Gus died the week after Heather's visit. To tell the truth, I half-expected him to last until the baby arrived. Heather went to the wake and the funeral; I had to work. As it turned out, we settled on Matthew—Matt—instead."

His break was over. Ransom exited the kitchen, turned down the hallway to the front door. On the walls to either side of him, photos of himself and his family, his son, smiled at photographers' prompts years forgotten. He peered out one of the narrow windows that flanked the door. The rocking chair he'd left on the front porch in a quixotic gesture stood motionless. Across the street, the charred mound that sat inside the burned-out remains of his neighbor's house appeared quiet. Ransom reached for the six-foot pole that leaned against the corner opposite him. Careful to check that the butcher knife duct-taped to the top was secure, he gripped the improvised spear near the tape and unlocked the door. Leveling the weapon, he stepped back as the door swung in.

In two months of maintaining the ritual every time he opened any of the doors into the house, Ransom had yet to be met by anything. The precaution was one on which his son had insisted; the day of his departure north, Matt had pledged Ransom to maintaining it. With no intention of doing so, Ransom had agreed, only to find himself repeating the familiar motions the next time he was about to venture out to the garden. Now here he was, jabbing the end of the spear through the doorway to draw movement, waiting a count of ten, then advancing one slow step at a time, careful not to miss anything dangling from the underside of the porch roof. Once he was satisfied that the porch was clear, that nothing was lurking in the bush to its right, he called over his shoulder, "I'm on my way to check the garden, if you'd like to join me."

A chorus of ringing announced the crab's extricating itself from the sink. Legs clicking on the wood floors like so many tap shoes, it hurried along the hall and out beside him. Keeping the spear straight ahead, he reached back for one of the canvas bags piled inside the door, then pulled the door shut. The crab raced down the stairs and to the right, around the strip of lawn in front of the house. Watching its long legs spindle made the coffee churn at the back of his throat. He followed it off the porch.

Although he told himself that he had no desire to stare at the remnants of his neighbor Adam's house—it was a distraction; it was ghoulish; it was not good for his mental health—Ransom was unable to keep his eyes from it. All that was left of the structure were fire-blackened fragments of the walls that had stood at the house's northeast and southwest corners. Had Ransom not spent ten years living across the road from the white, two-story colonial whose lawn had been chronically overgrown—to the point he and Heather had spoken of it as their own little piece of the rainforest—he could not have guessed the details of the building the fire had consumed. While he was no expert at such matters, he had been surprised that the flames had taken so much of Adam's house; even without the fire department to douse it, Ransom had the sense that the blaze should not have consumed this much of it. No doubt, the extent of the destruction owed something to the architects of the shape the house's destruction had revealed.

(*There's something in Adam's house*, Matt had said. The eyes of the ten men and woman crowded around the kitchen table did not look at him. *They've been there since before ... everything. Before the Fracture. I've heard them moving around outside, in the trees. We have to do something about them.)*

About a month after they had moved into their house, some ten years ago, Ransom had discovered a wasps' nest clinging to a light on the far side of the garage. Had it been only himself, even himself and Heather, living there, he would have been tempted to live and let live. However, with an eight-year-old factored into the equation, one whose curiosity was recorded in the constellations of scars up his arms and down his legs, there was no choice. Ransom called the exterminator and the next day, the nest was still. He waited the three days the woman recommended, then removed the nest by unscrewing the frosted glass jar to which it was anchored. He estimated the side stoop the sunniest part of the property; he placed the nest there to dry out. His decision had not pleased Heather, who was concerned at poison-resistant wasps emerging enraged at the attack on their home, but after a week's watch brought no super wasps, he considered it reasonable to examine it with Matt. It was the first time he had been this near to a nest, and he had been fascinated by it, the grey, papery material that covered it in strips wound up and to the right. Slicing it across the equator had disclosed a matrix of cells, a little less than half of them chambering larvae, and a host of motionless wasps. Every detail of the nest, he was aware, owed itself to some physiological necessity, evolutionary advantage, but he'd found it difficult to shake the impression that he was observing the result of an alien intelligence, an alien aesthetic, at work.

That same sensation, taken to a power of ten, gripped him at the sight of the structure that had hidden inside Adam's house. Its shape reminded him of that long-ago wasps' nest, only inverted, an irregular dome composed not of grey pulp but a porous substance whose texture suggested sponge. Where it was not charred black, its surface was dark umber. Unlike the house in which it had grown up, Ransom thought that the fire that had scoured this dwelling should have inflicted more damage on it, collapsed it. In spots, the reddish surface of the mound had cracked to reveal a darker substance beneath, something that trembled in the light like mercury. Perhaps this was the reason the place was still standing. What had been the overgrown yard was dirt baked and burnt brittle by the succession of fires. At half a dozen points around the yard, the large shells of what might have been lobsters—had each of those lobsters stood the size of a small pony—lay broken, split wide, the handles of axes, shovels, picks spouting from them.

(Matt had been so excited, his cheeks flushed in that way that made his eyes glow. The left sleeve of his leather jacket, of the sweatshirt underneath it, had been sliced open, the skin below cut from wrist to shoulder by a claw the size of a tennis racket. He hadn't cared, had barely noticed as Ransom had washed the wound, inspected it for any of the fluid (blood?) that had spattered the jacket, and wrapped it in gauze. Outside, whoops and hollers of celebration had filled the morning air. *You should have come with us*, Matt had said, the remark less a reproach and more an expression of regret for a missed opportunity. *My plan worked. They never saw us coming. You should have been there.* Despite the anxiety that had yet to drain from him, pride had swelled Ransom's chest. Maybe everything wasn't lost. Maybe his son . . . *Yes, well*, Ransom had said, *someone has to be around to pick up the pieces.*)

Ransom continued around the front lawn to what they had called the side yard, a wide slope of grass that stretched from the road up to the treeline of the rise behind the house. If the wreckage across the street was difficult to ignore, what lay beyond the edge of the yard compelled his attention. Everything that had extended north of the house: his next door neighbor Dan's red house and barn, the volunteer fire station across from it, the houses that had continued on up both sides of the road to Wiltwyck, was gone, as was the very ground on which all of it had been built. As far ahead as Ransom could see, to either side, the earth had been scraped to bare rock, the dull surface of which bore hundred-yard gouges. Somewhere beyond his ability to guesstimate, planes of light like the one on the other side of his house were visible on the horizon. Ransom could not decide how many there were. Some days he thought at least four, staggered one behind the other; others he was certain there was only the one whose undulations produced the illusion of more. Far off as the aurora(e) was, its sheer size made the figures that occasionally filled it visible. These he found it easier to disregard, especially when, as today, they were something familiar: a quartet of tall stones at the top of a rounded mountain, one apparently fallen over, the remaining three set at irregular distances from one another, enough to suggest that their proximity might be no more than a fluke of geology; from within the arrangement, as if stepping down into it, an eye the size of a barn door peered and began to push out. Instead, he focused on the garden into which he, Matt, and a few of his neighbors had tilled the side yard.

While Ransom judged the crab capable of leaping the dry moat and clambering up the wire fence around the garden, it preferred to wait for him to set the plank over the trench, cross it, and unlock the front gate. Only then would it scuttle around him, up the rows of carrots and broccoli, the tomatoes caged in their conical frames, stopping on its rounds to inspect a leaf here, a stalk there, tilting its shell forward so that one of the limbs centered in its back could extend and take the object of its scrutiny in its claw. In general, Ransom attributed the crab's study to simple curiosity, but there were moments he fancied that, prior to its arrival in his front yard the morning after Matt's departure, in whatever strange place it had called home, the crab had tended a garden of its own.

Latching but not locking the gate behind him, Ransom said, "What about Bruce? That was what we called our dog . . . the only dog we ever had. Heather picked out the name. She was a huge Springsteen fan. The dog didn't look like a Bruce, not in the slightest. He was some kind of weird mix, Great Dane and greyhound, something like that. His body . . . it was as if the front of one dog had been sewed to the back of another. He had this enormous head—heavy jowls, brow, huge jaws—and these thick front legs, attached to a skinny trunk, back legs like pipe cleaners. His tail—I don't know where that came from. It was so long it hung down almost to his feet. I kept expecting him to tip over, fall on his face. I wanted to call him Butch, that or something classical, Cerberus. Heather and Matt overruled me. Matt was all in favor of calling him Super Destroyer, or Fire Teeth, but Heather and I vetoed those. Somehow, this meant she got the final decision, and Bruce it was."

The beer traps next to the lettuce were full of the large red slugs that had appeared in the last week. One near the top was still moving, swimming lazily around the PBR, the vent along its back expanding and contracting like a mouth attempting to speak. The traps could wait another day before emptying; he would have to remember to bring another can of beer with him tomorrow. He said, "Heather found the dog wandering in the road out front. He was in pretty rough shape: his coat was caked with dirt, rubbed raw in places; he was so thin, you could've used his ribs as a toast rack. Heather was a sucker for any kind of hard case; she said it was why she'd gone out with me, in the first place. Very funny, right? By the time Matt stepped off the schoolbus, she'd lured the dog inside with a plateful of chicken scraps (which he devoured), coaxed him into the downstairs shower (after which, she said, he looked positively skeletal), and heaped a couple of old blankets into a bed for him. She tried to convince him to lie down there, and he did subject the blankets to extensive sniffing, but he refused to allow Heather out of his sight. She was . . . at that point, she tired easily—to be honest, it was pretty remarkable that she'd been able to do everything she had—so she went out to the front porch to rest on the rocking chair and wait for Matt's bus. When she did, the dog—Bruce, I might as well call him that; she'd already settled on the name—Bruce insisted on accompanying her. He plopped down beside her, and remained there until Matt was climbing the front steps. I would have been worried . . . concerned about how Bruce would react to Matt, whether he'd be jealous of Heather, that kind of thing. Not my wife: when Matt reached the top of the stairs, the dog stood, but that was all. Heather didn't have to speak to him, let alone grab his collar."

The lettuces weren't ready to pick, nor were the cabbages or broccoli. A few tomatoes, however, were sufficiently red to merit plucking from the plants and dropping into the canvas bag. The crab was roaming the top of the garden, where they'd planted Dan's apple trees. Ransom glanced over the last of the tomatoes, checked the frames. "That collar," he said. "It was the first thing I noticed about the dog. Okay, maybe not the first, but it wasn't too long before it caught my eye. This was after Matt had met me in the driveway with the news that we had a guest. The look on his face . . . he had always been a moody kid—Heather and I used to ask one another, *How's the weather in Mattsville?*—and adolescence, its spiking hormones, had not improved his temperament. In all fairness, Heather being sick didn't help matters any. This night, though, he was positively beaming, vibrating with nervous energy. When I saw him running up to the car, my heart jumped. I couldn't conceive any reason for him to rush out the side door that wasn't bad: at the very best, an argument with his mother over some school-related issue; at the very worst, another ambulance ride to the hospital for Heather."

A blue centipede the size of his hand trundled across the dirt in front of him. He considered spearing it, couldn't remember if it controlled any of the other species in the garden. Better to err on the side of caution— even now. He stepped over it, moved on to the beans. He said, "Matt refused to answer any of my questions; all he would say was, *You'll see.* It had been a long day at work; my patience was frayed to a couple of threads and they weren't looking any too strong. I was on the verge of snapping at him, telling him to cut the crap, grow up, but something, that grin, maybe, made me hold my tongue.

And once I was inside, there was Heather sitting on the couch, the dog sprawled out beside her, his head in her lap. He didn't so much as open an eye to me.

"For the life of me, I could not figure out how Heather had gotten him. I assumed she had been to the pound, but we owned only the one car, which I'd had at work all day. She took the longest time telling me where the dog had come from. I had to keep guessing, and didn't Matt think that was the funniest thing ever? It was kind of funny . . . my explanations grew increasingly bizarre, fanciful. Someone had delivered the dog in a steamer trunk. Heather had discovered him living in one of the trees out front. He'd been packed away in the attic. I think she and Matt wanted to hear my next story."

Ransom had forgotten the name of the beans they had planted. Not green beans: these grew in dark purple; although Dan had assured him that they turned green once you cooked them. The beans had come in big, which Dan had predicted: each was easily six, seven inches long. Of the twenty-five or thirty that were ready to pick, however, four had split at the bottom, burst by gelid, inky coils that hung down as long again as the bean. The ends of the coils raised towards him, unfolding petals lined with tiny teeth.

"Shit." He stepped back, lowering the spear. The coils swayed from side to side, their petals opening further. He studied their stalks. All four sprang from the same plant. He swept the blade of the spear through the beans dangling from the plants to either side of the affected one. They dinged faintly on the metal. The rest of the crop appeared untouched; that was something. He adjusted the canvas bag onto his shoulder. Taking the spear in both hands, he set the edge of the blade against the middle plant's stem. His first cut drew viscous green liquid and the smell of spoiled eggs. While he sawed, the coils whipped this way and that, and another three beans shook frantically. The stem severed, he used the spear to loosen the plant from its wire supports, then to carry it to the compost pile at the top of the garden, in the corner opposite the apple trees. There was lighter fluid

left in the bottle beside the fence; the dark coils continued to writhe as he sprayed them with it. The plant was
too green to burn well, but Ransom reckoned the application of fire to it, however briefly, couldn't hurt. He
reached in his shirt pocket for the matches. The lighter
fluid flared with a satisfying *whump*.

The crab was circling the apple trees. Eyes on the
leaves curling in the flames, Ransom said, "By the time
Heather finally told me how Bruce had arrived at the
house, I'd been won over. Honestly, within a couple of
minutes of watching her sitting there with the dog, I was
ready for him to move in. Not because I was such a great
dog person—I'd grown up with cats, and if I'd been inclined to adopt a pet, a kitten would have been my first
choice. Heather was the one who'd been raised with a
houseful of dogs. No, what decided me in Bruce's favor
was Heather, her ... demeanor, I suppose. You could see
it in the way she was seated. She didn't look as if she
were holding herself as still as possible, as if someone
were pressing a knife against the small of her back. She
wasn't relaxed—that would be an overstatement—but
she was calmer.

"The change in Matt didn't hurt, either." Ransom
squeezed another jet of lighter fluid onto the fire, which
leapt up in response. The gelid coils thrashed as if trying to tear themselves free of the plant. "How long had
that boy wanted a dog ... By now, we'd settled into a
routine with Heather's meds, her doctors' visits—it had
settled onto us, more like. I think we knew ... I wouldn't
say we had given up hope; Heather's latest tests had returned better than expected results. But we—the three
of us were in a place we had been in for a long time and
didn't know when we were going to get out of. A dog
was refreshing, new."

With liquid pops, the four coils burst one after the
other. The trio of suspect beans followed close behind.
"That collar, though ..." Bringing the lighter fluid with
him, Ransom left the fire for the spot where the affected
plant had been rooted. Emerald fluid thick as honey
topped the stump, slid down its sides in slow fingers. He

should dig it out, he knew, and probably the plants to either side of it, for good measure, but without the protection of a pair of gloves, he was reluctant to expose his bare skin to it. He reversed the spear and drove its point into the stump. Leaving the blade in, he twisted the handle around to widen the cut, then poured lighter fluid into and around it. He wasn't about to risk dropping a match over here, but he guessed the accelerant should, at a minimum, prove sufficiently toxic to hinder the plant from regrowing until he could return suitably protected and with a shovel.

There was still the question of whether to harvest the plants to either side. Fresh vegetables would be nice, but prudence was the rule of the day. Before they'd set out for the polar city with Matt, his neighbors had moved their various stores to his basement, for safe keeping; it wasn't as if he were going to run out of canned food anytime soon. Ransom withdrew the spear and returned to the compost, where the fire had not yet subsided. Its business with the apple trees completed, the crab crouched at a safe remove from the flames. Ransom said, "It was a new collar, this blue, fibrous stuff, and there was a round metal tag hanging from it. The tag was incised with a name, 'Noble,' and a number to call in case this dog was found. It was a Wiltwyck number. I said, *What about the owner? Shouldn't we call them?*

"Heather must have been preparing her answer all day, from the moment she read the tag. *Do you see the condition this animal is in?* she said. *Either his owner is dead, or they don't deserve him.* As far as Heather was concerned, that was that. I didn't argue, but shortly thereafter, I unbuckled the collar and threw it in a drawer in the laundry room. Given Bruce's state, I didn't imagine his owner would be sorry to find him gone, but you never know.

"For five days, Bruce lived with us. We took turns walking him. Matt actually woke up half an hour early to take him out for his morning stroll, then Heather gave him a shorter walk around lunchtime, then I took him for another long wander before bed. The dog tolerated me well enough, but he loved Matt, who couldn't spend enough time with him. And Heather . . . except for his walks, he couldn't bear to be away from her; even when we had passed a slow half-hour making our way up Main Street, Bruce diligently investigating the borders of the lawns on the way, there would come a moment he would decide it was time to return to Heather, and he would leave whatever he'd had his nose in and turn home, tugging me along behind him. Once we were inside and I had his leash off, he would bolt for wherever Heather was—usually in bed, asleep—and settle next to her."

He snapped the lighter fluid's cap shut and replaced it beside the fence. The crab sidled away along the rows of carrots and potatoes on the other side of the beans and tomatoes. Ransom watched it examine the feathery green tops of the carrots, prod the potato blossoms. It would be another couple of weeks until they were ready to unearth; though after what had happened to the beans, a quick check was in order. "On the morning of the sixth day, Bruce's owner arrived, came walking up the street the same way his dog had. William Harrow: that was the way he introduced himself. It was a Saturday. I was cooking brunch; Matt was watching TV; Heather was sitting on the front porch, reading. Of course, Bruce was with her. September was a couple of weeks old, but summer was slow in leaving. The sky was clear, the air was warm, and I was thinking that maybe I'd load the four of us into the car and drive up to the reservoir for an afternoon out."

On the far side of the house, the near curtain of light, on which he had watched the sunken island rise for the twentieth, the thirtieth time, settled, dimmed. With the slow spiral of food coloring dropped into water, dark pink and burnt orange spread across its upper reaches, a gaudy sunset display that was as close as the actual sky came to night any more. A broad concrete rectangle took up the image's lower half. At its other end, the plane was bordered by four giant steel and glass boxes, each one open at the top. To the right, a single skyscraper was crowned by an enormous shape whose margins hung over and partway down its upper storeys. Something about the form, a handful of scattered details, suggested an impossibly large toad.

The first time Ransom had viewed this particular scene, a couple of weeks after Matt and their neighbors had embarked north, a couple of days after he had awakened to the greater part of Main Street and its houses gone, scoured to gray rock, he had not recognized its location. *The polar city?* Only once it was over and he was seated on the couch, unable to process what he had been shown, did he think, *That was Albany. The Empire State Plaza. Those weren't boxes: they were the bases of the office buildings that stood there. Fifty miles. That's as far as they got.*

He was close enough to the house for its silhouette to block most of the three figures who ran onto the bottom of the screen, one to collapse onto his hands and knees, another to drop his shotgun and tug a revolver out of his belt, the third to use his good hand to drag the blade of his hatchet against his jeans' leg. The crab paid no more attention to the aurora's display than it ever did; it was occupied withdrawing one of the red slugs from a beer trap. Ransom cleared his throat. "Heather said she never noticed William Harrow until his work boots were clomping on the front stairs. She looked up from her book, and there was this guy climbing to meet her. He must have been around our age, which is to say, late thirties. Tall, thin, not especially remarkable looking one way or the other. Beard, mustache . . . when I saw the guy, he struck me as guarded; to be fair, that could have been because he and Heather were already pretty far into a heated exchange. At the sound of the guy's feet on the stairs, Bruce had stood; by the time I joined the conversation, the dog was trembling.

"The first words out of Harrow's mouth were, *That's my dog.* Maybe things would have proceeded along a different course . . . maybe we could have reached, I don't know, some kind of agreement with the guy, if Heather hadn't said, *Oh? Prove it.* Because he did; he said, *Noble, sit,* and Bruce did exactly that. *There you go,* Harrow said. I might have argued that that didn't prove anything, that we had trained the dog to sit ourselves, and it was the command he was responding to, not the name, but Heather saw no point in ducking the issue. She said, *Do you know what shape this animal was in when we found him? Were you responsible for that?* and the mercury plummeted.

"Matt came for me in the kitchen. He said, *Mom's arguing with some guy. I think he might be Bruce's owner.*

"*All right,* I said, *hold on.* I turned off the burners under the scrambled eggs and home fries. As I was untying my apron, Matt said, *Is he gonna take Bruce with him?*

"*Of course not,* I said.

"But I could see . . . as soon as I understood the situation, I knew Bruce's time with us was over, felt the same lightness high in the chest I'd known sitting in the doctor's office with Heather a year and half before, that seems to be my body's reaction to bad news. It was . . . when Matt—when I . . ."

From either end of the plaza, from between two of the truncated buildings on its far side, what might have been torrents of black water rushed onto and over the concrete. There was no way for the streams to have been water: each would have required a hose the width of a train, pumps the size of houses, a score of workers to operate it, but the way they surged towards the trio occluded by the house suggested a river set loose from its banks and given free rein to speed across the land. The color of spent motor oil, they moved so fast that the objects studding their lengths were almost impossible to distinguish; after his initial viewing, it took Ransom another two before he realized that they were eyes, that each black tumult was the setting for a host of eyes, eyes of all sizes, shapes, and colors, eyes defining strange constellations. He had no similar trouble identifying the mouths into which the streams opened, tunnels gated by great cracked and jagged teeth.

Ransom said, "Heather's approach . . . you might say

that she combined shame with the threat of legal action. Harrow was impervious to both. As far as he was concerned, the dog looked fine, and he was the registered owner, so there was nothing to be worried about. *Of course he looks good*, Heather said, *he's been getting fed!*

"If the dog had been in such awful shape, Harrow wanted to know, then how had he come all the way from his home up here? That didn't sound like a trip an animal as severely abused as Heather was claiming could make.

"He was trying to get as far away as he could, she said. Had he been in better condition, he probably wouldn't have stopped here.

"This was getting us nowhere—had gotten us nowhere. *Look*, I said. *Mr. Harrow. My family and I have become awfully attached to this dog. I understand that you've probably spent quite a bit on him. I would be willing to reimburse you for that, in addition to whatever you think is fair for the dog.* Here I was, pretty much offering the guy a blank check. Money, right? It may be the root of all evil, but it's solved more than a few problems.

"William Harrow, though . . . he refused my offer straightaway. Maybe he thought I was patronizing him. Maybe he was trying to prove a point. I didn't know what else to do. We could have stood our ground, insisted we were keeping Bruce, but if he had the law on his side, then we would only be delaying the inevitable. He could call the cops on us, the prospect of which made me queasy. As for escalating the situation, trying to get tough with him, intimidate him . . . that wasn't me. I mean, really."

With the house in the way, Ransom didn't have to watch as the trio of dark torrents converged on the trio of men. He didn't have to see the man who had not risen from his hands and knees scooped into a mouth that did not close so much as constrict. He didn't have to see the man with the pistol empty it into the teeth that bit him in half. And he did not have to watch again as the third figure—he should call him a man; he had earned it—

sidestepped the bite aimed at him and slashed a groove in the rubbery skin that caused the behemoth to veer away from him. He did not have to see the hatchet, raised for a second strike, spin off into the air, along with the hand that gripped it and most of the accompanying arm, as the mouth that had taken the man with the pistol sliced away the rest of the third man. Ransom did not have to see any of it.

(At the last moment, even though Ransom had sworn to himself he wouldn't, he had pleaded with Matt not to leave. *You could help me with the garden*, he had said. *You'll manage*, Matt had answered. *Who will I talk to?* Ransom had asked. *Who will I tell things to? Write it all down*, Matt had said, *for when we get back*. His throat tight with dread, Ransom had said, *You don't know what they'll do to you.* Matt had not argued with him.)

Its rounds of the garden completed, the crab was waiting at the gate. Ransom prodded the top of a carrot with the blunt end of the spear. "I want to say," he said, "that had Heather been in better health, she would have gone toe-to-toe with Harrow herself . . . weak as she was, she was ready to take a swing at him. To be on the safe side, I stepped between them. *All right*, I said. *If that's what you want to do, then I guess there isn't any more to say.* I gestured at Bruce, who had returned to his feet. From his jeans pocket, Harrow withdrew another blue collar and a short lead. Bruce saw them, and it was like he understood what had happened. The holiday was over; it was back to the place he'd tried to escape. Head lowered, he crossed the porch to Harrow.

"I don't know if Harrow intended to say anything else, but Heather did. Before he started down the stairs with Bruce, Heather said, *Just remember, William Harrow: I know your name. It won't be any difficulty finding out where you live, where you're taking that dog. I'm making it my duty to watch you—I'm going to watch you like a hawk, and the first hint I see that you aren't treating that dog right, I am going to bring the cops down on you like a hammer. You look at me and tell me I'm lying.*

"He did look at her. His lip trembled; I was sure he

was going to speak, answer her threat with one of his own . . . warn her that he shot trespassers, something like that, but he left without another word.

"Of course Heather went inside to track down his address right away. He lived off Main Street, on Farrell Drive, a cul-de-sac about a quarter of a mile that way." Ransom nodded towards the stone expanse. "Heather was all for walking up there after him, as was Matt, who had eavesdropped on our confrontation with Harrow from inside the front door. The expression on his face . . . It was all I could do to persuade the two of them that chasing Harrow would only antagonize him, which wouldn't be good for Bruce, would it? They agreed to wait a day, during which time neither spoke to me more than was absolutely necessary. As it turned out, though, Heather was feeling worse the next day, and then the day after that was Monday and I had work and Matt had school, so it wasn't until Monday evening that we were able to visit Farrell Drive. To be honest, I didn't think there'd be anything for us to see.

"I was wrong. William Harrow lived in a raised ranch set back about fifty yards from the road, at the top of a slight hill. Ten feet into his lawn, there was a cage, a wood frame walled and ceilinged with heavy wire mesh. It was maybe six feet high by twelve feet long by six feet deep. There was a large dog house at one end with a food and water dish beside it. The whole thing . . . everything was brand new. The serial numbers stenciled on the wood beams were dark and distinct; the mesh was bright; the dog house—the dog house was made out of some kind of heavy plastic, and it was shiny. Lying half-in the dog house was Bruce, who, when he heard us pull up, raised his head, then the rest of himself, and trotted over to the side of the cage, his tongue hanging out, his tail wagging.

"Heather and Matt were desperate to rush out of the car, but none of us could avoid the signs, also new, that lined the edge of the property: NO TRESPASSING, day-glo orange on a black background. Matt was all for ignoring them, a sentiment for which Heather had not a little sympathy. But—and I tried to explain this to the two of them—if we were going to have any hope of freeing Bruce, we had to be above reproach. If there were a record of Harrow having called the police on us, it would make our reporting him to the cops appear so much payback. Neither of them was happy, but they had to agree that what I was saying made sense.

"All the same, the second we were back home, Heather had the phone in her hand. The cop she talked to was pretty agreeable, although she cautioned Heather that as long as the dog wasn't being obviously maltreated, there wasn't anything that could be done. The cop agreed to drive along Farrell the next time she was on patrol, and Heather thanked her for the offer. When she hung up the phone, though, her face showed how satisfied she was with our local law enforcement."

Beyond the house, the scene at the Empire State Plaza had faded to pale light. Finished checking the carrots and potatoes, Ransom crossed to the gate. The crab backed up to allow him to unlatch and swing it in. As the crab hurried out, he gave the garden a final look over, searching for anything he might have missed. Although he did not linger on the apple trees, they appeared quiet.

On the way back around the yard, the crab kept pace with him. Ransom said, "For the next month, Heather walked to Farrell Drive once a day, twice when she was well enough. During that time, Bruce did not leave his cage. Sometimes, she would find him racing around the place, growling. Other times, he would be leaping up against one wall of the pen and using it to flip himself over. As often as not, he would be lying half-in the doghouse, his head on his paws. That she could tell—and believe you me, she studied that dog, his cage, as if his life depended on it (which, as far as she was concerned, it did)—Harrow kept the pen tidy and Bruce's dishes full. While she was careful not to set foot on the property, she stood beside it for half an hour, forty-five minutes, an hour. One afternoon, she left our house after lunch and did not return till dinner. When Bruce heard her footsteps, he would stop whatever he was doing, run to the nearest corner of the cage, and stand there wagging his tail. He would voice a series of low barks that Heather said sounded as if he were telling her something, updating the situation. *No change. Still here.*

"She saw Harrow only once. It was during the third-to-last visit she made to Bruce. After a few minutes of standing at the edge of the road, talking to the dog, she noticed a figure in the ranch's doorway. She tensed, ready for him to storm out to her, but he remained where he was. So did Heather. If this guy thought he could scare her, he had another thing coming. Although she wasn't feeling well, she maintained her post for an hour, as did Harrow. When she turned home, he didn't move. The strange thing was, she said to me that night, that the look on his face—granted, he wasn't exactly close to her, and she hadn't wanted him to catch her staring at him, but she was pretty sure he'd looked profoundly unhappy."

The crab scrambled up the stairs to the porch. His foot on the lowest step, Ransom paused. "Then Heather was back in the hospital, and Matt and I had other things on our minds beside Bruce. Afterwards . . . not long, actually, I think it was the day before the funeral, I drove by William Harrow's house, and there was the cage, still there, and Bruce still in it. For a second, I was as angry as I'd ever been; I wanted nothing more than to stomp the gas to the floor and crash into that thing, and if Bruce were killed in the process, so be it. Let Harrow emerge from his house, and I would give him the beating I should have that September morning.

"I didn't, though. The emotion passed, and I kept on driving."

Ransom climbed the rest of the stairs. At the top, he said, "Matt used to say to me, *Who wants to stay in the shallows their whole life?* It was his little dig at his mother and me, at the life we'd chosen. Most of the time, I left his question rhetorical, but when he asked it that afternoon, I answered him; I said, *There are sharks in the shallows, too.* He didn't know what to make of that. Neither did I." Ransom went to say something more, hesitated, decided against it. He opened the door to the house, let the crab run in, followed. The door shut behind them with a solid *thunk*.

At the top of the garden, dangling from the boughs of the apple trees there, the fruit that had ripened into a score, two, of red replicas of Matt's face, his eyes squeezed shut, his mouth stretched in a scream of unbearable pain, swung in a sudden breeze.

For Fiona

SUCH BRIGHT AND RISEN MADNESS IN OUR NAMES

Jay Lake

I

"Long have we dwelt in wonder and glory."

The passwords are ashes in my mouth. The last of the First Resistance was crushed eight years ago, when shoggoths swarmed the final submarine base hidden in the San Juan Islands at the mouth of Puget Sound, but the Second Resistance struggles onward, ever guttering like a starveling candle flame.

My contact nods, his—or her? Does it matter any more?—head bobbing with the slow certainty of a collapsing corpse. The Innsmouth Syndrome transforms so many of us who were once human. The voice croaking a response bespeaks more of the benthic depths than any child of woman born. "Such bright and risen days these are."

And simply as that, I am admitted to the tiled lodge here at the mouth of the Columbia, amid the ruins of Astoria. We meet with our rituals and our secret rooms in imitation of Dagon and the Silver Twilight, because their rites worked.

Oh, we were warned. Lovecraft, Howard, Smith—they had a glimpse of the truth, which they disguised as fiction. Who believed? People actually made up games about the Old Ones. As if the mile-long shattered corpse still rotting across the Seattle waterfront nine years after the U.S. Air Force's last bombing run could be made into a joke or a rattle of dice.

All that saves us now is inattention. Cthulhu, Yog-Sothoth, all are like children in their godhood. Dead, they lay so long dreaming that they lost the habit of attending to the world, except through such rites as move them.

The First Resistance fought the elder gods themselves. But how does a B-2 fly against something that can warp the very fabric of the stars with the power of its mind? The Earth's new masters did not need their priests to awaken them to those dangers, not after the Dunedin and Papeete nuclear strikes.

The Second Resistance struggles against the priests instead. Dread Cthulhu could snuff my life with the merest of thoughts, but he will no more bother to do so than I will snuff the life of a single amoeba deep within my gut. Traveling across six hundred million years of time and space, then slumbering eons beneath the waves in lost R'lyeh, does not equip one for such minutiae. His priests are the immune system, seeking to eradicate the last, hopeless glimmerings of human liberty and free spirit.

This lodge meets within the battered Sons of Finland hall along Astoria's deserted waterfront, in the shadows of the ruined Astoria-Megler Bridge. This was once a thriving coastal city of nineteenth-century sea captains' mansions, twentieth-century fisheries and twenty-first century tourism.

No more. Not a mile out on the bar of the Columbia river loom the unearthly non-Euclidian geometries of one of the cyclopean Risen Cities, strangely angled walls that endlessly glimmer a feeble green while screams echo across the water. Our priestly enemies hunt far and wide, but even under their noses we are scattered and furtive. We never see the stars any more, and little of the sun, for the Old Ones' emergence and the nuclear attacks of the First Resistance wrapped the Earth in permanent winter that varies only a little by season. A man may walk from Oregon to Washington across the frozen Columbia seven or eight months out of the year.

We are in the old ballroom now, a baker's dozen of

us. That number would once have been deemed unlucky, but Cthulhu and his fellow, rival gods have drained the world of luck.

The doorward drops his cowl. He is newly come among us, and must prove himself. Now I see he is a woman, as she lifts off a crowning mask that has misshapen her head. Beneath she is actually a reasonable-seeming human being, albeit as grubby and hunger-raddled as the rest of us. She slips from her robe as well, unhooks a padded hump, releases bindings on her legs, and stands straight, clad now in only blue jeans and a faded black t-shirt advertising a band called Objekt 775.

This is like looking at a piece of the past. I wonder where her parka is.

Inspired, I slip my cloak free and let it fall, along with my own fatigue coat, until I am clad only in ragged thermal underwear and combat boots. I am barely transformed, my hands overlarge and my fingers overblunt, but the change seems to have stopped there, as can happen with we who resist strongly enough.

Around me, others remove their cowls and hoods and cloaks, until we stand as an array of human and formerly human faces. Some eyes are bulbous and unblinking, others scowl furiously, but we all have the full measure of one another for the first time in years.

Also for the first time in years, as I look at our doorward, I feel stirrings in my groin. A natural woman . . .

"I am come from the lodge in Crescent City," she announces. Now her voice is blessedly normal as well. "Bringing news from Mendocino and further south." There are no lodges in the formerly great cities of the world, because none of those cities remain whole and unpolluted. "A lodge along the Sea of Cortez has made an important discovery. We have found a poison that will harm even the undying priests amid their armors and their spells."

"Despite the Old Ones' protection?" I ask.

"Yes." She smiles at me, and I am erect for the first time in years.

II

Just as foretold, the Old Ones are stripping the Earth from pole to pole. They are in no hurry, not by human standards—surely they perceive time so differently from us, this past decade may all be a single moment not yet passed to them, one thunderous tick of the clock of the long now.

Strangely, in places of some technology where electricity can still be induced to function, odd corners of the world away from the attention of the priests and their gods, we find that many of our space assets remain in order. Curiously, this is despite the abilities of the Byakhee and Mi-go to traverse the emptiness between planets. The last cosmonauts starved on the ISS seven years ago, and the station has since fallen burning from the sky, but their observations had proved invaluable. Likewise weather and spy satellites, not all of which have yet strayed from their courses or lost their mechanical minds.

The world's cities were crushed or blasted or sickened, sometimes by human effort in the First Resistance, more often by the Old Ones themselves when they finally stirred from their watery graves. Now great, slow waves of fungal rot progress across the continents like a nightmare tide, swallowing forests and prairies and bottomlands alike. I've been as far east as Estes Park, and looked down on the Great Plains being scoured to bedrock. The mountains and coastlines are yet spared, but surely that is only a matter of time.

With this data, and a tenuous network of wanderers and observers, the Second Resistance has our guesses about how many years are left to do something against the priests who focus the lamps of the Old Ones' eyes like mad projectionists beaming death about the world. That the gods themselves are narcoleptic was perhaps the world's saving grace, before someone, somewhere, finally succeeded in summoning them to shore in their fullest strength.

We must believe it happened thus, for if they returned

only because the stars were right, well, no one can fight the stars.

Even the most optimistic of us do not bet on more than two decades remaining, and the general consensus is less than ten years. The loss of biomass may have started an irreversible decline in the atmospheric oxygen budget. What isn't killed by the growing fungal tides freezes to death instead. We might win, by freakish luck and blind chance, only to perish as free men instead of slaves.

No, we are not even slaves, for slaves have value. We are but an infestation, an annoyance or perhaps a sport to the priests, less than dust to the Old Ones.

Still, we make our plans, and we gather our data, and we try. What else can we do? The human race is terminal, a cancer patient at full metastasis, every organ riddled with rot, the specter of death crushing a bit more air from every heaving of the lungs.

So I listen to this plan to cultivate an obscure type of jellyfish venom. Surely, like the fungi, it is those jellyfish who far more resemble the Old Ones than the cephalopods and amphibians old Howard Phillips Lovecraft was so fond of citing. This beautiful, as-yet untainted young woman—how?—whose name we will never know and who must have been a child when the end first came, explains how the vial she carries can be cultivated in long, low trays of saltwater, with an admixture of organic nutrients to sustain the jellyfish cells that produce the requisite toxin.

It is Julia Child by way of War of the Worlds. We plot the downfall of humanity's most vile traitors via kitchen science, and hope to blind the Old Ones back into restless slumber in doing so.

III

I stay that night in the lodge, for my string of boltholes doesn't begin until about fifteen river miles inland, at Knappa, Oregon. As is our usual practice, most of the others leave. Those far along into the transformation, including Madeleine Gervais, whom I'd known quite well back before the end, are far more nervous about this plan. The girl from Crescent City is unable to tell us how the poison might affect us, only that it has worked on captured priests, who cannot be slain except by extreme violence, followed by reduction and burning of the corpse.

We can make them die unknowing. Oh, the joy that thought brings me. These traitors who have already brought the deaths of billions are beyond any redemption of suffering or vengeance.

Curling in my little nest of borrowed blankets in one of the old basement saunas, I am quite surprised when the girl comes to me. I know her by her footsteps and her scent already.

Her fingers brush my shoulder, the light pressure of them through the fabric of the blanket the first human touch I have felt in almost nine years. We do not hug, or even clasp hands, in the Second Resistance. "I saw that you understood," she whispers.

The hairs on my neck prickle, as my cock strains like a clothyard shaft. "I do," I whisper, then immediately curse the echoed meaning of those particular words. I still wear my wedding ring, though my finger has grown around it until the band is almost invisible. Most days I cannot recall the faces of my wife and daughter.

"It is darker here." She squats back on her heels, shadows against shadow, barely an outline through some stray bit of light elsewhere in the basement. It is enough for me to notice the swing of her right breast beneath the concert t-shirt, and I recall enough of women to know she has done this on purpose.

"Darker than California?"

"Yes." She shivers slightly. I realize her nipple has stiffened to something pleasingly mouth-filling. "So many of the Old Ones love their cold."

"They are creatures of space, and night, and the darkest depths." For no good reason, I add, "Such bright and risen madness in our names."

That hand touches me again as the breast strains

against its enclosing fabric. "Are you lonely?" she asks
in a soft, lost voice. I am too taken up in her to wonder at
the question, for already I am lifting my blanket to show
her just how lonely I am.

IV

The woman is gone the next morning, a note telling
me she heads north for the Aberdeen lodge, if it can still
be found. Here in Oregon we've had no word from the
Washington side this year since the river thawed in May,
though in past years they've come across at Longview
two or three times a month by boat during the free flowing season. Priests burned out the Lincoln City Lodge
last December, the members stripped and broken and
laid before the dark tide of shoggoths, digital prints of
their deaths tacked to walls and telephone poles all up
and down the Northwest coast as a warning to the remaining feral humans.

No such word of Aberdeen, for good or ill.

I should go back to my own routines, but there are
vats of jellyfish toxin to establish. Someone will have to
scale the odd-angled walls of the Risen City and carry
the stuff in. Or allow themselves to be captured, and
pray for a slow enough death to be able to spread the
poison first.

In any case, the sauna room smells of sex and me and
her, and I know I shall never again experience the sweet
caress of a woman. The scent-memories are precious,
while they remain.

I work for days, as Madeleine stays with me after the
last stragglers depart. She knows that I touched the girl
with my body, just as I will never again touch her lidless,
staring eyes, and damp, spotted skin. The painful memory returns, that it was she who gave me the wedding
band I still wear.

Can she be jealous now, beyond the end of all
things?

Still, the little cells grow, the trays glowing slightly in
a curious echo of the walls just offshore. Madeleine's

lips are no longer well formed for speaking, and neither is her larynx, but she grunts her fears to me.

The toxins will kill us all, or at least those of us who are transforming. Her. Me. Everyone but the girl from Crescent City. Or perhaps the toxins will kill no one, and this is all but a cruel hoax. Maybe the Old Ones toy with us, even now.

Finally I take her into my arms one night in the old sauna. Though true coupling is not possible for us, I make love to my memory of who my wife once was, while her lidless eyes weep acid tears to scar my chest and shoulder.

V

In the morning, I find her shriveled corpse next to the toxin trays. A faint smear still glows around her lips. I wonder if I should cry, but tears are years gone.

There is nothing more to be done. I gather my strength and purpose. As we were instructed, I press the cells in old cloth, so the toxin can be more easily spread by air or contract. As it dries, I bottle the stuff into old light bulbs from which the metal stems have been broken off, then bind them with duct tape. If the priests beat me upon my capture, they will be very surprised.

I leave detailed notes and diagrams showing our work, for when others of the lodge return. Eventually I step outside into the chilled mist and stare across the water at the Risen City. I shall take a dory and row me down to that watery hell, bringing blindness to the Old Ones, and death to my immortal enemies.

As I ply the oars, I wonder if the girl and Madeleine planned this for me. The waters around me roil with evil, the sky is Armageddon-dark, and I find it does not matter.

"I love you," I tell the world. Then I row some more.

THE SEALS OF NEW R'LYEH

Gregory Frost

"**D**id you hear something?" Detwiler asked.
Stipe paused to listen.

Detwiler couldn't help himself; he glanced back down the tunnel. He could hear blood ringing in his ears; underneath that he wasn't sure if he heard wind or the "whump-whump" of leathery wings. It was paranoia. He needed confirmation of that.

"Besides wind, you mean?" Stipe asked.

"Yeah."

"Just them chanting upstairs. But you have to listen hard."

"Fine. Let's hurry up." Detwiler turned his attention back to his pry bar. He'd already chipped out the mortar around the massive stone block, enough room to wedge the bar in. Whatever else he had to say about life under Cthulhu, he appreciated the dependability of the architecture—dependable in the sense that it made the removal of one stone from the foundation wall a simple matter of physics. Fulcrums, levers, and offset stones. Stipe referred to the form as *Ugaritic*. In the old days, Stipe had read a lot on the toilet, mostly *National Geographic*s. Detwiler only cared that he could pull out one stone and not have the whole wall collapse on top of him.

Together they revolved the loosened stone. Then Stipe got a rope around it, and they pulled it out. It hit the floor of the tunnel with a boom that must have set

184

off seismographs in Mongolia, assuming either Mongolia or seismographs existed any longer.

They paused to listen again. No wings, no sound beyond the distant roar of wind. Nobody—more to the point, nothing—was crawling down the tunnel after them; and now there was a hole in the wall big enough to climb through.

"This better work," said Detwiler.

"John. If Cthulhu catches you inside the vault, what'll he do to you?"

"Pull me apart like your little brother torturing an insect?"

"And if you go back to living in the rubble of our dying world?"

"The same, I suppose. Just, you know, later on."

"So?"

"Yeah, great." Detwiler flicked on his halogen flashlight and pulled himself halfway into the hole.

Inside lay a vault exactly as Stipe had described, as huge as a cathedral, with twisted columns of stone supports. It was almost how he'd imagined Ali Baba's cave to look back when he was a kid. Ali Baba had been something of a role model. Thieves who rode in, got what they wanted, and rode out again to their secret lair. Detwiler figured a lot of his disappointments as a thief were because nobody rode in on horseback anymore. And that was before Cthulhu had shown up and pretty much flattened civilization. Try to find a horse *now*.

This time, however, things were looking up. The vault abounded with riches, and everywhere golden and silvery objects glinted in the light of his torch. Two enormous soapstone tubs presented heaps of cracked emeralds and what he dared to hope were uncut diamonds, a few as big as his fist. The tubs were covered with carvings, inhuman figures in relief. He wondered who had done the work. Some poor slob enslaved by the hideous Cthulhu, probably destroyed the moment he finished. "There are jewels in here, Stipe!" he called back. "We have to take some jewels. We can't break in here and not take some jewels."

"Okay, we'll get some jewels, but what about the stuff?"

Detwiler waved the flashlight around. Across the chamber, set on clawfooted displays stood five circular seals the size of garbage can lids. "Oh, yeah," he said.

"Let me see!" Stipe pulled him out of the hole. Detwiler handed him the torch, and Stipe leaped into the hole almost froglike. Then, "Oh," he said, as if a woman had just unexpectedly made a pass at him—which for Stipe would have been a life-changing event. He drew himself out. "The seals."

"They're worth a lot, right?" Detwiler asked doubtfully.

"Detwiler. They're so valuable nobody even believes they exist."

He considered that. "Good," he replied. "Then nobody will believe when they aren't there anymore."

Stipe bent down and picked up one of three duffels they'd brought, pushed it into the hole, and climbed in after it. Detwiler sighed. Grabbed the remaining two bags. So typical of Stipe that he had taken only his own duffel. Stipe the solipsist, a curse and a blessing; it meant that he was always looking for a score, but also that once he had his own, he lost all interest in everybody else's circumstance. This had resulted in Detwiler's one stretch in juvie two decades ago, and five months in Otisville more recently.

Now that Cthulhu had come along and shredded the fabric of society, not to mention time and space, everybody he'd known in the joint was free. A lot of them, he thought, probably shouldn't have been. And because of Stipe, Detwiler felt he bore some responsibility for Cthulhu in the first place, an opinion that was not going to make him popular with the remaining clusters of humanity.

Not unless his plan worked.

The cult of Glynn Beckman had caught Stipe's attention for a couple of reasons. First, most of its members were wealthy inbred loons too scabrous even for the Ayn Rand followers to tolerate, but like Rand's thugs, smug in their superiority, so much so that they tended to leave a lot of things unlocked—like for instance the walk-in safe in Beckman's study where the cult's finances and papers were kept—and available, like the valuable artworks decorating Beckman's walls. That appealed to Stipe so much he joined the cult before they'd finished buttering him up. Actually, they didn't know him as Stipe, but as Kellogg, the current and insanely wealthy scion of the cereal empire of the same name.

The cult was far more cautious and guarded about a book that Beckman claimed to have translated. He claimed that his was the only accurate translation anywhere. "All other followers of the mad Alhazred made mistakes. That's why everyone from Whately to Akeley—who refused to act, the fool!—ultimately failed to open the gate. *Yog-Sothoth* is indeed the gate, but it's only the first of six!"

It all had something to do with seals.

"Like at the circus?" Detwiler had asked.

Stipe had replied, "No, I don't think so."

All he expected Detwiler to do was pretend to be a rich refrigerator magnate and a total believer in Beckman's lunacy. "A couple nights in the house, we wait till everybody's asleep, load up all we can carry, and get out of there. By the time they notice we haven't shown up for mimosas, we're like in New Hampshire."

It sounded ridiculously simple, which was probably why Detwiler thought it couldn't possibly work. But once he was inside the house and, dressed in a rented tuxedo, was given a tour of the place, he had to admit it looked as simple as it sounded. The artwork wasn't wired. The safe was left ajar. And when he mentioned this to Beckman, the answer astounded him. "After we open the gate, my friend, there'll be no need for alarms, security, protection." As Beckman explained, he puffed on a cigar the size of the Hindenberg. "We shall rule the world!"

Yep, Detwiler agreed, nuts. There was no time to waste. The group was preparing for a big ritual the following night. Detwiler worked out the scenario: the two of them would pretend to get drunk while celebrating and pass out downstairs, allowing all others to go to bed. Then they would clean the place out. He determined the fastest route through the house while carrying priceless Miros and Picassos. He'd already gotten the code number that opened the front gate of the estate—the one security element Beckman did rely upon (and which Stipe had missed). All they had to do was join in the group's little event.

Of course things hadn't exactly followed the script. The ceremony with the weird stone seal, which Beckman split in two, had ripped open reality, a horrible, lightning-charged rending that Detwiler still couldn't believe he'd witnessed. From some other foul and pestilent dimension, Cthulhu slithered into this one. Unfortunately, he proved to be about the size of Godzilla, far larger than Beckman's house. The whole place came down, beams and ceilings caving in, circuits bursting into flame. Cultists were crushed left and right, including Beckman himself.

Detwiler hightailed it into the study as the building collapsed around him. He threw open the door of the walk-in safe, at which point something clocked him. Stipe later claimed it was a plumbing fixture from the second floor, just as he claimed that Detwiler had survived only because Stipe had dragged him into the walk-in safe. That had shielded them both. But Detwiler had awakened alone. True to form, Stipe had snatched half the cash from the safe and taken off.

Cash, of course, had already become a useless commodity. Cthulhu and the rest of his loathsome, wet, leathery entourage leveled Maine in an afternoon, and then settled in for a long stay, laying siege to the whole East Coast. The next week was like a bad B-monster movie, with various militaries throwing everything at them. Some of the lesser creatures were destroyed, but Cthulhu seemed only to devour the energy flung his way. Even the nuclear option failed, although nobody would be living in Baltimore again before 2400 A.D.

Like cockroaches that had lurked in the woodwork, a network of cults uncannily like Beckman's had emerged across the world, pledging their allegiance to the god. According to stories that he heard later, only some of them survived the contact. "Some people never learn," Detwiler mused. Granted, the ones who did survive had it better than most everyone else. The arrangement reminded him of trustees in Otisville.

Detwiler lived quite some time in the Beckman house safe. It provided protection against the weather, and the location remained undisturbed. Nobody wanted to come near.

From the remains of the house—notably the basement pantry—he managed to retrieve assorted canned goods and jellies. A plethora of jellies. It seemed that Mrs. Beckman had enjoyed canning jalapeño jelly for all occasions. In Detwiler's case, "all occasions" meant just that.

He scrounged boxes of crackers, but really missed not having some cream cheese. Somebody, probably Cthulhu, had stepped directly on the refrigerator.

The next weeks, he pulled up various parts of the house, occasionally finding someone's remains, including Beckman's. The cigar case and lighter from the suit jacket were about all that survived intact. Finally he came upon the broken seal and other objects from the ceremony.

When the food was about to run out, Detwiler gathered up the remaining supplies and recovered items in a large leather laptop satchel and over a period of months worked his way down the coast and back to the Bronx, or what it had become.

The creatures had taken over. They had marshaled the survivors of Beckman's inter-dimensional holocaust into an army of slaves to build monuments to the great Cthulhu, with cultists as their overseers. Already the landscape was starting to look like a representation of ancient Egypt, if the Egyptians had ingested a lot of magic mushrooms before constructing their pyramids.

He learned to avoid the barrel-shaped guardians with eyes on tentacles and huge bat wings, and subsisted mostly on canned goods while trying to ascertain what use somebody with his skills was in a world turned so upside down.

He came upon people hiding out in underground garages and former basements and shooting each other over who got to sleep on a dirty piece of cardboard. How good it was to see that we'd all settled our differences in the face of a common enemy.

The general opinion was that over a billion people had perished in the first week alone. Nobody knew what was true. It was merely the prevailing rumor. The future for Detwiler narrowed to encompass how to get food, how to survive the night without being shot, and how to stay warm as the weather turned cool. The last thing he expected ever again was to encounter Stipe.

One afternoon as he was creeping through some rubble, Detwiler came to an oddly fashioned tunnel. It wasn't a sewer tunnel or a subway. It was something that looked freshly carved and weirdly organic, glowing with an eerie rippling phosphorescence, as if the walls within were pulsating, a kind of living formation that produced patterns as he passed by—at least it seemed organic until he came to a wall of immense, roughly rectangular stones. Those appeared to be the foundation for something aboveground. Detwiler suspected that he'd blundered beneath one of the weird temples. He turned to leave, only to find his way blocked by a Twinkie.

As such creations went, this was the granddaddy of Hostess desserts, a slithering brown, granular lump the size of a Clydesdale that only moved when necessary— and very quietly at that. He was trapped, but instead of crushing him or absorbing him or whatever else he expected it to do, the thing let him sidle past, and then herded him back out of the tunnel and up to the surface, where three more joined it, offering him only one course to take. They drove him across a roughly hewn stalagmitic plaza toward one of the many ugly, off-kilter temples. Well, he thought, he'd had a good run, come about as far as anyone could hope in this twisted world. That's when he heard someone call his name, looked up, and found Stipe striding across the knurled landscape. Stipe, wearing a black suit and white shirt, looking for all the world like a beaming Jehovah's Witness come to lay on him a copy of *The Watchtower*; the Twinkie wranglers parted to let Stipe through.

Stipe slapped him on the shoulder, took him by the arm. "Man, I almost didn't recognize you with the beard. Good to see you. I was sure you'd do okay."

"Yeah, I was real safe in that safe."

"Safe in the safe, ha!" Stipe laughed, wiped at his eyes. "That's a good one. Here, come with me."

Detwiler eyed the clustered Twinkies.

Stipe insisted, "No, really, it's okay. They know you're one of us."

"Us?"

"You know what I mean. You're a Beckman."

"I'll have nightmares forever."

"Well, I think maybe I can help with that. You need a bath, John. A shave. Come on." They walked off across the plaza toward a group of humans, all dressed in much the same garb as Stipe, even the women. Some of them looked to Detwiler a little peculiar, as if maybe their parents had been spadefoot toads. Stipe explained to them that Detwiler was a surviving member of Beckman's group. The others oohed and aahed as if he was a lost treasure. They welcomed him to New R'lyeh.

Eventually Stipe dragged him off for a tour of the facilities.

"What's New R'lyeh?" Detwiler pronounced.

"It's what Cthulhu renamed New York. The parts he's had rebuilt, anyway."

"What happened to Old R'lyeh?"

"I think it sank into the Pacific. Anyway, this is where we all are now."

"Home, sweet ph'nglui."

Stipe chuckled. "Hey, you remembered some of the words from the ceremony."

"One or two."

As they entered through a gaping doorway, Stipe asked, "So, like, what d'you have in the bag?"

"Toothbrush," replied Detwiler.

"Right."

The inside of the place was just as rough and knurled. No surface was either exactly horizontal or vertical. The light came from more phosphorescence.

"Lichen," Stipe explained.

As they walked, something huge, brown, and repulsive flew by. Its stalked eyes turned to observe them. Its leathery wings flapped heavily. Then it shat something green and noxious. "Oh, great. Can we go another way?" Detwiler asked.

"It's just *fhtagn* poop."

"I'd say this whole *farkakte* setup's *fhtagn.*"

"Aw, don't be like that. We're gonna score hugely here, man, now that you're back."

"No kidding," Detwiler replied. "How do we define hugely in the universe of flying tentacled beer barrels?"

Stipe explained that Cthulhu's human followers were already hoarding all kinds of treasures: great works of art, things lifted out of what had been the Met and the MOMA: jewelry, gold, silver, anything that seemed like it might one day represent wealth for a new ruling class.

"Like that cash you made off with."

Stipe shrugged. "Yeah, that didn't play out too well. Why I had to rejoin the overseers."

"So where are they keeping all this wealth-to-be?"

"Inside the monuments. Well, underneath them, really."

"Like the tunnel I just came from?"

Stipe's eyebrows raised. "No wonder they nabbed you. Cthulhu's got a thing for tunnels. Loves 'em."

"Why? He's the size of the moon. He couldn't fit his left nut in one."

"And you know what else?" Stipe confided. "Some of the other groups showed up with more seals."

"Seals like Beckman's, you mean?"

"Absolutely. A shame Beckman's book got smushed."

"How so?"

"Well, see, that's the only translation that was accurate, just like Beckman claimed."

"So nobody can work the seals."

"Nope, and now they're not gonna get the chance."

"Why not?"

"Well, Cthulhu doesn't want anyone to have them. Every time somebody's shown up with another one, it's confiscated."

"He doesn't want to open the rest of the gates?"

Stipe shrugged. "Not yet, I guess. Probably wants to finish remaking the world in his image so he can show it off to the other gods."

Detwiler glanced around at the carved interior, the canted doorways, vaulted ceiling, rough and narrow steps. "Seems to be having some success with that."

"I got a place picked out we can move everything till we need it."

"Place?" Detwiler asked.

"Yeah, awhile back I found an old abandoned subway line that I don't think has been in operation since like forever. The tunnelers covered it up to bore one of Cthulhu's tunnels, but I made sure to leave one way into it. It's so close to the Temple of Yuggoth, though, that nobody else'll go near it."

"Why not?"

"You haven't been there, have you?" asked Stipe.

"How would I know?"

"'Cause if you had you'd be a gibbering mess now. The place exudes cosmic dread like a noxious gas. You hallucinate loathsome star clusters, and feel your very atoms come apart in slow motion, in agony so terrible that most people hurl themselves to their death at the very start of it."

"Yeah, I think I'd remember that."

"We only get together and chant there like once a year."

"How is it anybody's left?"

Instead of answering, Stipe went on, "I figure we can pull whatever we want out of the other temples, store it down under there. Sell it back to them if we have to, but otherwise we sit it out till we need some capital. Then we bargain."

"You're talking about the seals."

Stipe smiled broadly. "You always were a smart guy, Detwiler."

"Not smart enough."

"That's why you got me."

Detwiler closed his eyes and said nothing.

And so they'd spent days worshipping Cthulhu and his inhuman underlings at various sites around New R'lyeh, and their evenings scouting each elephantine temple and slimy tunnel until they'd located the collected Seals of Kadath, a matter made harder by the repeated denials they heard, mostly from the Cthulhulians themselves, that the seals had never existed at all.

With the stone pulled out, the two slipped into the unguarded vault beneath the Temple of Ultimate Chaos, which Detwiler observed looked like a greenish-black intestinal polyp.

They filled the duffels with the five seals, and Detwiler took time to add as many of the rough-cut diamonds as he could scoop up before Stipe nervously said, "They've stopped chanting."

It had indeed grown silent overhead. But no one was making their way down the Stygian stairways to this vault either. Detwiler snatched a few more jewels.

Stipe grunted as he hauled his duffel over to the hole. It took the two of them to lift it up and over, and lower it down the outside. The weight of the bag almost pulled Stipe out the opening. They repeated the act with the other two before climbing out. Stipe was dirty and sweating. Detwiler imagined that he looked much the same. "We're gonna have to come back for the third one of these."

"Just to the end of the tunnel for now," said Detwiler.

"You're crazy."

"I must be." He lifted his duffel and started walking, bow-legged and slow. Stipe followed him. At the mouth of the tunnel, Detwiler set his bag down and went back in for the third one. He carried that with less trouble, and set it on top of Stipe's bag. They looked out into the night. This was the part of the journey that presented the most peril. The duffels had to travel to the subway entrance, a good half a mile away. But Detwiler had worked that all out. After checking to be sure no one was watching from outside the glowing tunnel, he crept off into the dark and returned a few minutes later with a dinged up wheelbarrow.

"Where'd you find that?" Stipe asked.

"I used to move with it before your Twinkies caught me."

"You're a genius, John."

"Now and then." They loaded the last of the duffels and then Stipe's into the barrow. "We're still going to have to leave the third one here. Three's too heavy."

"Yeah."

"I'll stay with it," Detwiler said. "I know how you like to make off with the goods. And I can wait."

Stipe lifted the wheelbarrow onto its single wheel. "Yeah, I can handle this okay. I'll be back in under an hour."

"Be careful."

Stipe headed off, shortly disappearing over the rise and into the landscape. Amazing how dark it got without streetlights, Detwiler thought. No wonder we invented them.

He set to work. First he recovered his satchel, which he'd been careful to hide near the tunnel's mouth. Now, in the dull greenish glow of the fungi at the opening, he pulled out the battered copy of Beckman's *Necronomicon*, and with a few loose bricks set it up so that he could read from it. Next he unzipped the duffel. He'd put two of the seals in the bag in order to ensure that Stipe could transport the remaining duffels by himself. Now he hauled them out one at a time, afterwards rolling each to where he could see it clearly in the pulsating glow.

A low, shambling sound caught his attention, and one

of the Twinkies slid sluglike into the edge of the tunnel's luminescence. Detwiler edged back to the book and flipped through the pages. "Regna'd kesin," he read. The Twinkie flexed as if something invisible had poked it. "K'la ye'hah!" It turned and scuttled away. "Bugshoggoth."

Detwiler glanced from the book to the seals. The runes on each were distinctive, and only one bore the correct symbols as illustrated in Beckman's book. When he was absolutely certain he rolled the other one across the rubble to where an old fire hydrant still stood, anchored to pavement below the debris. Certain he'd end up with a hernia, he lifted the round stone over his head and then as hard as he could dashed it on the tip of the hydrant. The seal shattered. Somewhere, distantly in the night, something squealed like a lobster being immersed in a pot of boiling water. The sound faded. Thunder rumbled.

"Hey!" a voice called.

Detwiler turned. Stipe was approaching with the empty wheelbarrow.

Detwiler walked back over to his duffel and the remaining seal. He knelt beside the book and placed the seal face up on the ground in front of him.

Stipe set down the barrow. "Whatcha doing, man?"

"Oh, this and that."

Stipe stopped. "That's the *book*, Detwiler," he said. "Beckman's book."

"Yes, it is. Makes for interesting reading. For instance, I can tell you why Cthulhu's been hoarding all these seals."

"Really?"

"Oh, yeah. But give it twenty minutes and he'll be here anyway."

Alarmed, Stipe looked around, up at the sky, at the repulsive towers. "He will?"

"Yeah, I got his attention." He gestured toward the hydrant, the broken pieces of seal standing out in greenish contrast to the gray debris.

"John, you have any idea what even one of those is worth potentially?"

"Kind of. Pretty much all of humanity."

Distantly, the air vibrated, a quiet, slow rhythm.

Detwiler gestured with his thumb at the book. "According to Beckman, this world of ours used to be Cthulhu's domain. About eight or twelve millennia ago. He's responsible for this local area, which is big, but not compared to all space and time. The realm he got booted to from here was a kind of limbo between dimensions. Thing is, honestly, he's a cousin to the Old Ones. I mean the *real* Old Ones. They're not like him."

"No?"

"Infinitely worse," said Detwiler. "They'd likely have scorched the whole solar system by now, melted the planets and reassembled them as something you and I can't even comprehend, Stipe. We don't perceive enough dimensions."

"How you know this?"

"Well, I don't, exactly. It's what the book says. I mean, Beckman could just be nuts, like we both thought."

The "whump" of huge and unseen wings grew steadily louder.

"If that's the case, though," Detwiler continued, "we're in trouble here."

"What have you done?" Stipe stood as if ready to bolt.

"This—" he tapped the remaining seal "—this is the second seal. Your Old Ones think of Cthulhu as the cousin you don't invite to the wedding because he picks his nose and wipes it on the bride's gown, you know what I'm saying? They gave him our backwater swamp to manage, just to keep him off on his own. The gates are in place to keep him out as much as us in. *This* seal is Yog-Tetharoth."

The sound of wings seemed to be nearly overhead.

"You open this one" —he glanced at the book and yelled, "krel'bo'yni Kadath nar'whal Kaekeeba!" then went on as if nothing had happened— "and you'll re-open that buffer space between Cthulhu and the *rest* of the family. Suck him right back out."

Stipe's eyes were huge. "What are they like, the Old Ones?"

"All it says is, you can smell them, but you can't see them."

Something huge, writhing, with red glowing eyes emerged out of the clouds above. Detwiler drew the crowbar from his duffel.

"Of course, it requires a sacrifice. Nothing personal." He drove the sharp edge of the crowbar straight into the seam down the middle of the seal. With a flash, the greenish stone split in half.

Stipe put his hands out as if to push away from something. His mouth opened in a scream, but the more thunderous scream from the creature above him drowned him out. Cthulhu turned and vanished back into the clouds.

"That's not right," Detwiler muttered.

Stipe hadn't moved or vanished. A pure blackness arising from the broken seal spread up and out, surrounding him but leaving him untouched, save that his face contorted into a mask of revulsion, his eyes watered and he clamped both hands over his nose. The blackness rose like smoke upon a breeze and faded.

Lying flat on the ground, Detwiler glanced over at the book. He read the relevant passages again. "Krel'bo'yni Kadath nar'whal Kaekeeba—that's what it says. That's what *I* said. I don't get it." Then the stench reached him. It was like the distilled essence of sulphuric eggs run through an oil refinery and then fired out of a skunk's butt. He pressed his face into the dirt and groaned.

Stipe, on his knees, coughed and wheezed, "What did you do, John?"

"I—I was sending Cthulhu back to where he came from." He leaned up on his elbows. "You know when I said Beckman was nuts?"

"Yeah?"

"Well, his translation's screwy, too."

Overhead, clouds floated, drifted. Then, as if a titanic soap bubble had reached them, they flew apart. Moonlight spilled down, but distorted and sickly yellow as though projected through old celophane. Detwiler could feel phantoms nearby, invisible, amorphous things that swelled against the very fabric of reality.

"You let in the Old Ones," Stipe said.

"Uh, yeah. Let's not mention that to the others, okay?" He got to his feet. He wiped at his eyes, sniffled, choked. "Listen, if we're lucky, he was wrong about them melting the planets and stuff, too."

Stipe got up, shook his head like a dog. "I can't get that stink off me."

The ruin of a nearby building suddenly flexed and distorted. As if liquid it drew together, the top of it curled like an ocean wave and then stretched into the clouds. The night filled with distant piteous cries of horror, not all of them human.

"We, ah, we might want to go back into the tunnel awhile," Detwiler suggested. He bent down to pick up Beckman's book. The stars in the night sky shuddered. "Just till things settle down." He headed into the phosphorescence.

With a final glance at the world, Stipe stumbled into the mouth of the tunnel, too, but abruptly drew up. "Detwiler," he yelled, "what did you mean you needed a sacrifice?"

THE HOLOCAUST OF ECSTASY

Brian Stableford

It was dark when Tremeloe first opened his eyes, and he found it impossible to make out anything in a sideways or upward direction. When he looked down, though, in the hope of seeing where he was standing—for he had no idea where he was, and was sure that he wasn't lying down—he saw that there were holes in a floor that seemed to be a long way beneath him and that stars were shining through the holes.

There seemed to be a conversation going on around him, but there were no English words in it; the languages that the various voices were speaking all seemed to him to be Far Eastern in origin. The voices seemed quite calm, and in spite of the impenetrable darkness and not knowing where he was, Tremeloe felt oddly calm himself.

"Does anyone here speak English?" he asked. The words came out easily enough, but sounded and felt wrong, in some way that he couldn't quite understand.

For a moment, there was a pregnant silence, as if everyone in the crowd were deciding whether to admit to speaking English. Finally, though, a voice that seemed to come from somewhere closer at hand than all the rest, said: "Yes. You're American?" There was nothing Oriental about the accent, but that didn't make it any easier to place.

Tremeloe thought that the other might be near enough

to touch, and tried to reach out in the direction from which the voice had come, but he couldn't. His body felt strange and wrong. He couldn't feel his hands, and when he tried to touch himself to reassure himself that he was still there, he couldn't touch any other part of him with his fingers. The idea struck him that the conviction that he wasn't lying down, based on the fact that he couldn't feel a surface on which he might be lying, would be unreliable if he were paralyzed from the neck down.

"Richard Tremeloe, Arkham, Massachusetts," he said, by way of introduction. "Have I been in some kind of accident?" He tried to remember where he had been before falling asleep—or unconscious—and couldn't. "I think I've got amnesia," he added.

"More than you know," said the other voice, a trifle dolefully, "but the others are a little more relevant in their concerns."

"Can you understand what they're saying?" Tremeloe asked, knowing that it was the wrong question, but reluctant to ask one whose answer might provoke the panic that he had so far been spared.

"Some of it," the other boasted. "There's an animated discussion about reincarnation going on. The Buddhists and the Hindus have different views on the subject, but none of them really believes in it—especially the ex-Communists. On the other hand . . ."

"Who are you?" Tremeloe demanded, wondering why the anxiety that he ought to be feeling wasn't making itself felt in his flesh or his voice. "Where the hell are we?"

"If I'm not much mistaken," the other replied, "we've been reborn into the new era, beyond good and evil: the holocaust of ecstasy and freedom. I'm not at all sure about the freedom, though . . . or, come to that, the ecstasy. I shouldn't be here. This shouldn't be possible. The memory wipe should have made it impossible."

"Reborn?" echoed Tremeloe. "I haven't been reborn. I'm not sure of much, but I know I'm an adult. I'm fifty-six years old—maybe more, depending on the depth of the amnesia. I'm a professor of biology at Miskatonic

University, married to Barbara, with two children, Stephen and Grace . . . ." He trailed off. He was talking in order to test his memory rather than to enlighten the mysteriously anonymous other, but it wasn't an awareness of pointlessness or a failure of remembrance that had caused him to stop. It was the realization that the stars really were shining through gaps in . . . something that *wasn't* the floor. "Why has up become down?" he asked. "Why aren't I aware of being *upside-down?* Why can't I feel *gravity?*"

The voice didn't try to reassure him. Instead, the other said: "Miskatonic? Have you read the *Necronomicon*?"

"Don't be ridiculous," Tremeloe snapped—or tried to, since his momentary irritation was a mere flicker, which didn't show in his voice. "It's been locked in a vault for decades. No one's allowed to see or touch any of the so-called forbidden manuscripts, since the *unpleasantness* way back in the last century. Anyway, I'm a scientist. I don't have any truck with occult rubbish like that."

"Do you know Nathaniel Wingate Peaslee?"

That question gave Tremeloe pause for thought. He blinked and squinted—and was glad to know that he could still feel his eyelids, just as he could still feel the movements of his tongue—in the hope that he might be able to make out his surroundings now that his eyes were adapting to the extremely poor light. He couldn't. Above his head—or, strictly speaking, below it, since he seemed to be hanging upside-down—the darkness was Stygian. Around him, he had a vague impression of rounded objects that might have been heads, not very densely clustered, and wispier things that were vaguely reminiscent of fern leaves, but he couldn't actually *see* anything . . . except the fugitive stars, shining through gaps in what was presumably a dense cloud-bank. Occasionally, the stars were briefly eclipsed, as if something had moved across them: a giant bird, perhaps.

Around him, the chorus of foreign voice was still going on. If any of the others could speak English, they were content to listen to what Tremeloe and his companion were saying, without intervening.

What was remarkable about the other's question, Tremeloe reminded himself, when he came back to it reluctantly, was that Nathaniel Wingate Peaslee had died more than a hundred years ago . . . or, at least, more than a hundred years before Richard Tremeloe had turned fifty-six. He was long dead, but not quite forgotten . . . just as the university's famous copy of the *Necronomicon* was unforgotten, even though no one had clapped eyes on it since before Tremeloe had been born. Having no idea how to answer the other's question, Tremeloe prevaricated by saying: "Do you?"

"I did, briefly—but that was in another place and another time. I infer from your hesitation that he's long dead, and that you . . . died . . . sometime in the twenty-first or twenty-second century."

"I'm not dead," Tremeloe retorted, reflexively, although he did realize that if all the other hanged men in this dark Tarot space were earnestly discussing reincarnation, he might be in the minority in holding that opinion, and might even be wrong, in spite of *cogito ergo sum* and all his memories of Miskatonic, Barbara, Stephen, Grace, his hands, his legs, and his heart . . . .

His heart would have sunk, if he'd had one, and if its sinking had been possible. *I can't feel gravity*, Tremeloe thought. Aloud, he said: "Are you telling me that I really have been reincarnated?"

"Yes—probably not for the first time, although it's impossible to tell how many layers of amnesia we've been afflicted with."

"How?" This time Tremeloe succeeded in snapping. "When? *By whom?*"

"If you'd read the *Necronomicon*," the other voice replied, with a leaden dullness that probably wasn't redolent with panic because it had no more capacity to hold an edge than Tremeloe's own, "you'd know."

"And you have?" Tremeloe riposted.

"No," the other came back, quick as a flash. "I wrote it—and no, I don't mean that I'm the legendary Arab with the nonsensical name who penned the *Al Azif*. I mean that I too, like Peaslee, have lived in Pnakotus . . .

except that to me, it was a home of sorts, though not Yith itself, and I'm not supposed to be out of it any more. The human brain I inhabited for ten years was supposed to have been cleansed of every last trace of me. I shouldn't have been available for . . . *this*."

"Has it occurred to you," Tremeloe asked, "that you might be barking mad?"

"Yes," the other replied. "How about you?"

Good question, Tremeloe thought. *This is a nightmare— a crazy nightmare. There's no other explanation. Please can I wake up now?* Somehow, he knew that wasn't going to happen. He might well be dreaming, but he was very clearly conscious that he was living his dream, and that he was not going to be waking up to any other reality any time soon.

Even so . . .

"The cloud's getting lighter," he observed. "It *is* cloud, isn't it? That *is* the sky, isn't it? It only seems to be beneath us because we're hanging upside-down."

"Yes," the other answered. "It's dawn. Whether we're barking mad or not, this might be a good time to strive with all our might to lose our minds completely: to dissolve our minds into private chaos and gibbering idiocy, if we can. On balance . . ."

The other shut up, somewhat to Tremeloe's relief.

The dawn was slow. The shades of grey through which the bulk of the sky progressed as its patches turned blue and the stars were drowned seemed infinite in their subtlety, but Tremeloe soon stopped watching them, in order to concentrate on the tree.

The reason that he couldn't feel his body was that he didn't have one. He was just a head and a neck—except that the neck was really a stalk, and it connected him to the bough of a tree from which he hung down like a fruit, amid a hundred other heads that he could see and probably a thousand that he couldn't. The things he's intuited as leaves really were leaves, and really were divided up in a quasi-fractal pattern, a little like fern leaves but lacier. They were pale green streaked with purple.

The tree, so far as Tremeloe could estimate, was at

least a hundred feet high, and its crown had to be at least a hundred and fifty in diameter, but he was positioned on the outside of the crown, about five-sixths of the way up—or, as it seemed to him, down—and he couldn't see the trunk at all. He could barely see the ground "above" his head, but the thin streaks he could see between his head-fruit-tree and the next were vivid green and suspiciously flat, as if they might be algae-clogged swamp-water rather than anything solid.

The jungle stretched as far as his eyes could see. The birds in the sky really did look like giants, but that might have been an error of perspective.

There was no disintegration into private chaos, no hectic slide into gibbering idiocy. While not exactly calm any longer, and perhaps still capable of a kind of panic, Tremeloe felt that his consciousness was clear, that his memory was sound—so far as it went—and that his intelligence was relentless. He realized that he was no longer possessed of the hormonal orchestra of old. Presumably, he still had a pituitary master gland, which was probably still sending out its chemical signals to the endocrine glands that had once been distributed through his frail human flesh, but whatever was responding to them now was a very different organism. From now on, his feelings, like his voice, would be regulated by a very different existential system. Even so, he did still have a voice. He had no lungs, but he did have vocal cords, and some kind of apparatus for pumping air into his neck-stalk. He wasn't dumb, any more than he was deaf or blind.

All in all, he thought, only slightly amazed at his capacity to think it, *things could be worse*. Then he remembered what the other English-speaker had implied about losing his mind completely, and dissolving into gibbering mindlessness, probably being the better alternative . . . .

The head of the other English-speaker—the only Caucasian face amid a crowd of Orientals who occasionally glanced at him sideways, with apparent curiosity but no hostility, but showed no sign of understanding what he said—seemed to be that of a man in his mid-fifties, who might have been handsome before middle-aged spread had given him jowls and thinning hair had turned his hairline into a ebbing tide. The jowls seemed oddly protuberant, but that was because they were hanging the wrong way. Gravity still existed; it was just that Tremeloe no longer had any sensation of his own weight. He felt slightly insulted by that, having always thought of his intellect-laden head as a ponderous entity.

Tremeloe didn't see the bats until they actually arrived at the tree, wheeling around it in a flock that must have been thirty or thirty-five strong. This time, there was no possibility of any error of perspective; they were *huge*. Because Tremeloe was a biologist he knew that real vampire bats were tiny, and that the common habit of referring to fruit-bats as "vampire bats" was a myth-based error, but now that he was a human fruit, the difference seemed rather trivial—especially when he saw the bats begin to settle on his fellow human fruit.

Please, he prayed—although he was an atheist—*don't let it be me*. Because he was a biologist, though, he took note of the fruit-bats' eyes. The bats were obviously not nocturnal in their habits, so their eyes were adapted for day vision; these specimens were not as blind as bats even in their natural state—but that didn't explain why the unnaturally huge creatures had eyes that looked almost human in their fox-like heads.

After a few seconds, during which he saw one creature's needle-sharp teeth tear into the face of an Oriental man—who did not scream—Tremeloe was on the point of withdrawing the *almost* . . . but he never quite got there, because one of the bats suddenly descended upon him, as if out of nowhere.

He felt the monster's breath on his cheek, caught its rancid stink in his nostrils, and looked into its not-quite-almost-human eyes, and knew that it was about to pluck out his own as it groped with its clawed feet . . . but then it was suddenly gone again, snatched away as abruptly as it had arrived.

After the bats had come the huge birds . . . and they really were *huge*. They were eagles, or condors, or something akin to both but not quite either. At any rate, they were raptors, and they numbered human-fruit-bats among their prey of choice. There weren't as many birds as bats, so some of the bats were enabled to start their hasty meals in peace, but the birds were even fiercer, and they could easily carry a bat in each claw, so it wasn't long before the bats fluttered away, seeking the cover of the sprawling crowns.

The raptors too, Tremeloe realized, as he watched his own avian savior fall into the sky, clutching for its next meal with its terrible talons, had unnaturally large eyes: not eyes like a hawk's, but eyes like a man's . . . .

Tremeloe looked his white-faced neighbor in the eyes and said: "Is this hell?" He knew that it was a stupid question. He'd done much better before, when his not-quite-immediate response to the possibility that he had been reincarnated had been: *how? By whom?*

What the other said in reply, however, was: "That depends."

A phrase that the mysterious other had used while they were still enclosed by merciful darkness floated back into Tremeloe's mind: *the holocaust of ecstasy and freedom*. Except, the other had added, presumably knowing already that he was simply a head-fruit, there wasn't much freedom in their present existential state. *Nor ecstasy either, so far as I can tell*, Tremeloe added, privately. Although it might have been more exciting, now that he thought about it, to be reincarnated as a human eagle . . . better, at any rate, than being reincarnated as a human fruit-bat.

Are we all vampires now?

But the real questions were still *how* and *by whom?*

"I'm not who I think I am, am I?" Tremeloe said to the other, who seemed to know a lot more than he did. "I'm just some sort of replica, created from some sort of recording. This isn't the twenty-first century, is it? This is a much later era—maybe the end of time. Is this the Omega Point? Is this the Omega Point Intelligence's idea of a joke?"

"I wish it were," the other replied. "Perhaps it is . . .

but my suspicion is that it's not as late as you think. The Coleopteran Era is a long way off as yet, alas. This is Cthulhu's Reign . . . what the human race were designed to be and to become. But no, we're not just replicas reproduced from some sort of recording; we're actually who we think we are, shifted forwards in time. You are, at any rate. I shouldn't be here. I don't belong here. I only borrowed a human body temporarily, and then I returned to Pnakotus. I shouldn't be here. This isn't right."

Tremeloe thought that he had just as much right to protest as the other, but his mind—which was not only refusing to dissolve into incoherent idiocy but perversely insistent on retaining an emotional state more reminiscent of complacency than abject terror—was oddly intent on trying to pick up the thread of the narrative that the other fruit-head was stubbornly not spelling out.

"Pnakotus," he said. "That's the mythical city in the Australian desert, where some of the so-called forbidden manuscripts were found. You really believe that's where you're from?" He paused momentarily before adding the key question: "When, exactly?"

"Two hundred million years before you were born," the other replied. "But I seem to have been removed from the twenty-first century, where I spent ten years doing research. That memory was supposed to have been erased—not just blocked off, like some fraction of a computer hard disk whose supposed deletion is merely a matter of losing its address, but actually *wiped clean* . . . reformatted. I'm not supposed to be here. I'm supposed to live in Pnakotus for another hundred million years or more, and then migrate to the Coleopteran Era, in order to avoid *all this*. The Great Race of Yith are inhabitants of eternity. Chulthu and the star-spawn simply aren't relevant to us . . . ."

There was a rustling on the bough from which Tremeloe's head was hanging down, and he saw something moving behind the head that was talking to him. He couldn't see its body, so it might have been a lizard, or a snake, or neither . . . but he could see its head, and its suddenly-gaping mouth, and its forked tongue, and its oh-so-*human* eyes . . . .

However its body was formed, it had to be big: bigger than an anaconda. For a moment, Tremeloe thought that he was about to lose the only entity in this bizarre world that was capable of holding a conversation with him—that the un-man from Pnakotus was about to be swallowed whole by the monster—but then the leaves moved. The leaves were clever, it seemed, and surprisingly strong, given their apparent delicacy. They flipped the stealthy predator into the air, and it fell, crashing through the branches, seemingly moving up and up but actually tumbling down and down . . . until it hit the boggy surface with a glutinous semi-splash.

It was invisible by then, but when Tremeloe looked at the green streaks that were visible between the crowns of his trees and its neighbors, he saw multiple movements, as if creatures akin to crocodiles were homing in on the splash, in anticipation of a feast. He could not see the crocodiles' eyes and more than he could distinguish their bodies, but he did not doubt that they would be human.

As hells go, he thought, *it's not so bad to be a human-head-fruit, given that we have such defenders to prevent our being stolen and eaten.* As a biologist, however, he knew full well that the whole purpose of a fruit is to be eaten, and thus deduced that if he really were being defended, the purpose of that defense might only be to preserve him for the preferred fructicarnivore . . . except, of course, that he was not a seed-bearing entity at all, but a mind-bearing entity, which might or might not change the logic of the situation completely.

He suddenly remembered a line that everyone at Miskatonic knew, supposedly quoted—in translation, of course—from the mysterious *Necronomicon*: "In his house at R'lyeh, dead Cthulhu lies sleeping." There was a fragment of verse, too, which ended "that is not dead which can eternal lie," but the relevant point seemed to be, if the un-man from Pnakotus could be taken seriously—which was surely necessary in a world where

madness no longer seemed to be possible—that dead
Cthulhu was no longer asleep, but awake, and that his
awakening had changed the world out of all recognition,
maybe not overnight, but rapidly . . . and purposefully.

"What did you mean," Tremeloe said to his companion, "*this is what the human race was designed to be and
to become*?"

"Just that," the other replied. "That was why Cthulhu
and the star-spawn came to Earth: to produce and shape
humankind. The raw material was rather unpromising
when they first arrived, and seemed to be headed for
insect domination, but they're patient by nature, and we
saw immediately what the results of their project would
be, at least in the shorter term. They didn't bother us—
just worked alongside us for tens of millions of years.
Ours was a parallel project, after all. They create, we
record—we're complementary species. They seemed to
be leaving us alone, just as we left them alone . . . although I always had my suspicions about the flying pol-
yps. Maybe this is what they always intended, for all of
us . . . except that *we* already know that *we* escaped to the
belated Coleopteran Era after the Polyp Armageddon.
We were only ever present in spirit in the Human Era.
We never interfered, except to observe and record—
for our own purposes, of course. Nothing was supposed
to *leak out*. Maybe that's why Cthulhu took against us,
although I can't imagine how the garbled rubbish that
found its way from our records into *Al Azif* and its various supposed translations could have interfered with
the star-spawn's plans for shaping human intelligence."

Tremeloe had only the vaguest notion of who—or
what—Cthulhu and the star-spawn were supposed to
be, even though everyone at Miskatonic knew the basics
of what was, in effect, the university's own native folk-
lore. "As I remember it," he said to his companion, "this
Cthulhu character was supposed to be a sort of giant invisible octopus, which came to Earth from another star,
and whose eventual resurrection after a long dormancy
on the ocean bed was supposed to bring about the end

of the world as we knew it. You're saying that he's real, and it's actually happened?"

"It's difficult to describe Cthulhu in terms of shape and substance," the other replied, with a calmness that now seemed rather ominous. "He's primarily a dark matter entity. You know that ninety per cent of the universe's mass is non-baryonic, right? That it interacts with your sort of matter gravitationally, but not electromagnetically? Well, Cthulhu, the star-spawn, and most of the other life-forms in the universe are essentially dark matter beings, although they can transform themselves wholly or partly into baryonic matter when conditions are right and the whim takes them. Don't ask me what counts as right or wrong in that context—we Yithians can move our minds in space and time via hyperbaryonic pathways, but we're not creative. Exactly what the relationship is between Cthulhu's kind, matter and mind, we don't know—but they're certainly interested in them, simply because they *are* creative. Why they create, and how they select their creative ends, I literally can't imagine, but the simple fact is that Cthulhu spent hundreds of millions of years shaping the ancestors of human beings, partly in order to produce the kind of intelligence that my kind can borrow—but that was only a means, not an end."

"And *this* is the end?"

"Possibly. It's just as likely to be another phase in the grand plan, requiring something more than evolution by selection. The various cultists who decided, on the basis of leaked Pnakotic lore, that Cthulhu and his hyperbaryonic kindred are gods, looked forward to his return as a holocaust of ecstasy and freedom—a time when humankind would be freed from its self-imposed moral shackles and taught new ways to revel in violence and slaughter—but that was mostly wishful thinking."

Tremeloe thought about fruit with human brains, and eagles and crocodiles with human eyes, and extrapolated that imagery to the notion of an entire ecosphere in which human intelligence had been redistributed on a profligate scale, in order that human mentality might experience all of nature red in tooth and claw in all its horror and glory . . . and the notion of a "holocaust of ecstasy and freedom" no longer seemed so alien. As an individual, he was certainly not free, nor had he tasted anything akin to ecstasy as yet, but if one tried to see the situation from without, as a single vast pattern . . . .

"Are humans like the one I used to be extinct now?" he asked. "Has the harvest of minds taken place, so that all individual personalities could be relocated?"

"Probably not," replied the un-man who should not, in his own estimation, ever have been reduced to a mere fruit. "So far as our explorers could tell, original-model humans, living in societies of various sorts, lasted long into the intellectual diaspora . . . although they soon became as opaque to our technology of possession as entities like *this*. We only have a vague idea of the interim between the era a few millennia down the line from the time that you and I recall and the advent of the Coleopteran Migration."

There really might be things, Tremeloe thought, harking back to the Necronomicon again, *that man was not meant to know. Would I be better off on a tree where I had no language in common with any of my fellow fruit? Would I be better off trying to account for the situation by the force of my own unaided intellect, rather than listening to this bizarre lunacy? Except that it can't be mere lunacy, unless there are spoiled fruit here as well as healthy ones, whose sanity is being eaten away from within by mindworms . . . .*

He quite liked the idea of mindworms, although he knew that it ought to have frightened him. His "liking" was purely aesthetic, so far as he could tell. He thought that he was capable of feeling pleasure, just as he was probably *capable* of feeling panic, but his new hormonal orchestra was obviously in a quiet mood at present, tranquilizing his brain chemistry more efficiently than the intrinsically horrific thoughts he was formulating therein were disturbing it. If that remained the case, then his situation would surely be better than bearable and more akin to a heaven than a hell.

It would probably be painful if any bat ever got to bite into him or any snake were to swallow him whole, but while he remained safe, successfully protected by the leaves that surrounded him—whose photosynthesis was presumable producing the blood that nourished his flesh and thoughts alike—and the eagles who fed upon the bats, he was feeling no physical pain and no particular mental anguish. If his fate was to suffer eternal inertia, with no idle hands for with the Devil might make work, he thought that he might be able to cope—and since it was now proven that he could be reincarnated, perhaps he had an infinite and infinitely various future to look forward to, in which he would have abundant opportunity to fly and to swim, to squirm and to walk, always knowing that even if pain and death were to arrive, however hideous they might be on a temporary basis, there would be other lives to come: times to rest and times to ponder, times to eat as well as to be eaten ....

Or was it, he wondered, merely his reduced capacity to feel such emotions as horror and terror that made the future seem so promising? Might he, in fact, be better off as a gibbering wreck, consumed from within by mindworms, his very consciousness reduced to immaterial dust?

The invisible sun was climbing behind the cloud-sheet. Eventually, it began to rain. The drops seemed tropically large, but when they splashed on his chin and his cheeks the liquid explosions were more pleasurable than painful, and the moisture was welcome. The shower didn't last long. When it stopped the cloud was much lighter and thinner. Rapid shadows occasionally fluttered across Tremeloe's face, but no bats or birds came close to him. The eagles patrolling the sky were drifting lazily in slow circles.

"I know that you never expected to be here," Tremeloe said to his companion, "and that you'd rather be snug and warm in Pnakotus, dreaming of one day becoming a beetle, but this really isn't as bad as all that, is it?"

"I don't know," the other replied, "and *not knowing* is something that my kind aren't used to. I shouldn't be here. I've borrowed humanity in the past, for research purposes, but I'm not human. I wasn't designed for this. It's not my fate. You're a prisoner of time, so you can't begin to understand how Yithians think, any more than I can begin to imagine how Cthulhu and the star-spawn might think, but believe me when I say that *this is wrong*."

Tremeloe did believe him, after a fashion, but he couldn't sympathize. If all the silly rumors about Nathaniel Wingate Peaslee were actually true, and the professor's body really had been taken over by an alien time-traveler for several years way back in the 1900s, then the alien time-travelers in question evidently didn't observe the principle of informed consent, and could hardly complain if the tables were turned on them. They had poked their noses into human affairs, and had no right to bleat that they were only reporters, not creators, as if that somehow let them off the moral hook . . . except, of course, that the human world had moved beyond good and evil now, into an era when morality no longer had hooks, or claws, or censorious staring eyes.

Tremeloe remembered the bat's eyes then and the eagle's. No, they hadn't been censorious, or even judgmental—but he felt sure that they had been more than merely avid. There had been *something* in them that was more than mere sight or mere appetite, which might well have been "beyond good and evil," but held an emotion that was by no means entirely free of dread.

I'm just a head-fruit hanging on a tree, Tremeloe thought. *The birds and the crocodiles still have animal bodies and animal hormones. Perhaps I have the best of it, in this far-from-the-best of all possible worlds . . . but if the cycle goes on forever, I'll have it again and again and again*, ad infinitum.

Such was the comforting positive nature of that thought that he did not notice that the sky had become even bluer until the murmur of mostly incomprehensible voices altered him to the fact that something was going on.

At first, he thought that the cloud was simply clear-

ing, its remnants evaporated by the hot tropical sun that
was ascending towards its zenith—but then he saw the
bloated sun drift free of the brilliant white clouds to take
possession of the sky, and saw that its flames were red-
der and angrier than he had ever known them before.

It really is much later than either of us thought, he said
to himself, but then doubted the judgment, as he realized that the excessive blueness of the unclouded sky
and the excessive redness of the sun were both optical
illusions, caused by the fact that the sky was full of *creatures*; creatures that were not quite invisible, although
they had to be made of something other than the kind
of matter with which he was familiar: something so alien
as to be almost beyond perception. The big birds were
flying far away with rapid wing-beats.

Tremeloe was conscious of gravity now, although it
did not seem to be tugging him in the direction of the
green earth, but in the direction of the alien sky, whose
no-longer-kindly light hid all the multitudinous stars
of the incredibly, unimaginably vast universe within its
dazzling glory. "What are they?" he said, his voice little
more than a whisper.

The other heard him. "Star-spawn," he replied. "If
you could see them, the impression of shape they'd give
you would be much like Cthulhu's, on a much smaller
scale: vaguely cephalopodan, with a scaly tegument and
oddly tiny wings that shouldn't work but do."

Somehow, Tremeloe grasped what the other meant
by "the impression of shape." The star-spawn had mass,
but their matter was utterly alien, obedient to different
rules of dimension and form, whose relationship with
the kind of matter making up his own flesh and that of
the tree of which he was now a part, was essentially mysterious . . . and far, far beyond mere matters of good and
evil.

The raptors were nowhere to be seen now. If their
existential role was to protect the trees of human life
and their heady harvest from giant bats, they had played
their allotted parts and made their exit until the next
day.

But it's not yet noon, Tremeloe thought, wishing perversely that he were capable of terror, in order that he might feel a little more human, a little more himself. *Even mayflies live for a day*.

He had been a biologist, though, during his larval stage, and he knew that mayflies actually lived much longer than a day, even though their imago stage was a brief airborne climax to a life spent wallowing in mud. He knew, too, that from a detached scientific viewpoint, every mayfly had a living ancestry that stretched back through their larval stages and generation after generation of evolving living creatures, all the way back to some primordial protoplasmic blob, or some not-yet-living helical carbonic thread. Only its climax was ephemeral, and by comparison with the billion years it had taken to produce the fly, there was hardly any difference at all between an hour, a day, and fifty-six years.

Beyond good and evil, Tremeloe knew, human philosophers held that there ought to be a world in which good would no longer be refined by the absence of evil—of pain, of hunger, of thirst, and so on—but in positive terms, in terms of an active, experienced good whose mere absence would replace outdated redundant evil. But the good and evil that he had now moved beyond wasn't human good and evil at all, and the speculations of human philosophers were only relevant to it insofar as they had helped to shape his own consciousness, his own expectations, and his own intellectual flavor.

The good that the world embraced now was something essentially alien, and neither Tremeloe nor any of his fellow human fruit—nor even the reluctant Yithian refugee from legendary Pnatokus—had any words or the slightest imagination with which to describe or get to grips with it.

As the star-spawn descended to enjoy the crop that had been hundreds of millions of years in the creative shaping, and mere hours in the final ripening, Tremeloe still had time enough to realize that his new hormonal orchestra, quiet until now, was not unequipped with sensations akin to horror and terror, agony and fury . . . and to appreciate the irony of the fact that those sensations too, just as much as his thoughts, his memories and his knowledge and consciousness of history and progress, of space and time, of matter and light, and most especially of strangeness, were all elements of a nutritive and gustatory experience that something so very like him as to be near-identical would have to relive time and time again, from the wrong perspective, if not *ad infinitum*, then at least until the star-spawn had finally had their fill, and had abandoned earth to the long-delayed Coleopteran Era.

The star-spawn fed, like patient gourmets, and the blazing sun moved on in its patient arc, heading for a sunset that Tremeloe would not see . . . this time. He ran the gamut of his new emotions, reacting with his thoughts and his imagination as best he could, even though he wished, resentfully, that he was disinclined to do anything different.

There was a long future still ahead of him, but even that would merely be an eye-blink in the history of the New Eden that earth had become. Eventually, the multitentacled monsters of dark matter would pass on to pastures new, nature would reassert itself, and the primal wilderness would return.

The only thing we were ever able to deduce about the mind of the God who was in charge of Creation before Cthulhu arrived, Tremeloe reflected, with obliging but slightly piquant serenity, as the matter comprising his delectable freshness was chewed, absorbed, and digested without his ever quite losing consciousness, *is that he must have an inordinate fondness for beetles. And perhaps he had good taste.*

VASTATION

Laird Barron

When I was six, I discovered a terrible truth: I was the only human being on the planet. I was the seed and the sower and I made myself several seconds from the event horizon at the end of time—at the x before time began. Indeed, there were six billion other carbon-based sentient life forms moiling in the earth, but none of them were the real McCoy. *I'm* the real McCoy. The rest? Cardboard props, marionettes, grist for the mill. After I made me, I crushed the mold under my heel.

When I was six million, after the undying dreamers shuddered and woke and the mother continent rose from the warm, shallow sea and the celestial lights flickered into an alignment that cooked far-flung planets and turned our own skies red as the bloody seas themselves, I was, exiled-potentate status notwithstanding, as a flea.

Before the revelation of flea-ishness, I came to think of myself as a god with a little G. Pontiff Sacrus was known as Ted in those days. I called him Liberace—he was so soft and effete, and his costumes . . . I think he was going for the Fat Elvis look, but no way was I going to dignify my favorite buffoon by comparing him to incomparable E.

Ted was a homicidal maniac. He'd heard the whispers from the vaults of the Undying City that eventually made mush of his sensibilities. He was the sucker they, my pals and acolytes, convinced to carry out the coup.

218

Ted shot me with a Holland & Holland .50; blasted two slugs, each the size and heft of a lead-filled cigar, through my chest. Such bullets drop charging elephants in their tracks, open them up like a sack of rice beneath a machete. Those bullets exploded me and sawed the bed in half. Sheets burst into flame and started a fire that eventually burned a good deal of Chicago to the ground.

Bessy got a bum rap.

In sleep, I am reborn. Flesh peels from the bones and is carried at tachyon velocity toward the center of the universe. I travel backward or forward along my personal axis, never straying from the simple line—either because that's the only way time travel works, or because I lack the balls to slingshot into a future lest it turn out to be a day prior to my departure.

As much as I appreciate Zen philosophy, my concentrated mind resembles nothing of perfect, still water, nor the blankness of the moon. When I dream, my brain is suspended in a case of illimitable darkness. The gears do not require light to mesh teeth in teeth, nor the circuits to chain algorithms into sine waves of pure calculation.

In that darkness, I am the hammer, the Emperor of Ice Cream's herald, the polyglot who masticates hidden dialects—the old tongues that die when the last extant son of antiquity is assimilated by a more powerful tribe. I am the eater of words and my humor is to be feared. I am the worm that has turned and I go in and out of the irradiated skulls of dead planets, a writhing, slithering worm that hooks the planets of our system together like beads on a string. When all is synchronized and the time comes to resurface, a pinhole penetrates the endless blackness; it dilates and I am purged into a howling white waste. I scream, wet and angry as a newborn until the crooked framework of material reality absorbs the whiteness and shapes itself around me.

My artificial wife is unnerved at how I sleep. I sleep, smiling, eyes bright as glass. The left eye swims with yellow milk. The pupil is a distorted black star that matches its immense, cosmic twin, the portal to the blackest of hells. That cosmic hole is easily a trillion magnitudes larger than Sol. Astronomers named it Ur-Nyctos. They recorded the black hole via X-ray cameras and the process of elimination—it displaces light of nearly inconceivable dimensions; a spiral arm of dark matter that inches ever nearer. It will get around to us, sooner or later. We'll be long gone by then, scooped up into the slavering maw of functionally insensate apex predators, or absorbed into the folds of the great old inheritors of the Earth who revel and destroy, and scarcely notice puny us at all. Or, most likely, we'll be extinct from war, plague, or ennui. We mortal fleas.

The milkman used to come by in a yellow box van, although I seldom saw him. He left the milk bottles on the step. The bottles shone and I imagined them as Simic said, glowing in the lowest circle of hell. I imagined them in Roman catapults fired over the ramparts of some burning city of old Carthage, imagined one smashing in the skull of my manager and me sucking the last drops through the jagged red remnants while flies gathered.

I think the milkman fucked my wife, the fake one, but that might've been my imagination. It works in mysterious ways; sometimes it works at cross purposes to my design. I gave up fucking my wife, I'm not sure when. Somebody had to do it. Better him than me.

The flagellants march past the stoop of my crumbling home every day at teatime. We don't observe teatime here in the next to last extant Stateside bubble-domed metropolis. Nonetheless, my artificial wifey makes a pot of green tea and I take it on the steps and watch the flagellants lurch past, single file, slapping themselves about the shoulders with belts studded with nails and screws and the spiny hooks of octopi. They croak a dirge copped from ancient tablets some anthropologists found and promptly went mad and that madness eagerly spread and insinuated itself in the brainboxes of billions. They fancy themselves Openers of the Way, and a red snail track follows them like the train of a skirt made of meat. Dogs skulk along at the rear, snuffling and licking at the blood. Fleas rise in black clouds from their slicked and matted fur.

I smoke with my tea. I exhale fire upon the descending flea host and most scatter, although a few persist, a few survive and attach. I scratch at the biting little bastards crawling beneath the collar of my shirt. They establish beachheads in the cuffs of my trousers, my socks. And damn me if I can find them; they're too small to see and that's a good metaphor for how the Old Ones react to humanity. More on that anon, as the bards say.

At night I hunch before the bedroom mirror and stroke bumps and welts. It hurts, but I've grown to like it.

I killed a potter in Crete in the summer of 45 BC. I murdered his family as well. I'd been sent by Rome to do just that. No one gave a reason. No one ever gave reasons, just names, locations, and sometimes a preferred method. They paid me in silver that I squandered most recklessly on games of chance and whores. Between tasks, I remained a reliable drunk. I contracted a painful, wasting disease from the whores of Athens. My sunset years were painful.

The potter lived in the foothills in a modest villa. He grew grapes and olives, which his children tended. His goats were fat and his table settings much finer than one might expect. His wife and daughter were too lovely for a man of such humble station and so I understood him to be an exiled prince whose reckoning had come. I approached him to commission a set of vases for my master. We had dinner and wine. Afterward, we lounged in the shade of his porch and mused about the state of the so-called Republic, which in those days was prosperous.

The sun lowered and flattened into a bloody line, a scored vein delineating the vast black shell of the land. When the potter squatted to demonstrate an intricacy of a mechanism of his spinning wheel, I raised a short, stout plank and swung it edgewise across the base of his skull. His arms fell to his sides and he pitched facedown. Then I killed the wife and the daughter who cowered inside the villa between rows of the potter's fine oversized vases I'd pretended to inspect. Then the baby in the wicker crib, because to leave it to starvation would've been monstrous.

Two of the potter's three sons were very young and the only trouble they presented was tracking them down in a field on the hillside. Only the eldest, a stripling youth of thirteen or fourteen, fought back. He sprang from the shadows near the well and we struggled for a few moments. Eventually, I choked him until he became limp in my arms. I threw him down the well. Full darkness was upon the land, so I slept in the potter's bed. The youth at the bottom of the well moaned weakly throughout the evening and my dreams were strange. I dreamed of a hole in the stars and an angry hum that echoed from its depths. I dreamed someone scuttled on all fours across the clay tiles of the roof, back and forth, whining like a fly that wanted in. Back. And Forth. Occasionally, the dark figure spied upon my restless self through a crack in the ceiling.

The next morning, I looted what valuables I could from the house. During my explorations, I discovered a barred door behind a rack of jars and pots. On the other side was a tiny cell full of scrolls. These scrolls were scriven with astronomical diagrams and writing I couldn't decipher. The walls were thick stone and a plug of wood was inset at eye level. I worked the cork free, amazed at the soft, red light that spilled forth. I finally summoned the courage to press my eye against the peephole.

I suspect if a doctor were to give me a CAT scan, to follow the optic nerve deep into its fleshy backstop, he'd see the blood red peephole imprinted in my cerebral cortex, and through the hole, Darkness, the quaking mass at the center of everything where a sonorous wheedling choir of strings and lutes, flutes and cymbals crashes and shrieks and echoes from the abyss, the foot of the throne of an idiot god. The potter had certainly been a man of many facets.

I set out for the port and passage back to my beloved

Rome. Many birds gathered in the yard. Later, in the city, my old associates seemed surprised to see me.

Semaphore. Soliloquy. Solipsism. That's a trinity a man can get behind. The wife never understood me, and the first A.I. model wasn't any great shakes either. Oh, Wife 2.0 said all the right things. She was soft and her hair smelled nice, and her programming allowed for realistic reactions to my eccentricities. Wife 2.0 listened *too* much, had been programmed to receive. She got weird; started hiding from me when I returned home, and eventually hanged herself in the linen closet. That's when they revealed her as a replica of the girl I'd first met in Lincoln Park long ago. Unbeknownst to me, that girl passed away from a brain embolism one summer night while we vacationed in the Bahamas, and They, my past and future pals and acolytes and current dilettante sycophants of those who rule the Undying City, slipped her replacement under the covers while I snored. Who the hell knows what series of android spouse I'm up to now.

I killed most of my friends and those that remain don't listen and never have. The only one left is my cat Softy-Cuddles. Cat version one million and one, I suspect. The recent iterations are black. Softy-Cuddles wasn't always a Halloween cat (or a self-replicating cloud of nano-bots), though, he used to be milk white. Could be, I sliced the milkman's throat and stole his cat. In any event, I found scores of pictures of both varieties, and me petting them, in a rusty King Kong lunchbox some version of me buried near the—what else?—birdbath in the back yard. When I riffle that stack of photos it creates a disturbing optical effect.

The cat is the only thing I've ever truly loved because he's the only being I'm convinced doesn't possess ulterior motives. I'll miss the little sucker when I'm gone, nano-cloud or not.

During the Dark Ages, I spent twenty-nine years in a prison cell beneath a castle in the Byzantine Empire. Poetic justice, perhaps. It was a witchcraft rap—not true, by any means. The truth was infinitely more complicated, as I've amply demonstrated thus far. The government kept me alive because that's what governments do when they encounter such anomalous persons as myself. In latter epochs, my type are termed "materials." It wouldn't do to slaughter me out of hand; nonetheless, I couldn't be allowed to roam free. So down the rabbit hole I went.

No human voice spoke my name. I shit in a hole in the corner of the cell. Food and drink was lowered in a basket, and occasionally a candle, ink, quill and parchment. The world above was changing. They solicited answers to questions an Information Age mind would find anachronistic. There were questions about astronomy and quantum physics and things that go bump in the night. In reply, I scrawled crude pictures and dirty limericks. Incidentally, it was likely some highly advanced iteration of lonely old me that devised the questions and came tripping back through the cosmic cathode to plague myself. One day (or night) they bricked over the distant mouth of my pit. How my bells jangled then, how my laughter echoed from the rugged walls. For the love of God!

Time well spent. I got right with the universe, which meant I got right with its chief tenant: me. One achieves a certain equilibrium when one lives in a lightless pit, accompanied by the squeak and rustle of vermin and the slow drip of water from rock. The rats carried fleas and the fleas feasted upon me before they expired, before I rubbed out their puny existences. But these tiny devils had their banquet—while I drowsed, they sucked my blood, drowned and curdled in tears of my glazed eyes. And the flies.

Depending upon who I'm talking to, and when, the notion of re-growing lost limbs and organs, of reorganizing basic genetic matrices to build a better mousetrap, a better *mouse*, will sound fantastical or fantastically tedious. Due to the circumstances of my misspent youth, I evolved outside the mainstream, avoided the great and relentless campaigns to homogenize and balance every unique snowflake into a singular aesthetic. No clone mills for me, no thought rehabilitation. I come by my punctuated equilibrium honestly. I'm the amphibian that finally crawled ashore and grew roots, irradiated by the light of a dark star.

I pushed my best high school bud off the Hoover Dam. Don't even recall why. Maybe we were competing for the girl who became my wife. My pal was a smooth operator. I could dial him up and ask his quantum self for the details, but I won't. I've only so many hands, so many processes to run at once, and really, it's more fun not knowing. There are so few secrets left in the universe.

This I do recall: when I pushed him over the brink, he flailed momentarily, then spread his arms and caught an updraft. He twirled in the clouds of steam and spray, twisting like a leaf until he disappeared. Maybe he actually made it. We hadn't perfected molecular modification, however. We hadn't even gotten very far with grafts. So I think he went into the drink, went straight to the bottom. Sometimes I wonder if he'd ever thought of sending me hurtling to a similar fate. I have this nagging suspicion I only beat him to the punch.

The heralds of the Old Ones came calling before the time of the terrible lizards, or in the far-flung impossible future while Man languished in the throes of his first and last true utopian era. Perspective; relativity. Don't let the laws of physics fool you into believing she's an open book. She's got a *whole* other side.

Maybe the Old Ones sent them, maybe the pod people acted on their own. Either way, baby, it was night of the living dead, except exponentially worse since it was, well, real. Congruent to linear space time (what a laugh that theory was) Chinese scientists tripped backward to play games with a supercollider they'd built on Io while Earth was still a hot plate for protoplasmic glop. Wrap your mind around that. The idiots were fucking with making a pocket universe, some bizarre method to cheat relativity and cook up FTL travel. Yeah, well, just like any disaster movie ever filmed, something went haywire and there was an implosion. What was left of the moon zipped into Jupiter's gravity well, snuffed like spit on a griddle. A half-million researchers, soldiers, and support personnel went along for the ride.

Meanwhile, one of the space stations arrayed in the sector managed to escape orbit and send a distress call. Much later, we learned the poor saps had briefly generated their pocket universe, and before it went kablooey, they were exposed to peculiar extra-dimensional forces, which activated certain genetic codes buried in particular sectors of sentient life. So the original invaders were actually regular Joe Six-Packs who got transmogrified into yeasty, fungoid entities.

The rescue team brought the survivors to the Colonies. Pretty soon the Colonies went to the Dark. We called the hostiles Pod People, Mushrooms, Hollow Men, The Fungus Among Us, etc, etc. The enemy resembled us. This is because they *were* us in every fundamental aspect except for the minor details of being hollow as chocolate bunnies, breeding via slime attack and sporination, and that they were hand puppets for an alien intellect that in turn venerated The Old Ones who sloth and sleep (and dream) between galaxies when the stars are right. Oh, and "hollow" and "empty" are more metaphorical than useful: burn a hole in a Pod Person with a laser and a thick, oily blackness spewed forth and made goo of any hapless organics in its path.

The Mushroom Man mission? To liquefy our insides and suck them up like a kid slobbering on a milkshake, and pack our brains in cylinders and ship them to Pluto for R&D. The ones they didn't liquefy or dissect joined their happy and rapidly multiplying family. Good times, good times.

I was the muckety-muck of the Territorial Intelligence Ministry. I was higher than God, watching over the human race from my enclave in the Pyrenees. But don't blame me; a whole slew of security redundancies didn't do squat in the face of an invasion that had been in the planning stages before men came down from the trees. Game, set, and match. Okay, that's an exaggeration. Nonetheless, I think a millennium to repopulate and rebuild civilization qualifies as a reset at least. I came into contact with them shortly after they infiltrated the Pyrenees compound. My second-in-command, Jeff, and I were going over the daily feed, which was always a horror show. The things happening in the metropolises were beyond awful. Funny the intuitive leap the brain makes. My senses were heightened, but even that failed to pierce the veil of the Dark. On a hunch, mid-sentence, I crushed Jeff's forehead with a moon rock I used as a paper weight. Damned if there wasn't a gusher of tar from that eggshell crack. Not a wise move on my part—that shit splattered over half the staff sitting at the table and ate them alive. I regenerated faster than it dissolved my flesh and that kept me functional for a few minutes. Oh skippy day.

A half dozen security guards sauntered in and siphoned the innards from the remainder of my colleagues in an orgy of spasms and gurgles. I zapped several of the baddies before the others got hold and sucked my body dry.

I'd jumped into a custodian named Hank who worked on the other side of the complex, however, and all those bastards got was a lifeless sack of meat. I went underground, pissed and scared. Organizing the resistance was personal. It was on.

We (us humans, so-called) won in the end. Rope-a-dope!

Once most of us were wiped from existence, the invaders did what any plague does after killing the host—it went dormant. Me and a few of the boys emerged from our bunkers and set fire to the house. We brought the old orbital batteries online and nuked every major city on the planet. We also nuked our secret bunkers, exterminating the human survivors. Killing off the military team that had accompanied me to the surface was regrettable—I'd raised every one of them from infancy.

I could've eliminated the whole battalion from the control room with an empathic pulse, but that seemed cowardly. I stalked them through the dusty labyrinths, and killed them squad by squad. Not pretty, although I'm certain most of my comrades were proud to go down fighting. They never knew it was me who did them dirt: I configured myself into hideous archetypes from every legend I could dream up.

None of them had a noggin full of tar, either. I checked carefully.

I went into stasis until the nuclear bloom faded and the ozone layer regenerated. Like Noah, I'd saved two of everything in the DNA repository vault inside the honeycombed walls of Mare Imbrium. The machines mass produced *in vitro* bugs, babies, and baby animals with such efficiency, Terra went from zero to overpopulation within three centuries.

The scientists and poets and sci-fi writers alike were all proved correct: I didn't need to reproduce rats or cockroaches. They'd done just fine.

The layers of space and time are infinite; I've mastered roughly a third of them. What's done can't be undone, nor would I dream of trying; nonetheless, it's impossible to resist all temptation. Occasionally, I materialize next to Chief Science Officer Hu Wang while he's showering, or squatting on the commode, or masturbating in his bunk, and say howdy in Cantonese, which he doesn't comprehend very well. I ask him compromising questions such as, how does it feel to know you're going to destroy the human race in just a few hours? Did your wife really leave you for a more popular scientist?

Other times, I find him in his village when he's five or six and playing in the mud. I'm the white devil who appears and whispers that he'll grow into a moderately respected bureaucrat, be awarded a plum black ops research project, and be eaten alive by intergalactic slime mold. And everyone will hate him—including his ex-wife and her lesbian lover. Until they're absorbed by the semi-infinite, that is.

I have similar talks with Genghis Khan, Billie Jean King, Elvis (usually during his final sitdown), and George Bush Jr. Don't tell anyone, but I even visit myself, that previous iteration who spent three decades rotting in a deep, dark hole. I sit on the rim of his pit and smoke a fat one and whisper the highlights of *The Cask of Amontillado* while he screams and laughs. I've never actually decided to speak with him. Perhaps someday.

Dystopian days again. That fiasco with the creatures from Dimension X was just the warm-up match. Whilst depopulating Terra, our enemies were busy laying the groundwork for the return to primacy of their dread gods. Less than a millennium passed and the stars changed. The mother continent rose from primordial muck and its rulers and their servitors took over the regions they desired and we humans got the scraps.

It didn't even amount to a shooting war—occasionally one or another cephalopodan monstrosity lumbered forth from the slimy sea and hoovered up a hundred thousand from the crowded tenements beneath an atmospheric dome or conculcated another half billion of them to jelly. The Old Ones hooted and cavorted, and colors not meant to be seen by human eyes drove whole continental populations to suicide or catatonia. Numerous regions of the planet became even more polluted and inhospitable to carbon-based life. But this behavior signified nothing of malice; it was an afterthought. Notable landmarks survived in defiance of conventional Hollywood Armageddon logic—New York, Paris, Tokyo. What kind of monsters eat Yokohama and leave Tokyo standing? There wasn't a damned thing mankind could do to affect these shambling beings who exist partially in extra-dimensional vaults of space-time. The Old Ones didn't give a rat's ass about our nukes, our neutron bombs, our anthrax, our existence in general.

Eventually, we did what men do best and aimed our fear and rage at one another. The pogroms were a riot, literally. I slept through most of them. My approval rating was in the toilet; a lot of my constituent children plotted to draw and quarter their Dear Leader, their All Father, despite the fact the masses had everything. *Everything* except what they most desired—the end of the Occupation. I was a god-emperor who didn't measure up to the real thing lurching along the horizon two hundred stories high.

Still, you'd think superpowers and the quenching of material hunger might suffice. Wrongo. Sure, sure, everybody went bonkers for molecular modifications when the technology arrived on the scene. It was my booboo even to drop a hint regarding that avenue of scientific inquiry—and no, I'm not an egghead. Stick around long enough to watch civilization go through the rinse cycle and you start to look smarter than you really are.

On one of my frequent jaunts to ye olden times I attended a yacht party thrown by Caligula. Cal didn't make an appearance; he'd gone with a party of visiting senators to have an orgy at the altar of Artemis. I missed the little punk. I was drunk as a lord and chatting up some prime Macedonian honeys, when one of Cal's pet mathematicians started holding forth primitive astrophysical theories I'd seen debunked in more lifetimes than I care to count. One argument led to another and the next thing I knew, me and Prof Toga are hanging our sandals over the stern and I'm trying to explain, via my own admittedly crude understanding, the basics of molecular biology and how nanobots are the wave of the future.

Ha! We know how that turned out, don't we? The average schmuck acquired the ability to modify his biological settings with the flip of a mental switch. Everybody fooled around with sprouting extra arms and legs, bat wings and gigantic penises, and in general ran amok. A few even joined forces and blew themselves up large enough to take on our overlords of non-Euclidian properties. Imagine a Macy's Thanksgiving Day float filled to the stem with blood. Then imagine that float in the grip of a flabby, squamous set of claws or an enveloping tentacle—and a big, convulsive squeeze. Not pretty.

Like fries with a burger, this new craze also conferred

a limited form of immortality. I say limited because hacking each other to bits, drinking each other's blood, or committing thrill kills in a million different ways remained a game ender. The other drawback was that fucking around with one's DNA also seemed to make Swiss cheese of one's brain. So, a good percentage of humanity went to work on their brothers and sisters hammer and tong, tooth and claw, in the Mother of All Wars, while an equal number swapped around their primal matter so much they gradually converted themselves to blithering masses of effluvium and drifted away or were rendered unto ooze that returned to the brine.

It was a big old mess, and as I said, arguably my fault. A few of my closest, and only, friends (collaborators with the extra-dimensional monster set) got together and decided to put me out of my misery—for the sake of all concerned, which was everyone in the known universe, except me. The sneaky bastards crept into the past and blasted me while I lay comatose from a semi-lethal cocktail of booze, drugs, and guilt. That's where you, or me, came in. I mean, no matter who you are, you're really me, in drag or out.

Afterward, the gang held a private wake that lasted nearly a month. There were lovely eulogies and good booze and a surprising measure of crocodile (better than nothing!) grief. I was impressed and even a little touched.

For a couple thousand years I played dead. And once bored with my private version of Paradise Lost, I reorganized myself into material form and began a comeback that involved a centuries-long campaign of terror through proxy. I had a hell of a time tracking down my erstwhile comrades. Those who'd irritated me most, I kept trapped in perpetual stasis. Mine is the First Power, and to this day I, or one of my ever exponentially replicating selves, revive a traitor on occasions that I'm in a pissy mood and torment him or her in diabolical ways I've perfected in past, present, and future.

Now, it amuses me to walk among mortals in disguise of a fellow commoner. I also feel a hell of a lot safer—

the Old Ones sometimes rouse from their obliviousness to humanity and send questing tendrils to identify and extract those who excite their obscene, yet unknowable interest.

I'm going to wait them out.

Seven or eight of us still celebrate the Fourth of July despite the fact the United States is of no more modern relevance than cave paintings by hominids. Specialist historians and sentimental fools such as me are the only ones who care.   .

This year, Pontiff Sacrus, Lord High Necromancer, bought me a hot dog, heavy on the mustard, from an actual human vendor, and we sat on a park bench. Fireworks cracked over the lake. Small red and green paper lanterns bobbed on the water. The lanterns were dogs and cats and Paul Revere and his horse. The city had strung wires along the thoroughfares. American flags chattered in a stiffening breeze. I breathed in the smoke and petted Softy-Cuddles who'd appeared from no-where to settle in my lap.

The pogroms were finished. Pontiff Sacrus had over-seen the Stonehenge Massacre that spring and there weren't any further executions scheduled. According to my calculations, exactly six hundred and sixty-seven un-modified Homo sapiens remained extant, although none were aware the majority of the billions who populated the planet were replicants, androids, and remote-operated clones. Pontiff Sacrus's purge squads had eradicated the changelings and shifters and the gene-splicers and any related medical doctors who might conspire to reintro-duce that most diabolical technology. He'd reversed the Singularity and lobotomized the once nigh- universal A.I. Super job, pontiff old bean. He purported himself to be the High Priest of the Undying Ones, but they ig-nored him pretty much the same as every priest of every denomination has ever been ignored by his deity.

Now, the pontiff has been around for ages and ages. He's kept himself ticking by the liberal application of nano-enhanced elixirs, molecular tomfoolery, and outdated cloning tech. Probably the only remaining shred of his humanity lies within that mystical force that animates us monkeys. His is the face of a gargoyle bust or the most goddamned beautiful, dick-stiffening angel ever to walk the earth. He's moody, like me. That's to be expected, since on the molecular level he is me. Right?

Man oh man, was he shocked when I appeared in a puff of sulfurous smoke after all these eons. I'm a legend; a boogeyman that got assimilated by pop culture and shat out, forgotten by the masses. *Every* devil is forgotten once a society falls far enough..But Pontiff Sacrus remembered. His fear rushed through him like fire; he smelled as if he were burning right there beside me on the bench. He finally grasped that it was I who'd tormented and slain, one by one, our inner circle.

We watched the fireworks, and when the show wound down, I told him I'd decided to reach back and erase his entire ancestry from the space-time continuum. The honorable High Necromancer would cease to exist. The spectacle of the god's anguish thrilled me in ways I hadn't anticipated. Naturally, I never planned actually to nullify his existence. Instead, I made him gaze into the hell of my left eye. He shrieked as I manually severed his personal timeline at the culmination of the fireworks display and set it for continual loop, with a delay at the final juncture so he might fraternize with his accumulating selves before the big rewind.

Last I checked, the crowd of Sacruses has overflowed the park. He'll be/is a city of living nerves, each thread shrieking for eternity. My kind of music.

Crete, 45 B.C., again. The universe is a cell. I travel by osmosis, randomly, to and fro betwixt the poles that fuse everything. It's dark but for a candle within the potter's house. The blood odor is thick. My prior self snores within, sleeping the sleep of the damned. I alight upon the slanted roof; I peep through chinks and spy our restless form in the shadows. He whimpers.

Because I'm bored to tears with my existence, and just to see what will happen, I slip down through the cracks and smother him. His eyes snap open near the end. They shine with blind energy and his bowels release, and he is finished. Then I toss his corpse into the well, and return to the bed and fall asleep in his place.

I've gone back a hundred times to perpetrate the same self-murder. I've sat upon the hillside and watched with detached horror as a dozen of my selves scrabble across the roof like ungainly crows, and one by one enter the house to do the dirty deed, then file in and out, to and from the well like a stream of ants. This changes nothing. The problem is, the universe is constantly in motion. The universe stretches to a smear and cycles like a Slinky reversing through its own spine. No matter what I do, stuff keeps happening in an uninterruptable stream.

How I wish the Pod People could give me a hand, help me explore self annihilation or ultimate enlightenment, which I'm certain are one and the same. Alas, their alien intellect, a fungal strain that resists the vagaries of vacuum, light and dark, heat and cold, remains supremely inscrutable. That goes double for their gargantuan masters. Like me, the fungal tribe and their monster gods (and ours?) exist at all points south of the present. It's enough to drive a man insane.

After epochs that rival the reign of the dinosaurs, the stars are no longer right. Yesterday the black continent and its black house sank beneath the sallow, poison waves and the Old Ones dream again in the dread majesty of undeath. I wonder how long it will be before the dregs of humanity ventures from the bubble-domed metropolises it's known for ages beyond reckoning. The machines are breaking down and they need them since after the pogroms all bio modifications were purged. Just soft, weak homo sapiens as God intended. The population is critically low, and what with all those generations of inbreeding and resultant infertility I don't predict a bounce back this time. Another generation or two and it'll be over. Enter (again) the rats, the cockroaches and the super beetles.

I sigh. I'm shaving. Wife is in the kitchen chopping

onions while the tiny black-and-white television broadcasts a cooking show. The morning sky is the color of
burnt iron. If I concentrate, I can hear, yet hundreds of
millions of light years off, the throb and growl of Ur-
Nyctos as it devours strings of matter like a kid sucking
up grandma's pasta.

I stare at my freakish eyeball, gaze into the distorted
pupil until it expands and fills the mirror, fills my brain
and I'm rushing through vacuum. Wide awake and so
far at such speed I flatten into a subatomic contrail. That
grand cosmic maw, that eater of galaxies, possesses suf-
ficient gravitational force to rend the fabric of space and
time, to obliterate reality, and in I go, bursting into tril-
lions of minute particles, quadrillions of whining fleas,
consumed. Nanoseconds later, I understand everything
there is to understand. Reduced to my "essential saltes"
as it were, I'm the prime mover seed that gets sown after
the heat death of the universe when the ouroboros swal-
lows itself and the cycle begins anew with a big bang.

Meanwhile, back on Earth in the bathroom of the
shabby efficiency flat, my body teeters before the mirror. Lacking my primal ichor and animating force that
fueled the quasi-immortal regeneration of cells that in
turn thwarted the perfect pathogen, the latent mutant
gene of the Pod People activates and transmogrifies the
good old human me into one of Them. Probably the last
self-willed fungus standing—but not for long; this shit
does indeed spread like wildfire. My former guts, gan-
glion, reproductive organs, and whatnot, dissolve into a
thick, black stew while my former brain contracts and
fossilizes to the approximate size of a walnut and adopts
an entirely new set of operating principles.

Doubtless, it has a plan for the world. May it and my
android wife be very happy together. I hope they remember to feed the cat.

NOTHING PERSONAL

Richard A. Lupoff

The flashes on the surface of Yuggoth were so brilliant that they shorted out every bit of electronic equipment on *Beijing 11-11*. Dr. Chen Jing-quo was the sole occupant of the observation satellite at the time, and her own eyes were spared only through a lucky break. She had been showering when the flashes occurred, sealed off from the outer universe.

Still, she had a devil of a time extricating herself from the shower-stall, now that the fractional horsepower motor that rolled the door open and shut as well as the touch-sensitive keypad that controlled the motor were dead.

Dr. Chen found the manual override control by touch, got the door open, slipped into a jumpsuit and made her way to one of *Beijing 11-11's* visual ports. The series of flashes had caused the ports' photosensitive intracoating to darken dramatically. Dr. Chen stared at Yuggoth, a pulsing, oblate globe that filled the sky above *Beijing 11-11*. She studied the planet's surface and the flashes briefly; she intuited that the observatory's electron telescopes would be useless. Fortunately the station was also fitted with an array of old-style optical telescopes. Dr. Chen made her way to one of these, a 500-millimeter Zeiss-Asahi model, and trained it upon the site of the most recent flashes.

The flashes continued. Dr. Chen, at first alarmed and

confused by the unexpected events, was regaining her calm. She focused the Zeiss-Asahi on the apparent epicenter of the flashes and was rewarded by the sight of another flash. This time she observed a bright dot moving away from the surface of the planet. It flashed away into the black trans-Neptunian space, toward the tiny, distant jewel that she knew was the sun. She followed the brilliant dot as long as she could. When it disappeared from sight she set about repairing the assaulted electronics of *Beijing 11-11*.

As soon as she could she set up a hyper-lightspeed link with her superiors on earth's moon. As she did, she trained one of *Beijing 11-11's* powerful electron telescopes on Yuggoth's surface. She knew the planet's cities as well as—no, better than—she knew the cities of Earth. She had been born on the mother world but her recollections of the planet were only the vague images of a small child. Colors and sounds and odors. The feeling of her mother's arms, a flavor that she thought was that of her mother's milk. But she could not be sure.

She had been selected as a toddler and transported to the moon for two decades of training. She had emerged at the top of her class, triumphing in the final competitive examinations over a thousand young men and women who competed for positions in the world's ongoing scientific enterprises.

She had worked with joyous dedication on *Beijing 11-11* for the past decade, observing the enigmatic activities on Yuggoth. That huge planet and its four satellites, Nithan, Zaman, Thog, and Thok, rolled eternally in a counterplanar orbit, crossing the plane of the solar ecliptic only once in a thousand years. No wonder it had gone undiscovered for so long, for earthbound planetary astronomers had long concentrated their studies on the multi-billion-mile disk that surrounded Sol, containing the four rocky planets, the four gas giants, the asteroids and plutoids and the countless meteors and comets.

Barely a century ago, Yuggoth and its moons had actually crossed the plane of the ecliptic, and thus it had been detected at last. The discovery of a new major planet had sent shockwaves through the scientific community of earth. Probes had landed on the major solid bodies of the solar system, the four rock planets and the solid moons of the four gas giants. The variety of worlds was incredible. There were ice-covered bodies, volcanoes, nitrogen seas, mountain ranges and deserts and canyon-like beds of ancient rivers, long run dry.

Above all, there was life and the evidence of past life. Exobiologists on earth had long given hope of such discoveries. Their mantra: *where life can exist, it does!* The flaw in their argument lay in the fact that they had only a single model from which to draw their conclusion. True, life flourished in the most astonishing of environments, in water close to boiling, in fissures deep within the earth, on ocean floors where pressure reached tons per square centimeter and where neither sunlight nor oxygen could be detected. But it was possible—it was vigorously debated—that life had originated but once upon earth, and that all organisms, however varied their natures and locales, were descended from a single ancestor.

It took the exploration of dozens of moons to find jungles and prairies, natural gardens of unimaginable colors and forms, schools of swimming things that were surely not fish, and flocks of flying things that were anything but birds.

But no people. Not merely no humans like those whose robot explorers first landed on Callisto and Mimas, Miranda and Proteus and Galatea and all the others. The people of Earth both longed for and feared the discovery of alien intelligences, whether they looked like giant grasshoppers or self-conscious cabbages or whales with hands, whether they wrote epic treatises on the meaning of life or built machines to carry them across the dimensional barrier to other universes even stranger than the one from which they had come.

No people. No intelligent cabbages or whales with hands, no ancient cities to put the monuments of Thebes to shame and to make the mysteries of Rapa Nui and Stonehenge and the riddle of Linear B look like child's play.

Until Yuggoth.

Until the first robotic probe had circled Yuggoth, sending back to Earth images of structures that were undoubtedly artificial, yet that resembled no city ever built upon earth. They stretched for thousands of miles across the ruddy, pulsing surface of Yuggoth. They rose for hundreds of miles into the roiling, cloudy atmosphere of the planet. At the poles of the monstrous globe, black, glossy areas that must be ice caps reflected the light of a billion distant stars.

At this distance from the sun the amount of heat and light from that star was infinitesimal. Clearly, Yuggoth's ruddy pulsations emanated from within the planet, whether the product of radioactivity, of tidal or magnetic forces, or of some other source of unfathomable nature.

Controllers on Earth—for this was before the construction and orbiting of Chen Jing-kuo's observation station—tried sending messages to the occupants of those cyclopean cities, relaying them from their own base of operations on Luna to the satellites orbiting the gigantic "new" planet. There was no response.

Were the Yuggothi extinct? Were their cities like the dead cities of Angkor Wat and Yucatan?

But the satellites detected movement on the surface of Yuggoth. Great creatures of alien configuration, beings like nothing encountered on Earth or any other world of the solar system, moved between the buildings, between structures that had to be considered buildings, of those cities, which had to be considered cities.

Chen Jing-quo observed the Yuggothi with both electronic and optical instruments. They had heads and bodies and limbs. To that extent they resembled familiar species found both on Earth and elsewhere in the solar system. But where one might have expected to see facial features, the Yuggothi showed clusters of waving, polypoidal tentacular growths. Their limbs were tipped with vicious-looking claws, and on their backs were what appeared to be vestigial bat-like wings.

They were hairless, their skin of a scaly composition

that suggested a onetime marine origin, and indeed Yuggoth was covered in part with dark regions that appeared to be composed of a black, viscid liquid. If these were the seas and oceans of Yuggoth, the winged creatures might have evolved in their depths, using their wings to "fly" through the seas as earthly manta rays "flew" through the warm waters of the Caribbean Sea.

Once *Beijing 11-11* was launched from its construction site on Luna, it was piloted to the Oort Cloud by a two-member crew comprising Chen Jing-quo and Kimana Hasani. When *Beijing 11-11* settled into orbit around the ruddy pulsing oblate form of Yuggoth, Kimana Hasani informed Chen Jing-quo that he was going to take one of the station's EEPs for a closer look at the new planet.

Dr. Chen protested. *Beijing 11-11* carried only a limited number of EEPs—External Excursion Pods. They were meant to be used only in cases of extreme necessity. For servicing and repairs of the station, for transportation between space vehicles—although there were no other space vehicles within the better part of a billion miles of *Beijing 11-11*—or as lifeboats. They were emphatically not intended for exploration.

But Kimana Hasani would not be deterred. He suited up in protective gear and entered the EEP. He promised Chen Jing-quo that he would maintain a continuous video and audio link with *Beijing 11-11*. Once he had climbed into the EEP he waited for the interlock to click green, hit the launch button and dropped away from *Beijing 11-11*.

Dr. Chen watched twin video screens. On one she followed the progress of her partner's EEP as it dropped away from *Beijing 11-11* and drifted down toward the atmosphere of Yuggoth. On the other she watched Kimana Hasani's face. He in turn concentrated on the instruments and controls of the pod.

As the tiny craft entered the atmosphere of the planet, Chen Jing-quo heard her partner mutter something, but this phase lasted only a few seconds. She thought she heard Kimana Hasani say something like *sizzling,* heard him speak part of her name. Then she observed a flash. The screen that had carried Kimana Hasani's image went blank. The screen that had carried an exterior image of the EEP flared a brilliant golden-orange. A shock wave spread visibly through the atmosphere where the EEP had been, then rippled outward and downward toward the surface of Yuggoth.

And upward, toward *Beijing 11-11,* where Dr. Chen cried out in startlement and grief at what she had seen, and at what she suspected was its meaning.

The only phenomenon that she could think of that would produce so violent a discharge was a nuclear explosion. She knew the design of the EEP as she knew every surface, every weld, every circuit on *Beijing 11-11.* She knew that Kimana Hasani's pod carried no fissile material. She inferred what had happened: the atmosphere of Yuggoth was composed of SeeTee matter.

SeeTee. CT. ContraTerrene. Antimatter.

She experienced a flash of recollection, from her school days of a student joke: *what do you get if a normal matter boy makes it with an antimatter girl?*

Answer: *no matter.*

No matter. No matter, in truth. Just one hell of a release of pure energy.

Yuggoth was composed of SeeTee matter.

The mountains and plains of Yuggoth, its black, viscid seas, its ebony ice caps, its cyclopean cities with their towering, eye-wrenching structures, its monstrous inhabitants, all were composed of contraterrene matter. Of antimatter.

Chen Jing-kuo returned to the electron telescope. She trained it upon the Yuggothian city directly below the point where Kimana Hasani's pod and Kimana Hasani himself had been converted to pure energy. The city lay in ruins. Titanic structures had been toppled, crushed to rubble. The inhabitants of the city had died by the millions, their terrible bodies torn and scattered hither and yon.

Shaking her head, Chen Jing-kuo wiped her tears. She turned from the telescope and opened a hyperlightspeed link to Luna. The communications operator who received her call was a onetime classmate, Matyah Melajitm. For a moment Melajitm's smile filled Dr. Chen's screen. Then the comm-op saw the expression on Chen Jing-quo's face.

"What's the matter? Something's happened. What is it?"

"Get Dr. Jerom. Kimana is dead. We seem—I think we've started a war. The first interplanetary war!"

It seemed to take hours—more likely less than two minutes—for Harleyann Jerom to replace Matyah Melajitm at the Luna comm-link.

"Dr. Chen, tell me."

Chen Jing-quo gave her a quick summary of the event.

Harleyann Jerom groaned. "All right, Chen. Do nothing now. Better yet, batten down *Beijing 11-11*. Not that I imagine you can do much to defend the station if the Yuggothi choose to counterattack. They're likely to interpret the explosion as an attack. They surely will if they're anything like us."

"There was no way. I mean, how could Kimana ever imagine . . ." Dr. Chen's voice trailed away.

"Never mind blame," Jerom responded. "There will be plenty of time for that later on. Or maybe not. But not now, that's for sure. Keep the link open."

Chen Jing-quo saw Harleyann Jerom turn away, heard her give instructions to Matyah Melajitm. Chen knew that Jerom was going to talk with Earth, get a quick decision from the politicians who ran planetary affairs.

A quick decision.

Fat chance.

Jerom reappeared on *Beijing 11-11's* comm screen. "Chen, was there ever—ever—any indication that the Yuggothi were even aware of *Beijing 11-11?*"

Chen Jing-quo shook her head. "No. That's what was so—we tried—we tried to establish communication with them. They ignored us. Or—it wasn't even that. It was as if they were completely unaware of us. As if were bacteria, viruses, and they were humans. Or mammoths. How many bacteria does such a beast crush with every step? To the Yuggothi we were bacteria or less. They never even noticed us. Until Kimana hit their atmosphere. Then . . ." She spread her hands, helpless to continue.

Harleyann Jerom nodded. "An apt simile. They probably won't be angry with us. A mersa bacterium doesn't hate its host and a human doesn't hate a bacterium. They're just two kinds of organism, and one will kill the other in order to preserve itself and perpetuate its kind. The infection will kill the host or the host will kill the infection."

"Right." Chen Jing-kuo reacted with a manic grin.

Jerom's voice was harsh. "Get a grip!"

"Nothing personal," Dr. Chen went on.

"I said, *get a grip!* This is a crisis that could make all the wars in human history look like playground squabbles."

"I'm sorry," Chen said. She was calmer now. Her nerves were jumping. She could feel her heart pounding in her chest. It must be beating close to two hundred beats a minute. Her breath was coming in desperate gasps.

She recognized the phenomena. Some ancestor was reaching down to her, reaching through the genetic matter that carried ancient reflexes. Her body sensed her desperation, prepared itself for combat or for flight. Appropriate reactions for a Cro-Magnon, for Pithecanthropus Erectus, for an ancestor even more ancient. But hardly apt for Homo Interplanetarius.

She was in control of herself. "What are my instructions, Dr. Jerom?"

"For now, observe and report. What do you see on Yuggoth?"

Chen returned to the telescopes. She activated a third screen, one for an electron image, one for an optical image, one for a superimposed combination.

"It's daytime down there. You know, it's always daytime on Yuggoth. The planet rotates but its light comes from its core so it doesn't really matter. The city that was destroyed by the shock wave—I see Yuggothi arriving from all directions. I suppose they're rescue crews.

The devastation is terrible. The casualties—I can't even guess at the number. Some of them are still alive, though. I see Yuggothi crawling through the ruins. Some with dreadful injuries. Some are just—just—it looks as if their body parts, when they were ripped off by the shock wave, some of them didn't die and now they're flopping around, moving like torn starfish. And—and—I can't go on, Harleyann. I can't."

"That's all right, Jing-kuo. You've done what you can. And we're getting feeds from *Beijing 11-11's* instruments."

There was a pause, then Harleyann Jerom resumed. "You're convinced that Kimana Hasani's EEP set off the explosion on Yuggoth?"

Dr. Chen's eyes were still focused on the screens showing conditions on the surface of Yuggoth. "I'm certain, Harleyann. The only explanation—I'm convinced it's the only explanation, the only way that little EEP could cause the devastation—the only explanation is that Yuggoth is composed of antimatter. Once Kimana's EEP hit the atmosphere, that was all it took. The EEP and Kimana himself were canceled out. Converted to pure energy, along with an equivalent mass of Yuggothi atmosphere. He—"

Her words were cut off by a gasp from Harleyann Jerom. Then the voice of the woman on Luna said, "They're here!"

"Who? What are you saying, Harleyann?"

"The Yuggothi."

"Impossible. I just saw them leave their planet."

"They're here. They're circling overhead. Their ships are unlike anything else I've ever seen. They look like—like cyborgs. They're monsters, something like bats, something like octopuses, something like humans. And machines. They're machines, too."

"But—they can't have traveled that far in a few minutes."

"They can, Jing-kuo. They must have—I don't know—we manage to skip messages through wormholes or subspace or however our system works. We don't really understand, do we, we just know that it works. And they've found a way to travel, oh, not through space. Between space. Whatever. And they're heading toward earth, Jing-kuo. I can see. I can see waves of blackness sweeping across the planet. The atmosphere is burning, the oceans, forests, ice caps. Oh, my God, my God, my God. It's worse than—"

The transmission ended.

Chen Jing-kuo studied the surface of Yuggoth, pulsing red, filling the sky above *Beijing 11-11*.

The virus doesn't hate its host, she thought, and the host doesn't really hate the virus. There is nothing personal about it. Nothing personal. If the host doesn't destroy the virus in time, the virus will kill the host. But even if that happens, once the host is dead, the virus also will die.

Chen Jing-kuo turned the telescope toward Earth. The image was magnified until it filled a screen. As she watched, bits of black appeared on the blue-and-white disk. They spread from points to irregular blots. More of them appeared, and more, until they began to run together.

For a moment the planet disappeared against the solid black background of space. Then points appeared again, became blots, multiplied and grew until Earth was a red disk. Like Yuggoth, it began to pulse, to pulse like a malevolent heart. Now Chen Jing-kuo understood what she was seeing. The Yuggothi, she realized, had devised a means to convert the normal matter of earth, contact with which would have been instantly, disastrously fatal to them, into contraterrene matter. Antimatter.

Now they could live in earth, and now there remained no other life to compete with them.

But Yuggoth itself was also contraterrene. The Yuggothi had erected no shield against a potential plunging space station of terrene matter. For all Chen Jing-kuo could tell, the Yuggothi were as unaware of the station as a human would be of a single fatal bacterium.

Earth was dead. Chen Jing-kuo knew that now. The Yuggothi had wiped it clean. The atmosphere was gone.

The oceans, the forests. The ice caps were gone. The planet had been wiped clean. It now had new owners. Octopus-bat-man-machine *things* that even now were walking or slithering or flying across the black, dead surface of the once blue-green, beautiful world. The black surface that was now pulsing with a red, evil beat.

The oblate globe of Yuggoth spun beneath *Beijing 11-11*. Chen Jing-kuo set the controls, activated the verniers, sent *Beijing 11-11* plunging toward Yuggoth. This time, the sequence of events was reversed. The host had killed the virus, but the virus retained enough vitality for one final act. The virus would kill the host.

REMNANTS

Fred Chappell

I

Echo was thrashing and muttering in her sleep and would soon have cried out if Vern had not crawled over in the dark to her pallet and addressed her ear, making only a whisper-noise and no words. *"Psss, psss, psss."*

"Psss psss psss," she answered imitating his exact sibilance, as she always did.

"Hush now," he murmured. "Don't cry out."

These five words she repeated also, her inflection reproducing his. She had not wakened.

"What is it?" he said, speaking ever so softly. "Is it a shiny? Is it a waggly? Is it a too-bright?"

All this she mimicked.

"No," he said. "Say what."

"No. Say what." Then, in a while: "Dirt. Broke dirt."

"Broken dirt," her brother said. He was trying to lengthen the loop of her phrases so that more information would filter into its sequence of repetition. He was four years older than she; he was going on sixteen now, but he had learned to be almost tirelessly patient. He looked to see if Moms had been wakened by the girl's unrest, but she seemed to sleep soundly, lying in the leaf pile with her face turned away and covered with scraps of cloth and burlap and canvas. She shivered a little; it was impossible to sleep warmly in their cave behind the waterfall, and they were reduced to rags for blankets.

"Broke dirt," Echo said.

"Why broke-dirt? What for broke-dirt? Where is broke-dirt?"

"*Psss psss psss.* Hush now. Don't cry out. What is it? Is it a shiny . . ." She had started from the beginning again, her voice copying his in every breath, but not becoming louder, so probably what disturbed her sleep was not an Old One sweeping a thoughtprobe through the landscape in random search, as they so often did. The black mixed collie, Queenie, lay watching the brother and the sister, and she was peaceful, with her head on her paws and not bristling. Nor was she growling in that dangerous but almost inaudible manner that meant she understood that Echo had detected something perilous nearby.

Vern decided he could go back to sleep. Whatever Echo had encountered could wait till morning. She was a little easier to communicate with when she was awake, but communication required an immense store of calmness.

Which I have not got, he thought, as he lay down in his place and recovered himself with rags and leaves. I have just about run out of calm, the way I have run out of ideas about where to find food.

He thought about that, staring into the darkness above. The stream whose bed roofed the cave in which they lived offered fish, the small speckled trout native to these mountains. In summer there were berries and rabbits and other small game, but that season was dwindling and the trees were dropping their leaves so quickly they seemed to be racing to denude themselves. The family had not managed to put much by for the winter. The Old Ones and their shoggoth slaves had been active in this area all through the summer, so Vern and Moms had foraged less often than they desired. Also, Moms and Vern did not like to leave Echo alone in the cave, even with Queenie there to disguise her mind and to protect her.

This was the main reason they shared food with Queenie. The dog thought in the same way that Echo did. She thought in pictures and not in words; she thought in terms of smell and sound as much as in visuals, and this was true too of Echo. The Old Ones who swept a casual thought probe through would probably identify Echo as a dog or an opossum or raccoon. If Vern and Moms kept their feelings at a low level and were as careful as possible not to think in large generalizations like "weather," "time," "yesterday," "the future," and so forth, the pictures in the heads of Queenie and Echo would pretty well mask the ways of thought of Vern and Moms.

Of course, if the Olders—as Vern called them—set out to make a thorough and deliberate search, there would be no way to hide. And no way to defend themselves. They would be captured, examined inside and out, and when that bloody, shrieking inventory was complete, they would be discarded, unless the Olders found something in one of their minds to isolate and store in their cyborganic memory banks.

But this latter possibility was extremely unlikely. In their family, only their father, Donald Peaslee, had known anything that could have been of use to the Olders. They took it from him, whatever it was, along with his sanity first and then with his life.

Vern would not think about that. If he thought about the way his father, or what was left of him, had looked the last time he saw him, his emotions would rise like a scarlet banner run up a flagpole and then maybe an Older would notice and come hunting. Or maybe the Older would send a throng of their stupid and disgusting shoggoths to search them out. The cosmetic ministrations those creatures wreaked on humans prettified them no more than did the interrogations of the Olders.

But something had nudged Echo's sleeping mind with its strange faculties and it was needful to know what that might have been.

When morning came, he would make an attempt, if she had not forgotten ... Well no, Echo was incapable of forgetting anything. Everything that had ever happened to her, everything she had seen and felt and heard and smelled and tasted was all there in her mind. But it was hard to draw it out because she had no categories. You had to find a specific detail and then add that to another and then another and another until some sort of picture was suggested.

He sighed and turned to sleep and just as he was letting go, he fancied that something touched his own mind too, with just the whisper of a whisper. Then he decided he was only imagining; he lacked Echo's quick, delicate talent.

Vern wanted to question his sister the first moment the three of them were awake, but there was no chance of that. For Echo, everything had to fall into place in a customary routine. First, Vern had to go outside and "scout," as Moms put it—meaning that he had to find a tree and take a leak, fill a can with stream water, and look for dangers or for nothing until Moms had cleaned up Echo and brushed her hair as best she could and made her feel Echo-ish. This was one of the few times she enjoyed being touched by others, except for petting and hugging Queenie and guiding Vern's hand during the drawing sessions.

So out he went into a gray, chilly dawn with its sky streaked here and there with scores of dropping meteorites. This time he really did look about for signs of danger because of Echo's restlessness and his own vague feeling that something was waiting to happen. He toured the small, handy game traps he had set, but they were empty this morning. He had been seeing raccoon sign by a little streamlet that fed into the waterfall stream and was pretty sure he could capture it some soon morning before dawn. That would be glad news for the family, meat and pelt together. He did not bother to look into the fish trap set at the farther end of the waterfall pool; he had seen yesterday evening that a large brook trout was captured in the willow-withe cage and he would let it stay there to keep fresh. They already had stocked two smoked trout in the cave, one for now and one for the other meal of the day.

He let himself recall, for the most fleeting of moments, the great, lush blackberries he had gathered some forty-odd days ago, so juicy-sweet they had made Echo tremble as she crammed them into her mouth by handfuls while Moms watched her with teary eyes.

Then he turned the thought away. It might make his emotions rise to a detectable level. The Olders . . .

Time now to go back. Inside, he saw Echo all freshened up to the best of her mother's ability. She was hugging Queenie and singing her wake-up song: "All night all night all night . . ."

He found his length of steel—a flattened lever two feet long—and went to the ember hole, lifted off the slate covering, and dug out one of the cylinders of foil. The other he left for supper. He covered the hole over again and brought the trout to where Moms and Echo sat waiting.

Mom looked more tired than yesterday, he thought, but Echo was as happy as ever she could be. She liked the taste of the trout smoked in foil, but more than that, she liked the anticipation of eating it. She drummed her hands on her crossed legs, smiling and murmuring softly her song, "All night all night."

"Thank you, Vern," Moms said when he handed her the packet. "Did you sleep well?"

"Echo was hearing something," he said. "She was almost awake."

"I know." Moms took the one metal knife they possessed from her belt and divided the fish. Her belt held up the britches she had stitched together with nylon fishing leader from an old, mostly rotten tent they had found in the woods. They needed to find some more fabric soon or roam around naked. Echo would not like that; she must have her many-colored robe, cloth scraps of every kind held together with pins and wire bits and paper clips and whatnot. She would squall if she had to go naked.

"There is something she wants to tell us about," Vern said.

"The Old Ones?"

"I don't know. Should we try to find out?"

"Maybe we should. I heard once long ago that they make parts of forests like this one into preserves and stock them with all sorts of animals that might harm us. To this particular environment, they might import grizzly bears and gray wolves and panthers. Wolves and panthers used to inhabit here."

"I know," Vern said. But he didn't know and he wouldn't inquire. *I heard once long ago*—this was Moms' phrase to indicate something her husband had told her. Best never to say his name, for sorrow would rise in them and such a feeling—or any strong feeling—was so alien to the Olders that they could detect it at fairly long range.

His father had known many things: history and science and music and numbers and stars. He had known too much about the stars. He had known too much about everything. See what grief his learning had brought them . . . Vern turned aside these thoughts.

But Moms had remembered some of the history her husband knew. He had told her of the caves in this part of the mountains where remnants of the Cherokee nation hid out when the soldiers came to drive them away and to rape and kill and burn. Those who did not hide in the caves were herded on the Trail of Tears, to suffer and die on the brutal march westward. Vern had found signs and leavings in their own cave. A rose-colored flint knife was his special treasure.

Queenie had trotted out of the cave when they began eating the fish. She would scout the area, ranging farther than Vern had done, and then return for her own meal. It had taken a long time to reconcile her to this routine, but they needed a sentry in this hour. When Echo ate, she could concentrate on nothing else until the breakfast ritual was complete. When Queenie returned, Vern would feed the dog the smoked opossum buried in the ember hole. Now he passed to his mother and sister the can of water brought from the stream. Each drank, then both washed their hands and faces, Echo mimicking Moms' actions closely.

Tasks awaited Vern. He needed to fashion new traps from whatever pliable materials he could find. He already had a good-sized stock; the woods were full of discarded things, trash that was treasure for the family. He also needed to pile wood to dry for burning and to fashion into rude tools to dig and scrape with. But he was concerned about what Echo might have discovered. This was a good time to try to talk to her; she was calm and good-natured after feeding.

He sat on the earth floor beside her and began slowly. "Echo?"

She shook her head and would not look at him. Sometimes she was shy about contact; sometimes she seemed only to be teasingly coy, but of course she was incapable of such an attitude.

"Echo?" He kept repeating her name until she did look at him, her bright gray eyes staring into his face, her gaze now locked to his.

"Broke dirt. Do you remember? Broke dirt. Dirt broken. Do you remember?"

Yes, she remembered. She never forgot anything. But getting her to speak of one specific subject in the past was difficult because she knew no past. Everything was immediate.

"Broke dirt," he said again and, for a wonder, she repeated the phrase—three times in a row.

"What for, broke dirt?"

She repeated this phrase too for awhile and then interrupted the loop. "Go. Go broke dirt."

"Where is it?"

This question would make no sense to her and he regretted asking it. Sometimes when words made no sense, she would fall into a spooky silence and sit unspeaking, unmoving, for hours.

He had found out, though, that something had spoken in her mind, or to it, saying that the three of them must travel to Broken Dirt, wherever and whatever that was. He waited and then said, "Draw?"

She nodded, solemn-faced.

"Let's go to the drawing sand," he said and when she nodded again, he crawled over to a space toward the cave mouth where the light was brighter. Moms took Echo's hand and they joined him and Moms sat beside Echo, to be near and reassure her.

This space was a circle about four feet in diameter. Vern had cleared away the pebbles and smoothed the floor and brought fine sand from the bottom of the stream and poured it and spread it out. This was where they wrote and drew and Moms taught Vern mathematics and geometry and a little geography. Here too Echo and Vern drew the pictures that came into Echo's mind. Echo had many words in her head, but she could not order them into concepts; she could not abstract. Her world was made up of separate, individual things that could be, and sometimes had to be, placed in rote positions. She had no categories to put things into. Queenie did not belong to the family of dogs; she belonged to the family of Queenie and there were no other members. For all the masses of words heaped in her capacious, seemingly unlimited memory, Echo could not know what a *word* was.

It made everything extremely difficult, for she was their best detector of the Olders. She could hear sounds as acutely as Queenie, perhaps, and she could see even better, for the dog was less receptive to color. As for odors, there Queenie had it all over the girl. Queenie was particularly sensitive to the Old Ones' smell and if it became too strong she was uncontrollable, yelping and howling and snapping. She might bite even Vern in her terror.

"Let's draw how dirt is broken," Vern said. "Show me how." He took up the curved stick lying by the sand circle and held it in his right hand. It was a slightly arced, two-foot length of a sapling maple branch he had trimmed and sharpened.

It took some time before Echo would touch him, but at last she laid her small, porcelain-like hand on the back of his wrist and with slight but not tentative movements began to guide. The marks she directed Vern to make were incomprehensible, but he had learned to wait for the process to conclude. First a mark here by her knee, then one over there so that he had to lean to make it and then one to the left almost out of the circle ... Vern could not draw things in that way himself and he was always surprised when the marks joined together to form an image.

This time the picture would be of Broken Dirt, whatever that might be, but when Echo took her hand from his wrist and snuggled her face into Moms's shoulder, he thought that she must not have finished the picture and had given up. He had been struck by this fear before, that Echo was only making random scratches. She never closed her eyes to concentrate. It was as if she saw an image already in the sand and was merely tracing it out. So he leaned close and studied.

It was not a picture of an animal or a person or of one of the Olders. Echo could not have drawn one of the latter without crying out in terror and retreating into herself for a long time. It was no machine that Vern could puzzle out; the lines were too far apart. Maybe it was some building or monument the Olders had constructed or that they were constructing now. They were always busy, always remaking the world around them into something it should not be, something that made Vern queasy when he saw it. Echo's picture was of nothing that plied through the sky like the monstrous flying machines that whispered back and forth in the upper air on unguessable errands.

Maybe it was something in the stream. There was a wavy line between two sets of straight-line segments that were joined. There were squiggly circles and lines disposed about the line-segments. He peered more closely at the wavy line between the segment sets; it was broken in two places with small empty spaces.

Echo was watching him look, her face expressionless. When he pointed at one of the broken places and asked, "Is it a waggly?" she buried her face in Moms' shoulder. Then she looked out again to watch him examine it.

So, whatever, the hiatus indicated, it was not something that flapped or waved or fluttered in the breeze. Those irregular movements fascinated Echo; they were to her the salient parts of any landscape.

"Is it a too-bright?"

Echo rocked back and forth, excited, but she did not smile.

A too-bright would be something that flashed or glittered or glimmered. There were two of them, so it probably wouldn't be something that emitted a steady shine as an artificial light would probably do. What things in nature flashed or flickered intermittently?

Well, it was a stream, of course, or a river. When the three of them went to bathe in the stream in the warm summer, the thing that captured Echo's attention most firmly was the way the sunlight reflected off the wavelets. She was transfixed, watching these changing lights as fixedly as if she were trying to decipher a code.

So then, if the wavy line were a stream, the surrounding segments would represent the banks. The squiggly circles and other lines would represent bushes and grasses.

Except that Echo could not "represent" with abstract symbols. She always guided Vern's hand to draw, as closely as the sand-medium would allow, the exact lineaments of the thing to be seen. So his interpretation must be wrong and these disjointed marks composed a realistic picture of something he could not recognize.

Or—

Or maybe it was a true-to-life drawing of the picture that was in her mind. Maybe it had come to her just as it was laid out here in the sand, a schematic diagram of a place. In that case, it must have been sent to her as a message—and not from the Olders or any of their slaves. Their aura about it would ravage his sister. She would crouch with her face to the cave wall, clutching her knees and wailing.

He looked at her, safe in Moms' arms, watching him. She was not frightened. The message had come from something or someone else than they knew, an entity that had searched to find a receptive mind and had encountered Echo. This was not the first of her extrasensory episodes. Such experiences had been remarked as fairly widespread among autistics, even before the advent of the Olders had heightened, in greater and less degree, according to individuals, those powers among humans. Some person, or group of persons, was trying to make contact, either with Echo alone or with the whole family by means of Echo.

He examined the drawing again. Was he looking at a map? Did these scattered lines represent a specific place? He could not ask. "Place" would mean nothing to Echo. If she arrived at the location suggested by her drawing, she almost certainly would not be able to recognize it. It would be too detailed and, to her, would bear no resemblance to the lines in the sand.

Well then, supposing that this telepathic being, whatever it might be, really had transmitted a map to Echo's mind, and, supposing that Vern had interpreted the hiatuses in the wavy line correctly, how would the sender have known to include a representation of a "too-bright" in the scheme? The telepath would have to know her mind thoroughly, understanding the way Echo experienced things and reacted to them. But that would not be possible without her knowledge and if she had felt someone rummaging through her mind-pictures, her fear and trembling would alert her mother and brother.

If, however, the telepath understood the *kind* of mind it had touched, it would not need intimate knowledge of its contact. If she or he or it recognized autism and had had previous commerce with autistic personalities, it would know how to contact them and how to communicate information without distressing that person. Echo had been disturbed; she had murmured in her sleep, reacting to the encounter, but she had not been distressed. The telepath was not immediately threatening . . . But the further intentions might not be benevolent.

Now, supposing that his first two notions were not groundless, the situation would be that some being had made purposeful contact with the family, or at least with

Echo, and had transmitted a map, though one with limited geographical information. Perhaps it had transmitted only as much as it estimated that Echo could receive and pass on.

Why had it done so? Did it desire that the family travel to the mapped place?

He passed his hand above the sand drawing and looked at Echo, into her unwavering stare, and asked, "Go here?"

For a long time she did not respond and when she did, it was only to sing one of her songs. "All night all night all night . . ."

"Queenie, play with Echo," Vern said and the big black dog rose and came to his sister and nuzzled her elbow and suffered herself to be petted. This was one way to break Echo's verbal cycles, but it did not always work.

She had retreated from his question, Vern realized, because *here* meant to her not the place the diagram represented but the sand itself. Echo did not want to go sit in the circle and destroy her drawing; she was always proud when she had guided Vern to draw a picture that was in her head.

She would never be able to say, "Yes, let us travel to the place we have drawn the map of. Something wants us to be there and it is important." Those wishful sentences Vern furnished for himself in his anxiety to comprehend, and this fancy was a signal of his frustrated impatience.

There might be other explanations for the contact. Vern knew that others had retreated to these caves to escape the onslaught of the Olders. In their small university town, most people had been killed with dreadful weapons or left to the mercies of the slave-organisms called shoggoths that had no notion of what mercy might be, and so killed lingeringly, as if taking enjoyment from the spectacle and music of the final agonies. A number of persons had been taken away to the colossal laboratory structures the Olders had reared and there they were di-

vested of the knowledge the dire creatures judged might
be useful to their purposes—whatever those might be.

Among those who had managed to flee and hide in
the caves that had once sheltered the abused Cherokee
people, there might be another autistic with some of the
extrasensory powers that Echo possessed.

The question would still remain, however. Why should
such a person transmit a map? Whoever sent it had sent
an invitation. Or a summons.

They were as well prepared as they could be to leave
the cave and journey. Moms and Vern had made a list
and gathered the accessories necessary for travel. "Someday," she had said, "the Old Ones will come into our territory. They are always expanding their reach, tearing
down our world and rebuilding it to suit them, remaking
it in their own image. So we must gather supplies and
put them away in the cave and be prepared. *I heard once
long ago* that it is best always to be prepared."

So they had scavenged for twine and for whatever
other binding materials they could find, for cloth of any
kind that might warm, shelter, and hide them, and for
any handy pieces of metal that could be beaten into useful shape or sharpened to an edge. There was no way to
preserve foodstuffs, so Vern had laid several fish traps
in the stream below the waterfall. An early autumn rain
had washed away two of them, but there were three left,
though only one now contained a trout.

We have enough to travel a short way if we must, he
thought. He thought too about how people used to discard all sorts of good things, now useful for the family.
That time was a world ago and the kind of time it had
existed within could never return.

But if they were to travel, answering that summons,
where would they go?

He looked at the drawing again. The line segments
crowded near the wavy line upon its left-hand side, but
on the other side they were set farther away. So if the
wavy line was indeed a stream that sparkled intermittently, the right bank was farther from its center. Or

maybe that was just the angle of vision. If the right bank only appeared to be farther, it would mean that the stream was deep in a ravine and the map showed it from the right-hand side. The stream they lived beneath ran to the south and as it rolled down the mountainside, it had cut, over the millennia, deep declivities. Vern thought that if they decided to answer the summons, they should follow the stream, descending the mountain until they found a place that fit the map.

He sighed. It was all very chancy, but this was the best interpretation he could come up with. He would talk it over with Moms in the evening. Now he would go to his daily chores, gathering food and fuel where he could and collecting any shard or scrap or leaf or root that might help to keep them alive. Then this evening they would hold council and decide.

This was the best part of the day for them, although Echo, if she were overtired in the evening, would be fretful for a tedious time before settling to nestle in Moms' lap. Vern and Moms were by this hour good-tired, the cessation of the long, active day pleasant after their labors were accomplished. This was the hour they talked, making plans and sometimes recalling the good things they had stored in memory.

During this time they would also debate courses of action, and this evening Vern had asked Moms whether it would be wise to try to find the place Echo had depicted.

"You say it is an invitation or a summons from someone or some people we cannot know," Moms said.

"That's how I make it out."

"She is not in a state. She is not frightened by this . . . message."

They watched Echo. She had gone back to the circle and was playing with the sand, pouring the grains into one hand and then into the other and letting them spill through her fingers. Over and over she did this, over and over, while crooning a wordless song.

"That is one reason I think I should try to find it."

"You?" Moms asked. "That cannot be. It would have to be the three of us together."

"I could go find it and, if I can figure out what is going on and see whether it's safe, then I could take us there."

"But if you did not come back, Echo and I would perish."

"If we all go, we all might die."

"That would be better." Her eyes moistened and she turned her head away. Vern heard her taking deep breaths to calm her emotions.

"It would be hard traveling with three. Faster for me to go and come back and go again."

"But you can't be sure you have found the right place unless Echo is with you. She will know the place when she arrives there."

"She might not."

"Whoever is sending the message now will tell her when she has arrived."

"What if it is some plan of the Olders to draw humans out?"

"You have already rejected that idea or you would not even consider going. And if there was any slight hint of the Old Ones about it, Echo would smell them out. She is more sensitive to them than we are."

"Could they not find a way to disguise their presence?"

"I don't think so. I can't pretend to understand their psychology; I don't know that such a concept can even apply to them. But when I try to translate their 'attitude,' if I can call it that, to our terms, I would describe it as *contemptuous* in regard to humans. They probably hold us in less esteem than those amoebean slaves they created, those shoggoths. They think themselves invincible on our planet and maybe within the whole cosmos, as I heard once long ago. They would not think of hiding or disguising their presences. They do not confer upon us the dignity of being considered their opponents. We are, at most, mere nuisances."

"Yes." Vern let the image of the star-headed monstrosity slip into his mind and then imagined its disappear-

ance before it could bring up his emotional temperature.
But their handiwork, all those immense towers and cyclopean, steeply sloped pyramids with ridged ramps, all
that bewildering hyper-geometry of almost unvisualiz-
able angles—these images and many others he allowed
to register in his mind. They would not attract the attention of a probe, for they were only pictures of things
that existed and any animal might be gazing upon them.
"Yes," he said, "we are only minor pests to them. But we
know that they have enemies much more powerful than
we are. They have battled Cthulhu and triumphed and
were defeated and then triumphed again. This is something I heard once long ago. It may be that this call—this
invitation or summons—is intended to entrap an enemy
more dangerous than humans."

"But in that case the call would be cast in terms utterly alien to us. I do not think Echo could even react
to it."

Again Vern looked at his sister. The world outside
had darkened as the hour deepened and the sound of
the curtaining waterfall seemed to grow louder. Echo,
with her silvery long hair and porcelain-pale skin almost
glowed ghostlike in the dim cave. She had stopped pouring sand and was gathering it into little mounds spaced
out evenly from one another. After mounding a fifth
small pile, she stopped and sat up cross-legged with her
hands in her lap, looking toward the cave mouth.

"Well, what do you think we should do?" Vern
asked.

"It is time to go to sleep. Maybe you'd like to scout
around outside a little. Maybe when Echo goes to sleep
tonight, she will receive another message and maybe it
will be clearer than this map diagram she drew."

Moms' suggestion was what Vern had expected. He
supposed that prudence was probably their best policy,
but he was apprehensive. Someone or something knew
of their existence. They went on with their hardscrabble
daily lives as if the Olders did not know about them,
keeping as closely as possible to narrowly settled routines, to behavior that did not arouse their feelings or

require unusual degrees of mental activity. Quietude was their only camouflage. If they had to journey, the stress of traveling with Echo might rouse attention, but if pursuers were closing in, there would be no choice but to travel.

It was dark here; the detestable five-pointed orange moon was not in the sky—and he was grateful for that. Skirting around the waterfall by a familiar but barely traceable pathway over the rocks, Vern walked a little way down the stream edge. Then he stopped and breathed in the night air that was growing ever colder with the season. He shivered. The scraps of canvas and plastic and cloth Moms had spliced into a motley robe-like garment was draughty, to say the least. He hugged his chest.

And then he thought he heard a sound different from the customary night noises. A thin, high yelping far, far away. Perhaps the Olders had introduced an animal new to this forest, some strain of wolf, or an animal of their own engineering.

Then he heard it no more and decided that his imagination was overly exercised. He turned and headed back to the cave where Echo and Moms would be ready for sleep by now.

Despite his apprehensions, Vern was sleepy. Although his day had been physically a little less active than usual, anxiety had depleted his mental energy. He lay for a few minutes, listening. He could tell that Moms was not asleep; she was surely thinking through their discussion. Echo was asleep in her own way, though sometimes Vern wondered if she ever actually slept, the way that he and Moms and Queenie did—as Queenie was doing now, her large head laid on her large paws.

Almost as soon as he closed his eyes, he began to dream. His viewing floated like an invisible balloon, bodiless, and traversed one of the Olders' cities, if that was what they were to be called. He envisioned entering underground through a huge doorless opening. If he were making this journey in his body, his every nerve would be pulsing with fear as he passed tremendous pentagonal pools of unknown black liquids and drifted through rooms filled with curious and inexplicable utensils of myriad sorts. Then there were colossal caverns of intricate machines at whose purposes he could not guess. They were all motionless until he came to one larger than the rest. It was so large that the top of it must have extended through the cavern roof into the outside world. It seemed to buckle inward and outward continuously, the matte gray planes of its panels seeming to open and close simultaneously, as if it were a strange doorway allowing both entrance and exit in the same vertiginous movement. This machine uttered a high-pitched piping sound and it seemed to Vern that the noise was like the sound of the faraway yelping or baying he had thought he heard outside by the stream.

Then he woke.

Queenie was awake too, making her dangerous, nearly inaudible growl. And Echo was awake and Moms was sitting up straight, her eyes wide and glistening in the dark. The three of them listened to that piping; it was still far away, still small among the sounds of the waterfall and of the forest at night, but it was dreadfully intelligible:

Tekeli-li Tekeli-li.

II

"Ship?"

"Yes, Captain."

"Are all things well?"

"Very well. The mission is proceeding according to procedure."

"That is good," I said and truly I felt a happy relief in my organism. "Am I sober enough to take command?"

"You are not entirely cleansed of deepsleep narcosis," Ship said, "but you are rational and your body is highly operable, though it needs exercise, as do the bodies of the other crew members."

"Please find if they are well and sober," I said. "Doctor, Navigator, Seeker—how do they fare?"

"They fare well ... No. Disregard. Farewell is a phrase suitable for departures. The crew fare good. They are beginning to awake."

"I will address them when all is sober."

"The correct would be, when all are sober," said Ship.

"Are you certain?"

"Eighty-four point oh-two certain."

"Our mission dialect is difficult," I said.

"The English is," Ship said. "There are other planetary languages more difficult; there are others less so. Part of the problem is that we have taken our knowledge of these languages from what remained of the libraries of relic spaceships. The electronics were primitive and much has been lost to age-deterioration and other damage."

"But we must persevere," I replied, "for if our mission performance is well, we must be ready to converse."

"All the crew have been instructed during normal sleep periods and also during deepsleep, but that is not the same as speaking. We all must practice."

"I will write my account in English," I said. "That will be strong practice."

"We salute your pluck," Ship said, speaking for the Alliance, I presumed.

While Ship was waking the rest of the crew, I undertook the prescribed medicines and waters and endured the exercises. During the stretches and lunges, I reviewed the tasks that awaited. The Starheads had taken over the planet third from the sun to use as a base for offensive strikes and architectural experiment. As usual, they had almost eradicated the dominant intelligent species and there remained only scattered Remnants that were like my siblings and me. Our own home had been destroyed and the four members left of my family had been rescued by a small party of scientists who were members of the Radiance Alliance, the ancient foes of the Starheads. The Alliance are a highly advanced race (in our local mission world they were called the Great Ones) and they have thought it desirable to try to preserve all the different species of life that they could rescue. The Starheads (locally known as the Old Ones) regard every other species of intelligent beings but themselves as enemies, active or potential. For this reason, they kill all. But if any can be saved from slaughter, the Great Ones strive to that end and send out disguised spying machines where the Starheads are active to find if some few survivors escaped their attentions. Traces of Remnants had been detected here and Ship and crew had been dispatched.

So here we were. Our task was to find and rescue as many fugitives from the Old Ones as possible.

It was no easy job, and to accomplish it, we had only the four of us and Ship. We were not in direct contact with the Alliance for fear that the Starheads might trace signals back to our base and thereupon wreak destruction.

I desisted from my exercises and greeted my shipmates as they left their cubes and entered the control room one by one.

First there came my younger brother, whom Ship had designated navigator and now we used this title instead of his actual name. It is best to call him Navigator in this narrative in case information might be gleaned from his own name. Though he is younger than I, he is more muscled and usually bests me in the pan-agon arena where we exercise martially. Still, I have been designated Captain and he must receive my orders, which he does mostly patiently and sometimes not. His duty is to cooperate with Ship to keep knowledgeable of our spatial locations, of the happenstances in our space environment, and to locate and trace the movements upon the planetary surface of any Remnants we might contact.

My sister, who is only slightly younger than me, Ship names Doctor because it is her duty to tend the health of us three others. She monitors not only illness but also signs of emotional disturbance and of sudden, untoward changes in our mental states. She must keep watch that the thoughtprobes of Starheads do not disrupt our minds or displace them completely to make us to be crawlers and droolers, bereft of rationality, trying to do away with ourselves and with one another. She is always glancing at graph-screens and listening to corporal rhythms that Ship relays to her about our bodilies.

My youngest sister we call Seeker, a name not so pretty by far as her own true name. I should not write so here, perhaps, but she is my favorite person in the cosmos and also she is the favorite of all the crew. Whereas Navigator and Doctor are largish of corpus and darkly haired and complected, Seeker is as white as a gleaming mineral and her skin seems to glow, almost. Her eyes are green but become violet-like of color when she makes mind contact with others. Her hair is silver silk. All female telepaths belong to this physical type, Ship says, or at least the hominids do, though I believe none others universally can be so pretty as Seeker.

Her duty is the most demanding, for she must make mind contact with a Remnant group and persuade it to come to a place within the planet where we can guide them and let them know we are not perilous and mean them no injury and that we are all trying to escape and hide from the Old Ones now and maybe in time to come grow strong and do them grievous hurt so that the cosmos will not be only Starheads and their slaves and nothing else that thinks and feels.

Here now they stood before me, the three, still a little wrinkled in spirit from deepsleep and slightly confused. But they answered cheeringly when I spoke to each and congratulated on wakefulness. "Do we all know what is to come?" I asked.

They said Yes.

Then Ship directed us to the small mess hall and we partook solid food instead of veinous alongside some happy water and were much refreshed.

Then we returned to control and set up our routines.

Millions and millions of light years we had traveled, Ship had informed Navigator. Our vessel, disguised as a comparatively leisurely meteor, had skated across the orbit of the fourth planet and soon would pass the single moon of the third planet.

Navigator suggested that we call this third planet Terra, a word from an ancient and long deceased speech known as Latin. "We cannot very well call it Earth," he said. "All home planets are earths. Confusion must ensue."

"Terra is sound," I said. "Soon we shall be in its farther gravitation and perhaps Seeker can begin to search for whispers or traces of hominid Remnant mentation."

"I shall begin when our approach is closer," she said. "It would require powerful amplification of telepathic signal to scan the surface from here. Amplification of such magnitude the Starheads would notice."

"Now that we are in the Terran sun-system, let us call them Old Ones," I said. "We do not wish to confuse the Remnant group when we make contact."

"Very well, Captain," she said. She wore a pretty smile when she said that. I thought how it was or seemed unright that she, the smallest and most delicate of the crew, must perform the most difficult duties and engage the greatest risks. After all the millions of light years we had traversed through underspace, Seeker must calibrate her last tasks in terms of English yards, feet, inches and fractions of inches. It is a little like, I thought, leaping from an immensely tall tower and coming to rest lightly upon a grain of sand. While she was doing so, distractions would be taking place violently.

If any of us others could have done it for her, we would so, but we lacked the telepathic talents that are hers. We each possessed rudimentary telepathic ability, as Ship says that almost every intelligence must own, and Ship is able to link us tenuously with Seeker when necessary, but each faint contact is not voluptuously profitable. None could take Seeker's place, but we would be aiding in all possible ways, and eagerly too.

I read through the long list of protocols and drills that Ship inscribed on my screens and during the next eight waking periods, I went through them with the crew until it would no longer help to do so.

Thereafter we rested and played games among us, though Seeker and Ship kept alert.

Then on the next watch, Seeker reported that she detected mental activity nothing like that of the Old Ones. It was a small group hiding away, she said, three or four of them. Of three she was certain, but the fourth was unclear. One of the three was a telepath, sending strange, nearly random signaling, though of course not directed at Seeker. "This telepath is un-normal of mind," she said. She wrinkled her brow as she bent to her screens and scopes and auditories. Her console and all its instruments were nervily active, blinking and trilling, and her hands fluttered over them like white ribbons wafting in strong air convection.

"Is the Terran telepath deranged?" I asked.

"I do not know," Seeker said, and Doctor said, "Not exactly deranged." She was busy at her instruments also. Her console was collecting medical information from Seeker's instruments and filtering for Doctor.

"What then?" I asked.

She hesitated then said, "I believe the Terran term is *autistic*."

"Autistic?" I said.

She paused again, listening, and then repeated what Ship told her screen: "*Autistic* defines a mental condition or disposition lacking ability to generalize and to form conclusions aiding useful or even necessary actions. It is marked by a profound, imprisoning subjectivity. Many autistic individuals possess rudimentary telepathic capacities; some of them are well advanced in the talent."

"Profound, imprisoning subjectivity sounds like derangement," I said. "Is this autist able to travel distances?"

She studied for a while and then replied. "I think so, yes. But it will be difficult for her."

"The telepath is female?"

"Yes, a she."

"Being autistic, does she know she is telepathic?" I asked Seeker.

She studied. "We are too far. I cannot read. She may be mind-linked to a slave organism."

"That does not bode good," I said.

"We need to be nearer." Her face wrinkled as she concentrated and I recalled her description of the difficulties of receiving such mental fields or auras and the messaging therein. "It is like trying to feel a photon with a fingertip," she said. We marveled at that notion, Doctor and I. Navigator only shook his head impatiently. I think that he is sometimes a little envious of Seeker's abilities. It is good he keeps good temper, for if we quarreled and made spats, our concentration would suffer harm.

In the ruins of the old spaceship libraries there were many descriptions of Terra's moon. The scientific accounts put its orbital revolution at 271/3 days at a distance of 384,403 kilometers from the planet. Its bright albedo was remarked and attributed to its surface of glassy crystalline soil. There was a great amount of similar minutiae, important to Terrans because a moon base was in process of construction when the Old Ones came again. This satellite inspired poets to write of it incessantly, often in terms not faithful to astronomical fact. They frequently spoke of it in terms of silver, as "striding the night in silver shoon" or "gifting its silver smile to the still waters."

If there were any poets upon the planet still composing, they spoke no more of a "silver orb." The Old Ones had sculpted the satellite into a five-pointed construction, angry red-orange in color, mottled with pyramidal protrusions disposed in groups of five, a geometry vaguely suggesting the shapes of the crania of the Old Ones. The rubble from this immense project was still falling upon Terra in shower after shower of meteors and meteorites. This was one reason Ship was cloaked in the guise of a meteor. So many of such bodies were striking Terran atmosphere, it had been thought that we might be undistinguished amid the number of them.

On such frail hopes and forlorn details our enterprise depended.

I could not always keep my apprehensions at bay. The four of us, with no useful experience to rely on, dropping through its sun-system to an obscure planet, no more than a speck on the outer shoals of this galaxy, our vessel disguised and ridged and pocked as if by collisions, a mote thousands of times smaller than the watery world toward which we drifted . . . What madness had come upon the Great Ones to entrust us with so important a mission?

Then it came to me that our ignorance and inexperience were the factors that had determined the choice. We were a more expendable crew than most of the other search teams. Those who had survived encounters and rescued Remnant groups would be sent to more prominent fronts to undertake larger and more urgent missions. Our little family was dispatched to an odd little corner of the conflict. If the Old Ones exterminated us, the loss would be relatively unimportant—unless we let slip, through carelessness or under stress, information that might help tease out the locations of important Alliance posts.

Dreadful but necessary measures had been installed to prevent that from happening.

We kept gazing at the ugly orange moon-sculpture as it filled twelve of our visiscreens. I thought that it seemed to pulse its coloration, the orange brightening and darkening at irregular intervals, but set the impression aside as an illusions born of tensed nerves.

"Navigator," I said, "how fare we?"

He glanced at his instruments and sighed. "Well enough, I think, though there are some slight anomalies I cannot account for. Distances seem to change irrespective of our velocity."

"Seeker?"

"I think the Starheads—I mean, the Old Ones—may be distressing the local space-weave," she said. "They are probably constructing some of those colossal en-

gines we were taught about. The energies exchanged are
so enormous they may twist space-time here."

Navigator said this might account for his observations.

Then Seeker asked us to fall quiet. "I may be feeling
something," she said. "Silence will help me to concentrate. I am picking up fearful emotions. At least, I think
perhaps."

"The crew will silence," I said.

Seeker had spoken before of the fear the fugitives
on Terra must be enduring and I understood that these
would be stark and continuous, but I wondered how
they would feel if they knew the extent of the Old Ones'
desecrations. World on world, across all the cosmos,
were crumbled to rubble or blown away to radioactive
cloud, millions of nations, tribes, and civilizations were
mangled to bloody ruin, the grandest achievements of
art, science, religion, and philosophy had gone dark like
lights turned off on a space cruiser.

The Terrans had known something of the Old
Ones before this time. They had learned, but they had
forgotten—almost purposefully, it seemed. In one of the
relic spaceship libraries was a long document concern-
ing something called Miskatonic Expedition 1935. This
exploration project had discovered in land-mass Australia "certain traces" the Old Ones had left "in rocks even
then laid down a thousand million years . . . laid down
before the true life of [Terra] had existed at all." The Terrans, according to this history, knew about the struggles
of the Old Ones against the "spawn" of Cthulhu and the
abominable Mi-Go and about some of the interstellar
subjugations and massacres. These things they knew,
but when the ancient evils rose again from the sea or
"seeped down" from the stars, they were not prepared.

Their lack of realization had been pointedly described
by their best historian of Cthulhu and the Old Ones and
Great Ones. He spoke candidly of their failure, imput-
ing it to "the inability of the human mind to correlate
all its contents." He drew a dark, disheartening view of

his species: "We live on a placid island of ignorance in a black sea of infinity, and it was not meant that we should voyage far."

They had not voyaged far, but black infinity had come upon them, and few were left and those scattered few must endure miserable, terror-filled days and nights. These Terrans probably would not be counted among the greatest of races in the cosmos; they were not the widest thinkers or most accomplished builders or the most generous of spirit. Yet they had achieved things fine in their way, however modest. Their erasure would be a waste, pathetic if not tragic. They had struggled against the Old Ones, this planet full of nations. Now we four individuals must struggle against the same implacable force.

I ordered myself not to allow this mood of thought to dominate my spirit.

After the next sleep period, Seeker told us that she had located geographically the Terran telepath and her group. It was a family of four, including the mysterious ancillary member whose thoughts Seeker could partially read but only sometimes. "She too is a female, this other one, and, like the telepath, she has extremely limited language skills, so that it is difficult to understand her thought patterns. She mostly thinks without words and possesses sensory organs different from those of her companions. She may belong to a different species."

"Yet you say she is not enslaved," I said.

"It is an arrangement we do not have ourselves," she said.

"Does she see herself as part of the group?"

"Yes. But I need more information."

"We will now orbit-out three locator flyers," I said. "They will triangulate the source-point of the telepathic signals, just as we rehearsed."

Ship gave a slight lurch, having dispatched the flyers as I was speaking. Each flyer contained amplifiers to reinforce the signals from Terra. They transmitted simultaneously pictures of the planetscape to the ship screens and to Seeker's mind. If all performed according to scheme, we would have pictures of the close environs of the Remnant family in eight hours or fewer.

But it was a tiring interlude for Seeker. I watched her at work, her neck and shoulders tense in concentration. I could see the muscles strain as she bent to her console. Her lightweight white robe emphasized her taut slenderness and she frowned and smiled alternately, as the signal strengthened or faded. I could almost read Seeker's mind as she seined through the blasts of data she intook, making innumerable decisions almost instantaneously.

Doctor too was concentrating. Her mechanisms were now principally focused upon Seeker, monitoring her physical conditions to the finest detail. If something touched Seeker's mind, the event would show on Doctor's screens and she would decide whether Ship must go dark, maybe forever.

Navigator was occupied with directing the flyers, maneuvering them within the Terran atmosphere in accordance with the directionals of the Remnants' telepath.

All this went on for long and long.

"The signals are stronger now," Seeker said. Her voice was a musical whisper that floated above the steady mechanical humming of the control room. "I have a closely approximate placement. They are in a wilderness terrain. The locator flyers send pictures of the area. Can Navigator direct a beacon landing near?"

He considered for a time. "Yes," he said and described briefly the landscape at large, with particular emphasis upon a river in its midst and a high bluff that hung above its lower stretches. "But we must be secret and exquisite of touch. The plateau there is close upon a place where the Old Ones are laboring. I cannot make out exactly what they are constructing, but their presence will be strong there and the beacon cannot be placed any farther downstream. Even so, that plateau is the best choice."

"Have the flyers recorded pictures Seeker can send?"

"Yes," he said.

"Seeker?" I asked.

"Have forbearance," she said. "Contact is complex."

"The Old Ones are close upon them," I said. "There is a concern of time."

"Have forbearance."

Then in another while she said she was contacting and the rest of us could not help directing much attention, though we did not neglect our urgent duties. How could we not watch our most precious sister when she must undergo the rigors of contact with an alien species? The mind-frames of otherworlders are so different from ours that sometimes they can tatter the rationality of both telepathic parties. The Great Ones had described Terrans as being much like ourselves, but complete likeness was not possible and the margin of unlikeness, the forceful tension of sheer otherness, would cause a fearful strain on the mind-spirit of Seeker and perhaps a worse consequence. She once said it was like plunging down and down into a boiling sea within which unknown creatures drifted and darted, their shapes and sizes ungraspable until after long acquaintance. If the Terran telepath was indeed deranged, there was a possibility that her condition would infect Seeker's mind.

I believed I could not do the thing my sister was doing, even if I possessed her abilities. One must be strong of selfhood and sometimes that is insufficient. According to Alliance records, a number of telepaths have been contacted by Starhead minds. Those pale individuals lived out the rest of their days in the state that the English call catatonia, though the term falls short. In catatonia the mind is inoperable, but with Old-Ones' telepathic damage, the mind no longer exists. Some other indescribable mode of unconsciousness supplants it.

"I am receiving more strongly," Seeker said. "Is it nighttime where the signal emits? I think she may be sleeping. Some send stronger when they sleep, in particular if they are un-normal. Sleeping, they are less distracted."

"It is nighttime at the emission point," Navigator said.

"What does she signal?" I asked.

"She sends large smells of an animal friendly to her. It is not a slave organism, as we feared. It is a parasite or symbiote in complex and close relationship. I do not comprehend. Her name for it is a queenie. I think that must mean companion or helpmeet."

"May it be telepathic, this animal? Is it of normal mind?"

Seeker said nothing for long and then made a hand gesture of disappointment. "I cannot know," she said. "But the autist is calmly receptive while sleeping. As soon as we find a beacon place, I can tell her where."

"This Remnant group is safe from the Old Ones for the moment?"

Now she became more and more intent, enmeshed with Ship so closely in the mind-contact it was as if she were wearing the network of amplifiers and transceivers as a robe wrapped around her thinking. "Somewhere there is something perilous," she said. Her expression was darkening. "I cannot say what as of yet."

"Perhaps—" I began to say.

"Seeker, withdraw!" Doctor said.

Her face grew even more white and her eyelids fluttered. She thrashed her hands against her upper arms.

"Seeker, withdraw now!" Doctor said.

Her voice was high and thin and shrill when she said the words the autist on Terra must have been hearing. *"Tekeli-li."*

"Seeker!" cried Doctor and cried we all as well.

III

Vern was fairly pleased with the progress they had made today. His rough estimate was that he had brought Moms and Echo about a kilometer and a half along the streamside before evening came into the woods and visibility was hindered and the first faint pipings—*Tekeli-li—*

were heard from the west. Now it was time to find shelter, the best hiding place they could discover.

They were following the stream as it ran south down the mountainside. The decline was steep enough that it kept a fairly straight course, though it curled around the bases of some of the prominent hills and widened out in some of the more level hollers. He had reasoned that if the picture Echo had guided him to draw were indeed a ravine with a stream at the bottom, that water would almost necessarily be the same under which their cave was located and, if that were the case, it would be to the south where the force of its falling would have carved deeply between the hills.

That was a big *if* and Vern trusted his reasoning less than Moms did. She had more faith in him than he had in himself. Or perhaps she only pretended to, bolstering his confidence.

In any case, they must find a place to eat and sleep and to try to hide. Tonight was not as cold as last night and they would be warmer if they went into the woods a little way from the cold stream. He wanted to get some distance from the sound of it too, so that they might better hear anything moving through the forest.

That thin shrilling, the nerve-wracking piping of the shoggoths, had not come closer and Vern estimated that the group of them must be at least two kilometers away. The dreadful sound carried far, especially at night in these otherwise silent mountains. But the sound was close enough to cause Echo fearful distress.

He did not know if she had ever seen one of the creatures. Probably she had not, for the sound of their shrilling would recall their image and that would send her into paroxysms. He had seen them only once, two of them, as they fell upon a deer and did not devour so much as absorb it. Shapeless or nearly shapeless they were, composed of a viscous jelly which looked like an agglutination of bubbles, and these would be about fifteen feet in diameter when spherical. Yet they had a constantly shifting shape and volume, throwing out tem-

porary developments—arms, pseudopods, tentacles—
and forming, deforming and reforming organs of sight
and speech. *Tekeli-li* was the word, as nearly as Vern
could approximate the sound with human phonemes,
that they spoke to one another almost continuously,
though the slight variations in pitch and timbre he was
able to perceive suggested that this one utterance was
capable of a plenitude of meanings. That word had been
recorded by the old historians of the nineteenth and
twentieth centuries.

He had been stalking the same deer himself, a young
doe that had not learned caution, and had been so horrified when the monsters burst out of the foliage upon
their prey, that he swooned away for a few moments.
That was a piece of good luck. If he had cried out, they
would have made an end of him.

They would have ended the lives of Moms and Echo
too—and of Queenie, for there was an intense detesta-
tion of those creatures for dogs and of dogs for them.
Shoggoths, as the humans supposed, communicated tele-
pathically with the Old Ones their masters, and the presence of Vern in that glade where the doe was ingested,
or rather, digested, would have been made known. Then
the Old Ones would come to search this part of the forest and they would unfailingly find Echo, though they
might not comprehend the origin of her kind of mind-
pictures.

Echo had tired of walking and clambering over the
rocks and Vern and Moms had taken turns carrying her
for the past hour or so. She was in Moms' arms now and,
as the four of them came to the edge of a large streamside boulder, Vern signaled for Moms and Echo to stay
behind, while he searched for a suitable place to last out
the night.

They had arrived at a fairly level place on the mountainside. The stream widened out here and was less
voluble over its stones. If he could find a spot forty or
so yards from its edge, they ought to be able to hear forest sounds clearly and to distinguish those that signaled

danger. A cave would be ideal, but this place could offer nothing like that.

There was a dense laurel thicket bordering a ferny glade, and when he skirted it, he found a small opening. Echo would be frightened to crawl into this little tunnel in the foliage, but she would not be terror-stricken. He explored it for about fifteen yards and then could go no farther, the tightly meshed branches and twigs forming a prickly wall. Cozy, Vern thought. He realized that it had sheltered an animal not long ago, perhaps a fawn or maybe one of the black bears common in these hills. It would be a good place. Maybe they could even chance a tiny fire.

But when he brought the family inside this den, he decided against the fire. The smoke might not easily be visible at night, but they would have to crowd closely to the flame and Echo would be so transfixed by the sight of it that she might not be able to communicate. Flashing water, trembling fronds, twinkling lights—these sent her into a trancelike state, so fixedly that she could concentrate on nothing else.

So Vern and Moms tried their best to approximate the evening routine they had clung to when they lived in the cave. He crawled out of the brambly little tunnel to "scout," while Moms primped Echo and combed her hair. Then Vern returned with a tin flask of water and Moms opened the canvas bag with the decal that read University Bookstore and brought out jerky for Vern and herself and smoked fish for Echo. Sometimes Echo's teeth were painful and she would refuse to chew the dried deer meat.

After this meal, Vern and Moms arranged leaf piles for bedding. The fallen laurel leaves were thick here but made unsatisfactory mattresses, cold and slick and noisy. Uneasy sleep was guaranteed.

Now Moms took Echo in her arms and held her closely. This was their quiet time and Vern wanted to use it to question Echo, but he could not think how to ask what they needed to know.

"What voices do you hear inside?"

She shook her head, not meeting his eyes, and Vern looked to Moms for aid.

Moms said, "I know that we need to know what to look for, the source of the call or summons to her, but I don't know how to ask, either."

"If it is a person or a group of people, we must see them before they see us," Vern said. "If we don't like the look of them, we won't make ourselves known."

"But if we approach closely, they will sense we are there. It may be that they already know we are traveling toward their signal."

"Shiny," Echo murmured. Then she turned the word into a little song. "Shiny, shy-nee, shiny, shy-nee." She was carefully not looking at Vern or Moms.

"Shiny?" Vern asked. "What is shiny, Echo?"

For a long time she only repeated the word, but at last added another. "Wall. Shiny, shy-nee wall. Shine wall."

"Go there?" Vern asked. "Are we to go to a shiny wall?"

She nodded and looked at him and smiled. The picture in her mind of this shiny wall made her happy.

"Is it a too-bright?" Moms asked. "Does it hurt Echo's eyes?"

Slowly she wagged her head no. "Wall of shy-nee," she said.

"It must be a place," Vern said. "Maybe a building."

"Yes," Moms said. "A structure of some kind. Are there any buildings positioned by a ravine that would not be built by the Old Ones?"

"I don't know," Vern said. "I had thought that all the human things in this area had been destroyed. Maybe it is not a building but a machine. If it looks like a wall to Echo, it could be a big machine."

"Only the Old Ones have large machines now."

"They would not be sending a call to Echo. If they knew where she was, we would already be killed."

"Let us suppose that it is some sort of machine made by someone other than the Old Ones. If they wanted us to come to their machine, why didn't they place it or send it close to where we were?"

"I don't know," Vern said. Then in a moment: "Maybe because if things don't work out, if something goes wrong, we could still get back to our cave and be safe there, since the Olders don't know about it. If this shiny wall was discovered by them, they would search close by and find our cave."

"Perhaps," Moms said. "Anyway, we have decided that we should answer the summons. Does the singing of the shoggoths seem to be getting closer to us? It may be that we need to find this shiny wall soon."

"As soon as we can," Vern said. "Let us try to get some rest."

He had not said "sleep" and he suspected that Moms's night was as unrestful as his own. *Tekeli-li* had sounded continuously and the shrillness came from different quarters. It seemed to be advancing upon them, but perhaps that was an illusion brought on by anxiety. Queenie did not behave as if shoggoths were closing in and Vern trusted her senses.

The morning routine matched that of the evening, except that Vern actually did scout, trying to make sure the area was free of traces of the Olders and to acquire an idea of the topography they were to travel through. He found a tall poplar with one branch low enough to give access to the upper branches and climbed easily. The months of outdoor survival had given him a wiry, purposeful musculature and a sureness of foot, hand, and eye. He was not even breathing heavily when he made it to the nearly leafless top and stood on a sturdy limb.

From here he could see the stream as it wound out of the holler, disappeared around a bend, and reappeared below, all whitewater and jumbled rock. Above the stream at that point reared a cliff, its level top a treeless, grassy sward. He decided it would be more informative to leave the streamside and climb along the ridges to that cliff. Even if it did not border the ravine shown in Echo's map, it would offer a prospect of the southern reaches, so that if they did return to streamside, he would have some notion of where they were located in the forest.

Following the ridges would be no easy task, he thought, and indeed it was not. Echo found the trail-less climb hard going; she wanted to stop often and fix her attention on ragged leaves waving in the breeze upon ragged oak limbs. Then Moms would carry her for a while, shifting her from one arm to the other. And then Vern would carry, giving to Moms the book bag containing their provisions.

Still, they went forward, halting often to rest but then pushing on. Echo was not easy to manage, with so many new sights tugging at her faculties, but Vern and Moms got accustomed to her rhythms and Queenie showed canny trail-sense, finding openings and pathways that Vern would have overlooked.

A little after midday they came to a clearing full of goldenrod and orchard grass and Joe Pye weed and there, unexpectedly close, loomed the cliff face. There was a ridge leading close to the top on the western side; Vern thought that if they followed it at the rate of speed they had been making, they would gain the plateau before nightfall.

They did make pretty good time, but Vern had been deceived by the land-folds. The ridgeline led not to the cliff plateau but wandered off farther westward and there was no way to attain the top except by scrambling down to the very bottom and climbing the perilous-looking path that zigzagged up the face. Echo would not like those heights; the cliff looked to be about 250 feet high. She might struggle violently against being taken up, but their choices were nonexistent.

The climb was, however, steeper and more toilsome than he had counted on and, though Echo did not writhe and struggle, she refused to walk and proved a heavy burden. The day began to darken toward a chilly twilight and they had gotten only about halfway up. When they halted for a rest, Vern debated with himself whether to continue climbing or to go back down and find a night place.

Then when the ancient trail doubled back upward, there opened a hole in the cliff-wall, a cave that had not been visible from below because a projecting ledge hid it from the sightline. He motioned for Moms and Echo to stay in the trail and he and Queenie went toward the opening. Queenie sniffed all around the cave mouth, but she did not seem disturbed and Vern let her enter before him. The natural thing to fear in this spot was a rattlesnake den. Some of the caves in these mountains were filled with hundreds of serpents, coiled side by side among rocks and stretched out upon ledges. But Queenie went in without barking. She came out in a few minutes and gave Vern a quizzical gaze and he followed as she reentered.

This cave was handmade, like the path that had been carved into the cliff face. The Cherokee must have maintained this place to evade the soldiers that herded their nation so murderously westward. There were many hiding places like this, cellar-like holes dug out in the woods, large cubbyholes chopped into thorny blackberry thickets. In one of the latter Vern had found a flint hatchet. Other sites yielded shards of pots.

In here, though, he found no trace of the Cherokee and the one utensil was a pewter pitcher which lay in the deep dust. Disposed around it in disorder were eight skeletons. Three of these were of children and the others, to judge by size and structure, belonged to adults of varying ages. Clothing had rotted away, but remains of shoes and boots clung to the pedal bones of the adults. Two skeletons lay with some of the upper-body bones entangled, as if that couple had died in an embrace.

It was likely that they had died so. Vern imagined that here had come a family or an enclave of refugees from one of the scattered settlements; they would have been of like faith and resolve. They had killed themselves, Vern thought, and before him in the dust lay the pewter pitcher in which they has passed round the poison. This group of intimates had found it nobler and easier to die by their own hands than to be done in coolly, methodically, and agonizingly by the Old Ones—or in disgusting, viscous horror as victims of the shoggoths.

Here was a sorrowful sight and Vern spent a long minute in dark thought. There was a recess in the back of the cave, small but with adequate room to pile these bones in, and he did so, lifting them as carefully—and as tenderly—as he knew how. He deposited them in one place, all piled together, and mounded as much dust over them as he was able to gather. It was a sad task, but not the worst he had had to perform.

He felt that he ought to say some proper words over these rueful remains, but all that came to mind was the one familiar phrase and he mumbled it as he stood above the bones and poured over them a last scraping of dust.

"Rest in peace."

Well, they had made up their minds to do that and now they rested. The task for Vern was to try to make sure they did not disturb Echo's rest. If the toothy grins and hollow eye sockets frightened her, she might shriek for minutes, then moan for hours, rocking back and forth in Moms' arms. She would not be able to communicate information about the shiny wall or anything else. He removed all the other traces he could find of the sad departed. He would warn Moms to keep Echo away from the back of the cave.

For the evening meal, they had only a little water left in the flask, barely enough to wash down their nine mouthfuls of food. It was insufficient to slake Echo's thirst and she complained, whining and twisting her torso so that her makeshift dress was in danger of falling apart. Moms finally quieted her by crooning an improvised lullaby. Queenie got only a single strip of dried meat and no water. She was growing weak.

Vern and Moms were thirsty too—and hungry. Whatever the plateau might offer tomorrow, water and food must be found. How far could it be to the shiny wall of Echo's vision? They could last only a few more hours without some replenishment. When their scanty food

scraps ran out, they would share the fate of the last occupants of this cave, but in a more lingering fashion.

Unless they jumped.

Vern wondered about that misfortunate group. What
had been the final straw, the situation that convinced
them to effect their own ends? Might it have been the
shrilling of the shoggoths, *Tekeli-li*, from the streamside
below? His imagination failed in the attempt to picture
those amorphous, globular agglutinations climbing the
cliff side. Perhaps those people had heard the sound
from above, from the cliff top that Vern and Moms
and Echo and Queenie were trying to reach. That area
looked treeless from below and those pursued would be
exposed.

Best for Vern to reconnoiter the place just at day-
break. He did not know whether he could summon the
strength to climb the steep trail, observe the scene, and
then return and lead the others there. He would have to
decide about that in the morning; maybe sleep would
refresh him sufficiently.

Echo was still resting in Moms' arms. Her eyes were
closed and she seemed to be listening, though Moms had
left off her lullaby. Vern crept over to them and murmured "shiny wall, shiny wall," though he expected that
Echo was too tired and sleepy to be able to converse.

She did respond, though, repeating Vern's phrase in
his own intonation. "Shiny wall." Then she stopped and
a lovely, quiet smile came to her face. To Vern, this was
as surprising and delightful as a rainbow. Echo rarely
smiled—almost never.

Then, before he could speak further, she fell asleep
and Moms laid her down, just as she was, on the floor of
the cave and stretched out to sleep beside her. Queenie
slept, always with her head on her outstretched paws,
and only Vern was awake.

And then he was not.

The skeletons came crawling toward them, of course,
clacking their bones in this weary darkness in which their

nasty, eternal grins glowed and flickered. Vern knew that he was dreaming and was not frightened. He tried to dismiss the dream so that he could sleep more soundly, but it persisted, its loathsome images and sounds ever more vivid until he woke with a start and looked instantly to see if Moms and Echo were safe.

They had not moved from where they had dropped, but their breathing was excited and irregular, and he knew that they too were dreaming, though probably not of skeletons. The three of them had gathered enough nightmare material to furnish out bad dreams for the remainders of their lives.

He lay still for a long time. Just before sunrise a wind sprang up and the mouth of the cave resounded with strange humming. Vern listened hard but could hear no whistling of shoggoths in the wind. If only this cave were near water, he thought, it would be ideal to live in.

Best not to dwell on fancies . . .

When the light was bright enough to make out details—the paws of Queenie protruding from beneath her nose, the porcelain-pale hands of Echo on her tatter-demalion dress—he sat up and began to move about.

It was not easy to do. His muscles were sore and his knees ached. It would be miraculous if he could get them to the top. Moms would be even more exhausted than he, so he would have to carry Echo the larger part of the way.

Yet let them rest now, he thought, as long as they are able. He rose and went out onto the cliff-side path. In the early light the stream below seemed far away and he saw how it ran southward into the shadow of another cliff on the other side. It came to him that if they reached the top and went south upon the plateau, they would find a place that matched the map that Echo had drawn.

Maybe it is not hopeless after all, he thought.

But when he reentered the cave and saw Moms ministering to Echo, massaging his sister's swollen feet and crooning soothing encouragement, he felt anew the weight of the responsibilities he had taken on and doubt

crept over his spirit. Moms and Echo looked at him ex-
pectantly and he made himself smile as he began to ar-
range their scanty breakfast.

And so, in a short few minutes, they were out of their
shelter and struggling up the path that grew steeper with
every step. Vern realized that they would have to stop
often to rest and that the duty of mollifying Echo's fear
would grow more onerous, but there could be no turning back now.

The weather was in their favor, with a mild blue sky
and little wind, even at this height, and they made better going than he had reckoned they would. At the last
sharp turn before the top, Vern told Moms to stop for
a rest and mind Echo while he went up to see what lay
before them on the plateau.

The path they had been climbing was steeply graded,
but the last eight feet or so had been cut into steps. These
gave Vern an opportunity to peek over the edge, exposing only his head, so that his view of the prospect was at
ground level. The area before him extended about fifty
yards on three sides; the turf was short grass, composing
what was traditionally called a "bald" in these mountains. At its south end was a long border of wildflowers—
ironweed, jewelweed, bee balm, and the like—and these
water-loving blooms held the promise of a spring. Beyond the flowers was a stand of low firs which cut off the
long vista of the south.

There were no signs of shoggoths or other animals
or of the Old Ones. A preternaturally peaceful silence
reigned over this grassy bald.

Vern returned to the switchback in the path where
Moms and Echo and Queenie waited. Moms was crooning earnestly to Echo, and Queenie snuggled against the
pale girl, as if she, like Moms, were trying to stop Echo
from looking down toward the stream.

Vern did not know why he whispered the report of
his discoveries to his mother and sister. Maybe the information was too happy to speak of in normal tones.
Moms whispered too: "Oh, I do hope there is water."

"We will let Queenie go up first," Vern said. "If there is water, she will find it."

So it was Queenie who led the way to the gentle greensward, bounding up the weather-rounded steps and springing joyfully over the edge. By the time Vern brought Echo and Moms into the sky-tented field, the dog was already halfway to the border of flowers. She had smelled water.

Moms crawled onto the level surface, to sit cross-legged and receive Echo as Vern handed her up. Then Vern squirmed over too and the three of them sat for a few moments, to rest muscles and joints and to gaze back toward the way they had come, down the twinkling stream and over the tumbled, bushy hills, and through the shady glades and hollers to the foot of the treacherous but hospitable cliff. They shared a feeling of achievement. Whatever happened next, they had come this far safely, answering the summons. They had overcome great odds, greater than they had realized during their hard march.

Then Vern stood and turned toward the south and gazed upon a different world. Behind him was a landscape of forest, mountains, and green-blue valleys. Before him, beyond the flowers and the little firs, beyond the edge of this brief plateau, lay a vast panorama of immense, sky-spearing, cyclopean structures. So tall were these angular monuments, oblongs and cubes and spiry pyramids, that clouds obscured some of their tops. Their angles were all wrong, so that Vern experienced a fleeting vertigo.

Wrongness—that was the first salience that attacked his senses and his instincts. He could not estimate how far away these structures stood, piled one past the other in an infinitely regressing series, because they seemed to be erected in a different *kind* of space than that which obtained here on the plateau. They seemed also to inhabit a different kind of time, so that if you traveled toward them—that is, if you *could* travel toward them— you would leave behind the now you were in and stand in a different now, a kind of time to which your body, mind, and spirit were direly unsuited.

This knowledge flooded into his mind and gut all at once, as if from a suddenly unveiled black star.

He did not cry out; he did not swoon. But the sight of this monstrous, incomprehensible landscape, mindscape, was so alien that he fell to his knees. Then he fell forward on his hands, retching and heaving for breath and grasping the grass in his fingers as if these handfuls of turf were his only desperate handhold upon the planet.

I will not look up, he thought. I will not look at these things.

He heard from behind a muffled moaning and knew that Moms and Echo were gazing upon this nightmare prospect. It was Moms who had uttered that soul-stricken, heartsick moan. She was standing upright, hugging herself with both arms, and silver tears streamed gleaming upon her cheeks. There was an expression of desolate comprehension in her eyes. She must have known better than Vern could know what these gigantic shapes that crushed the southern horizon implied and that what was implied had to be the thing she most loathed and feared, except for the striking-down of her children.

"In their own image!" she cried.

Vern understood. The Olders were remaking the world, the whole planet, in accordance with their icy intellectual designs. They were not building machines and monuments upon the planetary surface; they were reconfiguring the molecular structures of the world, from core to crust, from pole to pole. Earth was in process of losing its identity. No longer would it be an earth; it would be an alien object, an implement or instrument, a tool whose purposes might be unimaginable.

Moms stood transfixed with horror, but Echo was not shrieking in terror, as Vern had supposed that she would be. She too was transfixed, but her expression was one of wonderment. Those unthinkably huge planes and angles and cleavages that folded inward and projected outward simultaneously in momentously slow formings and reformings exercised upon the autistic mind the same hypnotic fascination that a flickering light or a wind-trembled branch or a lightly dancing snowfall would produce. The fascination might be different by enormous degree, but it would not be different in kind from that which other and more familiar phenomena brought upon Vern's sister.

When he saw that Echo did not lose herself in terror, that she was not beating her face with her fists as she did when fear was too terrible in her, Vern came to himself a little. Even with the calming image of Echo before him, it took an effort almost beyond his powers for him to collect his senses and something of his reasoning power.

He walked slowly to where Moms was standing and knelt and took the canteen from the book bag she had dropped in the grass. He grasped it in both hands and, keeping his gaze firmly turned toward the ground, never raising his eyes to the mind-wrenching panorama, trudged into the little marshy area outlined by the ranks of wildflowers.

In a minute or so, he came to a thin, oily streamlet that oozed among clumps of marsh-grassed turf. He bent and filled the flask and tasted the water. Musky and muddy, it was not toxic. He drank a little more before carrying the flask back to the females. Queenie bounded out of the herbage and trotted along beside him. No more than Echo was she disturbed by the sight of the world in ruin.

He fed Echo a grateful swallow at a time and she looked at him with her bright gray eyes brimming with gratitude. Moms seemed to find it difficult to drink; she rinsed her mouth and took the humus-tasting liquid in small sips. Then she dropped to the grass and stretched her legs out before her.

She spoke to the air and the grass when she said, "We cannot live in a world like this." She shook her head. "At least, I cannot." She looked up at her son, into his weather-lined face with its sparse blond beard. "I feel I am on the verge of losing my sanity. I was afraid we would have no future. Maybe we can have one, but I do not want it. And now I think we have no past either."

"Last night we shared our shelter with some people who felt like you do," Vern said.

"What do you mean? I don't know what you mean. Don't talk in riddles." Her voice rose almost to a shout. "Say something that means something."

He shrugged. "Maybe nothing means anything."

He made himself look again, staring with renewed horror at the immensities of those grotesque cubes and cylinders, cube-clusters, and five-angled projections. His mind could not divide this phantasmagoric panorama into parts, but it seemed to him that gigantic bridges arched over seemingly limitless abysses. Those bridges did not attach to the surfaces they touched but penetrated into the stone with the continuous motionless movement that a great cataract of water presents to vision. The simultaneous opening and closing of the five-angled edges gave the impression that the matter of which those pinnacles were constructed was both material and immaterial. More dimensions than four were in play; that vertiginous rampart that struck its bulk over a half kilometer of empty space extended into time as well as into space. It was what it was—and yet it was in process of becoming what it already was, and becoming something other and beyond that also.

And it was all of a color that was no color at all.

Moms spoke more quietly than Vern had heard her speak before. "I cannot bear it," she said. "No one can."

Vern said, "Echo does not give up."

He pointed to his sister. Echo was clapping her hands and swaying in an excited dance, her face full of joy. "Shy-nee shiny shiny shiny shy-nee," she sang. She left off dancing and broke into a clumsy run. The air was bright there at the cliff-edge and Echo ran to enter into it, to plunge into empty space.

IV

Tekeli-li.

This transliterated approximation was the closest Terran English could approach to the piercing command-trilling the Old Ones' shoggoths made as they traveled, each telling its whereabouts to its sibling organisms. It had been anciently recorded in the unfinished narrative left by Arthur Gordon Pym and further attested by later writers and adventurers, and it always carried with it a nauseating feeling of dread.

Seeker held her face in her hands and drew deep, harsh breaths. She had not withdrawn from the Terran's mind and the sound of that trilling had shaken her.

"How close are the shoggoths to the Remnant?" I asked.

She was silent a space, gathering her thoughts. Then she said she could not tell. "That sound is vivid in her mind because of her great fear, but I cannot judge distance."

"Navigator?" I asked.

He studied his panel for some time. "Not so near as to be deadly, I think," he said. "It is very difficult to judge distances."

"We have found where this Remnant is," I said. "We also have pictures from the locators. Where shall we set down the beacon?"

"Not so close as to attract the Old Ones to them nor so far that the autist cannot travel to it."

"We must put the beacon down soon," Seeker said, "so that it can set the Gate in place. I will have to go down to the planet surface."

Three of us said no at once.

"The danger is too huge," I said. "If the Old Ones are close, your mind could be erased. A shoggoth could sense what you are. If you are lost to us, the Remnant is lost and so are we."

She looked at us steadily, each in turn. "If I do not exhibit myself in my own person, just as I have pictured me to the autist Echo and her queenie, they will not come through the Gate and we cannot bear them away. Then truly all will be lost."

"How have you pictured you?" I asked.

"Looking as I do, but with all pleasantness and all welcoming and offering safety to the family. I have tried to picture myself happily to the queenie, but I do not know if she knows and interprets in the same manner as the others. She has strong smell-sense; I would like to transmit odors to her but cannot."

"Are you certain it is needed for you to descend?"

"Yes," Seeker said.

"There is no other way?"

She indicated no.

"Then let us rehearse the protocols and do all speedily," I said, and once more and assiduously we bent to our tasks.

There was one procedure we could not rehearse.

If the Old Ones mind-touched Seeker, they would recognize our mission and why and how. Then they would try to trace us back and locate the Great Ones' operational point for this mission. The disaster that followed would endanger and probably result in the slaughter of many races on many planets and the Old Ones would then take care that no Remnants were left. They would scour clean every planet and sun-system.

To prevent, I would kill Seeker. That is, I would order Ship to kill her before her mind could reveal its contents or before the Old Ones could assimilate. If the instruments detected that I did not emit the order quickly enough, Ship would enact its final program and detonate itself and all of us to atomic gas. There would be nothing left for the Old Ones to trace—but they would have been warned, and there would be consequences of that.

But Seeker declared that she must descend in her own person and not by image transmission to planet surface. She knew the minds we others could not know. And she would not imperil the mission needlessly. So I reviewed the steps and all seemed to be in order and we had to do everything quickly and with no mistakes.

*   *   *

There was a complication. Navigator had found a desirable site; the locators furnished detailed pictures of a green plateau above a river and the unactivated beacon was on its way, disguised, like Ship, as debris. It hurtled toward Terra, along with a flock of moon-chunks, and once it was surfaced, Ship would activate it for a brief time so that Seeker's mind-signals could be amplified to the female telepath and directions would be vivid to her, though not a picture of the site, which Seeker explained would mean nothing or too much. Then the beacon would be deactivated, so as not to attract attention. When the time came, *the exact moment,* it would power up again and set the Gate in place and keep it open—again for the briefest of periods. In that short space, Seeker would appear to the autist and her queenie and welcome them through.

But Navigator was finding precise measurement difficult. We had thought that the distortion of the local space-weave was accidental, a product of the great interdimensional engineering the Old Ones were undertaking. As an ancillary quality, the distortion would remain constant and the anomalies could be taken into account. The distortion was increasing, Navigator told us, and he now thought it was not accidental. The Old Ones were transforming local space-time.

"They are not satisfied to remake the objects of the cosmos," he said. "They are changing the makeup of the vessel that contains the cosmos. It begins with Terra and will spread, wave upon wave, throughout the whole universe. We will be unable to ascertain when or where anything is."

"How can they change the nature of space without destroying themselves?" Doctor asked.

"I do not know," Navigator said.

"Perhaps underspace will not be affected," I said. "And this transformation—if it is really taking place—will require a very long time to complete. We must rescue this Remnant promptly and return to the Great Ones. They will understand how to halt the process."

"Perhaps," Navigator said. His voice was doubtful. "I will try to work out a mathematics for the rate of distortion and we will follow our plan whether it is useful or not."

"That is best," I said because I could think of nothing else to say.

And then it was time for Seeker to go down. The beacon was in place and had already proved its worth. The Terran telepath had received Seeker's pictures most clearly and Navigator reported that the family was marching toward the plateau. He suggested that we configure the beacon transceivers in a different way and thus access some of the energy the Old Ones were using to distort space-time. We could do so undetected, so much of that energy was surplus and not closely tabulated.

"It would require too long," I said. "Those shoggoths are too near, are they not?"

He watched his screens and scopes for a little and then agreed.

Seeker went into the Gate-entrance chamber. She had freshened her robe and made her long hair brighter. Doctor and I kept our gazes upon each other, for though our sister strode into the exchange chamber steadily and with all purpose, we knew that she must have been enduring most horrible fears. She was descending into the territory of the Old Ones and she absorbed the terror of them ferociously, being in contact with the Remnant that survived just outside the verge of their icy intelligences and had witnessed what things they had done.

We tested the communications and Seeker said she could well hear me.

"Good," I said, "because you must mark the instant for Navigator and for Ship. It has to be precisely exact."

"I know." She spoke bravely, but there was a quiver in her voice, only little, but it betrayed her slightly. I looked at Doctor and she was concerned but also smiled bravely to let me know Seeker would not lose consciousness.

We waited and waited but not, I now think, as long as it seemed we waited.

Seeker stood straight with her shoulders held back
and her eyes glowing now with more color than ever I
had seen in them. She brought her hands away from her
sides and rested them slightly on the Gate posts.

Then she said, *"Now,"* and I will not forget the sound
of that word, ever.

Ship heard and activated the beacon and the welcoming Shiny Wall-Gate was in place, so we thought.

V

Vern was certain that he could never get to her in
time. He sprinted as hard as he could, but though Echo
was severely uncoordinated and could often not walk
in a straight line, she had a long head start. She was
singing and babbling her Shiny Wall song and maybe
that slowed her. Yet when he caught her, only inches
from the fall that would crush her, and wrestled her
to the turf, he had to use all his strength to hold her
down. She struggled and cried and slapped at him.
She was scarlet-faced and weeping but still singing,
when she could find breath, "Shy-nee, shiny, shiny . . ."
Moms began wailing too, uttering a cry so full of grief
and horror, that it chilled Vern even in the heat of his
exertions.

And now in the midst of these commotions, Queenie
came bounding past. Vern hardly had time to turn his
head and follow her flight as she raced by him and the
caroling Echo and launched herself, as if arcing into a
lake to fetch a stick, over the cliff edge into the abyss.

Finally he was able to turn Echo on her back. He
knelt on her, pinning her shoulders with his knees. She
looked up at him with an expression of puzzled sorrow.
"Shy-nee," she said.

Then it was visible to Vern. It stood, or hovered, exactly upon the cliff edge, a rectangle of blue-white shim-
mer, mottled and interlaced with glowing threads that
pulsed silver and violet and orange-red. It looked as if
it ought to emit sound—a small sonic clap upon its appearance or the snap and sizzle of electronic static—but

it was eerily silent. Vern could feel that no heat emanated from this object that Echo called a wall.

He took his weight off his sister and stood her up and
clasped her tightly. She was not pushing him away now
or attempting to run. She was transfixed, hypnotized by
the shiftings and sparklings of the threaded workings
upon or within the seemingly flat surface. She even nestled a little in his embrace as she often did with Moms.

Moms came behind Vern and put her arms around
her shoulder, so that the three of them stood holding
tight in mutual embrace. Vern wanted to speak to Moms
but could not.

The girl who stepped out of Echo's Shiny Wall resembled Vern's sister in many ways. She was thin and her
skin was pale as porcelain and her hair was bright blond,
although it was not raddled and stringy like Echo's but
done up in feathery swirls that appeared to float about
her head. She was wearing a white robe that cupped
the sunlight into little pools of color, subtle yellows and
blues.

Then she spoke in a clear, treble voice, her syllables
like chimes. "You will be pleased to come away. The
shoggoths are near. There is small time before the gate
must shut."

Echo laughed delightedly. Vern could say nothing and
it was Moms who asked, in a quavering but determined
tone, "Who are you?"

"I am Seeker. Echo knows who I am. You can see
how she is not fearing. You must come. *Now*. They are
almost upon us."

Vern heard. They must have been advancing upon
them from the north ridge. *Tekeli-li Tekeli-li*. Those
beasts that looked like decomposing flesh could not
come up the cliff-side path. They must have come along
the other side of the bald.

Moms said, "We don't know how. We are exhausted
and frightened and you are strange to us."

"You must trust me," the girl said. "Your queenie is
already aboard."

"Queenie?"

"*Please.*"

The shrilling was very near. *Tekeli-li.*

"We have no choice, Moms," Vern said.

Her voice was vacant. "Maybe you were right, Vern, to say that nothing means anything anymore. I don't want to see this world the way it is now. How could anything be worse than what is here? So I will go first."

She walked to stand by the girl in the white robe. The girl motioned her forward and Moms did not turn to look at Echo and Vern but stepped into the sheet of silver fire that opened over the abyss.

"Now—so as to avoid those Old One things," the girl said.

Tekeli-li ...

Almost upon the greensward, almost within sight.

Echo was still frozen in fascination, so Vern scooped her up and carried her into the wall-sheet of energy and the girl in the colorful white robe followed, backing in and looking with horrified loathing at what was out there and then all that scene went away.

It was cold and sharp. It was like stepping through the waterfall that had protected their cave, except that it was not wet.

On the other side of the Shy-nee Wall was sleep.

VI

Ship had changed the combination of gases so that our vessel atmosphere conformed more closely to the Terran. For us crew members, the heavier air was not unpleasant, but it was a little more difficult to breathe. We wanted our Remnant guests to be as comfortable as possible, for all must seem highly strange to them. We were in space, where the Old Ones ranged abroad. That would be threatening, we thought, maybe.

As soon as the necessities were done with, we all went to our deepsleep berths and Ship filtered in the proper narcotics and we plunged into underspace. This happened in the shortest of times. We did not know if

we had been seen or, had we been, if we were traceable. We did not know if underspace were changed—or
"wrecked," as Navigator called it.

Ship was to awaken us after four periods. At that point,
we would be one hundred watches' flight from the Alliance Remnant Reclamation Consigning Base, a station
located where a sun system formerly had revolved. The
Old Ones had annihilated every planet and moon there
and the dim little central star now hung alone. There were
no outposts near this deserted space and it was a lonely
place wherein to stand waiting and planning.

After the crew had been awakened, Echo and the
queenie were brought to full consciousness and their
needs attended to. They required more bodily attention
than the young man and his mother. Seeker spent a long
time period communicating with the animal—"dog," it
was classified—and the autistic female; they could all
speak to each other in a rudimentary mental speech, and
Echo, once she was assured that her mother and brother
were alive and well, was happy. She no longer echoed,
repeating the phrases and words and sounds of others.
Now, with Seeker, she had her own voice.

Then Vern was wakened and he reported immediately that he felt wonderfully well. This was not surprising. Ship had massaged and exercised him and rid him
of unhealthy microorganisms and prepared healthful,
Terran-like food, which he ate with lavish enjoyment.

He asked a great many questions—as we had expected he would ask.

"You look so cool and white," he said. "You seem
delicate."

"We were rescued from our home planet by the Radiance Alliance almost two of your years ago. We have
been enclosed in the station and aboard ship since then.
So we have not . . . planetary . . . physiques. But now,
after we are restored to strength, we will be going to a
world like the one you left, like ours that the Old Ones
murdered. We will develop our physical nature on the
new planet."

"I like the clothes you gave me," he said. "I never wore a robe before. It is comfortable and very pink. It is very pink."

"I am glad you adore it," I said.

"There are lots of things I do not understand," he said. "I thought Echo would fall off the cliff and die. I thought Queenie had already fallen."

I explained that the scene was arranged to deceive the foe. "Echo is an autistic and sees *everything* the way it really is. You and I see what we expect to see, but autistics do not see predicted patterns. The Old Ones see only patterns, all things arranged schematically. If they saw the grass blades depressed by the edge of the gate, they would attribute that to the wind bending them over. But it was the gate pressing down, though it was not yet visible. Echo saw what it really was and went through the gate to Seeker."

"But the gate *was* visible," Vern said. "It was silver, with other colors. I saw it."

"Ship made it visual for you and your mother. Otherwise, you might not have entered."

He was silent for a while. Then he said, "Thank you for rescuing us. Thank you for saving our lives."

"It is our mission. In the world we are going to there are other Terralike Remnants hidden away. They were rescued too. The Alliance is trying to preserve as many species as possible. The greater number of them does not look like us." I could not help smiling. "Some of them look very different."

"Have you and the crew rescued many Remnants?"

"Only your family," I said. "We were all apprehensive because we had no experience. We are immature."

"What do you mean, immature?" Vern asked.

"In terms of Terran cycles, I am fifteen years old, Doctor is fourteen, Navigator is twelve, and Seeker is ten. We are orphans. We are Remnants, as you are. Our home was obliterated and we were rescued, though our escape was not so narrow as yours."

Vern thought, then wagged his head. "Why would

your Great Race send out children for such a mission? It seems not very brilliant."

"But if we were adults and thought in complicated patterns, the way older beings do, the Old Ones could detect us more easily. They are not so closely attuned to the thought-patterns of children or of animals—or of autistic beings."

"This is hard to take in," Vern said.

"Is it not better for you here than it was on Terra?"

"Yes. May we wake Moms now?"

"She had to stay asleep longer. Her mind is more torn because the world she lived in so long is unrecognizable to her now. She will take longer to recover."

"I had a sister younger than Echo," Vern said. "Her name was Marta. The Old Ones destroyed her when they murdered my father. We could never say her name because we would cry and become too upset. That was not safe."

Ship sounded some noises to signal that Moms had awakened.

Moms was sitting in a grand, plush chair shaped like a quarter moon beside her deepsleep rectangle. Queenie sat beside her in regal attitude. They looked as if they were granting audience. Moms' robe was of a softer-looking material than Vern's and Echo's, a dark, peaceful blue. It lapped over Queenie's paws. When she saw Vern and Echo and all the crew come to greet her, she began to laugh and cry. Her face formed different expressions and Vern saw how confused she was.

But she was happy.

"Oh children," she said. "How fine you look! And you are all dressed up! Is there going to be a party?"

"I don't know," Vern said.

So Ship announced that a celebration was scheduled in two hours in the large conference bay. Everyone is invited, Ship said. Please attend. I am proud to know you.

"And we are all cosmically proud of Seeker," I said. "She has done what all others could not."

"I am awfully grateful," Vern told her. "Is Seeker your real name?"

"In your English sounds, it would be something like Inanna," I said.

He tried to pronounce it.

"Seeker," I said, "say your name to Vern."

"In a moment," she said. She brushed the air with her hand. Her forehead was wrinkled and we knew she was mind-feeling something probably distant, but we could not know what.

ABOUT THE AUTHORS

Mike Allen works as the arts and culture columnist for *The Roanoke Times* in Roanoke, Va., where he lives with his wife Anita, a comical dog and three psychotic cats. He also writes poetry and fiction. The *Philadelphia Inquirer* called his verse "poetry for goths of all ages"—his poems have been reprinted in the Nebula Awards Showcase series and Ellen Datlow's *The Best Horror of the Year*—while his horror story "The Button Bin" was a finalist for the 2008 Nebula Awards. He is the editor of the critically acclaimed anthology series *Clockwork Phoenix* (Norilana Books) and also editor and publisher of the poetry journal *Mythic Delirium*. Like every other writer in the world, he's working on a novel.

Ken Asamatsu was born in 1956 in Sapporo, Hokkaidō. He graduated from Tōyō University to work at Kokusho Kankōkai, famous in Japan as the publisher of Lovecraft and many other works of horror and fantasy. His debut work as an author was *Makyō no Gen'ei* (Echoes of Ancient Cults), in 1986. He continues to be active in a wide range of activities, including writing extensively in the weird historical and horror genres. While remaining extremely interested in the Cthulhu Mythos, lately he has been concentrating on weird historicals set in the Muromachi period (1333–1573). In 2005 he was a candidate for the annual award of the Mystery Writers of Japan, Inc., in the short story genre, for his "Higashiyamadono Oniwa" (Higashiyamadono Villa Garden). He has also made considerable contribution to Japanese fiction as an anthologist, proposing a number of collections successfully published in Japan. The *Lairs of the Hidden Gods* series, which won high praise in the original Japanese, is now available from Kurodahan Press. http://homepage3 .nifty.com/uncle-dagon/

Laird Barron raced the Iditarod three times during the early 1990s. He migrated to the Pacific Northwest in 1994 where he became a strength trainer and studied martial arts. In 2000 he began to write poetry and fiction. Barron's work has appeared in places such as *The Magazine of Fantasy and Science Fiction, SciFiction, Inferno, Lovecraft Unbound!, Black Wings,* and *The Del Rey Book of Science Fiction and Fantasy.* It has also been reprinted in numerous year's best anthologies and nominated for multiple honors including the World Fantasy, International Horror Guild, Sturgeon, Crawford, Locus, and Shirley Jackson awards. His debut collection, *The Imago Sequence and Other Stories*, was recently rereleased as a trade paperback. A second collection, *Occultation*, and a novel, *The Croning*, will also appear in 2010 and 2011. He lives in Olympia, Washington, with his wife.

Matt Cardin has a master's degree in religious studies and writes frequently about the intersections between religion and horror. He is the author of *Dark Awakenings* (2009) and *Divinations of the Deep* (2002), the latter of which launched the New Century Macabre line of contemporary literary horror fiction for Ash-Tree Press. He is a regular reviewer for *Dead Reckonings*, and his work has appeared in *Lovecraft Studies, The Thomas Ligotti Reader, Cemetery Dance, The New York Review of Science Fiction, Icons of Horror and the Supernatural, The Encyclopedia of the Vampire, The HWA Presents: Dark Arts,* and elsewhere.

Fred Chappell is a prominent writer of Southern regional fiction, a retired university professor, a leading poet (who was poet laureate of North Carolina between 1997 and 2002), and winner of the Prix de Meilleur des Livres Etrangers, the Bollingen Prize, and the T. S. Eliot Prize. He is best known to Lovecraft fans for his novel *Dagon* (1968) which recasts the Cthulhu Mythos in a Southern Gothic mode, and for his collection *More Shapes Than One* (1991), which contains several stories directly related to Lovecraft and the Mythos including one of the very few prior to this anthology to take place (or at least end) after the Old Ones have returned. His work has appeared in *Weird Tales* and in *The Magazine of Fantasy & Science Fiction*. He won the World Fantasy Award in 1992 for "The Somewhere Doors."

Gregory Frost is author of the duology *Shadowbridge* and *Lord Tophet,* voted one of the best fantasy novels of the year by the American Library Association. It was also a finalist for the James Tiptree Jr. Award in 2009, and received starred reviews from *Booklist* and *Publishers Weekly*. His previous novel, the historical thriller *Fitcher's Bride*, was a finalist for both World Fantasy and International Horror Guild Awards for Best Novel. Author of fantasy, science fiction, and thrillers, he has been a finalist for every major fantasy award. *Publishers Weekly* proclaimed his collection *Attack of the Jazz Giants and Other Stories,* "one of the best fantasy collections." Other recent stories appear in *Poe*, edited by Ellen Datlow, and in *The Beastly Bride*, edited by Ms. Datlow and Terri Windling. He has taught writing at the *Clarion*, *Alpha*, and *Odyssey* workshops, and currently directs the fiction writing workshop at Swarthmore College in Swarthmore, PA.

John R. Fultz lives in San Jose, California. His fiction has appeared in *Weird Tales, Black Gate,* and *Space and Time*, as well as the comic book anthologies *Zombie Tales* and *Cthulhu Tales*. His graphic novel of epic fantasy *Primordia* is published by Archaia Comics (www.myspace.com/

primordiacomic). John's literary heroes include Tanith Lee, Thomas Ligotti, Clark Ashton Smith, Lord Dunsany, and William Gibson, not to mention Howard, Poe, and Shakespeare. When not writing stories, novels, or comics, he teaches English literature in the Bay Area. In a previous life he made his living as a wandering storyteller on the lost continent of Atlantis.

Jay Lake was born under an eldritch sign on a remote Pacific island. He now lives in Portland, Oregon, where he works on numerous writing and editing projects. His 2009 novels are *Green*, *Madness of Flowers*, and *Death of a Starship*. His short fiction appears regularly in literary and genre markets worldwide. Jay is a winner of the John W. Campbell Award for Best New Writer and a multiple nominee for the Hugo and World Fantasy Awards.

John Langan is the author of *Mr. Gaunt and Other Uneasy Encounters* (2008) and *House of Windows* (2009). He lives in upstate New York with his wife, son, and a pair of neurotic cats.

Richard A. Lupoff is the author of more than fifty books as well as uncounted short stories, screenplays, essays and reviews. His work spans a wide variety of fields including fantasy, horror, mystery, mainstream, and science fiction. His most recent novel is *The Emerald Cat Killer.* Recent collections include the trilogy *Terrors*, *Visions*, and *Dreams*, as well as *Quintet: The Cases of Chase and Delacroix* and *Killer's Dozen*. He first encountered a story by H. P. Lovecraft in a paperback anthology that he smuggled into church and hid in a hymnal. He has been fascinated by Lovecraft and his works ever since, and is the author of *Marblehead: A Novel of H. P. Lovecraft,* as well as many shorter contributions to the Cthulhu Mythos.

Will Murray is the author of over fifty pseudonymous novels and a lifelong Lovecraftian. He has been writing about HPL since the 1980s, chiefly in legendary journals such as *Crypt of Cthulhu*, *Lovecraft Studies* and *Nycta-*

lops. He was one of the three founders of Friends of H.
P. Lovecraft, which was organized to place the memorial
plaque on the grounds of the John Hay Library on the
centennial of Lovecraft's birth in 1990. As a contributor
to numerous anthologies, Murray's Mythos stories have
appeared in *The Cthulhu Cycle*, *Disciples of Cthulhu II*,
The Yig Cycle, *The Shub-Niggurath Cycle*, *Miskatonic
University*, *Weird Trails*, and the forthcoming *Cthulhu
2012*. He periodically threatens to write more.

Brian Stableford has two further Cthulhu Mythos stories due for publication in 2010: the short novel *The
Womb of Time* and the novella *The Legacy of Erich
Zann*, which will make up a book published by Perilous
Press. His other recent novels include *Prelude to Eternity*
and *Alien Abduction: The Wiltshire*. He is continuing to
issue a series of translations of classic French scientific
romances from Black Coat Press, including five volumes
of the work of Maurice Renard and five volumes of J. H,
Rosny the Elder, due in 2010.

Ian Watson's most recent collection of bizarre tales, co-
written with Italian surrealist Roberto Quaglia, *The Beloved of My Beloved* (NewCon Press, UK, 2009), may be
the only full-length genre fiction work by two authors
with different mother tongues, the product of much
travel and wine-fueled discussion in Hungary, Romania,
Spain, England, and Italy, including Genoa where "The
Walker in the Cemetery" is set. The UK's Immanion
Press recently rereleased Ian's earlier novels *Whores of
Babylon* and *The Gardens of Delight* in revised editions,
and his Balkan chess fantasy *Queenmagic, Kingmagic,*
which was perfect first time round, says he. Ian lives in
a tiny Middle English village, where black tulips waft
over his black cat's grave, at least in the spring, and his
website is www.ianwatson.info.

Don Webb has written books on the Greek Magical Pa-
pyri, computer security, and even a poetry collection. A
four-time loser (nominated for the Shirley Jackson Award,

International Horror Critics Award, Rhysling Award, and Hugo Fan Writing), he teaches English in a rural Texas reform school by day and online creative writing classes for UCLA by night. He is said to be working on a book of magic derived from the Mythos and is releasing a Kindle collection of his vampire fiction. He is generally disagreeable and funny-looking.

ABOUT THE EDITOR

Darrell Schweitzer is the author of the novels *The White Isle, The Shattered Goddess,* and *The Mask of the Sorcerer,* a recent novella published as a book, *Living with the Dead,* plus about three hundred short stories, hundreds of essays, reviews, and poems. His credits include *Twilight Zone Magazine, Alfred Hitchcock's Mystery Magazine, Interzone, Cemetery Dance, Postscripts, Amazing Stories, Publishers Weekly* and *The Washington Post.* He shared a World Fantasy Award with George Scithers, as coeditor of *Weird Tales* magazine, a post he held for nineteen years. With George Scithers he coedited *Tales from the Spaceport Bar* and *Another Round at the Spaceport Bar.* He is also the editor of *The Secret History of Vampires* (DAW 2007) and *Full Moon City* (2010, with Martin H. Greenberg). He has also edited many books of nonfiction, including the classic *Discovering H.P. Lovecraft,* which has been in print for over 30 years. He has also achieved a certain notoriety for rhyming the name of Cthulhu in a limerick, as follows:

> A cultist entranced with Cthulhu
> encountered a slavering ghoul who
> said, "Old Ones don't need me,
> they won't even feed me,
> and so in a pinch I guess you'll do."

But if this proves to be Schweitzer's most enduring work, we fear for the future of mankind.

Seanan McGuire

The October Daye Novels

"...will surely appeal to readers who enjoy my books, or those of Patrica Briggs." —*Charlaine Harris*

"Well researched, sharply told, highly atmospheric and as brutal as any pulp detective tale, this promising start to a new urban fantasy series is sure to appeal to fans of Jim Butcher or Kim Harrison."—*Publishers Weekly*

ROSEMARY AND RUE
978-0-7564-0571-7
A LOCAL HABITATION
978-0-7564-0596-0
AN ARTIFICIAL NIGHT
978-0-7564-0626-4

(Available September 2010)

To Order Call: 1-800-788-6262
www.dawbooks.com

P.R. Frost
The Tess Noncoiré Adventures

"Frost's fantasy debut series introduces a charming protagonist, both strong and vulnerable, and her cheeky companion. An intriguing plot and a well-developed warrior sisterhood make this a good choice for fans of the urban fantasy of Tanya Huff, Jim Butcher, and Charles deLint."
— *Library Journal*

HOUNDING THE MOON
978-0-7564-0425-3
MOON IN THE MIRROR
978-0-7564-0486-4

and new in hardcover:
FAERY MOON
978-0-7564-0556-4

To Order Call: 1-800-788-6262
www.dawbooks.com

DAW 70

Tad Williams

SHADOWMARCH

Volume One:

SHADOWMARCH
0-7564-0359-6

Volume Two:

SHADOWPLAY
978-0-7564-0544-1

Volume Three:

SHADOWRISE
978-0-7564-0549-6

"Bestseller Williams once again delivers a sweeping spell-
binder full of mystical wonder." —*Publishers Weekly*

"Williams creates an endlessly fascinating and
magic-filled realm filled with a profusion of memorable
characters and just as many intriguing plots and subplots....
Arguably his most accomplished work to date."
—*The Barnes & Noble Review*

To Order Call: 1-800-788-6262
www.dawbooks.com

DAW 47